PUFFIN CANADA

THE GUESTS OF WAR TRILOGY

Born in Edmonton, Alberta, KIT PEARSON graduated in English at the University of Alberta before going on to get her MLS at the University of British Columbia and an MA in children's literature at the Center for the Study of Children's Literature, Simmons College, Boston.

A former librarian as well as a writer, Ms Pearson has written several novels, including *The Daring Game, A Handful of Time*, and the acclaimed Guests of War trilogy: *The Sky Is Falling, Looking at the Moon,* and *The Lights Go On Again.* Her novel *Awake and Dreaming* won the Governor General's Award for Children's Literature. The recipient of many awards for her writing, Kit Pearson has also received the Canadian Authors Association/Vicky Metcalf Award for her body of work.

Also by Kit Pearson

The Daring Game

A Handful of Time

The Sky Is Falling

Looking at the Moon

The Lights Go On Again

Awake and Dreaming

This Land: An Anthology of Canadian Stories for Young Readers

Whispers of War

THE GUESTS OF WAR TRILOGY

The Sky Is Falling
Looking at the Moon
The Lights Go On Again

Kit Pearson

PUFFIN
CANADA

PUFFIN CANADA

Published by the Penguin Group

Penguin Group (Canada), 10 Alcorn Avenue, Toronto, Ontario, Canada M4V 3B2
(a division of Pearson Penguin Canada Inc.)

Penguin Group (USA) Inc., 375 Hudson Street, New York, New York 10014, U.S.A.
Penguin Books Ltd, 80 Strand, London WC2R 0RL, England
Penguin Ireland, 25 St Stephen's Green, Dublin 2, Ireland (a division of Penguin Books Ltd)
Penguin Group (Australia), 250 Camberwell Road, Camberwell, Victoria 3124, Australia
(a division of Pearson Australia Group Pty Ltd)
Penguin Books India Pvt Ltd, 11 Community Centre, Panchsheel Park, New Delhi – 110 017, India
Penguin Group (NZ), Cnr Airborne and Rosedale Roads, Albany, Auckland, New Zealand
(a division of Pearson New Zealand Ltd)
Penguin Books (South Africa) (Pty) Ltd, 24 Sturdee Avenue, Rosebank, Johannesburg 2196, South Africa

Penguin Books Ltd, Registered Offices: 80 Strand, London WC2R 0RL, England

The Sky Is Falling first published in Viking Kestrel by Penguin Group (Canada), a division of Pearson Penguin Canada Inc., 1989. Published in Puffin Canada paperback, 1991.

Looking at the Moon first published in Viking Canada hardcover, 1991. Published in Puffin Canada paperback, 1993.

The Lights Go On Again first published in Viking Canada hardcover, 1993. Published in Puffin Canada paperback, 1994.

First published in one volume as *The Guests of War Trilogy* in Puffin Canada paperback, 1998.

(WEB) 20 19 18 17

Manufactured in Canada.

NATIONAL LIBRARY OF CANADA CATALOGUING IN PUBLICATION

Pearson, Kit, 1947–
The guests of war trilogy

ISBN 0-14-038841-9
Contents: The sky is falling — Looking at the moon — The lights go on again.

I. Title.

PS8581.E386G84 1998 jC813'.54 C97-931665-0 PZ7.P42Gu 1998

CONTENTS

THE SKY IS FALLING

For my parents

It was a long journey they set out on,
and they did not think of any end to it . . .

"Alenoushka and Her Brother"
(Russian folk tale)

CONTENTS

PART ONE

1
THE PLANE

Norah, armed to the teeth, slithered on her stomach through the underbrush. She gripped her bow in her right hand and bit on a kitchen knife. A quiver of arrows made from sharpened twigs and decorated with chicken feathers slid sideways on her back, getting tangled with the string of her gas mask case. Pulling herself forward by her elbows, she finally reached the clearing.

There she stopped to wait for Tom's signal. The knife had an unpleasantly metallic taste. Spitting it out, she looked up and gaped in wonder.

In front of her, glittering in the August sunlight, was a shot-down German aeroplane—a Messerschmitt 109. Norah recognized its square-cut wing tips and streamlined fuselage. But it looked more like a squashed dragonfly than a plane. Its wings stretched lifelessly over the ground and its split body exposed its innards. One propeller blade was bent back and twisted. Bullet holes spotted the metal corpse and a burnt, sour smell like vinegar rose from it.

The mangled machine looked alien and out of place in Mr Coomber's peaceful field. Most sinister of all was the bold black swastika on the plane's tail. When the war had begun a year ago, the Nazis had been safely on the other side of the Channel. Then they had started flying over England. And now, here was one of their planes only a few hundred yards away. A choking fear filled Norah, as if there were a weight on her chest.

She took a deep breath and pulled herself to a sitting position, careful to stay concealed. In front of the aircraft, puffed with importance, stood Mr Willis from the village, his crisp new Home Guard emblem around his sleeve.

Across the field, Tom waved his arm. Norah waved back and watched the answering signals from Harry and Jasper. Tom pointed to Norah. Good, they were going to assemble here. Maybe if she weren't alone this strange new fear would leave her.

"Isn't it *smashing?*" whispered Tom a few minutes later. He and the younger two crept up to join her, dropping their weapons.

With three warm bodies pressing close to hers, Norah breathed easily again. They all stared greedily at the plane's parts: its instrument panel, machine guns, fuel caps and hanging shards of aluminum. Harry and Jasper were too awed to speak.

"The tailfin's completely undamaged," said Tom softly. "If only Mr Willis wasn't there and we had a hacksaw, we could cut it off."

Several older boys broke through the trees on the opposite side of the field and hurried towards the plane, halting with frustration when they saw Mr Willis.

"Get away!" he called. "This plane will be guarded until the lorry comes, so there's no use hanging about."

One of the boys darted behind the plane, snatched up some metal from the ground and bolted with his companions. Mr Willis shouted helplessly after them.

"I wonder where the pilot is?" mused Tom. "See his gear?" He pointed to the parachute pack, leather helmet and goggles abandoned in front of the wreck. "He could be lurking somewhere!"

Norah had trouble breathing again as she took this in. One of Hitler's men! The Enemy, the Hun, who wanted to conquer Britain, except Britain would never give up.

"He'll probably surrender," said Tom, "or they'll capture him. Or *we* will," he added. Norah glanced doubtfully at her fragile arrows and the dull knife lying in the dirt.

They watched the plane for an hour, until their arms and legs were cramped and Jasper complained he was thirsty. Finally, when it became obvious that Mr Willis was not going to leave his post, they crept through the trees to their waiting bicycles. Slowly they rode back to Ringden, squeezing through the side of the barbed-wire roadblock. The guards knew them well and didn't bother asking for their identity cards.

As they neared the edge of the village, they waved to old Mrs Chandler, who had had her noon meal in her front garden every day this week so she could watch the fighting planes in the sky. They parked their bicycles and crossed the lumpy grass behind her house to their tree fort.

Tom handed around weak lemonade. The four children sat in companionable, exhausted silence, each intoxicated with the thrilling danger of the plane.

II
THE SKYWATCHERS

Old Mrs Chandler didn't know there was a secret society in her orchard. Her house was the largest and highest in Ringden and looked out over the Weald. Last summer Tom and Norah had discovered the old tree fort hidden in an apple tree; it must have been built by one of her sons. They had reinforced it with scraps of wood and added a rope ladder to get in and out quickly.

At first, the fort had been a good place in which to play Cops and Robbers. But this spring it had been named the Lookout when the Secret Society of Skywatchers was formed. Now they were on the alert for real enemies: the Good Guys were the English and the Bad Guys the Germans.

Pinned on the walls of the Lookout were pictures cut out of the newspaper of the troop-carrying aircraft to look out for. They especially hoped to catch sight of a Junkers 52, the enemy plane most commonly used for parachute dropping. They owned a copy of *Friend or Foe? A Young Spotter's Guide to Allied and German Aircraft,* but Tom and Norah were such experts, they no longer needed it.

The Skywatchers looked at strangers suspiciously and longed to meet nuns, monks or nurses who might be Nazis in disguise with collapsible bicycles under their loose clothes. In the Lookout was a supply of grey, lumpy sugar, painstakingly saved from their rations, to pour into enemies' petrol tanks and neutralize them.

Norah sipped her sour lemonade and looked around the cluttered fort with satisfaction. Ranged along a shelf were their war souvenirs: twisted bits of shrapnel, uniform badges and tins of cartridge cases. It was too bad they hadn't been able to get anything new from the Messerschmitt.

A government leaflet was attached to the tree trunk: "If the Invader Comes". Her eyes focused on the words, "If you run away . . . you will be machine-gunned from the air." Again, Norah felt as if there were a weight on her chest.

"Whose turn is it to keep watch?" asked Harry.

"Mine," said Norah, glad of a diversion. She squatted on the edge of the Lookout, pressing her father's old field glasses to her eyes. They were so heavy they made her arms ache, and after a few seconds she put them down and scanned the sky and landscape without them.

Below her stretched the rolling Weald, dotted with sheep and the gleaming white caps of oast houses. She could just glimpse where the land levelled off, like the edge of a table, as it dropped to Romney Marsh. Beyond that was the Channel and from across the Channel the Germans came.... West of the Lookout was the village, its stubby church spire poking up past the rooftops. Norah could even see her own house and her brother Gavin playing with his wagon in the garden.

She stared so intently at the dazzling sky that her eyes watered. Never before had the weather been as consistently clear as in this summer of 1940. "Hitler and the rain will come together," the grown-ups predicted.

Then, for the last month things had been falling out of the sky: stray bombs meant for the coast or the airfields; German propaganda leaflets that ended up being sold at raffles; and distant, floating parachutes like tiny puffballs. During the air battles, showers of empty cartridge cases tinkled on the roofs of Ringden; last week one had splashed into Mr Skinner's bucket as he was milking.

Yesterday a pilot's boot had plummeted into the grass behind the Lookout: a worn, black leather boot with the imprint of a man's big toe creasing the top. They were certain it was a Nazi boot, and it now had the place of honour in their collection.

Every day this week they had seen dogfights, as the clean sky became covered with a cobweb of the tangled white contrails of fighting planes. This morning's battle had been the most exciting. The planes had come lower than usual, and they could pick out the tiny, silvery Messerschmitts circling protectively around the moth-like Dorniers. Then they had heard the growl of RAF fighters tearing in to give battle. For once they were Spitfires instead of the more familiar, hump-backed Hurricanes. The graceful Spits had tilted and twisted, machine-gun fire had sounded faintly and the children had cheered so wildly they'd almost pushed each other off the platform.

That was when one of the German planes had dropped through the blueness. The Skywatchers had scrambled to their bicycles, but it had taken hours to find it. While they'd paused to eat their sandwiches, a passing boy had told them the plane was in a field at Mr Coomber's farm.

There was no more activity now. The only sound was the purr of threshing machines and the raspy quarrelling of rooks. The countryside had been practically empty of cars since gas rationing, and the church bells would not ring again unless there was an invasion. Norah's eyes kept closing as she tried to concentrate on the sky. She was glad when her time was up and Harry took her place.

Behind her, the others had been reading comics and mending their bows. "We should write to Pete and Molly and tell them about the plane," said Norah. The Kemps had been active Skywatchers until, along with several other members, they'd been evacuated to Wales. Norah missed Molly; she had been her best friend. Now she supposed Tom was, although he was sometimes bossier than she liked.

"It would be better not to tell them," said Tom. "It'll just make them angry to know what they've missed."

"The Smiths are being sent away, too," Jasper said. "To Canada! My mum heard from their mum this morning."

"Canada?" Norah sputtered. She took down the Boot and examined it again, trying not to listen.

Tom looked disgusted. "Anyone who leaves England is a coward," he declared. "Derek and Dulcie and Lucy are so feeble, they probably *want* to go."

Harry turned around from his post. "Mum and Dad thought Jasper and me might go to our auntie's in Devon if the bombing starts. Now they've changed their minds, because it's just as dangerous there."

"*My* mum says that no place is safe, so her and me may as well stick it out together," boasted Tom. "She wouldn't even *consider* sending me away. And Norah's parents wouldn't either. We're lucky!"

"I'm going to fetch some water," said Norah abruptly, climbing down with the pail. She wove through trees heavy with ripening apples to the stream at the end of the orchard, thinking of everyone in Britain scurrying around like ants under a large, descending boot like theirs, all trying to find a safe place when there wasn't one.

She sat down by the water, took off her socks and shoes, and dangled her hot feet in the stream. She would linger here until they'd had time to finish talking about being sent away. For a few seconds the fleeting blue of a kingfisher distracted her. But she couldn't help brooding about evacuation.

Last fall her village had been considered safe. Hundreds of London children had been sent to the Ashford area, and one whole school had come to Ringden. They boarded with different families and had their own classes in the church hall. For four months the 'vaccies and the village children had waged a battle of hurled mud and words. The visitors complained about having to go all the way into Gilden to see the pictures; the village mothers objected to the bad language their children were learning. When nothing seemed to be happening in the war, the evacuees had returned to London.

But then the "phoney war" had ended and the danger had become real. When France fell and Churchill said the Battle of Britain had begun, Norah had helped pull up all the signposts in the village to confuse the enemy. "We shall fight in the field and in the streets, we shall fight in the hills," Churchill's solemn voice chanted from the wireless.

Norah was proud that her whole family was helping to fight. In January her older sisters, Muriel and Tibby, had joined the Auxiliary Territorial Service; they were stationed in Chester. "Not a nice thing for young girls, being in the forces like a man," said nosy Mrs Curteis next door. But Dad was proud. "My girls are as brave as any man," he boasted. He was too old to enlist, so he joined the Home Guard. Mum spent every morning in the church hall, marking blankets and sewing hospital bags for wounded soldiers. Norah, besides performing her Skywatcher duties, had donated sixpence to the village Spitfire fund—enough to manufacture one rivet. Gavin wasn't doing anything, but he was only five—too young and silly to count.

The war was the most exciting thing that had ever happened in Norah's ten years, and this summer was the best part of it. Other summers were a pleasant, mild blur of building sandcastles on the beach near Grandad's house in Camber.

But one day at the end of last August, Norah had found herself filling sandbags instead of playing.

Now there was a bright edge to everything; even the weather was exaggerated. The coldest winter in a hundred years was followed by a short spring and an early summer. As the war news grew worse and the grown-ups huddled anxiously around the wireless, day after day dawned hot and clear. At night, the sky's inky blackness was pinpointed with strangely brilliant stars, the only lights in Britain besides the searchlights that were not blacked out.

Every evening this week the news announcer had given out the "scores" of the battle in the sky as if it were a football match. Norah could hardly remember what life had been like before this war. How could anyone bear to be sent away from it? Tom was right—they were lucky that their parents were so sensible.

But then she felt afraid again, because she wasn't at all sure that *her* parents would remain sensible.

III
LITTLE WHITEBULL

After Norah had run back to the fort and swished out the lemonade cups, they all started home for tea. When they reached the middle of the village, Harry and Jasper gave the Skywatchers' secret signal—little finger and thumb extended like an aeroplane—and scampered down their lane. Tom and Norah put their fingers crossways under their noses and goose-stepped down the main street, singing loudly in time:

Whistle while you work!
Mussolini is a twerp!
Hitler's barmy
So's his army
Whistle while you work!

They passed the church and the stone vicarage beside it. The Smiths were probably inside, packing to go to Canada. Dulcie was in Norah's class. She was the sort of girl who fretted if she forgot her handkerchief. Lucy was a little older than Gavin and spent a lot of her time whining.

"Poor Goosey and Loosey," mocked Norah. "I bet they'll be afraid of wolves in Canada." Being nasty helped her calm down a bit. Then she felt sorry for them—they would be left out of the war.

She said goodbye to Tom at his mother's grocery shop and ran to her house. She was late for tea, but Mum probably wouldn't scold her.

That was part of Norah's increasing uneasiness. Her parents let her and Gavin stay up late, spoke to them in strange, gentle voices and gave them sad looks when they thought the children didn't notice. Gavin probably didn't. But every night Norah listened to Mum and Dad's worried murmur downstairs.

Norah paused at the front of her small, weather-boarded house. Its shabby exterior was brightened by the masses of zinnias and hollyhocks that flanked the door. A sign on the sagging gate said Little Whitebull in faded wooden letters. No one knew why their house was called that. It had been already named when her parents had bought it, just after Muriel was born.

The gate needed painting as well as mending, but Dad was too busy these days to do much work around the house. Norah studied the loose hinges; perhaps she could fix it and show them how useful she was. She could paint the sign again in bright red. And she would start to keep her room tidier and help with the washing up. Feeling more cheerful, she ran into the house.

"I'm home!" she shouted, clattering through the front room to the large kitchen where they spent most of their time. "Sorry I'm late, Mum."

Mrs Stoakes came out of the scullery and wiped back the lank hair that always hung into her eyes. "Where have you *been,* Norah?" she asked anxiously. "You weren't anywhere near that German plane, were you? I just heard about it."

"Not really," mumbled Norah. Not near enough to touch it, she added to herself.

Her mother shuddered. "It was terribly close. The next thing we know, we'll have one on top of us. Sit down, sweetheart, there's sausages."

Sweetheart? Mum never gushed; she was usually quick tempered and brusque. Now she was like a person in disguise.

If she was going to play-act, then Norah would too. "Thanks, Mum," she said politely. "Did you have to queue long at the butcher's?" She forced herself to eat slowly instead of wolfing down her food as usual.

Gavin was the only person who was himself. He sat at the table with his jammy bread divided into two, marching each one to collide with its twin and come apart in sticky strings. He hummed to himself with a dreamy expression, the way he always did in his private games.

Norah glanced at her mother. Surely she'd have to react to such a mess: there was jam all over the tablecloth. But all Mum said was, "Here, pet, let me wipe your hands."

Norah sighed. Gavin usually got away with a lot, but not sloppy eating. She bent over her milky tea, her brain buzzing. Something was definitely up.

The hens in the back garden chittered indignantly as Dad pushed through the scullery door. He removed the bicycle clips from his trouser legs, kissed Mum, ruffled Gavin's hair and grinned at Norah. "What have *you* been up to today? Seen anything interesting?" His green-grey eyes, which everyone said were exactly like hers, teased her as usual.

Norah forgot to be polite. "Oh, Dad, there was a crash-landed plane—a ME 109! You could see the bullet holes and the swastika and everything!"

"I passed it on my way home—the lorry was taking it away."

"Norah!" snapped Mum. "I thought you said you weren't close! You have to be more careful or I'll make you stay in your own garden, like the Smith girls. I really don't know what to do with you these days—the war is making you wild."

"Now, Jane, she couldn't come to much harm looking at a plane that's out of commission," said Dad mildly.

This was more normal. Norah relaxed and concentrated on her sausages, as Dad collapsed in his favourite chair with a groan. "Come and pull my shoes off, old man," he said to Gavin. He had only an hour between arriving home from his bookkeeping job in Gilden and setting out for his Home Guard duties.

Gavin picked up his small worn elephant and went over to his father. "Creature will pull your shoes off—he's very strong."

What a baby Gavin was, still playing with toy animals. Jasper was only three years older, but he was as brave as Tom. Gavin was such a namby-pamby brother. Everyone said he should have been a girl, and Norah a boy.

Dad looked up from the pages of the *Kentish Express*. "They're letting the hop-pickers come from London as usual," he said to Mum. "It says arrangements have been made for protection in case of air raids."

Mum opened the scullery door to cool off the steamy kitchen, which smelled pleasantly of hot fat and the clean clothes airing in front of the grate. Dad switched on the wireless and Gavin curled up in his lap. The familiar voice of Larry the Lamb filled the room.

Norah pretended to be too old for "The Children's Hour", but she still liked hearing Dennis the Dachshund talk backwards. As she listened, she surprised her mother by first helping dry the dishes and then sitting down to struggle with her knitting. The oily grey wool, which was supposed to be turned into a "comfort" for a sailor, cut into her hands.

"Good-night, children, everywhere," said the voice from the wireless.

"Good-night, Uncle Mac," said Gavin solemnly, as he always did.

"Dad," whispered Norah nervously, after the news was over and while Mum was still in the scullery. There was something she had to find out, even though it scared her to ask. "Do you know if they found the pilot?"

Dad gave her a warning glance, the one that meant Don't Worry Your Mother. "Yes," he murmured. "They picked him up near Woodchurch. He was wounded, poor lad—gave himself up easily."

Norah's chest felt lighter. At least she didn't have to worry about him wandering into their village.

Of course, if Hitler invaded Britain, as everyone thought he might, a *lot* of Nazis might come into Ringden—even into Little Whitebull! That thought made Norah feel choked up again and she shifted irritably. What was the matter with her? She had never been afraid before.

Her father stood up and stretched. "Time to get changed." He caught his wife's eye before he added, "Don't make any plans for the morning, Norah. Your mother and I want to discuss something with you. And I'll help you finish your kite tomorrow, Gavin, since it's Saturday."

"Can I stay up and listen to 'ITMA'?" Norah asked desperately. If he said no, everything would be ordinary.

"I don't see why not," said Dad gently.

After he left, dressed in his World War I uniform and carrying a shotgun, Norah made herself into a tight ball in his chair. Her suspicions were growing to a terrible certainty.

Before she had time to ponder further, the back door opened again and a tubby man with a snowy fringe around his otherwise bald head struggled in, loaded with packages and suitcases.

"Grandad!" shouted Norah and Gavin.

"Father! What on earth are *you* doing here?"

The old man chuckled as he let his luggage drop. He lifted Gavin into the air. "Bombed out! The drafted Hun put one right through my roof! All rubble, my dears, all rubble. So I've come to stay with you." He bent over to Norah and tickled her cheek with his stiff moustache. "What do you think of that, my fierce little soldier?"

Mum sank to a chair. "Bombed out... Father, are you all right? Are you hurt?"

"Don't fret, Janie. I'm right as rain, because I wasn't at home when they called. Came back from the pub to find a flattened house. So I just packed up what I could find and got on the bus. Better to live inland anyhow—the salt air was bad for my rheumatism." His sea-blue eyes sparkled under his droopy white eyebrows. "Got enough room for your old dad?"

"You know we have—we'd always give you a home. But you could have been killed! Oh, Father, this bloody war..."

Norah froze, shocked, as her mother, whom she had never seen cry, began to shake with sobs. Her mouth trembled and the tears slid over her thin cheeks as her weeping grew louder.

"*Don't,* Muv!" cried Gavin, pulling on her arm. "Did you hurt yourself?" Mrs Stoakes pulled him onto her knee and clutched him to her, burying her face in his neck. Gavin looked scared and tried to free himself.

"Now, now, Jane, enough of that." Grandad patted his daughter's shoulder awkwardly. "I *wasn't* killed. Never felt more alive, in fact. Nothing like a close call to make you see things in perspective! We'll weather this war out together now—that's how it should be, the whole family in one place." He released Gavin from his mother's grasp. "If you search my pockets, you might find a sweetie."

"To avoid watching her mother, Norah turned to the fire and lifted the heavy kettle of water onto the grate. She had never made tea on her own befoe, but she'd seen Mum do it often enough. When the water boiled she poured it carefully over the leaves and filled the cups with milk, sugar and tea. She offered one to Mum and one to Grandad.

"Norah, what a help!" Mum's tears had stopped and she gave a weak smile. "What would I do without you?" Then she looked as if she might cry again.

Norah poured herself a cup, surprised her mother hadn't said anything about using some of tomorrow's rations. They all sat around the kitchen table and, to her relief, the adults began to talk normally.

Norah stared incredulously at Grandad, hardly daring to believe he was here. The war was shifting people around too rapidly. Some, like Molly and Muriel and Tibby, suddenly went away; others turned up unannounced and homeless. A few days ago the whole of Mrs Parker's brother's large family had arrived on her doorstep. Their house in Detling had been bombed and they, too, had been lucky enough to be out when it happened.

Norah's throat and chest constricted with fear as she thought of Grandad's cottage, the one where she'd spent her summers, flattened to rubble. But Grandad was safe, and it would be wonderful to have him living with them. She wondered what Dad would think. Although Mum and Grandad often argued, they thrived on it. Dad was always polite, but Norah knew he and the old man didn't agree on much.

Grandad winked at Norah. "Now we'll have a good time, eh young ones?"

Norah winked back. She climbed onto Grandad's knee and began to tell him about the plane.

Later that night a commotion downstairs woke her up.

Dad had arrived home and was exclaiming about finding Grandad there. Norah lay rigidly in bed, listening to the usual murmur of worried adult voices. Then Grandad's rose above the rest, angry and accusing. She couldn't make out his words but the stubborn strength in his voice cheered her up. If her parents were telling him the decision she dreaded, Grandad was on her side.

IV
"I WON'T GO!"

They told her after breakfast. Mum had sent Gavin over to play with Joey, who lived across the road. Norah was dismayed when Grandad went out as well, a furious expression on his face.

She was invited to sit down in the front room. Muriel insisted on calling it the "drawing room". It was only used on special occasions—when Muriel and Tibby entertained their young men, or when the vicar came to tea. The flimsy chairs were too stiff to be comfortable, as if they proclaimed "only serious matters are discussed here."

Norah tipped back her chair and waited. Mum had just polished the windows and a faint whiff of ammonia came from them. For the rest of her life, Norah would never smell ammonia without a flutter of panic.

Dad began speaking in such a cheerful voice that she wanted to scream. "Well, Norah, you and Gavin are going to have a great adventure!"

"*No—*" said Norah at once, but he waved her to be still. "Hold your horses! Just listen for a moment, then you can have your say. You're going to travel on a big ship... all the way to Canada! Canadian families have offered to provide homes for British children until the war is over. Your mother and I would feel much more at ease if we knew you and Gavin were safe. And what an opportunity for you, to go overseas, to learn about another country..."

His voice faltered at Norah's expression. Mum looked as stricken as she was.

"I know it's upsetting," Dad continued gently, "but I think you knew we were considering it."

Of course she had known. After France had fallen in June, all the grown-ups had talked about sending the children away. That was when Molly and Pete had gone. She'd heard Dad read aloud the newspaper notice about applying for overseas evacuation, but she was too worried to ask if they'd actually done it. A few days later Dad had asked casually, "Norah, if you could visit another country, which one would you prefer—Australia, New Zealand, South Africa, or Canada..."

"None of them!" Norah had cried.

Then Norah and Gavin had had their photographs taken in Gilden. Norah had wondered why.

But after that, for a long time, nothing more had been said. She had almost forgotten about it in the growing excitement of the war. The possibility of being sent away had festered under the surface, however, and now at last it had burst open like a ripe boil. For a few seconds Norah sat in stunned disbelief. Then she jumped up, knocking over her chair.

"I won't go!"

"Calm down," said Dad. He reached out his arm, but Norah brushed it aside. Dad sighed. "Listen to me, Norah. You've had an easy, sheltered life up to now. Now we're asking you to do something difficult. I know you can—you've always been my bravest girl."

"But I don't *want* to!" She was astounded that they would force her. "I don't want to go away to another country and leave you! I'd miss you! I'd miss out on the war! It's braver to stay here, not to run away! And children are *useful.* I watch for paratroopers every day, just like the

Observer Corps. I helped pull up the signposts. And I'll do some of the housework so Mum can spend more time at the hall. I'll think of something for Gavin to do, too. I'll—I'll teach him to knit!"

Mum looked close to tears again. "Oh Norah, Norah, of course you don't want to go. I wish so much you didn't have to. But don't you see how going would be helping the war? You'd free Dad and me from worrying about you. And . . ." She paused, as if she weren't sure she should go on, "and if worse comes to worse, at least two members of the family will be safe and . . . free."

"And you'll be like ambassadors!" broke in Dad. "You'll meet children from another country and promote international understanding. That's the best way I can think of to end war . . ."

"Have you told her?" Grandad stood in the doorway, wiping his shining forehead with his handkerchief.

Mum turned to him impatiently. "Father, we said we wanted to be alone with Norah! Yes, we've told her—but we haven't finished. Please wait until we have."

But Grandad came into the room, muttering, "I'm part of this family too." He pulled Norah onto his knee and Norah's spirits lifted. Just in time!

With an irritated glance at Grandad, Dad continued to explain to Norah why it would be safer if she and Gavin left England.

"What will *Hitler* think if we start fleeing the country?" interrupted Grandad. "We're supposed to be sticking together and fighting!"

"Norah and Gavin are only children," said Dad patiently.

"Then what will he think about us panicking so much that we send away our children? I suppose you'll send *me* next! Get rid of the young and the old! We're useless, so send us away!"

"Father!" Mum turned bright pink. "They're our children—let *us* decide, and stop interfering. If you can't keep quiet, then leave the room."

Grandad scowled at her, but he shut up. He and Norah listened to the rest of Mum and Dad's reasonable arguments. And, slowly, Norah realized that they had lost. Grown-ups could always make children do what they wanted them to. She felt Grandad give a long sigh. Old people had to do what grown-ups decided, too.

Norah slid down to the floor, drew her feet up and clutched her knees to her chest. Her eyes prickled but she forced them wide open—she would *not* cry.

Desperately, she tried one last argument. "Even the princesses aren't being evacuated!" she protested. "The Queen said in the paper that they wouldn't send them out of the country—Tom's mum read it to us." Norah had always felt a special link with Princess Margaret Rose, who was almost her age. She was sure Margaret Rose had refused to go, and that's what had convinced the King and Queen.

But Mum and Dad just smiled, the way they did when they thought Norah was being amusing. "The princesses are in a safe part of the country somewhere, not right in the path of an invasion as you are," said Dad. "And a large number of well-off children *have* been sent overseas. Why should they be the only ones? Now the government has finally decided to pay for those who can't afford it."

Norah felt small and lost and wounded.

"You must have some questions," Dad prompted.

"When do we go?" she asked weakly.

"On Monday. Mum will take you to London, and an escort will meet you there. I wish it wasn't so sudden, but they only let us know a few days ago."

"There will be lots of other children with you," said

Mum. "It will be like a church picnic! And the Smiths are going too, so you'll have someone from your own village along. Derek can keep an eye on all of you."

"Where—where shall we *live* in Canada? How long will we have to stay?"

"You'll be living somewhere in Ontario," Dad told her. "I believe it's the largest province. You won't know who you'll be staying with until you get there, but I'm sure they'll be good people. Anyone who offers to do this must be kind. And we don't know for how long..." He looked apologetic. "Perhaps a year."

A *year?* When they came home she would be eleven! And leaving the day after *tomorrow?*

Dad was watching her. "Norah, I think that's enough to absorb for now. You go out and play and we'll talk about it again later. Send Gavin home, will you? I don't know how much he'll understand, but he has to be told."

As Norah left, her parents were arguing with Grandad again, but his voice sounded old and defeated. It was no use. They were sending her away and there was nothing she could do about it.

V

TOO MANY GOODBYES

"But you can't!" Tom cried.

"I have to. I told them all the reasons they shouldn't send me, but they don't understand."

The four Skywatchers sat in gloomy silence. They were used to grown-ups not understanding.

"Do you—do you think I'm a coward?" Norah asked Tom. She couldn't bear it if he did.

"Of course not—you don't want to go. But it's a rotten shame." Tom glanced at the two wide-eyed little boys. He looked deflated. "Everyone's leaving! First Pete and Molly and the Fowlers, and now you. How are we going to keep up our work with just three of us?"

They sat in a row without speaking, watching the sky as usual. But there had been no battles today and the air was ominously still, as if the war had stopped to hold its breath.

Norah already felt like a stranger. "Can I pick some shrapnel to take?" she asked finally.

Tom nodded and she chose some jagged pieces from their collection. She yearned for the Boot, but it was much too big to pack, and it belonged in the Lookout.

"You can have the plane book if you like," said Tom.

"What for?" said Norah. "There won't be any enemy planes flying over Canada—there's no war there." A country without a war seemed a very dull prospect.

Then the goodbyes began. Dad sent a telegram to Muriel and Tibby and they returned one immediately. HAVE WONDERFUL TIME KEEP CHEERFUL it said, as if Norah and Gavin were going on a holiday. It was so long since the older girls had left Ringden that receiving a farewell message seemed unnecessary; Norah had *said* goodbye to them.

That afternoon the friends and neighbours Norah had known all her life began dropping in with advice.

"I've given your mother some of my camomile tea," said Mrs Curteis. "If you sip some every morning until you board the ship, you won't be seasick."

"Aren't you a lucky girl, to see the world!" said Norah's headmaster. "You must observe everything carefully."

"You'll have to be a little mother to Gavin now," Joey's mum clucked at her.

Norah was told to dress warmly, not to pick up Canadian slang and to remember she was English. And again and again she heard the words, "Take care of Gavin."

Gavin told everyone that Creature was excited about going on a train and a ship. That was as much as he seemed to grasp. "They're sending us away!" Norah wanted to shout. But there was no point in upsetting him.

Grandad glowered at the visitors from a corner of the kitchen, where he sat with his pipe and newspaper. He was allowed to sulk; Norah had to be polite and submit to all the kissing, patting and advice.

Not all the neighbours approved. "I couldn't send my children so far away," whispered Mrs Baker to Mrs Maybourne. "What about German torpedoes—have they considered that?"

"Shhhh!" her husband warned, with a glance at Norah, who was getting used to pretending she didn't hear things.

Why couldn't Mrs Baker tell that to Mum and Dad? But

Grandad had mentioned it too, and Dad said that staying in England was a greater risk than U-boats.

In church the next day the Smith girls waved at Norah importantly, as if their shared fate made them allies.

"The last hymn is for our five young travellers who are about to start on a great adventure," announced Reverend Smith. "Number 301". His eyes glistened as he gazed at his three children in the front pew.

"O hear us when we cry to thee / For those in peril on the sea," droned the congregation.

"How could he!" hissed Norah's mother. She refused to sing and glared at the vicar, whom she had never liked.

Norah could sense the whole churchful of sympathetic eyes fastened on her back. She gripped her hymn book and sang without thinking of the words.

After church, more people milled around the door to say goodbye. Dulcie and Lucy, dressed alike as usual, skipped over. Dulcie, who often acted afraid of Norah, was unusually forward. "Oh, Norah, isn't it exciting! I'm so glad we're going where it's safe. I wish Mummy and Daddy could come too, but they have to stay and help win the war."

"*We* should be staying to help win the war," said Norah coldly.

"But we're not old enough! Daddy says children are better out of the way."

"Not old enough": that's what Norah's sisters had said to her all her life. Even after Gavin had arrived, she had had to spend a lot of time proving she was old enough. She scowled at Dulcie, who had always reminded her of a calf, with her mild, bulging eyes and dull expression. Just because they were stuck together on this journey, it would never do to let Dulcie think they were going to be friends.

"Are you bringing all your dolls with you, Goosey?" Norah taunted.

Dulcie wilted at the familiar nickname, the way she did at school. Norah felt as guilty as she always did when she teased her. The guilt made her even more irritated.

"Thank you, we would appreciate a ride into town," Mum was saying to Mrs Smith. "Are you sure you can spare the petrol? Come along, Norah, we still have a lot of packing to do"

Everyone at church had commented on the unusually calm sky. But the air-raid siren sounded right in the middle of Sunday dinner. Dad rushed off and Mum made them all go into the shelter in the garden.

"Can't I watch?" begged Norah. "It might be the last fight I see."

"Not after that German plane," said Mum grimly.

Norah and Grandad peeked out of the low entrance of the corrugated steel structure while Mum read to Gavin on one of the narrow bunks. Grandad had hardly spoken since Saturday morning, but he squeezed Norah's shoulder as they watched the planes soar over.

There was fighting on and off for the rest of the day. Norah was made to stay either inside the shelter or in the house, helping to pack. They were only allowed to take one piece of luggage each.

"I can't fit in any more," sighed Mum that night. She sat on the end of Norah's bed, folding the last of the freshly washed and ironed clothes into the small brown suitcase. "I hope I've packed enough woollies. We'll send more clothes to you later."

She glanced around Norah's room. It had belonged to Muriel and Tibby, but Norah had claimed it after they left.

Three neglected dolls sat demurely under the window. The ceiling was hung with balsa-wood aeroplanes, twisting slightly in the warm night air. Mum looked back at Norah, already in bed and escaping into a *Hotspur* comic.

"Is there anything else you want to take? One of your planes, perhaps?"

"No thank you," said Norah stiffly. She had already packed her shrapnel and a few comics. Mum was in disguise again, as bright and cheerful as if this weren't Norah's last night at home.

"I wish I knew more about Canada to tell you. I imagine it will be beautiful, though—like *Anne of Green Gables.* And the Dionne Quintuplets live in Canada. Just imagine, five little girls exactly alike! Perhaps you'll see them!"

She looked desperate when Norah didn't answer. "Wait..." Mum left the room and returned in a few seconds with the family photograph that always stood on the mantelpiece. "I want you to have this, Norah. I'll wrap it in your blue jersey."

Norah just grunted. Mum sat down again, patted her hand and sighed. "I know you're angry with us. I don't blame you, but wait until you get on the ship and start having a good time! It won't be as bad as you think, I promise. I wish I knew who will be taking care of you, but Dad's right—they're sure to be kind. Just don't judge them too soon. You know how stubborn you can be." She smiled. "And try not to lose your temper. You've inherited that from me, I'm afraid. But you've always been so sure of yourself, I'm not really worried about you, Norah. *You're* tough, but Gavin isn't. He's so sensitive, and he's very young to be going so far away. You'll have to take especially good care of him." Her voice broke.

Norah yawned deliberately. "I'm going to sleep now." She flopped over and buried her face in her pillow. What about *her*? She, too, was young to be going so far away, wasn't she? Gavin had always been Mum's favourite, though, just as Norah was Dad's.

Mum kissed the back of Norah's neck. "Good-night, sweetheart. Go right to sleep—you have a big day tomorrow."

The Smiths were supposed to pick them up after dinner. Norah spent the morning hanging about outside the house. She looked for the hedgehog they left bowls of milk for, but he had disappeared—perhaps the air-raid sirens had frightened him away. She filled the stirrup-pump with water from the red fire bucket by the back door and sprinkled the carrots with it. Finally she sat glumly on the step and watched the silly chickens scratching in the dirt.

Mum made her and Gavin have a bath before dinner. She washed their hair, cut their nails and dressed them in clean clothes from the skin out. Dad had polished their shoes until they were as glossy as chestnuts. When he arrived home for dinner, they sat down to an extra-special meal. But Norah could only push her fishcakes around her plate.

"The Smiths' car is going to be awfully crowded," said Dad. "Why don't you cycle into town with me, Norah? If we leave now, we'll have plenty of time before the train."

"Oh, yes, please!" she said. In the holidays she often went into Gilden with her father.

"But you'll get your dress dirty," protested her mother. "I want you to look nice. You know how tidy Dulcie and Lucy always are."

"She'll get grubby on the train anyhow," said Dad. "Say goodbye to Grandad and we'll leave now."

But Grandad was nowhere to be found. "We already said goodbye," mumbled Norah. Last night he had hugged her fiercely and pressed a sixpence into her hand. "You keep fighting, young one," he whispered. Norah couldn't answer. It seemed so unfair that Grandad had come to live with them just as she had to leave.

She and Dad rode down the main street side by side. Norah tried to fix the familiar landmarks in her mind. The village pond, where she and Tom fished for tench. The wide green that was now littered with old bedsprings, hayricks and kitchen ranges to stop enemy planes from landing. Tom's mother's shop, where she spent most of her pocket money on sweets and comics.

As they reached the edge of the village and Mrs Chandler's house, she kept her head down in case the Skywatchers were in the Lookout, watching her go by. She hadn't seen them again; there were enough good-byes to say as it was.

They rode through the peaceful countryside in silence. The early afternoon sky was overcast and grey. "Maybe it will rain at last," said Dad. "There won't be any fighting today." Norah looked up automatically, but there was only a flock of black and white lapwings overhead, veering like Spitfires and crying plaintively.

"Let's rest here a minute." Dad pulled over to the stile leading to Stumble Wood. Norah leaned her bicycle against it and Dad lifted her up to sit on top. A cloud of white butterflies hovered in the cool air.

"How will you get my bicycle back to Ringden?" she asked, gazing sadly at its worn leather seat. It was old, black and ugly, a hand-me-down from Tibby, but it was her favourite possession.

"Someone from work can ride it back. Don't worry, I'll keep it shipshape for your return. Now, Norah..."

Norah tried to avoid his eyes; not *another* pep talk.

"I want you to remember three things," said Dad gravely. "Most important, of course, is to take care of Gavin. I don't think he really knows he's going away from us and perhaps that's for the best. But when he realizes, he may become very upset—you'll have to comfort him. The second is that you aren't just going to Canada as yourself. You're representing England. If you're impolite or ungrateful, the Canadians will think that's what English children are like. So remember your manners and whenever you're in doubt, think of how Mum and I would expect you to behave. And third . . ." He finally smiled, "Have a good time! I know you will. Just think, you're the first one in the family to go overseas! I wish *I'd* had the opportunity to travel more when I was young."

He really was envious, Norah realized, not just jollying her along. Dad had worked for most of his life as a book-keeper in the tannery in Gilden; the only time he'd been away was in the first war.

Norah swallowed hard. "Oh, Dad . . . do I *have* to go?"

Dad looked sympathetic, but said softly, "Yes, Norah—you have to go. I'm sorry, but you just have to believe me when I tell you it's for the best. Come along now, we'd better carry on."

They reached the Gilden railway station just as the Smiths' blue car drew up. Dulcie and Lucy jumped out, wearing smocked pink dresses and pink straw hats. Derek was in his grammar school uniform. Gavin rushed over to the engine.

"I wish I could come to London with you," said Dad. He pulled Gavin back from the tracks and picked him up. "Goodbye, old man. You do exactly what Norah says."

"Say goodbye to Creature," ordered Gavin. Dad shook the elephant's trunk solemnly.

He handed Norah a twisted white bag. "Sweets for the

train," he winked. "Now remember what I told you. And have a safe and happy journey, my brave Norah." He kissed her quickly and turned his head, but Norah had seen his tears.

She stomped after her mother onto the train. If Dad was so upset, then why was he doing this to her? She glared at the Smiths in the opposite seat, chattering to their father, who was able to spare the time to come to London.

Steam drifted by the window and Norah could hardly make out her father's waving arm. When the mist cleared, she waved back and forced herself to smile.

For the next two hours, Norah almost forgot why they were going to London. The only other time she had been was the Christmas before last, when Muriel and Tibby had taken her to see *Peter Pan.* This journey seemed the same. The train still chuffed along sounding important, they still waited until after Ashford to eat their sandwiches and she couldn't shake off the familiar train feeling of having a treat.

But there were differences too: the large number of men and women in uniform, the whited-out station signs they passed and the fine netting on the windows in case of flying glass. There was only a small hole left in the middle to peek through.

And this time she didn't even see London. They went straight from one train station to another via the underground. Dozens of other children and parents waited for the train north. The children were all, like Norah, carrying luggage and coats and gas mask cases, and they all had large labels attached to them, as if they were going to be sent through the post. Some of the younger ones, like Gavin and Lucy, also clutched stuffed animals or dolls. Most of the crowd babbled in high, excited voices; others were quiet and wary. "Is Your Journey Really Necessary?" asked a poster on the wall.

Norah was introduced to a fat, flustered woman called Miss Nott. "I'm your train escort," she explained. She consulted a list. "Is this all the Kent and Sussex children? Say goodbye, then—we must go on board."

The train waited, a snorting black dragon. Norah gulped and took her mother's hand.

"Oh, Norah..." Mum smoothed Norah's hair, refastened it at the side, and pulled down her felt hat. "Hang onto your coats carefully," she said. "Remember that your five pounds and your papers are sewn inside." She kissed Norah's forehead. "Make sure you both clean your teeth every night." All she said to Gavin was a choked "Goodbye, pet—you take care of Creature." Then she helped him on with his rucksack and put his hand in Norah's.

"Come on," muttered Norah, pulling Gavin's arm as Miss Nott beckoned.

"Are we going on the other train now?" asked Gavin with delight. They were whisked into the compartment with the rest of their group and couldn't get close enough to the window to wave goodbye.

VI

"ARE WE DOWNHEARTED?"

The eight children under the charge of Miss Nott were crammed into one compartment. Derek was the eldest and Gavin the youngest. Two of the children across from Norah were boys around Lucy's age. They had brought along cards, and Lucy and Gavin joined their game of snap on the floor. The other stranger was a cheerful older girl called Margery. She tried to talk to them, but Dulcie was too shy to answer and Norah didn't feel like being friendly.

She read all her comics, and then there was nothing to do. She couldn't even look out the window, which had been closed and blacked out for the evening. "Do you know where we're going?" she asked Derek. He was also being unsociable, his face hidden behind his book.

Derek looked insulted at being spoken to by someone his sister's age. "Liverpool, I imagine," he said shortly, in the posh accent he'd picked up at his school.

They all ate their sandwiches, and the compartment became a smelly mess of greasy papers, crumbs and spilt milk. Miss Nott and Margery darted around trying to tidy up. Then Miss Nott's plump figure swayed in the corridor while she led a singalong: "Run Rabbit Run", "Roll Out the Barrel" and "There'll Always Be an England". Dulcie joined in dutifully, but Norah refused.

The singing began to falter as the children grew drowsy. Gavin fell asleep and Norah tried to pull her cramped arm from under him. Finally she dozed off herself, the train's chant intruding into her dreams: Don't *want* to go, don't *want* to go, don't *want* to go...

They arrived in Liverpool early in the morning. Miss Nott said goodbye, looking relieved to be free of them. The dazed and hungry children were driven to a hostel at the edge of the city where they spent the next few days, eating at long tables and sleeping in long rows on straw pallets on the floor. The hostel filled up with children from all over Britain, many with strong accents that were hard to decipher. Norah began to feel like a performing puppet. Again and again she was asked to follow someone, to get ready for bed, to get up, to eat, to play games and to sing rousing songs.

On the first day a doctor examined her and pronounced her "scrawny but fit". The next morning an earnest and important-looking man told the assembled children, as Dad had, that they were little ambassadors. "When things go wrong, as they often will, remember you are British and grin and bear it. Be truthful, brave, kind and grateful."

Norah stored this advice at the back of her mind along with all the other she had received and promptly forgot it. The only person's she followed was Mum's: she carefully cleaned her teeth every evening. It was somehow soothing to do such a simple task.

As for looking after Gavin, she left that up to the women in charge. She waved to him in the morning and reminded him to clean *his* teeth at night. But she had too much to brood about to consider him in between. Besides, he wasn't making a fuss, although he looked bewildered and whispered a lot to Creature.

On the third morning they were taken on a bus to the wharves. It took most of the day to board the ship. First they were herded into a cavernous shed called the Embarkation Area. Hundreds of children raced about while harried-looking escorts tried to find their groups.

Norah's escort was Miss Montague-Scott. She was an enthusiastic, strong woman with springy brown curls, much livelier than the frazzled Miss Nott. Norah had already met her at the hostel; Miss Montague-Scott would take care of them all the way to Canada. There were fifteen children in her group, including Dulcie and Lucy, all of them girls. But now Miss Montague-Scott was leading Gavin up to them.

"Here she is! Norah, we've decided Gavin's too young to go with the boys. He'll stay with us and sleep in your cabin."

Norah looked over her brother doubtfully; now she'd *have* to look after him. She'd never had to before; Mum or Muriel or Tibby always had.

Gavin's cheeks were as flushed as if he had a fever. "Are we going on the ship now, Norah? Will Muv and Dad be on the ship too?"

Oh *no!* Didn't he realize? Norah looked around frantically for Miss Montague-Scott, but she had hurried away to organize someone else.

She couldn't tell him—then he'd cry and everyone would expect her to do something. "Hold on to me, we're supposed to follow the others," she muttered, ignoring his question.

A woman fastened a small hard disc stamped with a number around Norah's neck. Another official checked their identity cards and passports and made sure they didn't have too much luggage. Then someone collected all their gas masks. "You won't need these any more," she smiled.

Norah clutched hers possessively. "Can't I keep it as a souvenir?"

"You have enough to carry," said the woman. Norah

handed over the cardboard case she'd taken with her everywhere for the past year. She was surprised to discover she felt attached to it; she'd always hated wearing her gas mask for school drills. It smelled like hot rubber and made her want to gag. But you could produce rude noises and spit by puffing into it, and once she'd sent her whole class into convulsions by pretending to blow its long "nose". Without it she felt naked and vulnerable.

Miss Montague-Scott led her group to the wharf. They sat down and waited for hours to board the ss *Zandvoort.* Sandwiches were passed down the long lines of children, and then a man started them singing. Were they going to have to sing all the way to Canada?

"Come along, everyone," the man exhorted through his megaphone. "Stand up and take some d-e-e-e-e-p breaths. Now, all together . . . 'There'll *al*-ways *be* an *Eng*-land . . .' "

It sounded like a dirge. A group of boys behind them broke into the singing loudly: "There'll always be a SCOTLAND . . ." Norah turned around and grinned with surprise.

The leader looked startled, then he smiled too. "Good for you, boys, that's the spirit! Now, kiddies, you're about to start on a marvellous adventure. I see some sad faces in the crowd—that will never do. Are we downhearted?"

A few voices called out "No!"

"I can't hear you! *Everyone,* now—are we downhearted?"

"NO!" roared the children.

Dulcie was standing beside Norah; her hysterical scream pierced Norah's right ear. Again and again the man led the crowd to yell "NO!"

Norah pressed her lips tightly together. This was as bad as being asked to clap if you believed in fairies.

"That's much better!" laughed the jolly leader. "Now,

before you sit down again—thumbs up! Come on, everyone, show me how!"

"Thumbs up, Norah!" said Dulcie, closing her fists and pointing her thumbs. She looked puzzled when Norah ignored her.

Finally they were allowed to walk up the gangway to the huge, grey ship. Norah sniffed in a mixture of tar, steam and salt water. In spite of herself, she felt a twinge of excitement. She'd never been on a ship before.

"Smile, everyone!" They were asked to lean over the railing, wave to the photographers and drone once again, "There'll Always Be an England".

Norah held onto Gavin's small hot palm and took a last look at Britain. Everything was grey: the dirty water below, the smoking chimneys of Liverpool and the leaden sky. Slender beams of searchlights crisscrossed the dusk and high in the air floated the silvery, pig-shaped barrage balloons.

Then the engines thrummed, the whistles blew and the ship began to move. Norah turned her back on home and faced the other way.

VII
THE VOYAGE

Norah and Gavin were assigned to the same cabin as Goosey and Loosey. "Isn't this nice for you!" boomed Miss Montague-Scott, popping her head in to tell them to get ready for bed. "Four friends from home bunking together!"

It was awful. Dulcie giggled as they banged into each other in the cramped space. Lucy complained because her nightdress was wrinkled. Worst of all was Gavin. He looked around the cabin frantically, then shook Norah's arm. "Where are Muv and Dad? Why haven't they come yet?"

Norah wanted to shake him. How could he be so dim? "They aren't *here,*" she said impatiently. "Don't be so silly. They're at home in Ringden and we're going to Canada without them."

"Didn't you know that, Gavin?" said Lucy with all the superiority of someone seven years old. "We aren't going to see our mothers and fathers for a long, *long* time, not until the war is over."

"Of course he knows," snapped Norah. "Clean your teeth, Gavin." She tried to find their toothbrushes in the clutter.

But Gavin just sat on his bunk looking stunned. He fingered his elephant. "Creature said they would be on the ship," he whispered.

"Well, they aren't." He continued to sit passively, so Norah undressed him, put on his pyjamas and tried to tuck him into his bed.

"I want to sleep with you," said Gavin in a small voice.

Norah tried to control her irritation. "Oh, all right." It was difficult to find enough room for both of them in the narrow space, but finally they slept.

Norah woke up with a start a few hours later. Where was she? Her bed was vibrating and there was a low, humming sound. Then she remembered and moved her leg from under Gavin's. She brushed across a cold, wet patch.

"Gavin!" Norah sat up and shook him angrily. "Look what you've done!" She made him get up and stand shivering on the cabin floor while she stripped the sheets and covered the damp mattress with blankets.

"Gavin wet the be-ed, Gavin wet the be-ed," crowed Lucy in the morning. "He's a *baby.*"

He did it every night. Because he insisted on sleeping with Norah, she made him curl up at the other end of the bed, but she still woke up every morning to the wetness. Miss Montague-Scott helped her rinse out the sheet and his pyjama bottoms every morning in the tiny sink, but they never dried properly and she could never get it all out. Soon there was a perpetual sharp odour in the cabin, and Norah spent as much time as she could away from it.

Gavin followed her around like a lost puppy. After Norah had pulled his grey balaclava helmet over his head on the first windy day, he refused to take it off. He wore it to meals and even to bed. It made his round blue eyes look even larger and more frightened. He had become strangely silent and didn't even talk to Creature. Norah knew she should soothe him, but what could she say? She couldn't tell him they'd see their parents soon—they wouldn't. She couldn't think of anything comforting about Canada to offer him. And she couldn't help nagging him to stop being so babyish.

Then she got a reprieve. On the third day at sea, she and Gavin sneaked up to the upper-class decks. The government-sponsored children were supposed to stay below, but no one noticed if they didn't. Many of the children above were under five and several had mothers, nannies and other adults travelling with them. Norah found a place to sit beside a friendly looking mother with a baby in a carry-cot beside her.

"Hello, you two." She smiled at Gavin. "Aren't you hot in that hat?"

Gavin shook his head, but he took out Creature for the first time since they'd boarded and held him up to the woman.

"What a very nice elephant. What do you call him?"

"Creature," whispered Gavin.

The woman laughed. "That's an unusual name. Where does it come from?"

Norah explained how Gavin had named the elephant after the line in the Sunday school hymn: "All Creatures Great and Small."

"He's very small for an elephant, you see," said Gavin. "What's *your* name?"

"Mrs Pym. And this is my little boy, Timothy. We're going to Montreal to live with Timothy's grandparents"

After that, Gavin spent all his time trailing after Mrs Pym. She didn't seem to mind; she even took him into meals with her and came down to kiss him good-night every evening. Norah felt vaguely guilty about abandoning him, but he seemed much happier with Mrs Pym than he was with her.

Now that she was free of Gavin, she longed to spend the whole of each day exploring the ship. But Miss Montague-Scott had other ideas. You could tell she was a teacher; she seemed to forget that it was still the holidays. Some of the other escorts were lax and spent a lot of their time in the lounge or flirting with the officers, but Miss Montague-Scott made her group conform to the ship's schedule. First there were prayers, then a lifeboat drill, then a different activity each day: singalongs on the poop deck, art classes, spelling bees, Physical Training or memorizing poems. "No grumpy faces allowed in *my* group, Norah," she cried heartily as they performed their morning jack-knives. "*One,* two, *one,* two . . ."

Then Miss Montague-Scott got seasick. So did Lucy and many other children. Some threw up on the deck as they ran around, but most spent their days moaning in bed.

Now Norah was free to do as she pleased. Dulcie wasn't seasick either, and when she wasn't looking after Lucy, she hung around with Margery and some other prissy girls who had formed a society called the "Thumbs Up Club".

"Don't you want to join us, Norah?" Dulcie asked. "It keeps our spirits up. Every time one of us feels homesick or scared she says 'thumbs up!' and we all do it together. It's a great help."

"*I'm* not homesick," lied Norah, who lay beside Gavin every night trying to block out the images of home that flooded her mind. "I'm busy with much more important things, thank you."

She was watching for periscopes. Every day she leaned over the railing and gazed out to sea. Ahead of the ss *Zandvoort* steamed a whole convoy of ships, protecting them until they were far enough away from England to be safe. The escorts pretended to ignore the presence of the convoy, but Norah remembered Mrs Baker's comment. *She* knew they were in danger of being torpedoed. She watched the unbroken line of grey water on the horizon every day for an hour, until she got too chilled to stand still. The problem was, she didn't know what a periscope or a U-boat looked like.

Sometimes, if she let herself think too much about torpedoes, the suffocating fear would come again. Once she groped beside her in panic—where was her gas mask? Then she remembered. Instead of a gas mask, she now had a lifebelt she had to carry everywhere: scratchy orange canvas filled with cork. At least it made a good pillow.

The ship was like a moving island and Norah explored every inch of it, happy to be able to go where she wanted after the regimented hostel. The Dutch crew indulged the children and let them help polish brass and coil ropes. Sometimes the captain would stop and speak to them in his halting English, or inspect their lifeboat drill. Wherever he went, he was followed by a gang of admiring small boys.

The best part of the voyage was the unrationed food. Everyone gorged on unlimited supplies of sugar, butter, oranges and ice cream. Some of the meals had seven courses and there were five a day. Norah thought of the doctor who'd said she was scrawny, and ate as much as she could.

The ten-day trip became a soothing, timeless space between the war behind and the unknown country ahead. Everything had happened so fast that Norah still couldn't believe she was leaving home. Sometimes she tried to imagine "Canada". She thought of ice and snow, red-coated Mounties and *Anne of Green Gables.* None of it fit together.

Miss Montague-Scott recovered but, except for the daily lifeboat drills, she gave up trying to organize them. "They may as well run free while they can," Norah heard her tell another escort. "The poor kiddies are going to have enough red tape when they arrive."

What was red tape? Norah wondered.

She made friends with one of the boys from the Scottish group. His name was Jamie, and he had collected far more shrapnel than she had. He helped her watch for periscopes.

"I *do* wish we'd be torpedoed," Jamie said longingly, as they stared at the blank expanse of water. When they got tired of keeping watch they held up biscuits for the hovering gulls to snatch out of their fingers.

Jamie introduced Norah to his older brothers. She envied them when they told her they were going to live with their uncle on the Canadian prairies. The Smiths, too, were "nominated". That meant they knew whom they were going to stay with in Ontario. "It will be in a vicarage in Toronto, just like at home," said Dulcie. "The Milnes are old friends of Daddy's." Norah wondered where she and Gavin would be sleeping in a week.

Norah and Jamie were standing together on the deck one morning when Norah cried, "Look! Is that land?"

Far in the distance was a thin blue line, as if someone had painted a dark outline along the horizon. As the day progressed it got darker and closer, and the next morning it had broken up into islands.

Then a thick fog obscured their vision. Jamie's brother, Alistair, who seemed to know everything, told them they were off the Grand Banks of Newfoundland. As they leaned over the railing into the mist, Norah was astonished to see an enormous grey-white shape loom out of the fog.

"What's *that?*"

"It's an iceberg!" said Alistair. "There's something to write home about!" They watched in awe as the ship glided by the ghostly mountain of ice.

Soon they entered a huge estuary; Alistair said it was the St Lawrence River but its banks were so far apart it seemed more like a small sea. Then it narrowed to a proper river, its high shore dense with firs. Jamie kept a close watch. "Maybe we'll spot an Indian war dance," he told Norah.

"What a little idiot!" scoffed Alistair. "Canada isn't like a wild west film."

But Jamie and Norah kept examining the cliffs hopefully. Now they were passing small villages, each with a lighthouse and a white-spired church. In the distance rose the green roofs of Quebec City. The ship docked there briefly and all the children crowded at the railing, pushing each other in their excitement. Below them men shouted to each other in French.

"Don't they speak English in Canada?" Norah asked Margery nervously. What would it be like to live with a new family she didn't understand?

Margery looked bewildered but Miss Montague-Scott assured them that, although Canada had two languages, most of the people in Ontario spoke English. "The children who will be living in Montreal are lucky," she added in her school-teacher tone. "Some of them will probably learn French." But Norah thought it was going to be difficult enough to adjust in her own language.

The ship continued through the dusk to Montreal. That evening there was an excited atmosphere aboard. They had a special banquet, and the escorts led the children in a chorus of "For they are jolly good fellows." The captain stood up and told them what good sailors they'd been.

They were allowed to open the darkened portholes for the first time, and all the ship's lights streamed out into the darkness. "You're safe now," laughed Miss Montague-Scott. "There's no need for a black-out any more." She had come in to help their cabin pack. "Make sure you have all your papers ready. We'll be in Montreal in an hour and will stay there for the night. Then I'll have to leave you—someone else will be in charge."

"Where will you go?" asked Norah. Miss Montague-Scott already seemed to be an established part of their lives.

"Back to Britain and, I hope, back here again with another load of evacuees," she said cheerfully. "Let's hope I can conquer my seasickness next time! Now, Gavin, can't you take off that dreadful hat? You'll get some kind of skin disease, you've worn it so long." She pulled at his balaclava.

"No!" wailed Gavin, pressing his hands to his head.

Miss Montague-Scott sighed. "You'll have to find a way to get it off him, Norah. It's not healthy."

Norah didn't have time to worry about it. It was hard enough getting Gavin to leave Mrs Pym the next morning. She gripped his hand tightly when he started to run after her. "I'm your *sister!*" she hissed. "She's not even related to you. You have to stay with me, so do what I say."

The timeless peace of the voyage was over; now everything was confusing and difficult again, the way it had been in Liverpool. Baggage was piled everywhere. All morning they lined up on board the hot ship, until their landing cards were checked and their passports stamped. Then they waited again, in the observation room, where at least they could sit down. Some journalists came on board to take their pictures.

"Isn't this exciting, Norah?" said Dulcie. "It's as if we were famous!" Her voice had an hysterical edge to it and there was an ugly rash all around her mouth from constantly licking her lips. A reporter came up to them and Dulcie began telling him about the 'Thumbs Up Club'."

Finally they were allowed to walk down a covered gangway. A large crowd clapped and cheered, throwing them sweets and chewing gum. Then their papers were checked again by customs officers with soft accents. "What a brave little girl, to travel all the way from England by yourself!" said the man helping Norah. He spoke as if she were Gavin's age.

"Over here, Norah!" called Dulcie. Norah frowned. Dulcie was getting much too bossy.

The Ontario group was moved towards a bus that was to go to the Montreal train station. Norah peered through the noisy crowd for Jamie and spotted him in another line, too far away to call to. But she'd never see him again, anyway; what was the use in saying goodbye?

Mrs Pym hurried up and gave Gavin a last kiss. "You do what your big sister says," she told him. "Cheerio, Norah, and the best of luck to both of you." She looked as if she felt sorry for them; Norah thrust out her hand quickly so Mrs Pym wouldn't kiss her as well.

She dragged her brother onto the bus before he had time to whimper. The bus pulled away from both Mrs Pym and Jamie, leaving Norah and Gavin alone with each other once again.

The Montreal train station was a vast, clean hall with a slippery marble floor; the enormous space echoed with voices. Margery pointed to the ceiling. "There's the Canadian flag," she said knowingly. Norah gazed at the tiny Union Jack lost in a sea of red. It was like England now—small and far away.

The train to Toronto was different from British trains: there were no compartments and all the seats faced the same way. Norah and Gavin sat across the aisle from a stout man with a checked hat. He seemed very curious about them.

"All the way from England, eh? How old are you? Did you get bombed yet? Where's your village?"

He asked so many questions that Norah wondered if he were a spy. "I can't say," she said loudly, the way their headmaster had told them to answer suspicious strangers. She stared so hard at him that he got up and moved to another seat.

Seventy children from the ship were going to Toronto.

There were new women in charge and one of them went up and down the carriage, passing out coloured armbands. Norah's was blue and Gavin's green. She supposed they signified their ages.

"Will we be staying with our new families tonight?" Norah asked her.

"Oh, no, dear. You'll be put into residences at the university for a while, until we get you vetted."

"Vetted?"

The woman laughed. "Just checking you over to make sure you're healthy. Then your hosts will come and pick you up. Don't worry, we have lots of fun planned. Singalongs and games and movies and swimming."

Norah sighed... *more* singing.

"My sisters and I won't have to go there, will we?" asked Derek behind her. "We know who we're living with."

"That's nice, dear, but you still have to stay at the university at first. Regulations, I'm afraid."

Norah was glad; the Smiths needed to be taken down a peg.

Gavin had fallen asleep. He twitched awake when the train drew to a stop. It was already dusk—where had this blurry day gone? Many of the children had dozed and someone had pulled down the blinds to keep out the rays of the setting sun.

Now one of the adults pushed up the blind beside them. "There you are! Welcome to Toronto!"

Lights blazed outside the window, some in beautiful flashing colours. Norah gaped, amazed.

Gavin took one look and screamed. "Turn out the lights, turn out the lights!"

"It's all *right,* Gavin!" Norah pushed him back into his seat. "Remember what Miss Montague-Scott said? There's no black-out here. There's no war. We're in Canada, now, not England."

She choked on the last words. Now what would happen? Gathering up their things wearily, she got up to leave the train.

VIII
GUESTS OF WAR

At Union Station another set of adults conducted them off the train and asked them to line up two by two. They were led into a large waiting room where a man gave orders.

"Welcome to Toronto, children!" He made the name sound like "Trawna." "We want each of you to look at the colour of your armband and line up behind the leader with that colour."

He didn't need to shout; the whole group was tired and subdued. Norah looked around for the adult wearing a blue armband. Then she remembered that Gavin had a different colour. Her brother clung to her dress, his grimy face spotted with tear marks.

"Please..." she entreated an adult. "My little brother's supposed to go with the green group, but he has to stay with me."

The woman looked worried. "Oh, but he's supposed to go with the boys. You can visit him later." She gently loosened Gavin's fingers and led him away. He looked back over his shoulder at Norah, his eyes brimming.

"I'll see you later, Gavin!" called Norah. If only Mrs Pym were still here.

"He'll be all right, Norah," said Dulcie. Norah felt almost envious of her. She never seemed to have any problems with Lucy, but Lucy was far more confident than her big sister. And they both had Derek to look after them, even if he was usually lost behind a book.

That morning Dulcie had dressed Lucy and herself in their pink dresses, which she'd hung up and kept clean for the whole journey. Norah's dress was stained with food and her feet were moist and gritty inside her socks.

"Come along, Blues." The group of girls followed their leader out of the station to a waiting bus decorated with a blue pennant.

Just as in Montreal, a crowd across the street began to applaud. They strained against a rope as they called out greetings. "Welcome to Canada!" "Rule Britannia!" "Look at them, aren't they sweet?" As the blue group came closer, a sigh rose in the crowd. A woman near Norah said, "Do you see those two? The ones in matching pink dresses and hats? They look just like the Princesses!" Lucy smiled and waved as if they were.

The bus ride was short and soon they were unloaded at an old stone building the adults called Hart House. It was like a church inside, with dark ceiling beams and high windows of coloured glass.

Gavin rushed up from a group of boys. "You went away," he sniffed. His nose was running disgustingly. Norah tried to mop it with the corner of her dress; she had lost her handkerchief long ago.

A jovial man led Gavin back to his group. "Come along, youngster, you're eating with the big fellows!" Norah lost sight of him as they were taken into a vast dining room called the Great Hall. It had large golden letters painted around its walls.

Supper was boiled chicken and mushy cauliflower. By the time dessert arrived, some of the children had begun to revive. They called to one another down the long tables and bolted their ice cream. But Norah wasn't hungry.

Immediately after supper the girls were taken into a gymnasium where they had to stand in their vests and knickers while women doctors checked their throats, ears and chests. "We need to put some flesh on you," the doctor told Norah. She felt insulted—hadn't she eaten a lot on the ship? She'd always been small for her age, but no one had ever made a fuss about it before.

While she got dressed again, she heard the doctor tell the little girl behind her that she had a cold and would have to go straight to the infirmary. "But I want to stay with my sister," the child wailed.

A nurse opened the door and hurried across the room. "Is Norah Stoakes here?"

Norah waved her arm. "Can you come and stop your brother from crying?" the nurse asked her. "He's having hysterics because we took off his hat, poor little tyke."

Gavin's screams filled the corridor. He was outside the other gymnasium, thrashing and kicking on the floor. "I want my s-sister!" he blubbered.

Norah wasn't at all sure she wanted *him.* His cheeks were smeared with dirt and mucus and his fair hair looked dark where the balaclava had covered it. What would Mum do? She was suddenly furious that her mother wasn't there to cope.

"Shut *up,* Gavin!" She shook him so hard that his head wobbled.

The nurse looked shocked and reached out to stop her. "Don't be so rough, Norah! That's no way to treat your little brother!"

As Gavin's cries turned into hiccups, Norah whirled around and faced the woman. "You *asked* me to stop him, and I did! It's your fault he was crying, anyway—you shouldn't have taken his hat off! Didn't you realize that would upset him?"

The nurse looked indignant. "We had to take it off—it

was filthy! We've thrown it away and now he'll have to have his hair washed thoroughly. You look as if you could do with a bath too, Miss—come with me. And I think you're forgetting your manners. In Canada, children don't speak like that to their elders."

She led them outside and across the grass to another building, where there was a row of bathtubs. Norah lay dazed in the soothing hot water, listening to Gavin having his hair shampooed in the next cubicle. He had turned silent again.

"Do I have to bathe you as well?" grumbled the nurse, coming in to check on her. "Imagine, a girl of your age who can't wash herself!" She did Norah's hair and scrubbed her all over with a rough flannel. Then she handed her a kind of gown to put on.

"Now say good-night to your brother," she ordered. "I'll take him to his room and come back for you. Yours is in a different building."

A stubborn voice forced itself up through Norah's exhaustion. "No."

"What did you say?"

"He has to stay with me."

"Don't be difficult, Norah. You can see him all you want during the day, but the boys and the girls are sleeping in separate residences."

"No," said Norah again. Part of her wondered why she was being so insistent; she didn't really want the care of Gavin. But he looked so pathetic with his wet hair skinned back and dark circles under his eyes. She tried to forget about how her hands had made his thin neck bend like the stem of a flower.

The nurse stared at her for a few seconds, then gave up. "Stay here," she sighed. "I'll see what I can do. But you're upsetting our system."

In ten minutes Norah got her way. The nurse returned and took them both to a building called Falconer House, to a room with four beds in it. Norah's luggage was already there and a boy arrived with Gavin's just as they did. The beds were labelled and Norah noticed that the others belonged to Goosey and Loosey.

"I have to go, but someone will check on you in a few minutes," said the nurse. Her voice was kinder now, but Norah was too tired to answer her.

"Get into bed," she told Gavin after the nurse had left. He obeyed mutely, curling into a tight ball. Norah tucked the blanket around him. She felt the mattress and was relieved to find a rubber sheet.

She buried herself in her own stiff, clean sheets. She was so worn out, she scarcely heard the Smiths when they came in a few minutes later.

They stayed at the university for a week. Everyone was very kind and welcoming, but Norah began to feel she was in prison. The campus grounds were spacious and she longed to run on her own under the large trees or cross the busy street, where the cars drove on the wrong side. The bustling city surrounding the university seemed as big and exciting as London. But Boy Scouts stood on guard all day outside Hart House, where the children ate and played. "They're to keep away curious strangers," the adults said, but Norah thought they were to keep them in.

The only time the children left the campus was for a visit to a hospital, where each of them was examined in much more detail than in either Hart House or Liverpool. Norah had to take off all her clothes while a doctor checked every inch of her body, from her hair to her toes, including the embarrassing parts in the middle. She was X-rayed, her knees were hammered and a blood sample was taken from her finger. Then she was given several injections and pushed and prodded until her body didn't seem to belong to her any more. Canadians seemed to think that British children carried some dreadful disease.

Another doctor asked her questions: what her parents were like, who her friends were at home, and what she liked to do best. It was so painful to talk about home that Norah answered him in short, clipped sentences. When he asked her in his kind voice how she felt about being evacuated, she just mumbled "Fine" to keep from crying. "I guess you're a shy one," said the doctor. "You'll soon feel more talkative in your new family."

Once more, Gavin was taken off her hands. Now he trailed after Miss Carmichael, who looked after their dormitory and, as well, was in charge of all the children under nine. She was a softer, prettier version of Miss Montague-Scott; not as hearty, but just as school-teacherish.

"What a well-behaved child Gavin is!" said Miss Carmichael. "And such an attractive little boy, with those huge eyes and delicate features." She kept the younger children constantly occupied. Gavin came back to the room each evening with paint on his clothes and grass-stained knees. He seemed calmer, but he kept wetting his bed every night and he was strangely still, as if a light had gone out inside him.

The woman in charge of the older children kept encouraging Norah to participate in the organized activities. Part of Norah wanted to forget her troubles and run relay races and swim in the pool with the rest. But a kind of stubbornness had set in her, a mood that had always exasperated her mother—she called it her "black cloud" mood. When Norah felt like this she almost took pleasure in not enjoying or being grateful for what the grown-ups offered.

"You should join in more," Margery told her. "You'd like it here better if you did."

Norah knew she would, just as she knew she should be paying more attention to Gavin. But the black cloud engulfed her and she couldn't escape it.

The first day she squatted sullenly on the grass and watched a new game called baseball. There were new games, much more food and different accents. Still, it was difficult to believe she was really in Canada. Being here was much like being in the hostel in Liverpool: a tedious interlude of waiting for the next thing to happen.

The baseball bounced to a stop beside her. Norah threw it back and was suddenly gripped by a memory of bowling a cricket ball to her father—the sharp smell of newly cut grass and her father's encouraging, patient voice.

"Are you sure you don't want to play, Norah?" a woman asked kindly. Norah shook the memory out of her head as she refused.

After that she escaped from the daily activities by spending as much time as possible in the large room that had been stocked with children's books and set aside as a library. Norah had never been much of a reader. At school she was better at arithmetic than English, and at home there was too much to do outside to waste it on reading. But now she curled up with a book every day in one of the comfortable leather armchairs. Derek was always in there as well, along with several others. No one spoke; they were isolated like islands all over the room, each sheltering in a story.

The first book Norah picked out was called *Swallows and Amazons.* It was about a group of children who camped all by themselves on an island. They reminded her of the Skywatchers. The book was good and thick and lasted for three days. After she'd finished it, she found an even thicker one,

Swallowdale, about the same children. She became so lost in their adventures that whenever the meal gong sounded she looked around, startled, as if she'd been a long way away.

One afternoon Miss Carmichael found her and shooed her outside. "It's too nice a day to be cooped up with a book. Come out to the grass. We're having a lovely time blowing bubbles and there are some journalists here who want to meet you all."

Reluctantly Norah put aside her book and followed Miss Carmichael to the lawn. She was handed a piece of bent wire and invited to dip it into a pail of sudsy water. Iridescent bubbles floated around her in the warm air. The weather was hot for September; the heat pressed on her skin like a wet sponge. Blinking, she watched her bubble rise, feeling like a mole who had emerged from under the ground.

Beside her, Lucy was being interviewed. "Now tell me what you think of Hitler," a journalist asked her.

"Hitler ith a nathty, nathty man," said Lucy coyly. Her lisp was newly acquired.

A family of five was being lined up for a picture. The star of the group was Johnnie, who posed in the middle of his older brothers and sisters. "We've come to Canada to help win the war," he declared proudly.

"Why do you say that?" a journalist prompted.

"'Cause children are a *nuisance* at home. If we're out of the way then the grown-ups can fight better!"

The journalists leaned forward eagerly. "Tell the nice people what you said on your first night when I asked how you were feeling," coaxed Miss Carmichael.

Johnnie looked confused until Miss Carmichael whispered to him. "I said—I said I was eager and brave!" he shouted. "I'm so brave I'll—I'll"—but his eldest sister dragged him away, her hand over his mouth.

Two women carrying cameras had been listening on the edge of the group. "Excuse me," one said to Miss Carmichael. "We're visiting Toronto from the United States and we couldn't help overhearing this adorable little boy. He's just too precious to be true! These children are evacuees, aren't they? How can we get one?"

"We don't call them evacuees," Miss Carmichael corrected. "That sounds as if they have no homes to return to. They are Canada's war guests. We're hosting them for the duration. If you want to sponsor a child you'll have to ask your own government."

The next day Miss Carmichael brought them the evening paper. Lucy's and Johnnie's pictures were included, among many others, over a story headed "Young British War Guests Blowing Peaceful Bubbles at Hart House."

"We'll have to send this home!" cried Dulcie. "Do you see how they put in your words, Lucy?"

Norah couldn't find herself or Gavin in the photographs. It made her feel more than ever that she wasn't really here.

IX
ALENOUSHKA

Towards the end of the week the "nominated" children left to go to their friends and relatives. "Goodbye, Norah," said Dulcie hesitantly, as Miss Carmichael helped her carry her luggage to the door of Falconer House. "Do you think we'll see each other again?" She ran her tongue over her raw lips; her rash was worse.

"I'm sure you will," said Miss Carmichael. "The Milnes can find out from us where Norah is living, and there's going to be a party for all of you at Christmas."

Norah walked with Dulcie as far as the door and waved, surprised at feeling sad. Goosey and Loosey were a trial, but they were faces from home.

"When will Gavin and I go?" she asked Miss Carmichael that night. "Do you know who we'll be living with?"

"Not yet, but we'll match you up with someone as soon as possible. We need your beds for the next batch of children and school has already started. But don't worry, the response has been tremendous."

That was on Thursday. On Saturday, Norah heard her name mentioned as she came down the corridor to their room. Miss Carmichael was helping Mrs Ellis change the sheets.

"They've decided on a place for Norah and Gavin," Miss Carmichael was saying.

Norah froze and listened intently. She knew it was wrong

to eavesdrop, but this was important. She couldn't catch the name Miss Carmichael gave in answer to Mrs Ellis's question.

"The family only wanted a boy," Miss Carmichael continued, "but they've persuaded them to take Norah as well. I do hope she'll settle in. Gavin is so sweet, but Norah can be difficult. She's such a loner, it isn't natural."

Norah was enraged. Gavin was the difficult one, not her! Did Miss Carmichael *enjoy* changing his sheets and washing out his pyjamas every day?

"I thought they'd be sent to the country," said Mrs Ellis. "They come from a small village, don't they?"

"I would have thought that would be more suitable, but apparently the woman was very specific about having as young a boy as possible—and Gavin's the only five-year-old left. I shouldn't be saying this, but I imagine they couldn't very well refuse her, she has so much money."

Norah shuffled her feet to let them know she was approaching.

"There you are, Norah!" Miss Carmichael smiled. As with Mrs Pym, Norah had the feeling she felt sorry for her. "I have wonderful news! A family called Ogilvie would be delighted to have you and Gavin be their guests for the war. There are two ladies—Mrs Ogilvie, who's a widow, and her daughter. You'll be staying right here in Toronto—isn't that nice? You're lucky—the Ogilvies are very well off and you'll be living in a grand house in Rosedale. What do you think of that?"'

It was far too much information to absorb at one time. Besides, the Ogilvies didn't want *her*—just Gavin. All Norah could say was, "When do we go?"

"Someone will pick you up tomorrow after lunch. Now come and help me pack your things."

Early Sunday morning the children were taken to church. The night before, Norah's dwindling group had been enlarged by a contingent of evacuees fresh from the ship. Norah felt sorry for them as they trooped out after supper for their medicals. At least she was finally leaving, however frightening her new home sounded.

In church the minister prayed for the British people "bravely carrying on their struggle alone." Norah prayed too, naming each member of her family carefully. She tried not to think of what they would be doing. Instead she imagined a family called Ogilvie; her chest grew heavy.

When they got back to Hart House they were told that a librarian had arrived to tell them stories before lunch.

"You take Gavin in," said Miss Carmichael. "I have all these new children to deal with."

Stories sounded babyish, but Norah took Gavin's hand and went into the room they used for recreation. Children were scattered all over, playing with toys and puzzles. A small woman with very bright eyes sat on a low stool in front of the fireplace, watching them calmly.

"Once upon a time there was a farmer and his wife who had one daughter, and she was courted by a gentleman . . ." she began slowly. Her vibrant voice cut through the chatter. As she carried on, the children drew closer and squatted on the floor in front of her.

When she reached the point where the people in the story were all wailing in the cellar, some of the children began to smile. By the time the man was trying to jump into his trousers, they were giggling. Gavin laughed for the first time since they'd left England, and Norah felt a chuckle rise inside her.

". . . and that was the story of 'The Three Sillies,' " the woman concluded.

"Tell us another!" demanded a fat little girl called Emma.

"Once upon a time Henny Penny was picking up corn when—whack!—an acorn fell on her head. 'Goodness, gracious me!' said Henny Penny. 'The sky is falling! I must go and tell the king.'"

She came to the part about "Goosey Loosey," and Norah grinned, looking around for Dulcie. Then she remembered she had gone.

There was a satisfied silence in the room after Foxy Loxy had finished off his witless victims. "Of course, the sky wasn't *really* falling," said Emma knowingly.

"It is at home!" declared Johnnie. "It's falling down all over England, and that's why we had to go away."

The librarian looked startled, but only for a second. She showed them how to do a game with their fingers called "Piggy Wig and Piggy Wee" Then she told them "The Three Little Pigs". All the younger children huffed and puffed with the wolf, even Gavin. They moved closer to her and one of them stroked her shoes. Emma wriggled onto her knee.

"And now, I want to tell you the story of Alenoushka and her brother." Her tone had become sad and solemn and the rollicking atmosphere changed to hushed expectancy. "Once upon a time there were two orphan children, a little boy and a little girl. Their father and mother were dead and they were all alone. The little boy was called Ivanoushka and the little girl's name was Alenoushka. They set out together to walk through the whole of the great wide world. It was a long journey they set out on, and they did not think of any end to it, but only of moving on and on..."

The back of Norah's neck prickled. She was pulled into the story as if by a magnet and she *became* Alenoushka, trying to stop her little brother from drinking water from the hoofprints of animals, and desperate when he did and turned into a little lamb.

The other children were as spellbound as she. They sat like stones while the rich voice went on, forgetting the storyteller in their utter absorption in the story itself.

O my brother Ivanoushka,
A heavy stone is round my throat,
Silken grass grows through my fingers,
Yellow sand lies on my breast.

Norah didn't realize her eyes had welled with tears until one rolled down her cheek.

The story ended happily. Alenoushka was rescued from a witch's spell, and when she threw her arms around the lamb he became her brother once more. "And they all lived happily together and ate honey every day, with white bread and new milk."

The haunting voice stopped and the room was still. Norah's body was loose and relaxed. She felt the rough rug under her legs and Gavin's warm thigh pressing against hers.

The librarian stood up and left the room without acknowledging them or saying goodbye. It was as if the stories had used her to tell themselves. The children got up quietly and went in to lunch.

Norah's ease ended after they'd eaten. She and Gavin, dressed in cleaned and pressed clothes, waited in the front hall.

"Where are we going to live *now?*" whispered Gavin.

Norah was struggling to secure her hair-slide. "What do you mean, silly? We haven't lived anywhere yet."

"Yes, we have. First we lived in the hostel. Then we lived on the boat with Mrs Pym and then we lived here with Miss Carmichael. Now where are we going to live?"

"With a family called Ogilvie who have a posh house. You know that, Gavin, we've already told you."

Miss Carmichael came up to say goodbye. "Now, be sure to behave like polite guests and everything will be fine. Someone will come and visit you in a while to see how you're getting along."

The front door opened and into the hall stepped a plain, plump woman. She wore a brown linen suit and a beige hat; her beige hair was twisted into a tidy knot and her brown eyes looked anxious. "How do you do? I am Miss Ogilvie. And this must be Norah and Gavin. I'm very pleased to meet you both." Her voice sounded more frightened than pleased.

Norah shook the woman's limp hand. It was covered with a spotless beige glove.

"I want to stay here," whimpered Gavin, hiding behind Miss Carmichael.

"Off you go, Gavin." She handed him a large boiled sweet. This was such a surprise that Gavin sucked it busily instead of crying.

Miss Carmichael kissed them both. "I'll see you at the Christmas party," she smiled.

Miss Ogilvie led them out to a sleek grey car. "Perhaps you'd prefer to sit beside each other in the back," she said hesitantly.

Norah watched the university become smaller and smaller behind them. Then she turned around and watched the neat back of Miss Ogilvie's hair as they drove wordlessly through the still Sunday streets to their new home.

PART TWO

X
THE OGILVIES

The car turned into a quiet, leafy street and stopped at the house at the end, a house so tall and enormous it looked like a red brick castle. There was even a tower. The windows stared down at Norah like a crowd of inquisitive eyes. She carried her suitcase up wide white steps flanked by green pillars.

Inside, the house was even more resplendent. The front hall was as large as two rooms in Little Whitebull. It looked even bigger because it was almost empty of furniture, except for a mahogany table on one side with a silver bowl full of roses on it. Arched doorways led to several rooms off the hall; a curved staircase disappeared upwards.

Miss Ogilvie stood in the hall beside them as if she, too, were a stranger who didn't know what to do next. "Now, let's see . . ." Her timid voice rang out in the silence. "Mother is anxious to meet you, of course, but this is her rest time. I'll show you your room and you can unpack before tea."

She led them up two levels, first on thickly carpeted stairs, then on bare, slippery ones. At the very top there were only two rooms: a small one containing a huge bathtub and a large, circular bedroom with built-in seats around its windowed walls.

"This is the tower!" cried Norah. She ran to the windows and looked out at the lush tops of trees.

"Yes . . .I hope you don't mind being up here alone. Is it all right?" Miss Ogilvie's voice was shy. "I prepared it myself."

Norah had never encountered a grown-up who was so nervous. She walked around the room carefully, trying not to make sudden movements that might startle her.

Two narrow beds were along one wall, each covered in a satin eiderdown. New-looking curtains hung from the windows. On a table were piled boxes of jigsaw puzzles and games. Some battered tin cars and trucks were parked in a row under the table and a shabby rocking horse with a real horsehair mane stood in a corner. Gavin went over to it and stroked the mane gently.

"I'm afraid they're mostly boys' things," Miss Ogilvie apologized. "You see . . ." Her voice faltered.

Norah thought she was about to reveal they had only wanted a boy. Her excitement over the lofty room subsided.

" . . .you see, this was our nursery—my brother's and mine. Most of these toys belonged to him, but I found one of my dolls for you, Norah." She pointed to a small doll with a chipped plaster face lying on one of the beds. "I used to love dolls, but of course not all girls do," the soft voice continued anxiously.

Norah fingered the doll's yellowed eyelet dress. Miss Ogilvie watched so hopefully that she tried to sound enthusiastic. "Thank you. She's very nice. Where's your brother, then? Does he still live here?"

The woman's plain face seemed to collapse upon itself. "Oh, no! Hugh was killed in the war. Not this war, the first one."

"Oh. I'm sorry."

There seemed nothing more to say after that. Miss Ogilvie looked as if she wanted to leave. "You get yourselves settled," she said, "and I'll come up for you when it's time for tea. We have a formal tea on Sundays and an informal supper later. Perhaps you could change into your best clothes. And could you wipe his mouth?" she added hesitantly. Gavin's lips were smeared red from the sweet Miss Carmichael had given him. "First impressions are important, don't you think? I'll see you later." She disappeared down the stairs.

The horse creaked as Gavin rocked on it slowly. Norah took out all their clothes and put them away in the wardrobe and the chest of drawers. There was lots of space left over when she'd finished. She placed the photograph of the family on the small table between the beds. At the bottom of her case she found her bundle of shrapnel and ran her hands over the smooth, iridescent metal before she decided to hide it under her mattress.

Then she made Gavin wash his face and go to the toilet. That was in with the bathtub; at home it was a separate room attached to the scullery. She had already become used to pressing a handle instead of pulling a chain.

She picked out some clothes for them. The only dress she had that was fancier than the one she wore was a very rumpled winter one of flowered Viyella. She tried to get rid of the wrinkles with a wet flannel.

"I'm too hot," complained Gavin, after Norah had made him put on his grey wool shorts and knitted waistcoat. At least the waistcoat partly covered up his wrinkled white shirt.

"Stop whining. You heard what she said about first impressions." Norah looked for a ribbon and tied a sloppy bow on one side of her head. Even the ribbon was wrinkled.

"Let's take these horrid things off." She unfastened the identification disks around their necks and threw them into the wastepaper basket, feeling lighter.

They sat quietly on the window seat and looked down on the rooftops below them. Norah began to feel hopeful. Perhaps it wouldn't be so bad, living here. Even if the Ogilvies only wanted Gavin, this marvellous room was an unexpected pleasure. And if she were as polite as possible, they might want her as well.

Miss Ogilvie knocked at their door. "Oh," she gulped, as she inspected them. "You should have asked the maid to iron your clothes. Never mind, it's too late now. Mother likes people to be punctual and she's already waiting in the den."

She acted as if they were about to be greeted by royalty. Norah's chest felt constricted as she and Gavin descended the long staircase and followed Miss Ogilvie into a room off the hall.

"Come in, come in," a resonant voice called impatiently. "Let's have a look at you."

In contrast to the stark hall, the cosy room overflowed with fat chintz chairs, more bowls of flowers and tables crowded with ornaments and silver-framed photographs. "Den" was a suitable word; it was like stepping into a scented, muggy cave.

The voice had come from a woman reclining in a chair by the window. Her full face was circled by a thatch of curly silver hair. Her wide grey eyes almost matched her hair. An ample bosom swelled under her red silk dress, like the breast of a well-fed robin. In contrast to her stout body, the long legs which stretched out on the Persian carpet were slim and elegant.

"Come and shake hands," commanded Mrs Ogilvie. Norah shrank from the extended fingers, but she had to take them. A ring with sharp stones bit into her own wet palm.

"You must be Norah—and this is little Gavin, of course. Do sit down. I'm delighted to meet you both."

Mrs Ogilvie assumed they knew who *she* was. Norah sat, waiting for her next instructions. A throbbing energy came from the woman, as if she were an engine running in perfect order. No wonder her daughter was so pale and subdued; her mother seemed to have sucked all the colour from her.

Gavin gazed at Mrs Ogilvie's splendour as if he were bewitched. Mrs Ogilvie looked him over and purred with pleasure. "Aren't *you* a handsome little boy! You come over here by me." She pulled a low stool close to her feet. "I won't eat you! You and I are going to be great friends."

Gavin advanced slowly, his eyes never leaving her face. One hand burrowed in his pocket.

"You're five, aren't you. And what do you have in your pocket?"

"Creature," whispered Gavin, pulling out the elephant to show her.

"Creature! What a charming name! Look what I have for you and Creature." She opened a drawer in the table beside her and took out a small tin aeroplane. "There! *I* know what little boys like."

Gavin stroked the aeroplane with shining eyes. Norah gazed at it jealously. It was a very good model of a Blenheim. She wondered if she would get a present too. "Say thank you," she hissed.

"Now, now let him be," admonished Mrs Ogilvie. "This is a new and strange experience for him." She looked at Norah again. "What part of England was it that you're from?"

"Kent," mumbled Norah. She offered a few details about the village when Miss Ogilvie questioned her. Mrs Ogilvie had immediately turned her attention back to Gavin, who was telling her about the ship. Norah shifted irritably. How could he talk so easily to a stranger when he had hardly talked to his own sister the whole trip?

"How frightening it must have been when the German planes flew over," shuddered Miss Ogilvie. "You must be so relieved to be safe."

"*I* wasn't frightened," declared Norah, still watching Gavin. "I didn't *want* to be safe."

Mrs Ogilvie looked over and frowned. "She's awfully small for her age, Mary. Are you sure she's ten?"

"I'm ten and a *half,*" said Norah indignantly. "You needn't speak as if I wasn't here."

Miss Ogilvie gasped. Norah regretted her words when she saw Mrs Ogilvie's expression.

"Sauce! We won't have rudeness in *this* house, my girl."

Norah knew she should apologize, but something in those determined grey eyes made her want to be just as stubborn back. She sat in angry silence, all her resolutions to be polite flown away.

Mrs Ogilvie waited for a few seconds, then she gave a knowing glance at her daughter. She picked up a little brass bell and rang it.

A maid in a ruffled white apron wheeled in a trolley with an elaborate tea on it: egg sandwiches and chicken sandwiches, warm scones with butter and raspberry jam, thin lemon biscuits and a heavy spice cake blanketed with maple icing. Norah ate rapidly. It was tricky to balance everything on her knee; she finally copied Gavin and squatted on the floor. Mrs Ogilvie made them drink milk. "Tea's not good for children," she said when Gavin asked for some.

"Now, let's get ourselves organized," she said, setting down the silver teapot. "I thought you might feel more comfortable if you called me Aunt Florence and my daughter Aunt Mary. I know you'll feel at home here—we follow the good old British traditions. And in this terrible war, especially, we're eager to help our mother country as much as we can. That's why I decided to take on war guests—to do my part." She looked at Norah as if she expected her to be profoundly grateful, then smiled at Gavin. "And, of course, I wanted to have a little one around again." Turning back to Norah, she continued. "You will have to do your part, too. I expect you to be quiet, clean and well mannered. You'll be treated like members of the family, and I'm sure your parents will be glad to learn you've come to such a good home. Do you have any questions?"

"No," muttered Norah.

"No, what?"

"No... Aunt Florence." The name stuck in her throat like dry crumbs. Why should she have to call someone "aunt" who wasn't even related to her? Then she remembered she did have a question. "What about...school?" That was a hurdle she wasn't at all prepared for, but she had to find out about it sometime.

"You'll begin school on Tuesday. The people at Hart House suggested you stay home for a day first to get used to your new family."

The maid arrived back and removed the trolley. Then there was an awkward silence. Norah pushed up her sleeves; her winter dress made her feel hot in the stuffy room.

"Well, now, what shall we do next?" Aunt Florence smiled kindly, but Norah only looked at the carpet. "Why don't you have a game of cribbage with Norah, Mary, and Gavin and I will play fish."

Her daughter obediently rose and led Norah to a table in the corner. On it lay a long narrow board with ivory pegs stuck in its holes, a pack of cards and some paper and pencils. Norah tried to pay attention as Aunt Mary taught her the game, but she couldn't help listening to Gavin's gleeful voice as he ordered "Fish!" again and again.

Cribbage was so confusing that she was relieved when Aunt Florence finally told them to go back to their room. "When Mary fetches you, you can have a light supper in the kitchen. Sunday is our bridge night, and I'd like you to come in and meet everyone." She dismissed them with a regal wave of her arm.

"Aunt Florence is beautiful!" said Gavin when they were back in the tower. "Do you think she's the Queen of Canada?"

Norah scowled. "Don't be such an idiot, of course she's not. And how can you possibly like her? She's mean and bossy and *fat*."

"Oh." Gavin looked deflated. "Does that mean we aren't going to stay here, if you don't like her?"

"Do you think it's up to me? If it was, we'd never have left England! Of course we're staying. There's nowhere else to go."

Gavin climbed onto the horse and hummed, zooming his plane in the air. "Creature thinks he might *like* to stay here."

Aunt Mary came up at six-thirty and told them to get into their pyjamas. Norah wanted to protest about getting ready for bed so early, but she knew that anything she said to Aunt Mary would just make her all the more nervous. They put on their dressing gowns and slippers and followed her down to the kitchen.

Aunt Mary left them with the cook, Mrs Hancock. She was an older, good-natured woman with red hands and untidy hair she kept pushing under a hairnet. "All the way from England you've come!" she marvelled. "I've always wanted to visit the old country. I saw the King and Queen when they visited Canada last year. Real close they were, I could have touched them. Sit down here and try my tomato soup."

They ate soup, toast and pudding at a scrubbed pine table. The kitchen was much like theirs at home, except it had a large refrigerator and no fireplace. Mrs Hancock was comfortable to talk to. She showed them how the refrigerator made its own ice cubes.

"Call me Hanny," she said. "Everyone in the family always has. This is just like the old days, when Mary and Hughie used to eat their Sunday supper in here. That must be thirty years ago! What a treat to have young ones in the house, isn't it Edith?"

Edith, the maid, who was slouched over a novel at the other end of the table, ignored Hanny's comment. "It's my evening off. How soon can I leave?" she asked sulkily.

"Not until you carry in their sandwiches. Have some more pudding, Gavin."

Norah was sorry to leave the kitchen when Aunt Mary fetched them again. She led them to the door of the living room. At one end of it, seven adults were sitting around two square tables. Mrs Ogilvie looked up from a pack of cards she was shuffling expertly. "Here are our young war guests! Come in and meet everyone."

All the adults got up and moved towards the children with broad smiles and outstretched hands. Norah's hair was ruffled and her arm pumped vigorously. "How do you do?" "Welcome to Canada!" "Where do you live in England?" "Did you have a good voyage?" "Are you beginning to feel settled?"

Since it was impossible to answer so many questions, Norah kept silent. When Gavin began to talk timidly about Creature the adult voices froze.

"What a darling accent!" one woman cooed when he'd finished. Norah frowned—didn't Canadians realize *they* were the ones with accents?

"And what do you think of Canada, Norah?" a man asked. "Is it very different from England?"

Once again there was an expectant hush. Norah stared at the beaming faces and blurted out the first words that came to her. "Everyone in Canada has very white teeth."

The adults roared with laughter and Norah blushed with confusion. What had she said that was so funny?

"Off to bed with you now," said Aunt Florence. She kissed Gavin and began to approach Norah but when Norah backed away she changed her mind. "And turn out your lights at once. You must both be very tired."

They were sent back upstairs by themselves. "Creature understands now," said Gavin when they were in bed. "We're going to live here for a long time, until I'm eight, and then we're going to live with Muv and Dad again."

"Not until you're eight! Maybe almost seven."

"Miss Carmichael said eight."

"Well, she's wrong! Dad said 'perhaps a year'. Those were his *exact* words."

Gavin soon fell asleep. Norah tossed for a while, then got up and sat on the window seat. A warm wind had risen—it turned the trees into a surging leafy sea. Rosedale was much quieter than the university. Occasionally a car passed or a dog barked, but in between all she could hear was the steady burr of some insect. It wasn't quite dark, much too early to go to sleep. Norah stared out the window with a sad finality.

This was it, then, their home for the duration, however long that might be. The war and England seemed far away from the cushioned luxury of the Ogilvies' life—their life, now.

She noticed that there was a hinge along the back of the window seat, and when she lifted it up she found a cavity stuffed with blankets. That would be a better hiding place for her shrapnel. After she'd placed it there, she got her coat and uncovered the five pounds Mum had sewn in the lining. She hid it under the blankets as well and closed the lid. Mum and Dad had told her to give the money to her new family for safekeeping, but Norah decided she would rather have it close at hand—just in case.

She got back into bed and thought of her abandoned room at home, with her parents sleeping below. She began to cry softly, but even that seemed useless, so she lay and listened to the night until her eyes closed.

XI
MONDAY

Breakfast was a formal meal in the dining room. Norah and Gavin and Aunt Mary sat at one end of a long polished table, eating the porridge and eggs and bacon that Hanny brought in. "Mother never gets up for breakfast," Aunt Mary explained. She seemed more relaxed without her mother.

In front of each plate was a piece of long yellow fruit. "What's this?" asked Gavin.

"It's a banana, silly," Norah told him. "We haven't had bananas since before the war," she explained to Aunt Mary. "He doesn't remember."

"Ouch!" Gavin had bitten into the skin without peeling it.

"You poor child—let me help." Aunt Mary showed him how to take off the skin. "Now, what would you like to do today? We should think of something nice before you start school tomorrow, Norah."

"And Gavin," Norah added.

"Isn't Gavin too young for school? I thought he was five. I suppose he could go to kindergarten, but I think Mother would rather have him at home...."

"He'll be six in November and anyway, he's already been to school. He was in the Infants last year. So he's old enough, aren't you Gavin?" Norah felt proud of her brother this morning; for the first time since the hostel, he hadn't wet the bed.

"I don't think Mother knows he's almost six," said Aunt Mary doubtfully. "I'll have to tell her, I suppose."

"I don't like school," said Gavin.

"You did after you learned to do up your buttons," Norah reminded him. Gavin used to come crying to her at playtime after he'd been to the lav, and she'd have to button up his trousers behind a tree. Thinking of that made her resent him again; she would have to look after him even more at a new Canadian school.

"Your school is only six blocks away," Aunt Mary was saying. "I found out at church yesterday that you'll have some friends from England there—the Smith girls. They and their brother are war guests of our minister, Reverend Milne."

Norah put down her spoon. She had forgotten about Dulcie and Lucy. It seemed odd to associate them with the Ogilvies.

"Would you like to invite them for lunch?" asked Aunt Mary. "They haven't started school either and Mrs Milne decided to keep them home today so you could all begin together."

"No, thank you." Norah tried not to sound rude. "Could I—could I just go out for a walk instead?"

"All by yourself? I wonder what Mother would say." Aunt Mary looked at Norah's pleading face. "I suppose it's all right. Everyone in the neighbourhood knows who we are, so if you get lost just knock on someone's door. Don't go too far, though, and wear your hat. I'll expect you back in an hour."

Norah tried to be still enough to listen to the rest of Aunt Mary's cautious directions. Then she dashed upstairs to use the toilet and fetch her hat.

On the way down, she paused on the landing outside Aunt Florence's bedroom. Despite her impatience to be out, she couldn't help stopping to listen when she heard a voice. She was doing a lot of eavesdropping these days, but it seemed the only way to get information.

Aunt Florence couldn't be talking to herself. She must have a telephone in there. Norah had never heard of anyone having a telephone in her bedroom. In Ringden, the only people who had one at all were the doctor, the policeman and Mrs Chandler; the rest of them used the call box on the main street.

"The girl?" said the throaty voice. "Well, she's cheeky, but we'll work on that. Girls are so sly—I had to be much stricter with Mary than I was with Hugh. But wait until you see Gavin! He's such a character, with an adorable accent. And such rosy cheeks! The girl is thin and pale—you'd never guess they were brother and sister. And their clothes... well, you can see they're not well off. I'm going to take Gavin shopping tomorrow. With his fair colouring, he'd look so fetching in a navy-blue sailor suit. Would they still carry them at Holt's, do you think? It's been so long since I've bought children's clothes. I'm telling you, Audrey, this is all making me feel young again."

Aunt Florence wouldn't be able to take Gavin shopping when she found out he'd be in school tomorrow, Norah thought as she continued down the stairs.

As soon as she stepped outside, she forgot her resentment. A delicious sensation of freedom swept through her. It was the first time since the day she'd left England that she could go where she pleased. And it was the first time since the war began that she'd gone out with nothing to carry—no gas mask, identity card or lifebelt.

She left her hat on the steps and walked along the sidewalk slowly, savouring the sun on her bare arms and legs. It was going to be a scorcher, Hanny had told them, but the morning air was still fresh. The winding street divided around islands of flowers. Ranged along it were houses as grand and impassive as the Ogilvies', some of brick and some of stone. Norah wondered why none of them had names. In one she saw a curtain twitch, as if someone had peeked out at her.

The twisting streets were like a maze. Norah noted each turn carefully so she wouldn't get lost. She was proud of herself when she found her way back to the Ogilvies'. Then she went around again the other way. At one house a small, wiry dog rushed up to her from behind a wrought iron fence. When she crouched down it licked her fingers, pushing its nose through the railings.

After she'd completed the circle again, it didn't seem like an hour yet, and she didn't feel like leaving the bright outdoors for the Ogilvies' dim house. Their garden was tiny; it seemed odd to have such a large house on such a small property. But there was something much better than a garden behind the house: a thick patch of trees that spilled down the bank into a valley.

Norah plunged into the trees, thrusting through bushes and pushing aside branches, until she reached a clearing at the bottom. High above her stretched a bridge; she could hear the rumble of cars driving over it. Someone had written rude words on one of the concrete supports.

You could make a good fort here; but it would be lonely to build a fort all by herself and she felt too lazy to start. She sat on a log and scraped the ground with a twig. When she thought of school tomorrow her chest felt heavy, but she breathed deeply and scratched pictures in the dirt of all the aeroplanes she knew.

When she had been there for a long while Norah suddenly remembered the time. She scrambled up the bank and rushed into the Ogilvies' house. For a second she almost thought she was at home, for from the den came a familiar voice: "This is the BBC news coming to you directly from London." She paused outside the door; would Aunt Florence be angry?

The Ogilvies were sitting around a large wireless. Aunt Florence switched it off quickly as soon as she saw Norah—as if she didn't want her to hear. "Where have you *been*, young lady? We were just about to call the police!"

"Out for a walk," Norah mumbled. She raised her head and tossed back her hair defiantly. "Aunt Mary said I could."

"She said you had gone around the block, but you've been away for hours! And just look at you—you're covered in leaves and dirt. Where have you been? You've scared us half to death. If I had been consulted, you wouldn't have been allowed out alone at all!"

"I went into the woods behind the garden and I forgot about the time." Aunt Mary looked so stricken that Norah added, "I'm sorry."

"You went into the *ravine?*" said Aunt Florence crisply. "This won't do, my girl! The ravine attracts rough boys and it's muddy and dangerous. You are never to go there again, do you understand? Get yourself cleaned up for lunch."

As Norah shook out her twig-covered dress and changed her dusty socks, she resolved to go back to her secret place in the ravine as soon as she could. She would just have to be careful not to get caught.

The rest of Monday crept by so slowly, that Norah thought she would burst with boredom. Aunt Mary suggested a drive, but her mother said it was too hot. All afternoon they sat listlessly on a screened verandah at the back of the house, sipping lemonade. Norah lay on the floor beside Gavin, helping him construct houses out of cards. She thought longingly of *Swallowdale,* which she'd had to leave unfinished at Hart House. Then she remembered Aunt Mary pointing out a bookcase in their room. Could she just leave and go up there by herself—as if she were at home?

"Excuse me," she mumbled. "I'm going to my room."

"Of course, Norah." Aunt Mary smiled at her. Aunt Florence didn't even look up from her needlepoint. She had been sulking ever since Mary had told her that Gavin would have to go to school.

Norah decided to explore the house first. No one had offered to show her around, but she could see it for herself while the Ogilvies were safely on the verandah and Hanny was off.

She wondered why two people needed so many rooms. On the main floor, behind the den, she found another room, with a photograph of a sober-faced, whiskered gentleman on the desk: Mr Ogilvie, she decided. Upstairs were five bedrooms, connected by spacious halls covered in slippery rugs. The rooms were crammed with dark furniture. They smelled stale and their heavy curtains were pulled tight against the sun. Aunt Florence's and Aunt Mary's doors were firmly closed.

She found a set of back stairs leading up from the kitchen. When she put her head around a curtain at the top, she gasped. Edith was stretched out on a cot with her stockings off, fanning herself with a folded paper. She sat up and shouted at Norah, "What do you think you're doing, poking your nose up here! Get away!"

Norah scuttled down the stairs, through the kitchen and hall, and up the other staircase to the tower. She collapsed on her bed, her heart hammering. She knew that Hanny came in to work every day; she hadn't realized that Edith lived right in the house. From the brief glance she'd had at her room, it looked smaller and barer than any of the unused ones.

The tower was hot, but Norah decided it was the best room in the house. When she'd caught her breath she examined the books. Most of them were old schoolbooks; there was nothing by the man who wrote *Swallowdale.* The only story she found was called *Elsie Dinsmore.* Its spongy pages were spotted with mildew; "Mary Ogilvie" was written on the flyleaf in careful round handwriting. It was a strange book, about a repulsively good little girl who was very religious. Norah struggled along with it until dinner.

That evening Norah had a telephone call. "For me?" she asked with disbelief. Who knew her in Canada?

"Hello, Norah, this is Dulcie!" said the high, nervous voice.

"Hello, Dulcie," said Norah without enthusiasm. Still, it cheered her up to hear someone familiar.

"Isn't it super that we live in the same neighbourhood? The Milnes are ever so nice. We've had a holiday since we arrived. What I was wondering was... do you think we could try to sit next to each other at school tomorrow? It's quite a large school, Aunt Dorothy says..."

What she was really asking was if they could stick together as if they were friends. The Smiths had only come to Ringden two years ago. Norah remembered how scared Dulcie had looked on her first day of school and how the other children had taken advantage of this to tease her.

Norah had never been a new girl. She had always been one of the most popular people in her class—surely that would carry on. It was flattering that Dulcie recognized her superior position.

"I'll see what I can do," she said grandly.

"Oh, thank you, Norah!" said Dulcie. "See you tomorrow!"

Aunt Florence came into the hall. "Off to bed with you, now," she said briskly. "You and Gavin have a big day tomorrow. I don't know how that delicate little boy is going to bear it."

XII

"NOW IN SCHOOL AND LIKING IT"

As if Aunt Florence had willed it, Gavin woke up the next morning too sick to go to school. His nose streamed, he had a croaky cough and his forehead was hot.

Aunt Florence moved him downstairs into the bedroom opposite hers and settled him against lofty pillows under a mountain of blankets. When Norah left with Aunt Mary she could hear the rich voice coaxing, "Would you like me to read *Winnie-the-Pooh* to you? I once knew a little boy who loved that story."

The walk to Prince Edward School was not long; they reached the two-storey red brick building much sooner than Norah wished. She tried not to flinch from the curious stares of the children standing around in noisy groups. Aunt Mary took her inside to look for the headmaster; she called him the "principal".

The principal's secretary told them to wait in the outer office. They sat on a hard bench and listened to a deep voice talking on the telephone from behind a frosted glass door. Soon Dulcie and Lucy bounced up, accompanied by a complacent-looking, smiling woman.

"Good morning, Miss Ogilvie," she said. "This must be Norah. I'm so pleased that Dulcie and Lucy will have friends from home. But where's your little brother?"

Aunt Mary explained about Gavin. Mrs Milne introduced her to the Smiths and said that Derek was going to high school. "He's such a clever boy, they've put him ahead a year. Isn't it a privilege to have the care of these children, Miss Ogilvie? The Reverend and I didn't realize how empty our lives were until they came. Already I feel as if they are part of the family." She plumped the bow in Lucy's hair and kissed her fondly.

"Mr Evans would like to talk to the ladies first," interrupted the secretary. She led Aunt Mary and Mrs Milne behind the glass door and then left the office. "You wait here quietly," she told the children. "He'll see you in a few minutes."

"Miss Ogilvie seems very nice," said Dulcie. Her rash, like Lucy's lisp, had disappeared. "What's *Mrs* Ogilvie like? Uncle Cedric says she's a dragon, but a pillar of support for the church."

Norah shrugged. She couldn't think of any words to describe Aunt Florence, although "dragon" and "pillar" certainly seemed right.

"Aunt Dorothy and Uncle Cedric aren't at all strict," said Lucy, trying to balance on one leg. "They let us do whatever we want and they've taken us to all sorts of interesting places. Have you been on a streetcar, yet, Norah? Have you seen the Toronto Islands and Casa Loma? *We* have."

"Isn't it odd how they shop for food here?" Dulcie giggled. "Everything in one store! Does your house have a refrigerator? Ours does, and we can have as much water as we like in the bath. Do stop that, Lucy, we're supposed to be sitting quietly."

Goosey and Loosey babbled on and Norah only half-listened; she kept her eyes on the glass door. At home the headmaster—*principal,* she corrected herself—was also her teacher. He didn't have an office or a secretary, or a mysterious glass door.

"It's an enormous school, isn't it?" said Dulcie. "Aunt Dorothy says it goes up to age fourteen!"

In the village school their age group had been the oldest. As Norah contemplated this, the glass door opened a crack. "Come in, girls," called Mrs Milne.

They stood in a row in front of the principal's desk. He leaned across it and shook their hands. "Welcome to Canada," he said vaguely. He was a sleepy-looking man who seemed preoccupied, as if none of them were really in the room with him.

"Yes, um, war guests—there are already twenty-four in the school and they're settling in well. We're glad that Canada has been able to help you at this difficult time. Now, about your grade levels." He told them that Lucy would be in grade two, and Norah and Dulcie in grade five. "Say goodbye to your guardians now and I'll take you to your classrooms."

"I'll meet you at the front door at 12:30," whispered Aunt Mary.

The three girls followed Mr Evans's back down the hall. The wooden floor made their footsteps echo loudly. Everyone else was already in class. Norah and Dulcie waited outside while the principal took Lucy by the hand into a room labelled Two B—Mrs Newbery. Then he continued to a door that said Five A—Miss Liers.

He knocked before poking in his head. "Miss Liers, your war guests—Dulcie Smith and Norah Stoakes." They stepped through the doorway and he closed them in.

Miss Liers was a thin, bitter-looking woman with dark hair scraped back so tightly in a bun that it pulled on her skin. Although her words were kind, her tone was sarcastic, as if they had done something wrong. "How do you do, Dulcie and Norah? We've been expecting you. I've given you desks next to each other over there. Five A is proud to have some war guests. We felt deprived without any, didn't we, class?"

Five A stared at Norah and Dulcie as if the multitude of eyes were one big eye.

Miss Liers handed them each some pencils and notebooks, continuing to talk in a strained, cold voice. Why did she resent them? Norah wondered, lifting up the lid of her desk to hide from all those eyes. She found out at once.

"Dulcie and Norah are extremely lucky," Miss Liers was saying. "*All* British evacuees are lucky that Canada has invited them here for the duration. But we mustn't forget that there are other children in Europe who aren't so lucky. Little Belgian and Dutch and Jewish children whose circumstances are far graver than British children's. Let us hope that our government will act to bring those children over to safety as well."

She paused expectantly and the class droned, "Yes, Miss Liers." But no one was listening. They were all peeking at the two new girls.

Norah bent her head over her arithmetic book as the interrupted lesson continued. It wasn't her fault she had been sent to Canada instead of a European child. Perhaps she could tell Miss Liers sometime that she would have been happy if one could have been evacuated in her place.

She discovered quickly that the problems were ones she had done last year. Beside her, Dulcie gave a small sigh of relief. Arithmetic had been her weakest subject.

Miss Liers didn't call on either of them. When some of the pupils went to the blackboard to write down their answers, Norah felt safe enough to raise her head and examine the room.

It was as large as their whole school in Ringden. The five rows of desks had wide spaces between them and at one end there was a raised platform with a piano on it. The walls were hung with rolled-up maps and a picture of the Royal Family, just like at home. Norah's desk was beside high windows; she could see out to the houses across the street.

Next she looked at the pupils. Everyone was too busy concentrating to return her stare. They didn't *seem* any different from English children, but there were so many of them. In Ringden there had been only thirty-two children divided into two age groups. Here there were—she counted quickly—twenty-seven, including her and Dulcie, and everyone seemed to be the same age. If there were two rooms for each of the eight grades, there were over five hundred children in the school!

A loud bell interrupted Norah's private arithmetic. She looked around to see what they were supposed to do next. All the children put down their pencils and sat up alertly.

"Before you go out for recess, I want two volunteers to look after our war guests," said Miss Liers.

All the girls shot up their arms. One large, smartalecky boy with red hair waved his wildly, while his friends hooted and cheered.

"That will do, Charlie!" There was instant silence; Miss Liers commanded respect.

"Babs Miller will look after Dulcie, and Ernestine Gagnon, Norah. Show them where to go and what to do for the next few days. Make them feel at home here."

Babs Miller started asking Dulcie eager questions as soon as they were allowed to talk. Ernestine looked longingly after Dulcie as they left the room, as if she had wanted her instead of Norah. She was a very pretty girl with glossy brown curls held back with a huge bow.

Norah was desperate for a toilet. "Where's the lav?" she asked, as she and Ernestine started out to the playground.

"The lav? What's that?"

Oh, help—what would they call it? At the Ogilvies' they said "bathroom" but surely there weren't any rooms with baths in them at school.

"The WC," Norah tried next.

"The WC? Are you asking riddles or something?" Ernestine looked annoyed, as they stood inside the door and everyone surged past.

"The—the *toilet!*" burst out Norah, flushing with embarrassment.

"Oh, the *washroom*—why didn't you say so? Follow me." Looking even angrier, Ernestine led her to a large room with a long row of cubicles in the basement. Norah had to stay there awhile. By the time Ernestine had waited for her and taken her out to the playground, recess was almost over.

The boys and girls seemed to have separate play areas. Ernestine and Norah went up to the grade five girls, all standing around Dulcie in an eager crowd.

"How long did it take you to get over?"

"What was it like on the ship?"

Dulcie beamed at all this unusual attention. "The ship was *scary,*" she said importantly. "Some other girls and I started a club to keep up our courage."

"I love your dress, Dulcie," said Ernestine, pushing past Norah and forgetting her.

Norah assessed the situation quickly. This would never do—Dulcie was the one who was supposed to be unpopular! And she wasn't describing any of the interesting parts. Norah opened her mouth to tell someone about the German plane, but another bell clanged and they all swept past her to line up at the girls' entrance.

Very well, then, she thought angrily. If they were going to like Goosey better than her, she would not tell them anything.

"You come from the same village as Dulcie, don't you?" asked the girl in front of her. Norah mumbled "Mmmm," and looked the other way.

For the rest of the morning Norah returned any friendly looks she received with proud reserve. She glanced at the picture of Princess Margaret Rose, standing regally in her Coronation robe beside her sister and parents. Norah pretended she was a princess as well, too elevated to mix with Canadian children

During English, Miss Liers read them a poem called "How They Brought the Good News from Ghent to Aix." Norah listened intently. It was the first poem she'd ever liked, about the kind of noble deed the Skywatchers would do. Miss Liers asked her to read the first verse again. Norah stood up and recited it in a fierce, animated voice:

I sprang to the stirrup, and Joris, and he;
I galloped, Dirck galloped, we galloped all three;
"Good speed!" cried the watch, as the gate-bolts undrew;
"Speed!" echoed the wall to us galloping through;
Behind shut the postern, the lights sank to rest,
And into the midnight we galloped abreast.

At the last word Charlie gaffawed, until Miss Liers's sharp glance silenced him. "Good, Norah!" she said in a surprised tone, as if her admiration had got in the way of her resentment. "I wish the rest of you could read with such expression."

The rest of them, of course, looked sulky and some of them scowled at Norah. When Dulcie read the next verse in a halting monotone and Miss Liers corrected her, the class smiled in friendly sympathy.

"How was it?" Aunt Mary asked her anxiously, when Norah came out at lunchtime. "Is it very different from your old school?"

"It's bigger," was all Norah replied.

Hanny served her lunch all alone at the polished table. Aunt Mary had to go to a Red Cross meeting.

"Oh, Norah," she said on her way out. "Someone phoned to tell us you are allowed to send home a free cable each month—but you have to select from prewritten messages. The man read them out to me and the most suitable seemed to be 'Now in school and liking it.' Mother agreed that they would send that message to your parents for this month from you and Gavin—isn't that nice? It will get there before any letters. Can you find your way back to school by yourself?" When Norah nodded, she hurried out the door.

Aunt Florence didn't notice her leave for school again; she was upstairs feeding Gavin. "The doctor's been and it's a bad cold," said Hanny. "He's to stay in bed for a week, poor child."

Norah thought he was lucky. And she was glad she didn't have Gavin to worry about at school—taking care of herself was going to be difficult enough.

XIII

MISERY UPON MISERY

For the rest of the week Dulcie became more and more popular and Norah grew more and more aloof. She pretended she didn't care if no one spoke to her and assumed a cold, proud expression if anyone tried. Ernestine abandoned her. "What a snob," Norah heard her whisper to the others.

It was a relief not to have to go to school on the weekend, but Norah had a hard time finding something to do. Gavin was still in bed, cosseted with tempting food, new toys and Aunt Florence's undivided attention. Aunt Mary seemed to be on a lot of committees.

At least there was Hanny. Norah spent most of Saturday in the kitchen, helping her cook. Hanny asked a lot of questions about England. She was very interested when Norah told her about rationing.

"Two ounces of tea a *week*? However did your mother manage? Why, sometimes I drink three pots a day! What did you do if you ran out?"

"We never did," said Norah with surprise. "I suppose Mum was just careful." For the first time she realized how difficult it must have been. "Sometimes we were short of sugar and once Dad put one of my acid drops in his tea—because sweets aren't rationed yet. He said it tasted horrible."

"Let's just hope we don't get rationing in Canada," said Hanny, creaming butter and sugar together.

When she'd finished, Norah picked up the eggbeater and licked it. She tried to think of something to ask so they could stop talking about home. "Why hasn't Aunt Mary got a husband?"

Hanny sighed. "Poor Mary. Stifled all her life, then the one chance she had ..." She pressed her lips closed.

"What?" prompted Norah.

"It's not for young ears. Let's just say she has a secret sorrow." She wouldn't say any more about it.

A Secret Sorrow; it sounded like one of Muriel's romances. Dull Aunt Mary suddenly seemed more interesting.

The cake was put into the oven and Hanny made a pot of tea. "May I have some?" Norah asked hopefully.

"Do you like tea? Sure, I don't see why not." She handed Norah a cup of half-milk, half-tea.

Norah curved her fingers around it and sipped. "*Thank* you!" Hanny smiled at her.

"What about *Mr* Ogilvie?" Norah asked. "What was he like?"

"Ah, what a sad loss to this house when he went. A real gentleman, he was—I don't mean uppity, but a *gentle man*, always kind and thoughtful. He didn't speak much but when he did he said things you wanted to remember. Mary was his favourite—she was absolutely stricken when he died. And so was *she*, of course."

They both knew who "she" was. Norah couldn't imagine Aunt Florence married to a gentle, quiet man.

"She shut herself up for weeks," continued Hanny. "I felt sorry for her, I must admit. First her son, then her husband—the two people she loved best. But that was fifteen years ago and she's long since recovered. She's a strong woman, Mrs O is—too strong for her own good. She was softer when Mr O and Hughie were alive. She needs someone to think about besides herself. Maybe having you two here will use up some of her energy."

Norah shuddered—she didn't *want* Aunt Florence to think about her. "What about you?" she asked, to change the subject. "Did your husband die too?"

"Not him," laughed Hanny. "He's a retired CPR brakeman. Spends his time making model railways now—one day I'll take you and Gavin home to see them. But goodness me, look at the time and I haven't even started the vegetables! You better go and join them in the den—they'll be wondering where you are."

Norah put down her cup and slowly walked out of the comfortable, fragrant kitchen.

Hanny didn't come in until eleven on Sundays, so Norah couldn't escape to her. Instead she had to go to church with the Ogilvies. At least it passed the time. The service was almost the same as at home, with the Smiths sitting in the front pew as usual. Norah found out why Aunt Florence and Aunt Mary turned off the radio whenever she was near: Reverend Milne talked about the terrible bombing London was experiencing. "It's all right, Norah," whispered Aunt Mary, exchanging a worried look with her mother. "I'm sure the bombs weren't anywhere near where your family lives."

Norah's throat felt so constricted that she had a hard time swallowing the huge Sunday lunch. Another dreary afternoon stretched ahead of her and once again she took refuge in the kitchen.

Aunt Florence came in to get some milk for Gavin. "You're in here far too much, Norah," she scolded. "Hanny has work to do—you're getting in her way. And is that tea you're drinking? I'm surprised at you, Hanny—she's much too young for tea."

Hanny pretended not to hear the last part of her sentence. "She doesn't bother me at all, Mrs Ogilvie," she said calmly. "In fact, she's a great help."

"Norah isn't here to be a servant. What would her parents think if we had her doing housework? I want you to stay out of the kitchen, Norah—except for Sunday supper, of course."

Norah opened her mouth to protest, but Aunt Florence silenced her. "No arguments, please. Can't you find anything to do? What about all the puzzles Mary put in your room? Have you done your homework?"

"We didn't have any," said Norah sullenly. "And I've *done* all the puzzles." If she was only to be allowed to talk to Hanny once a week, what *would* she do?

"I know," said Aunt Florence briskly, as she whipped an egg into the glass of milk. "It's time you wrote home. You can do that *every* Sunday afternoon," she added, looking relieved to have thought of a way to occupy Norah.

She settled her in the room behind the den with a pile of thick white monogrammed paper. Norah knelt on the chair drawn up to the oak desk, chewing the end of her pen. She had already written once from the university, but that was just a short note to tell them they'd arrived safely. Now she didn't know what to say. Mr Ogilvie watched sympathetically from his gold frame.

She longed to pour out the truth, to relieve her misery with a litany of complaints. How she had to ask permission every time she left the house and was allowed to explore only within a four-block area. Being forbidden to go into the ravine—although she went there almost every day on her way home from school. Being scolded for biting her nails, for climbing the tree in the front yard and, yesterday, for trying to slide down the laundry chute that led from the second floor to the basement. And school—her isolation and loneliness and the continued resentment of Miss Liers. Just to be able to tell them all this would be a huge relief.

But she couldn't. It would only worry them, when they had the war to worry about. And she knew how disappointed Dad would be if she complained. Grandad would understand, but if she wrote to him separately her parents would wonder why.

Finally Norah thought of a way to fill up the page. She dipped her pen in the crystal bottle of ink and began.

Dear Mum, Dad and Grandad,

Here is what is different about Canada. The cars drive on the wrong side of the street. The robins are huge. There is no rationing of food or petrol. There's no black-out. Canadians have different money and they speak a different language. Here is a list of the words I know so far.

Biscuit__________________________Cookie
Sweet ___________________________Candy
Lollipop_________________________Sucker
Wireless__________________________Radio
Shop _____________________________Store
Flannel_______________________Washcloth
Jersey _________________________Sweater
Lav __________________________Washroom
Headmaster ___________________Principal

Dinner is called lunch and tea is dinner. We only have tea on Sundays but we aren't allowed to drink it. Could you tell Aunt Florence that we can?

Did the bombs come near Ringden? Are there still dogfights? Did any more planes get shot down? Did Mr Whitlaw's mare have her foal? Did the hedgehog come back? Have you heard from Muriel and Tibby? Please answer soon.

By the end of the letter she was limp with homesickness. Her hand shook as she wrote "Love and kisses from Norah" and added a postscript: "I am cleaning my teeth every night."

At least writing the letter had taken a good long time, especially the list. She'd drawn careful straight lines with the edge of a paper-knife and hadn't made any blots.

"When do you suppose I'll get a letter from England?" Norah asked Aunt Florence, going to her in the den for stamps.

"Not for a while, I'm afraid—the war has made the overseas mail very slow." Aunt Florence took Norah's letter and frowned, as if she were displeased it was sealed. "I hope you didn't mention Gavin's cold, Norah—we don't want to worry your parents unnecessarily."

"I didn't." Guiltily, Norah realized she hadn't mentioned Gavin at all.

"I've written as well," said Aunt Florence, holding up an envelope. "I've told your parents all about our family and sent them a photograph of the house. I'm sure that will reassure them. I'll get Gavin to draw a nice picture to enclose."

Norah was sure that *her* letter talked about Gavin. She looked just as curiously at Aunt Florence's envelope as Aunt Florence had looked at hers, wondering what had been said about herself.

On Monday, Norah woke before dawn—something was wrong. "Oh, Gavin—not again!" she groaned, half-asleep. Her bed was cold and wet, as it had been on the boat.

Then she was fully awake and remembered that Gavin wasn't in her bed or even in the room—he was asleep on the floor below. Who had wet the bed?

When she realized, Norah hopped out as quickly as if the bed were on fire. She tore off her wet pyjama bottoms, balled them up and hurled them on the floor.

What was the matter with her? She was ten years old, not a baby! Maybe she was sick. Even so, she didn't want anyone to know what she'd done.

At least no one was up here to see. She took her sheet and pyjama bottoms into the bathroom and rinsed them. She hung them in the wardrobe and closed the door. Then she scrubbed the mattress and made the bed without a bottom sheet. With luck, it would all be dry by evening.

Everything was still damp that night, but Norah put the sheet back on the bed and curled around the wet patch in her other pyjamas. "*Please* don't let it happen again," she prayed. But it did. And the next day after school, Aunt Mary called her into her room.

Norah looked around for evidence of the Secret Sorrow, trying to distract herself from what she guessed Aunt Mary was about to discuss. As in the rest of the house, the room was muffled with dark furniture and curtains. A large Bible lay on the table beside the bed. On the chest of drawers was a photograph of a little girl in a white dress and black stockings, gazing up with adoring eyes to a stalwart-looking boy in a sailor suit. He had one arm circled protectively around her. The boy was handsome, with a thick crop of hair, while the girl was plain and plump. It must be Aunt Mary and her older brother Hugh.

"Sit down, Norah," began the soft voice. "When Edith was doing your room this morning she found a wet sheet and pyjamas hanging in the wardrobe. Did you—did you have an accident?"

Norah nodded unable to speak.

"Do you do this often?"

"Never! I never have before now. Perhaps I'm ill."

"I suppose you're just adjusting. They told us to expect this, but I thought it might happen with Gavin, not a child your age. You'll probably stop eventually." Aunt Mary sighed. "Edith will put a rubber sheet on your mattress. If it keeps on happening, please don't hang your sheets upstairs—put them down the laundry chute. If you leave your bed stripped, Edith will make it up again. And Norah . . . perhaps we won't say anything about this to Mother."

Both their faces were red when Norah left the room. At least Aunt Florence didn't know. It would be a point on her side if she did.

Norah almost became used to scuttling down the stairs with her wet bundle before breakfast each morning. She was relieved Aunt Florence was never up at that time. Edith began to give her resentful looks and mumbled about extra work. Aunt Mary seemed resigned that bed-wetting was part of having war guests, and Norah felt more and more lost and ashamed.

School, too, grew worse instead of better. Miss Liers never praised Norah again; in fact, she seemed to take pleasure in criticizing both her and Dulcie. "Surely it isn't necessary to crowd your words like this," she said coldly, handing back their first compositions. They weren't brave enough to explain that, in England, they'd been encouraged to fill every corner of the page to save paper.

Norah spent recesses standing alone in the corner that was neutral territory between the girls' and boys' playgrounds. She was tired of acting like a princess. She wouldn't mind having a friend, but making friends had always just happened; she didn't know how to be deliberate about it. And by now, everyone had her labelled as stuck-up anyhow.

There was another loner in the schoolyard: a pale boy with glasses and mousy hair that stuck out all over his head like a mop. As Norah watched how the other boys plagued him, she was thankful that at least the girls didn't do things to her; they just ignored her. She wondered why they picked on that particular boy so much.

On Thursday she was just leaving after school when she heard a rhythmic banging come from the middle of a crowd of grade five and six boys. "*Sauer*kraut, *sauer*kraut," the group chanted. Norah moved closer; she'd heard them call the boy that before.

The boy with glasses was sitting in the dirt in the middle of the group, a bucket inverted on his head. Two boys held him down, while Charlie beat on the iron bucket with a stick in time to the chant.

Norah pushed through the crowd before she had time to think. "Stop that! You're hurting him!"

The group turned with surprise at the sight of a girl interfering. Their victim saw his chance; he pushed off the bucket and fled.

"Why did you *do* that?" Norah asked angrily. She clenched her fists, but her chest constricted at the unfriendly glares of the others.

"Because he's an enemy alien, stupid," said Charlie.

Norah was confused. What did he mean? She didn't have time to ponder, as the group began to close in on her.

Charlie was obviously the ringleader. He was bigger than any of them, and his bright red hair commanded attention like a flag. "You think you're really something, don't you, Limey?" he jeered. "Do you know what *we* think? We think you're a coward. You couldn't take the war, so you ran away to Canada. *We* wouldn't have let them send us away. We'd *like* to be in the war, wouldn't we?" The other boys nodded and waited.

Norah spluttered with fury. "Why—you—you're just a bunch of—of *colonials!*" she finally spat. "I'm *not* a coward! I didn't have any choice about coming here. And I saw a lot of things you'll never see. I saw a crashed Nazi plane!"

A few of the boys looked interested, but Charlie jeered again. "Naaah, you couldn't have. Enemy planes wouldn't come down that close." He sounded so authoritative that the others looked threatening again.

"They did too!" cried Norah. "They were all around us! And I helped watch for them. What do *you* do? You're the cowards, safe from the war. You wouldn't even know there *was* a war here!"

But they were already moving away. Norah couldn't stop shaking. How was she going to survive this school? The girls ignored her and now the boys despised her. She stopped in the ravine on the way home, first letting herself cry, then thinking for a long time.

She got home late, but no one noticed her sneak upstairs. All of Gavin's belongings, including the rocking horse, had disappeared. Suddenly Norah felt concern. Was Gavin seriously ill? He'd been out of school for almost two weeks, too long for a cold. With shame, she thought of how she'd hardly seen him all that time. Had they taken him to a hospital? She dashed downstairs and into the room where he'd been sleeping.

Gavin was stretched out on the rug, surrounded by a troop of toy soldiers. He was dressed in a navy-blue sailor suit and shiny new shoes.

"Are you still sick?" Norah demanded.

Gavin shook his head. "No, but I'm going to stay in this room all the time now, because I'm delicate. See my new soldiers, Norah? Aunt Florence took me to an enormous shop today called a department store. There was a lift—'cept it's called an elevator—and six floors. She bought me all sorts of clothes and things and these wizard soldiers. Tomorrow we're going to the museum to see the dinosaurs!"

"Don't be ridiculous, Gavin. If you're better, you'll go to school tomorrow. And you're *not* delicate—you hardly ever get sick."

"He most certainly is." Aunt Florence stood in the doorway, beaming at Gavin. "Don't lie on the floor, sweetness, you'll catch cold again. Norah, there's something I wanted to discuss with you." She hesitated strangely. "I have decided not to send Gavin to school this term. He's been through a great ordeal, coming all the way over here. That large school would be too much for him. I'll build up his strength until Christmas and then we'll see. Perhaps your parents would let me pay for a private school. We'll go on educational outings and I'll read to him every day. He won't be missing anything—they can't do much in school at his age. If he's not going to be six until November, nobody is going to object if he waits until January to start. I've told your parents that it's not customary in Canada to send five-year-olds to school. I know we sent that cable, but my letter will reach them soon." She spoke as if all her arguments had been prepared beforehand; her imperious grey eyes dared Norah to contradict her.

Norah sat down and picked up a lead soldier while she digested this news. It was wrong, of course. It was bad for Gavin to be so pampered, and he would forget everything he had learned last year. Her parents would be upset if they knew that Gavin really could go to school at five. Aunt Florence had lied to them!

She could threaten to write to her parents; Aunt Florence knew she could. The longer she waited for Norah to speak, the more uneasy she looked.

But it would be much handier for Norah if Gavin was kept out of school and out of her care. Because now she had a plan.

Finally she shrugged wearily. "Lucky you, Gavin—school's *awful.*"

Aunt Florence didn't seem to have heard the second part of her sentence. "That's settled, then," she said cheerfully. "And *you're* lucky, Norah, to have that big room all to yourself."

Norah couldn't disagree about that. She trudged back up to the tower that was now her own little kingdom and stared out the window at the darkening sky.

XIV
BERNARD

Norah woke up early and peeled off her wet sheet before she had time to think about it. Then she got back on top of the bed and reviewed her plan, listening to the slow clomp of the milkman's horse in the street.

She had decided to play truant. Never before had she done something so risky. In Ringden, where everyone was aware of everyone else's affairs, she would be spotted immediately if she were out of school. But Toronto was a large city; no one would know or care.

She had noticed that when Babs had forgotten to bring a note last week, Miss Liers hadn't insisted on one. "Try to remember next time," was all she had said. Perhaps Norah could get away with pretending she'd been ill.

But what if she didn't? What if she were caught? The worst consequence she could imagine was the Ogilvies and the school being very angry. Maybe she would even be sent to live with another family. It had always been upsetting to have her parents or her headmaster angry with her, but she had no warm feelings towards either the Ogilvies or Prince Edward School. And being sent to another family couldn't be any worse than being here; it might even be better.

The black cloud mood descended and she felt reckless and defiant. She could have a whole day of freedom, without the aggravation of either the Ogilvies or school.

"May I take my lunch to school?" she asked at breakfast, trying to keep the nervousness out of her voice.

Aunt Mary looked pleased. "That would be a help today. Mother and Gavin will be at the museum and I have an Altar Guild meeting. It would give Hanny more time to do the grocery shopping."

Norah left the house as usual and went straight to her retreat in the ravine. She still hadn't made a fort, but she'd pulled logs together to form a kind of chair. She perched on it jubilantly, stripping the leaves off a twig and trying to ignore guilty thoughts of her parents.

What would they think if they knew? Well, they didn't; they were too far away. What if Aunt Florence knew? The fact that *she* didn't made Norah grin with triumph. The only people she wished could see her now were Charlie and his gang—then they'd know she wasn't a coward.

She stayed in the cool glen for a long time, hugging her knees to her chest. She had only planned as far as not going to school; how to fill the day in front of her was a challenge. It might be interesting to explore Toronto, as long as she avoided the museum. But she didn't know where that was, anyway. Perhaps she could go for a ride on a streetcar. Aunt Florence had begun to give her pocket money—she called it "allowance"—every week. She could have a streetcar ride, then go somewhere to eat her lunch. There was still the afternoon, but by then she might have thought of something else.

Hiding her school books under a bush, Norah scrambled out of the ravine. She walked rapidly away from the Ogilvies', her legs trembling. Someone could still come out and see her.

When she reached Yonge Street, the busy main thoroughfare that she wasn't supposed to cross, she stood and blinked with uncertainty for a few seconds. Streetcars moved up and down amidst the cars, but she didn't have the courage to board one yet. She began to walk.

She was right about being anonymous in a big city. No one seemed to find it unusual to see a ten-year-old girl walking along the street on a Friday morning. All the same, she tried to look purposeful.

After about ten minutes, she reached another busy street and realized she was in a much more bustling area. They had come by here on their way from Hart House. This was like exploring Stumble Wood with Molly and Tom, only the landmarks were signs and buildings instead of trees.

It was even easier not to be noticed here. Norah gazed in store windows and wove in and out among crowds of women carrying shopping bags. Her ears rang with the screech of cars and the bleat of horns; she marvelled how quiet it was in Rosedale, with all this activity so close.

A red and yellow streetcar clattered along a track in the middle of the road and stopped, its bell dinging. Norah noticed how people walked right out onto the street to board. She followed them as the doors unfolded.

"Do you have a ticket?" asked the driver.

Norah shook her head. "How much is it, please?" He told her, and she counted out the change carefully. Even though Miss Liers had given her and Dulcie a lesson in Canadian money, she still wasn't used to it.

"Pay the ticket-taker," said the driver. Norah moved down towards the middle of the car, where she gave her fare to the ticket-taker. She took a seat on one side of the long, thin car. It rocked from side to side as it rumbled along. When someone glanced at her curiously, Norah tried to look as if she belonged to the woman beside her.

She had boarded at Charles Street. After she'd travelled about ten blocks, she got off the streetcar and ran across the road to catch a car going back. Anxiously she peered out at the imposing brick and stone buildings, each one jammed with windows. What a lot of people must be inside! She reached the sign saying Charles Street again, and got off for good.

Exhilarated by her success, Norah almost skipped as she made her way back to Yonge and Bloor. She'd done it! Now Goosey and Loosey weren't the only ones to have ridden on a Toronto streetcar.

As she paused for a red light, she glanced across the street and saw a large woman pulling a small, sailor-suited boy by the hand. Aunt Florence and Gavin! Norah pelted into the doorway of a store and hid.

Aunt Florence stopped to talk to an elegant lady in a flowery hat. She seemed to linger there forever. Norah pretended to be absorbed in a display of women's shoes. Her heart raced as she imagined Aunt Florence's voice cutting through the traffic noise as she shouted, "Norah, *what* are you doing out of school?"

Finally Aunt Florence began walking again, Gavin trotting along behind. He looked unhappy, Norah noticed with surprise—dazed and passive, like a puppy on a lead.

As soon as she thought it was safe, Norah hurried in the other direction. She trudged up Yonge Street with relief. She was getting tired, but she couldn't stop with nowhere to sit. Her stomach gurgled and the soles of her feet stung from the hard pavement. Finally she reached a park. Resting on a bench far away from the street, she ate all the food Hanny had packed for her lunch. A mangy-looking black squirrel and two pigeons shared it with her.

Now what? Norah sighed, wishing she owned a wristwatch. Perhaps she could miss only the morning, but she didn't know when the lunch bell would go. And it was going to be tricky arriving back at the Ogilvies' at her usual time after school. She began to walk again, feeling flat; seeing Aunt Florence had wilted her enthusiasm.

When she reached her own neighbourhood, Norah decided to keep walking north. There was nowhere else to go besides the ravine, and she didn't feel like sitting down there for the rest of the day. By now her legs felt like two lead sticks, but she passed no more parks.

Then she noticed, a few doors down a side street, a sign saying Toronto Public Library—McNair Branch.

Anyone could go into a library. This one was larger than the one in Gilden, but it looked inviting; there was even a sign at a side door saying Boys and Girls.

She pushed open the door timidly and went down the stairs to a long room filled with books and tables. At one end there was a fireplace and a puppet theatre, and at the other a desk with a young woman bent over it. She lifted her head as Norah hesitated by the entrance.

"Good morning!" she greeted. With surprise, Norah saw that the clock on the wall said it was only eleven. "Is there anything I can help you with?" asked the librarian. Her round face smiled eagerly.

"May I look around?" asked Norah shyly.

"Of course! Look around as much as you wish and take any books you want to a table. Are you one of our young war guests?"

How did she know? Norah flushed with confusion until she realized: her accent, of course. "Yes," she said as calmly as possible. "I'm staying with a family in Rosedale but I've been ill, so I don't have to go to school today."

The friendly woman accepted this easily. "My name is Miss Gleeson. I'm very fond of England, because that's where all my favourite authors are from. Would you like to apply for a library card? You can take the form home for your hosts to sign."

"Oh, no—I'll just look at the books here," Norah said hastily. Then, because Miss Gleeson looked disappointed, she added, "My name's Norah."

"Well, Norah, and what would you like to read?"

"Do you have a book called *Swallowdale?*"

Miss Gleeson shot out of her chair, ran to a row of green-backed books, snatched one from the shelf and darted back with it. She held the book aloft as if it were a sacred object.

"Arthur Ransome! My favourite author! Isn't he *wonderful?* Have you read the first one? Have you ever been to the Lake District? The first thing I'm going to do after the war is over is to go there and try to find the places in the books."

Norah wished she could just have the book. She mumbled an answer and the librarian finally handed over *Swallowdale.* Norah sat down at one of the tables and found the place where she'd left off. Miss Gleeson had returned to her desk, but every time Norah looked up, the librarian was gazing reverently at her and the book.

She forgot about Miss Gleeson as the story drew her into it. For the next two hours Norah scarcely moved. She was so involved in the escapades of the Walkers and the Blacketts that she jumped when the door opened.

"Come in quietly, Bernard," said Miss Gleeson to the boy who entered. "There's someone reading."

Norah turned over *Swallowdale* and stretched the stiffness out of her arms and legs. She was close to the end and wanted to put off having to finish. She looked at the newcomer more closely; then she quickly held up the book to cover her face.

It was the boy with glasses. She peeked at him over the top of her book, as he went straight to the section marked Other

Lands, chose a book and settled with his back to her at the table in front.

Norah studied the washed-out flannel of his plaid shirt. Miss Gleeson had called him Bernard. What was he doing here? Would he recognize her from yesterday and tell someone she wasn't in school? Then it occurred to her that he must be playing truant too; she relaxed and went back to her story.

"Excuse me, children." They both looked up. "I have to go to a meeting. If anyone wants help, could you send them up to the adult department?"

They nodded, and Miss Gleeson left through a door by the fireplace. Norah had finished her book. She closed it with a sigh and sat for a few minutes wondering what to do next. It was only two o'clock; this was the longest day she could remember. She could pick out another Ransome book, but her eyes burned and her head was so full of *Swallowdale* there was no room for a new story.

"Do you mind if I ask why you aren't in school?" The boy had turned around and was looking at her steadily through his round glasses. His eyes were a muddy brown, like the faded colours of his shirt.

Norah could repeat her lie about being ill, but a person her age was much less likely to believe it than a grown-up. And there was something about the boy's freckled face she trusted.

"I'm playing truant," she said. Then, after a pause, she added. "I hate school."

Bernard grinned. "So am I and so do I! You're one of the grade five war guests, aren't you?"

Norah nodded. "And you're in Mr Bartlett's class. I'm Norah Stoakes."

"I'm Bernard . . . Bernard Gunter." He looked sheepish.

"Thanks a lot for rescuing me yesterday. I would have come back to thank you then, but I'm not very brave, as you may have noticed." He spoke in a wry, grown-up tone, as if he were older than grade six.

Norah shuddered. "It must have been horrid, all that banging. Charlie's in my class—he's awful!"

"My ears didn't stop ringing until this morning! But I don't care about them. Charlie's such a pea-brain. He's supposed to be in grade seven, but he's flunked twice. How did you get out of going to school today?"

Norah explained how she'd hidden in the ravine and gone for a ride on a streetcar. When Bernard told her he'd convinced his mother he had a stomach-ache that was too painful for school but not painful enough to stay away from the library, they both giggled.

"Why do *you* hate school?" asked Bernard.

It was too complicated to explain. "You first," said Norah.

"Nobody likes me," said Bernard matter of factly. "I guess it's not surprising, with the war on and my last name. We—my mother and I—are beginning to get used to it. Some of the stores in our neighbourhood won't give her credit any more, and sometimes we get anonymous letters telling us to move."

"But what has your last name got to do with it?"

"Gunter is German. Both my parents come from Munich, but I was born in Kitchener. That's where we lived until my father died and we moved to Toronto. My mother thought it would be easier to find work here. She cleans houses for rich ladies."

Norah struggled to take all this in. German! German like Hitler—like the Enemy. She remembered Charlie's words: "an enemy alien".

But Bernard was just an ordinary boy, like Tom. Not really ordinary, though. He'd called himself a coward, but there was something special about him, a kind of dignified inner assurance that wasn't cowardly at all.

"Are you going to not like me too?" asked Bernard calmly, when she didn't reply. "It would be understandable if you didn't, being English. But kind of stupid, I think. I'm a Canadian. I hate Hitler and the Nazis as much as you do. My aunts in Germany don't like them either. We wanted them to come over here, but they're too old to move."

Norah's qualms vanished. If Bernard hated the Nazis, he must be all right. She certainly didn't want to act as stupid as Charlie. And besides, she liked him. Surely that was all that mattered.

She smiled. "I don't care what your last name is." Bernard looked relieved, and Norah suddenly began telling him how she hadn't wanted to come to Canada.

"I can see why you wouldn't want to leave your family," said Bernard. "You're lucky to be able to travel, though. And Canada's a great country—maybe you'll get used to it. What are the people like where you're staying?"

Norah didn't want to talk about them. She shrugged, and Bernard showed her his book about Australia.

"I'm trying to find out about every country in the world. When I grow up, I'm going to visit them all and write articles about them for the *National Geographic.* Mr Bartlett lends them to me. What are *you* going to be?"

"I don't know—I'm only ten!"

"You should decide," said Bernard gravely. "It gives you something to look forward to. When I'm a famous journalist, it won't matter that those guys put a bucket over my head."

Norah listened to him with growing admiration, as he explained more about the countries he'd studied. He knew as much as a teacher. Miss Gleeson smiled at them when she returned; she didn't seem to mind them talking in a library.

Norah noticed the time. "I should go," she whispered. "I have to be home by three-thirty so they won't suspect anything." The two of them exchanged a conspiratorial look and walked out together.

Bernard gave her a ride on the back of his bicycle to her street. "Are you going to school on Monday?" he asked, as if Norah played truant whenever she felt like it.

"I suppose so. Miss Liers might not believe me if I stay away too long." She remembered something and gulped. "Do you think, if she finds out, I'll get the Strap?" The grade fives were always whispering about the Strap. One day when Charlie had started a fight in the playground, he'd come back from Mr Evans's office with red puffy hands.

"Only boys get the Strap," Bernard assured her. "And I won't, because Mum will give me a note. She knows I have to have a break sometimes. Would you like to come over to my place tomorrow?"

"Sure!" said Norah, trying out some Canadian slang. "I'll have to ask, though."

"Phone me in the morning and let me know." He wrote down his number for her.

Norah skipped down the leafy street, her insides light and airy. Now she remembered how friendship sometimes happened—so quickly that, a little while after you'd met a person, you couldn't believe you hadn't always known each other. Just before she reached the Ogilvies' she remembered to retrieve her books from the ravine.

"May I go over to a friend's house tomorrow?" she asked at dinner.

"How nice, Norah!" smiled Aunt Mary. "I'm glad you've made a friend."

But her mother frowned. "What's her last name?"

"It's a boy—Bernard Gunter."

"Gunter? That's not a name I know. Is this boy in your class?"

"He's in grade six," said Norah. "May I go?" Why did Aunt Florence have to make such a fuss over a simple request?

"I think you'd better have him over here first, then I'll decide. I'm sure your parents wouldn't want you associating with anyone unsuitable."

"They would leave it up to me," blurted out Norah before she could stop herself.

"Enough sauce, my girl! If you'd like to ask this Bernard over for lunch tomorrow, I'll ask Hanny to prepare something special. Then we can all meet him."

Norah finished her dessert in deflated silence. All her elation over having a friend was spoiled. She was sure Bernard would never want to come to the Ogilvies' to be inspected like something from a store brought home on approval.

But to her surprise, he didn't seem to mind. "Mum says they live in a big house," he said on the phone the next morning. "Sometimes she lets me come along to the places she works in—once I found a secret passage! How many rooms are there?"

Norah said she wasn't sure.

"Maybe we can count them," said Bernard. "See you at noon."

She felt better after he had hung up. Lunch was sure to be an ordeal, but it would pass quickly. Then, surely, Norah would be allowed to play with Bernard alone. She decided to show him her shrapnel.

Norah waited on the front steps for Bernard to arrive.

"This place is gigantic!" he exclaimed on the way in. He

was very clean and tidy. His unruly hair was somewhat subdued with water, and his blue shirt looked freshly ironed. He was even wearing a tie.

He was also very polite. He said "please" and "thank you" in all the right places and chewed his macaroni in careful small mouthfuls.

"What does your father do, Bernard?" asked Aunt Florence.

Bernard swallowed before he answered. "My father died two years ago. He was a garbage collector."

Aunt Florence gave a small cough as Aunt Mary said gently, "I'm sorry, Bernard. You must miss him."

"Where do you live?" Aunt Florence asked next. "How does your mother manage on her own?" In five minutes she seemed to have found out everything she wanted to know. For the rest of the meal she sat in unusual silence.

Gavin shifted his chair closer and closer to Bernard's. "Do you want to come and see my rocking horse after lunch?" he asked eagerly.

"He wants to look at *my* things," said Norah. "May we please be excused?" Gavin trailed after them, but Norah ignored his wistful look and shut the door of her room before he reached it.

For an hour she and Bernard examined the shrapnel and the old books. Bernard was properly impressed and wanted to know all about the Battle of Britain. He found an old geography book and asked if he could borrow it. "Let's try to count the rooms now," he suggested.

"Not today," said Norah uneasily. "We'd better just stay here." She couldn't decide whether Aunt Florence had approved of Bernard or not. Her silence had been perplexing.

She found out the verdict at dinner. "Your young friend seems very well brought up," said Aunt Florence. "Obviously his mother has absorbed the standards of the homes she works in. But I'm afraid I can't allow you to associate with him, Norah. His background is quite unsuitable—why, his mother works for my friend, Mrs Fitzsimmons! It would just make him uncomfortable to mingle with a family like ours. And then there's his nationality. I don't know why I didn't realize at once that he was German."

"He's Canadian!" cried Norah, throwing down her fork. "And what does it matter what his mother does? At home my friends' parents do all sorts of things!"

"Kindly lower your voice, Norah," commanded Aunt Florence. "A small village is different than a large city—you can't be too careful." Her voice became less harsh. "I'm doing this for your own good. You are part of this family now and it's my duty to take care of you." She sighed. "You should really be going to Brackley Hall, where Mary went."

Norah bristled. "I don't *want* to go to a snooty school! And I'm *not* part of your family! I didn't choose you and I wish I didn't live here!"

There was a shocked silence. Aunt Mary pressed her linen napkin to her lips and Gavin stared at Norah with round, frightened eyes.

Finally Aunt Florence spoke, her voice icy. "Might I remind you that we didn't have a choice either? If we had, I'm sure we would have picked a child who was grateful for the opportunity to live with a privileged family, instead of rude and inconsiderate. We have to put up with *you,* so you had better put up with us. I don't want you to have anything to do with Bernard. That's my decision, and I don't want to hear any more about it."

Aunt Mary took a deep breath. "Mother, isn't that a little hard? He seemed like such a *nice* boy."

"Mary, really! I think Norah had better miss dessert and

go straight up to bed." Aunt Florence looked as if she'd like to order her daughter to do the same.

Up in her room Norah tugged on her pyjamas violently, shaking away her angry tears. She glanced at the photograph of her family. Dad's eyes looked reproachful and she remembered his parting words: "If you're impolite or ungrateful, the Canadians will think that's what English children are like." But he'd also said the people she'd be living with would be kind.

She picked up the photograph and shut her parents' faces into her top drawer. Aunt Florence was wrong. Norah couldn't and wouldn't obey her. Bernard would have to be a secret. She would just have to work out a way to see him without Aunt Florence knowing.

Late that night she woke up when she heard a noise on the second floor. It sounded like singing. She crept downstairs and saw a light on in Gavin's room.

Was he ill again? Norah tiptoed along the hall and listened outside his door. It was Aunt Florence who was singing, in a rich, tender voice.

> Dance to your daddy,
> My bonnie laddie.
> Dance to your daddy,
> My bonnie lamb.
> You shall have a fishie
> In a little dishie.
> You shall have a fishie
> When the boats come home.

"When will I see *my* dad?" asked Gavin. "And my muv. . . ." He sounded as if he had been crying.

"As soon as the war is over, sweetness. But you're with me now, and I'll keep you safe. Is the nightmare all gone now? No more bogeyman? Lie down, then, and I'll sing to you again."

Norah peeked in as the vibrant voice crooned. Aunt Florence was wearing a pink silk dressing gown that made her look soft in the dim light. She was stroking Gavin's hair and her expression was sad and yearning.

"Why are you angry with Norah?" asked Gavin sleepily. "You made her unhappy."

"Your sister has to learn to control her temper," said Aunt Florence stiffly. "But don't worry about Norah, sweetness. She's such a strong girl, I'm sure she's not that upset. Go to sleep, now."

Norah slipped upstairs before Aunt Florence caught her. Gavin didn't *belong* to her, she thought angrily. And what a babyish song for a five-year-old. But she couldn't forget that look of longing. Perhaps Aunt Florence had once sung the song to Hugh.

XV
NEWS FROM ENGLAND

Norah stood beside her desk on Monday morning, her chest so heavy she could hardly breathe. Around her, the rest of the class mumbled their way through the Lord's Prayer and "God Save the King." Miss Liers left the piano, returned to her desk and took the roll call.

Why did she have to have a last name so far along the alphabet? Norah sat on her hands to stop them from shaking and Dulcie looked over with surprise. If only Bernard were in her room, someone would understand her agony.

Finally Miss Liers called "Norah Stoakes" in her tight voice.

"Present, Miss Liers."

The teacher raised her head. "You weren't here on Friday, Norah—did you bring a note?"

"I'm—I'm sorry, Miss Liers. At home we didn't need to bring a note when we were sick."

Her voice was so strained, it must have sounded convincing. Miss Liers appeared to believe her. "Here you *do* need one," she said coldly, "but we'll let it go today. Kindly remember next time you are ill." She frowned at the rest of them. "That goes for the whole class. Far too many of you are forgetting."

Norah slouched with relief. It was over, and she'd hardly had to lie. She knew she'd never play truant again. It was too nerve-racking. But now school would not be quite so bad, not when she had a friend to meet at recess.

She found Bernard at the flagpole, as they'd planned. They both looked around warily for Charlie, but he was at the other end of the schoolyard playing football.

Norah didn't know how to tell Bernard he couldn't come to the house again. "Aunt Florence says we're not allowed to see each other," she blurted out awkwardly.

"My mother *said* she might not approve of me. That's why she made me get all dressed up." Bernard's voice was nonchalant, but his eyes looked hurt. "Does this mean we can only meet at school?"

Norah shook her head, grinning. "I've thought of a place we can meet every day, and no one will ever know—the library!"

She got a form from Miss Gleeson that afternoon and took it home for Aunt Florence to sign. From then on, she was allowed to go to the library every day after school. It was a perfect solution, because it was almost legitimate. Norah *did* choose books every day and brought them home. Miss Gleeson had a knack of knowing exactly what she would like and saved new ones for her. When Norah got home she went straight to her room and read until she had to join the Ogilvies in the den before dinner. She often read long into the night as well. No one ever checked on her after she'd been sent upstairs. In school she became sleepy and inattentive, but the work was easy enough that she didn't fall behind.

Aunt Florence seemed pleased that Norah had found an activity that kept her occupied and out of the way. Norah even heard her boast about it to one of the Sunday evening bridge players: "Norah's turned into a real bookworm," she said, with surprising pride.

But Aunt Mary began watching her anxiously. "You're

looking peaky, Norah. I think you spend too much time alone."

What she didn't know, of course, was that Norah wasn't alone. She now took her lunch to school every day; after she gulped it down in the classroom, she and Bernard had half an hour to talk in the playground. It never took her long after school to choose her books. Then they had a whole hour to play.

Often they went to the ravine, descending into it well before they reached the Ogilvies', to be out of sight. They were building a fort under the bridge and carried down old scraps of lumber and cardboard. Bernard had invented a complicated method of making a roof by weaving thin branches together. It took a long time because the branches kept snapping.

The trees were changing colour rapidly and the air was as tart as new apples. Horse chestnuts littered the ground in their split green cases. They collected them to make conkers—Bernard called them bullies. At Bernard's place, they baked them hard in the oven, bore holes through them with Mrs Gunter's meat skewer and threaded Bernard's skate laces through the holes.

But their beautifully tough conkers were wasted as they stood on the sidelines of the bully matches that now happened daily in the schoolyard. No one invited Norah and Bernard to compete. Instead, they had to be content with swinging at each other's.

Charlie and his gang seemed reluctant to beat up a girl, so Norah's presence protected Bernard. The boys still shouted "Hun" and "Limey" after them, but they ran away together and tried to laugh.

Bernard lived in one quarter of a "fourplex" on the other side of Yonge Street. "My mum cleans the building, so the rent is cheap," he explained. Sometimes Mrs Gunter was finished work by the time school was out. Then she would greet them with cupcakes and cocoa. She was a large woman who sighed a lot. Her doughy face was always creased with a tired smile, but somehow it still looked sad. "I'm so glad Bernard has a friend," she said the first time Norah met her. Norah hoped he hadn't told his mother that their friendship was forbidden; she didn't want to add to her sadness.

Norah told Mrs Gunter all about her family and her journey to Canada. Even though she was tired of telling the story to the Ogilvies' friends, she didn't mind repeating it to this comfortable woman.

"It's not right that children should have to go through so much," sighed Bernard's mother. "What trying times these are for us all. And your little brother, how is he liking Canada?"

Norah shrugged. "All right, I suppose." It made her uncomfortable to think of Gavin. Yesterday afternoon he had appeared in the doorway of the tower.

"What do *you* want?" Norah had asked, startled from her book. He hadn't been in her room since they had shared it.

"Nothing. I just came up." As if that explained everything, Gavin came in and sat on her bed, swinging his legs.

"*What?*" asked Norah irritably, wanting to get back to her story.

"Norah, do you think Hitler's captured England yet? Will Muv and Dad and Grandad and Joey be prisoners?"

Norah couldn't answer for a second, her throat was so tight. She took a deep breath and tried to sound calm. "No, I don't. We'd hear about it, wouldn't we? And there might not even *be* an invasion."

Suddenly her brother's trusting face made her want to shake him. How was *she* expected to know? He should have asked Aunt Florence.

"Go away now, Gavin, I'm trying to read." She picked up her book and turned her back on him.

But she couldn't read any more. Instead she listened to his slow footsteps descending the stairs and almost called him back.

"Norah?" asked Bernard. "I said, do you want to go to my room now?"

"Sure!" Norah shut Gavin out of her mind and followed Bernard. As usual they pored over the maps which covered his walls, and then they stretched out on his rug to play Parcheesi and checkers. Norah felt much more at home here than at the Ogilvies'. "Come over as often as you like," urged Mrs Gunter, but she was seldom there herself—she was usually out working.

Escaping into books and having a friend made being a war guest more bearable. But now Norah lay awake worrying about her family. The radio reports from England were worse and worse—London was bombed every night now. She checked the hall table each day for mail, but still no letters came.

On the same Monday she had given her excuse to Miss Liers, Norah heard some shocking news. She was lying on the floor of the den, finishing off the Saturday funny papers. At home, most of the newspaper comics had disappeared because of the paper shortage. "Rupert," her favourite, was still published, but even his adventures had been reduced to one panel at a time. But here there were such thick wads of comics from all the different papers that it often took her several days to get through them. Superman, the Lone

Ranger, Tarzan and Flash Gordon—they were all new to Norah and she devoured their adventures with relish.

Aunt Mary was sitting beside Norah reading the *Evening Telegram*. "Oh, *no!*" she gasped.

Aunt Florence jerked up her head. "Gavin, would you go and fetch my needlepoint?" she said quickly.

As Gavin left the room, Norah jumped up and scanned the front page over Aunt Mary's shoulder. "Children Bound for Toronto Victims of Hitler's Murder," said the bold print.

"What does that mean?" she whispered.

"Let *me* see." Aunt Florence snatched the paper from her daughter. "Disgraceful!" she fumed, when she'd read it. "What I would do to that man if I had a chance..."

"*Please,*" choked Norah. "What happened?"

Aunt Florence and Aunt Mary held a kind of silent conversation with their eyes. "I suppose we can tell you, since you're safely over here," said Aunt Florence, "but when Gavin comes back we must stop talking about it. What's happened is that a ship was torpedoed by the Nazis. It was full of evacuees on their way to Canada and many of them were drowned."

"How many?"

Aunt Florence seemed reluctant to answer. "Eighty-seven children and two hundred and six adults," she said finally, her voice unusually thin.

Aunt Mary touched Norah's shoulder. "Thank God it wasn't *your* ship!"

Norah was stunned. All those days at sea she had looked for periscopes she'd never really *believed* the Germans would attack their ship. She remembered Jamie saying he wished they'd be torpedoed. He hadn't believed they would either. It had just been a game—but this was real.

Then she remembered Miss Montague-Scott, who was

hoping to come back again on another ship. "Does it give the names?" she asked in a small voice.

Aunt Florence shook her head. "Not yet—I expect the families haven't been notified." She looked at Norah with sudden, unexpected concern. "I don't want you to brood about this, my dear. I'm sure there was no one you know. Let's just be thankful that you and Gavin made it over here safely."

The two women tried to change the subject, but in the next few weeks Norah kept hearing more about it on the news. The ship was called the *City of Benares* and some of the children thought drowned were rescued after spending days in a lifeboat.

In the meantime, she finally got a packet of letters from home. She whisked it off the table and flew up to the tower. Three letters tumbled out, from Mum, Dad and Tibby. "Dear Norah and Gavin," they each began, but she had to read them by herself before she could share them with him.

"What lucky children you are—it looks as if you're living in a mansion!" said Mum. "We've shown the picture of the house to everyone in the village. Mrs Ogilvie sounds very pleasant—she wrote a reassurng letter. It's too bad Gavin isn't old enough for school but it sounds as if he's having some splendid outings. We feel much better knowing you're both in such a secure home."

Both her parents continued in the same way, expressing relief at their safety, saying how much they missed them and answering some of Norah's questions. "We still see lots of planes and another one crashed near Smarden," said Dad. "It's London that's really getting it now. Everyone is bearing up, though. People are sleeping in the tube. We can sometimes see the reflection of the fires from here. We go into the shelter most nights but don't worry, there's been no damage in Ringden."

Grandad sent his love in a postscript. Tibby told her she and Muriel were being trained as mechanics, which was much more interesting than all the scrubbing and cooking they had been doing. Her letter was spotted with words that had been blacked out, words that looked like place names. "You will probably find that parts of this have been censored," Tibby warned. It was unsettling to think that someone else had already read her words. Muriel had added a note to the bottom of Tibby's letter. "I've met a dreamy lieutenant and we're very much in love." Norah grinned; that was what Muriel always said.

She read the letters again and again, extracting every morsel of news. The only part that made her uncomfortable were some questions for her from Dad: "Norah, we are delighted to know you're learning so much about Canada. Mrs Ogilvie told us all about Gavin, but we'd like to hear more about *you.* Are you happy at the Ogilvies'? Is school all right? Please tell us everything."

But she couldn't. As she wrote home again the following Sunday, Norah still had trouble finding enough to say. She couldn't tell them Gavin was being kept out of school deliberately. She couldn't tell them about Bernard, in case they mentioned him to Aunt Florence. Her letters, too, were censored.

XVI
GAIRLOCH

One Thursday in October, Norah couldn't go to the library to meet Bernard; she had to come straight home from school to help pack. The Ogilvies were driving north for the weekend, to a place called Muskoka.

"You'll like it there Norah," said Aunt Mary eagerly. Her voice was much more animated than usual. "Hugh and I spent all our childhood summers at Gairloch—that's the name of our cottage, and it's on the most beautiful lake in Ontario. Our family has been going there for generations."

Aunt Florence had told Norah she could miss school from Friday to Tuesday. "I'll write you a note—I'm sure your teacher won't mind," she said grandly. "We always go to the cottage for Thanksgiving. It's our last time before next year."

Norah was surprised to learn that Dulcie had been invited to come along. "I thought you'd like someone your own age to explore with," explained Aunt Mary. Dulcie was so busy being popular, Norah hardly spoke to her in school. But when they picked her up early Friday morning, she acted as if nothing had changed.

"Isn't it super to be missing school!" she whispered to Norah. "It was so kind of the Ogilvies to ask me. I hope you don't mind," she added timidly.

Norah shrugged. She was reluctant to admit that it would be a nice change to have someone else to talk to, although she wished it could be Bernard.

Aunt Florence was at the wheel of the long, grey Cadillac. Aunt Mary sat on the other side, with Gavin in the middle; Norah and Dulcie had the whole back seat to themselves—the suitcases and boxes of food were in the trunk. Hanny and Edith were staying behind to look after the house.

The drive took most of the day. The houses in the city became smaller and sparser, then gave way to farms. There were rolling hills and fields dotted with bright orange pumpkins. Norah was astonished at the leaves. In the open country they formed a sea of scarlet and golden hues, wave upon wave glistening against the blue sky. The trees were so radiant, they didn't seem real.

"I do believe the colour this fall is the best we've ever had," said Aunt Florence with satisfaction. She spoke as if she had personally ordered the brilliant display.

For lunch they stopped at the side of the road and had a picnic: chicken and mayonnaise sandwiches on soft white bread, sticks of celery, poppyseed cake and milk. Everyone, even the two women, took turns going behind a bush. "You probably think we're being very primitive," said Aunt Florence, "but it's cleaner than a gas station." Norah and Dulcie looked at each other and stifled a giggle at the thought of Aunt Florence squatting in such an undignified position. The farther north they went, the more the two Ogilvies lost their Toronto stiffness.

After lunch, the fields and hills turned to rock and trees, broken by sheets of water. When they drove over a small bridge, Aunt Mary burst into song:

> Land of the silver birch
> Home of the beaver,
> Where still the mighty moose

Wanders at will.
Blue lakes and rocky shore;
We have returned once more.
Boom didi ah dah...

She stopped with embarrassment when she noticed the three children staring at her, their mouths open. "Hugh and I always sang that once we'd crossed the bridge," she explained sheepishly. "He learned it at camp. That river was the boundary for Muskoka."

The car plowed northwards. Gavin and Dulcie fell asleep and Norah's eyelids drooped. But Aunt Florence didn't tire. She was talking to her daughter about storm windows and the luck of an Indian summer. What was an Indian summer? Norah wondered drowsily, looking out on the empty landscape.

Canada was so big! She had never gone so far in a car. Her parents had never owned one, although Grandad had once fixed up an old Morris. Obviously Aunt Florence liked driving; she stretched her long legs to the pedals and leaned back in the seat as if she were in a comfortable armchair. Norah imagined how it would feel to have the control of such a powerful machine in your hands. Perhaps that's what she would be when she grew up, someone who drove cars.

Finally they pulled into a tiny town that was really just a store, a gas station and a few scattered, shabby houses.

"Everybody out," ordered Aunt Florence. "Now we're going on a boat, Gavin!"

The children woke up again. The little store was beside a vast, ripply lake. Norah breathed in the fresh-smelling air as a man came out of the store and led them to a moored motor launch.

"It's the only way to get there," explained Aunt Mary.

"Mr McGuigan always takes us over in his boat. Sometimes we have to make several trips with the food, but it's worth it to be on the island."

Norah whirled around to face her. "Are we going to an *island?*"

"Why yes, Norah, didn't I tell you? It's not a very large one, but it's all ours."

Her expression was as excited as Norah's. An island! Like *Swallows and Amazons . . .*

All the luggage, food and people were loaded into the boat, then it putted across the water. Norah sat at the bow, her hair blowing back and her face showered with cold spray. The water was as clear as green glass; when they slowed down she could see rocks in the depths of it.

In front of them was a hill; on top perched a large circular house with a verandah all around it. "There's the cottage!" beamed Aunt Mary. "There's Gairloch!"

A cottage? It was as big as the Ogilvies' house in Toronto. But it looked friendlier, perhaps because it had a name. They got out onto a wharf and helped carry things up steep steps to the house. Its wooden walls were a faded white and its turreted structure was higgledy-piggledy, as if it had been added on to over the years.

Aunt Florence unlocked the front door. Inside, the cottage was dark because the windows were shuttered. The children helped remove them, and bars of late afternoon sunlight streamed through the space. Unlike the formal Toronto house, the furniture was a colourful conglomeration of mismatched chairs and cushions. An immense stone fireplace filled one wall; the others were patterned in strips of contrasting wood.

"Let me see . . ." mused Aunt Florence. "I think Gavin had better sleep on this floor with Mary and me. You girls take your bags upstairs and you can have your pick of any rooms up there. Mary will make up your beds when you've decided."

There were six enormous bedrooms on the second level. The biggest had two double beds in it. "Would you mind... can we both sleep in here?" asked Dulcie. "I'd be frightened sleeping alone."

Norah was worried she'd wet the bed as usual; it would never do for Dulcie to know about that. But it would also be pleasant to have company for a change; she decided to risk it. "All right. You take that bed and I'll have the one by the window." She threw her suitcase in a corner, impatient to get outside.

They clattered downstairs again. The Ogilvies were unpacking food in a large kitchen with a black wood stove. Both women had changed into faded calico dresses; Aunt Florence's even had a hole in it.

"We'll have supper in about an hour," she told them. "It will take us a while to get the stove going. Why don't you all go out and explore? Be careful of Gavin near the water, Norah—it drops off very quickly."

Norah dashed out the front door, followed by Dulcie and Gavin. She peered through the veil of leaves; all she could see was sky, water and trees. "Come on!" she yelled, catapulting down the hill to the water.

The Ogilvies' grey boathouse had a balcony with an ornate white railing skirting its upper storey. It was as big as Little Whitebull. More fancy boathouses and huge "cottages" dotted the shoreline opposite. The children dipped their hands in the icy water and ventured gingerly onto the diving board that jutted off the wharf.

Then Norah had to run. She led the others up the steps. First they circled the steep shore until they came back to their starting place; it really *was* an island. Then they scrambled up over the rocks until they collapsed on a promontory. The lake was spread below like a wrinkled blue sea. Along the horizon the trees blazed like a fire, here and there broken by dark firs and the white lines of birches.

"I'm tired, Norah," complained Gavin. "You went too fast."

"You're just lazy," laughed Norah. "You've been pampered too much."

Dulcie panted. "I'm tired too. May we rest here a minute? Isn't it gorgeous? You *are* lucky to be able to come here all summer."

"All summer?" repeated Norah. In the summer the water might be warm enough for swimming.

"Aunt Dorothy said the Ogilvies stay here from June to September. Maybe they'll even let you out of school early! The Milnes go to a cottage too, on Georgian Bay, but only for two weeks."

Norah couldn't imagine next summer—would they still be in Canada?

"Children! Suppertime!" Aunt Mary's voice floated up to them.

The meal had been cooked by Aunt Florence herself. There were sausages and baked potatoes and huge McIntosh apples. They ate around the kitchen table. "A very good supper, if I do say so myself," said Aunt Florence. "Don't you think I'm a good cook, Gavin?" Norah looked at her curiously. If Aunt Florence liked her own cooking so much, why did Hanny always do it at home?

Aunt Florence handed Norah a cup of tea. Mum had written to her and given permission for Norah and Gavin to have it.

"Are *you* allowed to drink tea, Dulcie?"

"Oh *yes,* Mrs Ogilvie. Aunt Dorothy says we can have whatever we're used to at home."

Aunt Florence sniffed disapprovingly and Norah tried not to grin as she slurped the familiar milky liquid.

"This is a very large cottage, Miss Ogilvie," said Dulcie to Aunt Mary. "Did you used to have more people in your family?"

Aunt Florence answered for her daughter. "It doesn't just belong to us, Dulcie. My father and his brothers built it. Their name was Drummond, which was mine too, of course. All the Drummonds share Gairloch. In the old days they travelled up by train and steamer and brought lots of servants. Hanny and her husband come with us in the summers, but we always rough it in October."

"There are so many relatives that some of them stay in cabins down the hill," said Aunt Mary. "The older children either sleep in the old servants' quarters in the back or on top of the boathouse. We call them the Boys' Dorm and the Girls' Dorm. You'll be over the boathouse, Norah—there are several girl cousins your age."

Norah digested this. "Why aren't they here now?" she asked, although she was glad they weren't. It was far better to have Gairloch to herself.

"Most of our family lives in Montreal," explained Aunt Mary. "It's too far for them to come for just the weekend, but you'll meet some of them at Christmas."

"Mary and I stay in the main cottage, of course," said Aunt Florence. "I am the oldest living Drummond, so I'm the head of the clan, so to speak." She puffed herself up like a peacock.

Norah felt herself grow proud too. Even though she was only a war guest, if Aunt Florence was the head of the family her reflected glory would surely give Norah some status among all those cousins next summer. If she were still here next summer, of course.

"It's almost time for little boys to be in bed," said Aunt Florence fondly. "Norah, you help Gavin find his pyjamas and you and Dulcie get ready yourselves. We'll tackle the dishes."

After she was in her pyjamas and dressing gown, Norah wandered onto the verandah and sat down on a seat that swung from chains. The night was as black, and the stars shone as brightly, as at home. She searched the sky for the Great Bear, surprised to find it looking exactly the same. Could *they* see it while she saw it? she wondered. The air was brisker than in the city: her breath clouded in front of her.

"Norah, come in—you'll catch cold!" called Aunt Mary. Norah stayed a few more minutes to chill her skin thoroughly, then ran in to enjoy it tingle in front of the roaring fire.

"Now I will read aloud," announced Aunt Florence. "We always do at the cottage." She picked out a worn, leather-covered book from a low bookcase. "This is called *The Jungle Book.* You should enjoy it, Gavin, it was Hugh's favourite." She opened the book, made sure everyone was attentive, and began. "'It was seven o'clock of a very warm evening in the Seeonee hills when Father Wolf woke up from his day's rest, scratched himself, yawned, and spread out his paws one after the other to get rid of the sleepy feeling in the tips.'"

Gavin soon fell asleep, leaning against Aunt Florence, but the story kept Norah awake. Aunt Florence was a wonderful reader. Her resonant voice made the story of the wolves and Mowgli come to life. Sitting here like this was so much nicer than after dinner in the city, being bored while the Ogilvies read the paper, played cards or listened to the radio.

Aunt Florence closed the book and Norah and Dulcie stumbled upstairs. They both fell asleep instantly.

To her relief, Norah woke up in a dry bed. The morning was gloriously sunny, with a hint of wind. After breakfast Gavin played contentedly with his soldiers in the dirt under the verandah. Norah and Dulcie tried fishing with some old poles they found in the boathouse. Norah dug up some worms, but Dulcie made so much fuss about putting them on the hooks, they had to stop. They climbed as high as they could go onto the rocks, then went down the hill and peeked into the windows of the locked family cabins.

In the afternoon Aunt Mary took them out in the rowboat. It had velvet cushions and three sets of oarlocks. Each of them tried rowing and Aunt Mary surprised Norah by being very good at it. Her face seemed serene and somehow young. "In the summer we use the motor launch and go on picnics to some of those other islands," she said, pointing them out. "All the children know how to run the motor—you'll learn quickly, Norah." Every time next summer was mentioned, Norah wondered anew about this unexpected future she hadn't thought about.

That evening a few neighbours, also here to close up their cottages, arrived in their boats. They all asked Norah and Dulcie how they liked Canada.

"Isn't it tiring how they always do?" whispered Dulcie at supper. "I always just say 'fine.'" Norah nodded, pleased that Dulcie felt the same way. Dulcie really wasn't a bad sort—if only she were braver.

After the guests had left, they went to bed late; but Norah and Dulcie weren't tired. They lay awake and talked about school.

"I wish Miss Liers liked us better," sighed Dulcie. "I can't do anything right for her."

"She hates Charlie even more than us," said Norah. "I thought she was going to hit him with the pointer when he was so rude last week."

"I wish she had! I'm scared of Charlie. He pulls Ernestine's hair and he calls me 'Limey.'"

"He does?" Norah thought she was the only one in their class he taunted.

"Even so, I like this school better than the one in Ringden," continued Dulcie. "The work's far easier and nobody calls me Goosey here. Babs and Ernestine are ever so nice. I go over to their houses almost every day and we dress up and pretend we're movie stars."

If that was what they did, Norah was glad they didn't like her.

"I know this isn't my business, Norah," said Dulcie slowly, "but everyone notices that you're friends with Bernard Gunter. Girls don't play with boys here. They would like you better if you didn't. And you shouldn't associate with someone who's German. What if he's a spy?"

"He's not! He's a *Canadian,* not a German. And I can be friends with whoever I choose!"

"Of course," said Dulcie quickly. She prattled on, changing the subject. "Mrs Ogilvie really isn't that bad. And *Miss* Ogilvie is kind."

"She's all right, I suppose. But Aunt Florence is a bossy snob. She may seem nice here, but in the city she's horrid! I'll never like her."

"Oh." There was a long, awkward silence.

"Have you had many letters from Ringden?" asked Norah. And suddenly their words tumbled over each other's as they told what they'd heard from home. Norah had almost forgotten that Dulcie came from the same place.

Finally they finished talking about everybody in the village. "Do you know what, Norah?" Dulcie asked, sounding drowsy.

"What?" Norah lay on her back and stared at the moon through the trees.

"Sometimes I forget what Mummy and Daddy look like. I try and try, but I can't imagine their faces. And it hasn't even been two months since I've seen them. What if we stay in Canada for a year? I might not know them at all!" Dulcie's voice was small and scared. "Do you remember what your parents look like? And your sisters and grandfather?"

Norah said loudly, "Of course I do! Anyway, I have a picture of them. Don't you?"

"No, but that's a good idea. I'll ask Mummy to send one." Dulcie sounded more cheerful. Her voice stopped and her breathing became regular.

Norah sat up in bed to lighten the weight on her chest. She tried to picture her mother's face. Thin blonde hair and blue eyes—or were they grey? Panicking, she tried her father. The different parts of his face came clear—his dark hair streaked with grey and his long, beakish nose—but she couldn't make them fit together.

She did have the photograph, but it was a few years old. Norah fell asleep trying to conjure up the images of her sisters.

The weather was clear for the next two days, too sunny to dwell on thoughts of home. They spent the time in blissful, wandering freedom. Aunt Florence said that, as long as they wore life jackets, the three of them could take out the row-boat alone. They went for long, slow rides around the island;

the boat was so heavy, it was a struggle to move it at all. There was a near disaster when Creature fell overboard, but Norah scooped him out before he sank.

At noon on Monday they all gathered around an ancient radio to listen to a message from Princess Elizabeth to the evacuated British children. "My sister Margaret Rose and I feel so much for you, as we know from experience what it means to be away from those we love most of all..." said the clipped voice.

Norah listened intently as Margaret Rose obeyed her sister's instructions to say good-night. It was the first time she'd ever heard her voice. She wondered where *they* were spending the war. A month ago, Buckingham Palace had been bombed. Would Princess Margaret Rose feel glad to have been safely away from it, or would she wish she'd been there for the excitement?

"Isn't that touching?" said Aunt Mary when the message was over. "That must be a comfort to you, girls."

Norah and Dulcie glanced at each other self-consciously. It felt both embarrassing and important to have a radio broadcast directed especially to them.

That night more neighbours came in to help celebrate Canadian Thanksgiving. They ate turkey, mashed potatoes and pumpkin pie, a new kind of food. Dulcie whispered that it wasn't sweet enough and only touched the whipped cream, but Norah liked its raw, rooty taste.

Aunt Mary looked sad as Norah helped her close the shutters early Tuesday morning. "Gairloch always looks so desolate when it's shut up like this. I hate to think of how long it will be until we come again."

"When will that be?"

"The Victoria Day weekend in May. That's when everyone opens up their cottages. There are fireworks and a big bonfire at the Kirkpatricks'." She smiled. "I'm glad you and Gavin will be sharing that with us. And in June we'll have three whole months! Just wait until you try the water—it's so clean, you hardly have to wash your hair all summer."

"But will we still be in Canada then? Dad said we'd stay for *perhaps* a year."

"Oh, Norah . . . did you think it was only for a year?" Aunt Mary looked apologetic. "It could easily be for years, now. It looks as if this war will go on longer than any of us expected. Do you mind very much? It's so hard for you, I know, but you already feel like part of the family. And every summer we'll be at Gairloch. You do like it here, don't you?"

"Yes. I like it *here,*" said Norah angrily. She ran away before Aunt Mary could say more. Sullenly she helped load the boat. All the way back to Toronto she ignored Dulcie's hurt look as she refused to talk the way they had earlier.

"For years." That was an eternity. Surely Aunt Mary was wrong. As soon as they got back to Toronto Norah took out her family photograph again, but the faces looked too far away to be real.

XVII
PAIGE

After Norah's outburst, Aunt Mary began to pay more attention to her, as if Norah were as much her concern as Gavin was Aunt Florence's. Every night she came up to the tower to say good-night, which made Norah feel guilty when she switched on the light later to read. She inquired about Norah's bed-wetting, which had returned, and took her to see a doctor. They told Aunt Florence they were going for a drive.

"That's not really a lie," said Aunt Mary in the car. "We *are* driving, and after the doctor I'll take you along the lake." She tittered nervously; Norah was amazed at her defiance.

"There's nothing physically wrong with her," said Dr Morris, after an examination that made Norah blush all over with shame. "I'm sure it will disappear in time." He advised nothing to drink from dinner until bedtime, and occasionally that worked.

"Mary thinks you should get to know more children your own age," Aunt Florence told Norah one Saturday morning. "I've been meaning to have you meet the children of some family friends, but they've been away, visiting in Massachusetts. Frank Worsley was my son's closest friend; he's the editor of one of Toronto's newspapers. They only live a few blocks from here, and you and Gavin have been invited for lunch today. They have three little girls, aged ten, eight and seven."

Norah had planned to sneak off to a Gene Autry movie with Bernard. "I have something to look up in the library for school," she tried.

"It can wait. Go and change, please. The Worsley girls are always perfectly dressed."

They sounded awful. Sulkily, Norah stood beside Gavin a few minutes later to be inspected.

"I wish you'd let me buy you some clothes, Norah." Aunt Florence sighed at the skimpy Viyella dress that Norah wore every Sunday for church. "Wouldn't you *like* a pretty new dress?"

"No, thank you," said Norah haughtily. She was not going to be beholden to Aunt Florence for more than she had to.

They were allowed to walk by themselves to the Worsleys'. Aunt Florence gave them directions and waved goodbye from the steps. "Remember to say thank you," she called. Norah scowled; did she think their mother hadn't taught them any manners?

She shuffled through the crunchy carpet of leaves on the boulevard. Some drifted down from the tall branches, turning slowly in the sun. "Fall" was a much better word than "autumn", Norah decided. The air was acrid and smoky; it reminded her for some reason of the downed Nazi plane, but then she realized it was only the smell of the heaped, burning leaves in the street. She and Gavin dawdled along the curb, poking sticks into the smouldering piles. A man walked along the other side of the street with a wheelbarrow, calling out "Dry wo-ooo-oood!"

"What's it like at school, Norah?" Gavin asked suddenly.

Norah shrugged. "As boring as school usually is. You're lucky you don't have to go this year."

"I'd like to," said Gavin.

Norah glanced at her brother's wistful face; it was like looking at a stranger. She was almost never alone with Gavin any more. When she got back from playing with Bernard she went straight to her tower and the rest of the time they were with the Ogilvies. Could Gavin be unhappy? Of course he wasn't—he was being given treats and outings every day. "You said you didn't like school," she reminded him.

Gavin looked confused. "That was before. Norah, could you ask..."

But they'd reached the Worsleys'. "I know this house!" interrupted Norah.

It was the one where the friendly dog had greeted her on her first walk. What a long time ago that seemed! Now the dog yapped inside as they stood hesitantly on the doorstep. Norah lifted one leg at a time and brushed off the bits of dry leaves that stuck to her socks.

"Aren't you going to knock, Norah?" asked Gavin, but he quickly took her hand when she did.

A very tall, narrow man holding a pipe opened the door. He looked as if he had been squashed vertically; even his hair was tall. "You must be Norah and Gavin," he smiled. The wiry terrier leapt up at each of them, trying to lick their faces. Gavin pushed it away with a whimper.

"Off, Thistle!" the man ordered. The little dog ignored him and continued to bounce up and down as if it were on springs. Norah bent and picked it up; it wriggled in her arms and slobbered all over her face.

"I'm Mr Worsley," said the man. "Aren't you brave to dare to eat lunch with my daughters! From the sounds of things, they might be planning to eat *you!* Follow me and I'll introduce you."

Gavin gripped Norah's hand as they climbed a winding staircase. The inside of the house was as grand as the

Ogilvies', but its white walls and pale furniture made it seem airier.

Squeals and shrieks came from an upstairs room. "Peace!" laughed Mr Worsley. "Come and meet your guests. Norah and Gavin, here are my three wild daughters."

Paige, Barbara and Daphne Worsley were in identical tartan dresses, with navy-blue bows tied at the ends of their long blonde braids; they were like three matching dolls in descending sizes. But Daphne had ink smeared on her leg, one of Barbara's ribbons hung in a streamer and Paige's cheeks were daubed with slashes of red paint. Norah's spirits rose—they looked as if their ladylike outfits were disguises.

"Be merciful," admonished their father. "I'm going to pick up your mother from the hairdresser's. Ellen is in the kitchen if you need anything. We'll be back in time for lunch." He left the room.

"Oh good, another *small* person!" The eldest, Paige, pinched Gavin's thigh. "How would you like to be a dinner for cannibals? We've just finished eating Daphne and we're still hungry."

"No, thank you," whispered Gavin, but Paige had already begun to tie him up with a skipping rope.

"Here, I'll help you," said Norah, delighted. "Don't worry, Gavin, it's only a game."

Gavin was trussed and set in the middle of a table, while the cannibals leapt and whooped around it. He smiled uneasily, not sure if he was enjoying this or not. Then they untied him and each chose a part to eat.

"Not as fat as Daphne!" said Barbara.

"I'll take this arm," said Paige, making munching sounds from his wrist to his neck. "Yum, yum!" Gavin looked relieved after all of him had been eaten.

"Let's play cowboys now," suggested Paige. "Norah and

I will be the Lone Ranger and Tonto, and Barbara and Daphne will be our horses. Gavin, you and Thistle can be little colts who follow along."

Gavin enjoyed being a colt much more than he had being a cannibals' dinner. They fashioned reins out of dressing-gown belts and drove their horses up and down the stairs and all around the huge house, shooting imaginary guns all the way. Thistle raced circles around them, barking frantically and trying to grab the ends of the reins.

"Whoa!" said Mr Worsley, as he came in the front door with his wife. "Chow time."

At lunch, each Worsley girl competed to say something in a high, shrieking voice. Norah sat beside Mrs Worsley and answered the usual questions.

"I'm sure you'll like it in Canada," she said quietly. She was a glamorous woman, with large green eyes and thick smooth hair like a movie star's. "We're delighted you're living so close. I hope you'll consider our house yours, although you might find my girls overwhelming." She gazed at them with puzzled affection, as if she were not sure they were really hers. They were badgering their father loudly for their allowance.

"Come on, Norah," said Paige, who had already claimed her as her property. "Let's leave the babies and go to my room."

Paige's bedroom was a wonderland of every conceivable toy, game and book that anyone would want. As in Norah's room at home, there was a shelf of pristine dolls and some model planes hanging from the ceiling.

"I have planes like this!" cried Norah.

Paige took out her collection of coloured pictures of British aeroplanes. "They're free—just ask your cook to save your syrup labels, and you can send away for some too."

Norah told Paige about the Skywatchers and the crashed

plane. Paige was entranced. "We could start something like that here, except there aren't any enemy planes to watch for. You were *lucky,* being right in the middle of the war." She made Norah feel like a hero and said nothing about anyone being a coward for leaving England.

"What school do you go to?" Paige asked.

"Prince Edward."

"I wish I could go to a public school. Brackley Hall is really strict—I'm always getting into trouble. There's lots of sports, though. I'm very good at basketball because I'm so tall. If only we went to the same school! All the girls in my class are so boring."

Norah thought of Dulcie, Babs and Ernestine. "They are in mine, too."

"I tried to make friends with some of our war guests. A whole school of them came to Brackley with their teachers. But they stick to themselves."

Paige then startled her by climbing onto a stool and hanging upside down by her knees from the door of the wardrobe. The ends of her braids trailed on the floor. "How would *you* like to be friends with me?" she asked casually.

They were so easy together already that it seemed unnecessary to ask. But Norah felt an uncomfortable twinge of betrayal: what about Bernard? He was probably in the library right now, wondering where she was.

"Sure," she answered, just as casually. She paused. "I have one friend at school who's not a bore. He's a boy."

Paige put her hands on the stool and flipped her legs off the door to the rug. "Well, obviously *he* is!" she panted, her face red. She didn't seem to find it unusual to be friends with a boy.

"And he's . . . German," continued Norah. "His parents

came from there, anyway. But he's not a Nazi," she added hastily.

"A Nazi! I wouldn't think so. Lots of Germans have come to Canada. Dad has a friend called Mr Braun who works with him at the paper. Sometimes he gets threatening phone calls telling him to leave the country—and he's a Canadian! People are so dumb."

"Aunt Florence—Mrs Ogilvie—doesn't like Bernard. I don't know if it's because of his last name or because his mother's a cleaning lady."

"Probably both! Dad says she's a terrible snob. When he and her son Hugh were young, there were boys he wasn't allowed to see and he had to meet them in this house—Dad grew up here."

"That's just like me!" Norah felt a sudden link with Aunt Mary's brother. "Aunt Florence says I'm not allowed to associate with Bernard. But I do anyway—we meet secretly at the library. Maybe you could meet us there too and we could show you the fort we're building."

"Sure! Or you and Bernard could come here!"

"We couldn't do that—not when your parents know the Ogilvies. They might say something."

"I'll tell you what," said Paige eagerly. "We'll give Bernard another name and pretend he's *my* friend. Then if Mrs Ogilvie ever hears about him she won't know. Bring him over on Monday. I'll show you our secret hideaway in the basement."

Paige was certainly bossy, but she was bossy in such an enthusiastic way that Norah couldn't help being swept up in her plans. She took Norah up to a cavernous attic, where they tried on old clothes from a trunk. Barbara followed them and the three of them played gangsters. Paige and Norah put on slouchy hats and talked out of the sides of their mouths. Barbara wanted to wear one of the elegant dresses and be their girlfriend. "She's sometimes like this," Paige apologized. "It's handy, though, when you need a girl. She's always Maid Marian when we play Robin Hood."

The afternoon sped by so fast, Norah couldn't believe it when Mrs Worsley called up to them that it was time to go. Gavin waited in the hall, holding Mrs Worsley's hand. He looked as if he had been crying blue tears.

"That Daphne..." sighed Mrs Worsley. "She tried to dye Gavin's hair—luckily it was washable ink. But I've sent her to her room and we've had a peaceful time playing the piano together, haven't we, Gavin? It's such a nice change to have a quiet little boy in the house. I'm sure I got all the ink out, Norah. Please tell Mrs Ogilvie that I'm very sorry and that I hope she'll let you come again."

When Norah explained why Gavin's hair was wet, Aunt Florence just chuckled. "Frank's children are certainly a handful—just like *he* was as a boy. How did you get along? Would you like to have them all over here sometime?"

"Not Daphne!" whispered Gavin. "I don't like her, and Barbara tried to dress me up like a girl."

"We won't have them if you don't want to, sweetness," soothed Aunt Florence. "What about you, Norah? Would you like to invite Paige over? She would be a suitable friend for you."

Norah didn't understand how wild Paige could be more suitable than polite Bernard. But she smiled at Aunt Florence in spite of herself. "That would be nice, thank you."

When Paige and Bernard met on Monday, they took to each other at once. The two were so different that they filled in each other's gaps: Paige's loud and lively nature was balanced by Bernard's thoughtful calm. Norah fit neatly in between, like the filling in a sandwich.

The three of them met almost every day after school and every weekend, sometimes at the library and more often at Paige's. This was easy to arrange because Norah was allowed to go to the Worsleys' whenever she wanted. They called Bernard "Albert", his middle name, and said Paige had met him at the library—which was the truth, of course.

Mr and Mrs Worsley accepted "Albert" as easily as they did everything their daughters did and only interrupted their long afternoons of play to suggest snacks. Norah thought Paige's parents were practically perfect. The only conflict Paige had with them was about clothes. Lined up in her wardrobe was a long row of dresses that matched her sisters'.

"When I'm thirteen I won't have to look like Barbara and Daphne any more." She sighed. "That's still so far away. It's such a trial, but it amuses Mother. You'd think we were the Quints!"

"Who?"

"The Dionne Quintuplets." Now Norah remembered her mother mentioning them.

"We went to see them once," said Paige. "We drove up north and lined up for hours, then we went through a kind of tunnel and watched them through a screen. They were riding around on five tricycles. It was really weird, like looking at animals in a zoo."

"Are they really exactly alike?"

"Exactly. Like five Daphnes—yeech!"

Dressing alike seemed a small price to pay for belonging to such a happy-go-lucky family. If only she and Gavin had been sent *here* to live! Norah spent as much time as she could at the Worsleys'. So did Bernard; he told her he liked going there instead of to the empty house he came home to almost every day.

Paige had come over to the Ogilvies' a few times, but it

was hard to think of something to do in their silent house. And they all preferred to play outside, either in the ravine or in the Worsleys' large backyard. Paige thought of a new, elaborate game each week. They played at being Captain Marvel, Knights of the Round Table and all the characters in *The Wizard of Oz.* They tried to train Thistle to be as obedient as Toto, but the stubborn little dog was as rowdy as his owners. At first Norah wondered if Bernard would think he was too old for pretending, but he joined in.

It was Norah who made up the game of Spitfires and Messerschmitts, but both she and Bernard insisted upon being RAF pilots.

"There's no way I'm being a Nazi," said Bernard quietly.

"It's only a game," said Paige. "Okay, *I'll* fly a Messerschmitt—so will Barbara."

It *was* only a game, thought Norah as they roared around machine gunning each other. It didn't really matter which side she was on. But she thought of Tom and proudly piloted her imaginary Spitfire. Then she roared even louder to drown out the painful thoughts of what he and the other Skywatchers would be doing.

Sometimes they went exploring on bicycles, when they could persuade Barbara to lend hers to Norah. It was too small, and her legs became cramped from being bent in the same position. She thought longingly of her own bicycle. Would it be rusted by the time she got back to Ringden?

"If only you had a proper bike, we could go all the way to the beach," complained Paige. "Couldn't you ask for one for Christmas?"

Ask Aunt Florence for something as expensive and important as a bicycle? It was impossible. Norah was sure that Aunt Florence would never approve of her having one anyway, not if she suspected how free it would make Norah.

Once the three of them had even ventured downtown, carefully avoiding cars and the treacherous streetcar tracks.

"Come right home from school today, Norah," said Aunt Florence one Thursday. "A social worker is coming to see how you're getting along."

Reluctantly, Norah told Paige by telephone and Bernard at recess that she couldn't meet them. After school she was made to wash and put on clean white socks. Then she and Gavin were brought into the living room and introduced to Mrs Moore, a merry, round woman in a tight dress that was popping its buttons. Around her were the remains of tea; she must have already spoken to the Ogilvies. Aunt Florence left Norah and Gavin alone with her.

"Well!" she began, a bit too cheerfully. "Aren't you lucky to have come to such a luxurious home! Are you happy living here? Is there anything you'd like to tell me?"

If she had been asked this a few weeks ago, Norah might have unloaded the burden of her misery and homesickness. Now she was filled with confusion.

She only used the Ogilvies' house for sleeping, eating and reading. She still wet the bed almost every night and, most of all, she still wanted to go home. But if she said these things they might send her to another family—then she would lose Bernard and Paige.

"I have a smashing room," she said, trying to be as truthful as possible, "and Hanny is a very good cook. And I've made two friends," she added proudly.

The woman laughed. "Two friends already! Well done! And how are you getting along at school?"

"Fine." She could only lie about that. Even with Bernard as an ally, school was as lonely as ever.

"That's good. And I can tell Gavin is thriving here—

look at those rosy cheeks! I'm sure that next year he'll be strong enough for school." Gavin sat quietly, stroking his elephant.

He was *too* quiet, these days, Norah thought uncomfortably. It probably wasn't good for him to spend so much time following Aunt Florence in and out of stores. He was often left alone, as well—sometimes when she came in he was playing by himself in the hall. She remembered him saying he wanted to go to school. She could tell Mrs Moore that he should go there now—and that he always had rosy cheeks. But she remembered again that then she'd have to take care of him. It would be a waste of her precious after-school time to have to bring Gavin home every day.

Mrs Moore passed them the cake and nibbled on a huge piece herself. "The Ogilvies' cook *is* excellent," she said. "This is delicious! I think we can assume that this home was a good match for you two. You seem to have adjusted very well. Are you looking forward to our Canadian winter? You'll find our weather much colder than yours. We have *snow* here—you'll love it!"

"But we have snow," said Norah. "Last winter there was so much that the roads were blocked and all the stores were closed. It was so cold that some birds were frozen to the branches."

"Oh." Mrs Moore looked disappointed. Then she brightened. "Is there anything at all I can do for you? Anything you need?"

Could Mrs Moore get her a bicycle? Would she pay for it, so she wouldn't have to ask Aunt Florence? Norah knew she wouldn't. She shook her head and said politely, "No thank you, there's nothing we need."

Mrs Moore spoke privately to the Ogilvies again. After she left, Aunt Florence looked relieved. "I'm glad you didn't find anything to complain about, Norah," she said awkwardly.

"You *are* happier, aren't you?" Aunt Mary's face was so pleading that it was for her that Norah answered. "Yes, thank you. May I go over to Paige's now?"

XVIII
THE WITCHES ARE OUT

Towards the end of October, the last of the leaves blew off the trees and the weather became colder; one morning there was even an icing of snow on the ground. Norah's bare legs tingled when she came in, and she puffed on the tops of her fingers to warm them. Mum had sent the long knitted leggings Norah wore last winter under her skirts, but none of the Canadian girls seemed to wear them, so she left them in her drawer.

Then Aunt Florence took her and Gavin to Simpson's to buy them winter clothes. They picked out two-piece snowsuits, close-fitting hats called toques, wool scarves and mitts, and buckled rubber galoshes lined with fleece. There were knee-length britches for Gavin and, for Norah, itchy wool stockings that were held up by complicated garters.

Aunt Florence wanted to buy Norah a new party dress as well. "You can have your choice of any of these," she said grandly.

Norah looked curiously at the bright dresses hanging in the girls' department. She'd never had a store-bought dress; she usually wore hand-me-downs from her sisters. She thought of how the Viyella dress chafed her armpits. But she'd already accepted enough of Aunt Florence's charity; she could ask her mother to make her a new dress.

"No, thank you."

"You're being very stubborn, you know. I *like* buying you things."

Did she? Or did she just want Norah to look respectable... Norah couldn't decide. And she had more important things to think about than clothes: in two days it would be Hallowe'en.

"What's Hallowe'en?" she had asked when Paige and Bernard had gone on about it.

"Don't you *know?*" They interrupted each other in their eagerness to tell Norah about dressing up and going out at night to collect treats from the neighbourhood.

"Isn't there Hallowe'en in England?" asked Bernard.

"I'm not sure—not where I live, anyway. But in November we have Bonfire Night."

"What's that?"

"It's for Guy Fawkes Day. We make a Guy—like a big rag doll—out of old clothes, and we put him in a wagon and take him through the village for a few days, calling 'a penny for the guy.' Then we use the money to buy fireworks. We stuff the Guy with the fireworks and burn him in a huge bonfire on the green—everyone dances around it. Except last year we weren't allowed to have one because of the black-out."

They wouldn't be able to this year, either, she thought sadly. But Hallowe'en sounded just as thrilling. She joined in the excited plans about costumes.

"We could be Guys!" suggested Paige. "Aren't they sort of like tramps? All we'd have to do would be to wear old clothes—you could ask the Ogilvies for some, Norah."

Norah wondered if she would be allowed to participate in such lawless-sounding activities. Aunt Florence, however, seemed to approve of Hallowe'en. She had bought Gavin a fancy clown suit trimmed with yards of orange and green ruffles. A bright orange wig went with it. After dinner on

Hallowe'en night, she painted Gavin's face with rouge and white make-up.

"Doesn't he look precious, Mary?" Aunt Florence held Gavin out at arm's length, then kissed him. "Now I'll take your picture and send it to your parents. Come along, Norah, you get in it too."

Aunt Mary had helped Norah find some old clothes. She wore a pair of Hugh's tattered fishing pants, a shapeless shirt and Mr Ogilvie's felt hat. With glee at being allowed to be so messy, she'd daubed her face and hands with a burnt cork.

"Don't stand too close to Gavin," warned Aunt Florence. "You might get him dirty." She focused the camera on them. "There!"

Norah blinked from the flash as the front door knocker sounded. Into the hall walked another tramp, a witch and a black cat with a bedraggled tail: Paige, Barbara and Daphne.

"I want you back by nine o'clock, Norah," said Aunt Florence. "I'll lend you my watch. Do you have rules about where you're allowed to go, Paige?"

"Yes, Mrs Ogilvie," said Paige politely. "We aren't allowed to cross Yonge Street." She winked at Norah when Aunt Florence's back was turned.

"Let's go, then, Gavin." Aunt Florence was planning to drive him around to all her friends' houses. His cheerful wig and make-up were a sharp contrast to his doleful expression. He turned to Norah and said plaintively, "Can't I come with you, instead?"

"You're too young," muttered Norah.

"Of course not, sweetness," agreed Aunt Florence. "You'd have trouble trying to keep up."

"Why can't he?" asked Paige. "We'll take care of him."

"Thank you, Paige, but I don't think he'd enjoy it." Gavin looked back longingly as Aunt Florence led him away.

Norah was surprised he wanted to come; she thought he was afraid of the Worsleys. But she forgot his hurt face when they went out into the street. Shadowy figures hurried past them in the darkness: ghosts, cowboys, pilots, soldiers and pirates. A spooky breeze swirled dead leaves around their feet. They met Bernard, as planned, at the corner. He made an odd-looking tramp in his glasses.

"Shell out! Shell out! The witches are out!" The thin cry echoed around them as gangs of purposeful children tramped up the steps of houses lit with leering pumpkin faces.

In school they had been asked to collect pennies instead of candy for the war effort, but they carried pillowcases along with their milk bottles. At almost every door they received a treat as well as a donation.

Paige refused to ask for money. "It's not fair. I've already collected the most bottle caps in my class for the Red Cross. Tonight's supposed to be *our* night! If they don't give us any candy, we'll play tricks on them."

"Like what?" asked Norah.

"Like soaping their windows or taking off their gates or filling their mailboxes with horse buns," said Paige. "At least, that's what the older kids do. I've never actually done a trick—but that doesn't mean I wouldn't."

They crossed Yonge Street to cover Bernard's neighbourhood as well. On one corner Charlie and his friends were noisily overturning garbage cans. They watched from a distance, careful to stay far enough away to run. Then they dared one another to ring the bell of an unlit old house. Daphne was the only one brave enough, but no one answered.

"Hello, Norah!" Norah jumped as a white gloved hand tapped her shoulder. It was Dulcie, in a lacy dress and jewels. Her face was thick with make-up.

"Isn't Hallowe'en super? We're all film stars—I'm Betty Grable." Behind her lurked Babs and Ernestine, their galoshes peeking out from under their long gowns.

Babs frowned at Norah and Bernard. "Come *on* Dulcie, we have to go home now."

"*We* refused to accept candy," said Ernestine righteously, at the sight of Norah's bulging pillowcase. "You're supposed to be collecting money."

"I did!" Norah shook her bottle of coins angrily.

"*Dulcie . . .*" Babs was moving away. "Don't you remember the party at my house? Mum's made scads of fudge, and we're going to bob for apples—you'll like that."

Dulcie hesitated. "I don't feel like going in yet. You go ahead. I'll see you there."

Her friends looked surprised but left quickly. Dulcie seemed surprised herself at her daring. "Can I come with you for a while?" she asked timidly.

Norah grinned. "Sure!" She introduced Dulcie to the Worsleys. Paige inspected her warily, but soon forgot Dulcie as they collected more candy.

When their bags were almost too heavy to carry, they rested under a streetlight and compared their booty. Best were homemade popcorn balls; worst were ordinary apples you could get anytime.

"We still have an hour before we have to go home," said Paige, pulling out a long string of toffee from her teeth. "I know something you'd like, Norah. Why don't we have a bonfire? Then we could celebrate Guy Fawkes too."

"But we don't have a Guy!" said Norah.

"And we don't have matches," said Bernard, looking worried. "Anyway there's nowhere safe to make a fire."

But Paige, as usual, was unstoppable when she had an idea. "I took some matches from the living room before we left. And I have a Guy." Out of her pocket she pulled a small, wilted rag doll. "It isn't very big, but it'll do."

"That's mine!" protested Daphne.

"You haven't played with it for years—you never did. It doesn't even have a name. Wouldn't you like to see it burn up?"

Daphne thought for a second and then nodded, a wicked gleam in her eye.

Up to now, Dulcie had seemed to be enjoying herself. Now she looked scared. "I think I'll go to the party, now—Babs's house is just around the corner." She hurried away.

"She's a chicken," remarked Paige, digging in her pockets again.

Norah thought of how Dulcie had done what she wanted in spite of her friends' disapproval. "No, she's not. She likes doing different things than us, but she's all right really."

"If you say so. Now watch." She had found a pencil and marked a moustache under the doll's nose. "There, we'll turn him into Hitler—then it will be even more fun to burn him. We'll make the fire by the fort. If we pile dirt around it, it'll be safe. Come on, while we still have time!"

Bernard still looked reluctant and Norah felt a twinge of fear. But the Worsley girls were at their wildest. They whooped and pranced as they ran along the streets and into the ravine. It was difficult to find their way to the fort in the darkness and they held onto one another as they slithered down the bank. Gradually their eyes adjusted and they could see by the dim glow of the streetlights on the bridge above them.

"I'm freezing!" complained Barbara. "Hurry and make the fire, Paige."

First Paige ordered them to gather up twigs and branches while she and Bernard dug a circular trench with a board from the fort. When they had a large pile of fuel she struck a match on a rock and held it to the smallest twigs.

The flame flickered and went out. Norah breathed easily again, but Paige looked around impatiently. "Paper... that's what we need. Can we use some old comics? We've read them all."

Before they could answer she had grabbed an armful of comics from the fort. She tore out the pages, wadded them up, fit them under the kindling and tried again.

The wind rose and the paper caught at once and whooshed into a blaze. Soon the twigs ignited, then the larger branches. The sparks flew up into the darkness and the dancing yellow flames illuminated their grimy faces.

"Yaaay!" Paige threw the doll into the fire and seized Norah's hand. Hollering like banshees, they all circled the flames as they grew stronger.

The crackling fire made Norah feel reckless and powerful. She stopped being afraid. She almost forgot she was in Canada and for a few seconds was at home in Ringden before the war, dancing around the Guy.

> Guy, Guy, Guy
> Poke him in the eye.
> Put him in the fire
> And there let him die.
> Burn his body from his head,
> Then you'll say Guy Fawkes is dead.
> Hip, Hip, Hooray!

The others joined in with her chant. "Then you'll say that *Hitler's* dead!" added Paige. The flames leapt defiantly and they hurled wood on the fire to feed its mounting rage. Even Bernard had lost his usual calm. "This is Charlie!" he shouted, throwing on a large branch.

Norah added more comics. "And this is Aunt Florence!" she screamed. Even Paige looked a little shocked at that. Then she grinned and shouted, "School! Dresses! GROWN-UPS!" They circled and jumped and shrieked, the fire roaring with them.

Suddenly Bernard gave a different kind of scream. "LOOK!" He pointed and they froze. Part of the fire had leapt across the trench and caught on one of the cardboard boxes they used as a table. The dry box flared instantly and then the flames travelled to the fort itself.

"Stop it!" cried Paige. "Put dirt on it!"

They threw on handfuls of dirt and tried to beat down the flames with branches. But the fire continued to snarl like an angry beast at the wood of the fort.

Daphne sobbed hysterically and Barbara clung to her, her face white with terror. "*Do* something!" she entreated the older children.

Bernard turned to Norah. "Run up to the Ogilvies' and call the fire department. Hurry! Paige and I will keep throwing dirt on it."

Norah didn't know how she made her legs work. She tripped and stumbled up the steep bank. When she reached the front door, she felt as if she were suffocating and struggled for air.

"Norah! What's wrong?" Aunt Mary sprang up as Norah appeared in the den.

"Fire. In the ravine," Norah gasped. "The others—are—down there." Then her arms and legs turned boneless and she collapsed in a chair.

The rest of the evening had the foggy, unreal quality of a dream. The fire engines came quickly, their whining wail as insistent as an air-raid siren. In a daze, Norah stood in the backyard and watched as long hoses sprayed onto the flames from the bridge. The firemen led or carried Paige, Bernard, Barbara and Daphne up the hill as the fire was extinguished.

None of them could speak. When Aunt Florence and Gavin got home, all five children were sitting in the kitchen, with Aunt Mary and Hanny trying to get them to have some cocoa. The firemen were standing in a corner drinking theirs, looking sternly at the children.

"*What* is going on?" the majestic voice asked. Aunt Florence directed her question to Norah, after glaring first at Bernard.

Fortunately Mr Worsley arrived before Norah had to answer. "Are you all right?" he cried, inspecting each daughter as if she might be broken. Then he looked grave. He said he would drive Bernard home and hustled him and his daughters out the door.

"Obviously there's a lot of explaining to do," he said to Aunt Florence, "but I think it can wait until tomorrow. They'd all better stay home from school. I'll ring you in the morning and we'll try to sort out what happened."

Norah was sent to bed. She didn't even wash her filthy face and hands but curled up into a tight ball and tried to quiet her breathing. The dangerous, leaping flames and Aunt Florence's outraged expression filled her dreams.

The next morning, it all came out. The Worsleys arrived after breakfast and the girls had to stumble through the story together in front of the four adults.

Aunt Florence blamed a lot of it on Bernard. "I told you he was unsuitable! And why were you with him at all, Norah, after I forbade you to see him?"

Then she discovered that Norah had been seeing Bernard all along. "We didn't know she wasn't allowed to play with him," said Mrs Worsley timidly. "We thought his name was

Albert. He seems so sensible for his age, it couldn't have been his idea."

"It was *my* idea," said Paige. "Not Bernard's."

"I'm sure it was," said her father grimly.

But Aunt Florence didn't seem to believe her. "Now, Paige, you couldn't have thought of such a dreadful thing by yourself. And it was extremely deceptive of you, Norah, to pretend Bernard was someone else."

Mr Worsley gave them a long, serious lecture on how foolish they had been. He told them exactly the same sorts of things Norah's father would have. It was painful to listen to—Barbara cried and Paige pressed her lips together and pretended not to—but everything he said was so true that Norah felt cleansed at the end.

Then Mrs Worsley and Aunt Mary had their turn. They wrung their hands and carried on about how they might have been burnt to death. Then Norah and Paige were told they weren't allowed to see each other all weekend.

Throughout all this, Aunt Florence was suspiciously silent. Norah guessed she was saving the rest of her comments for her alone.

Sure enough, after Paige, Barbara and Daphne had been marched home again, Aunt Florence had her say. She kept Norah in the living room for half an hour and told her over and over how ungrateful and disobedient she was.

She even brought up Norah's bed-wetting. Before breakfast, as if she had decided to pick a time when Norah was already in everyone's bad books, Edith had come to Aunt Florence to tell her she refused to wash Norah's sheets any longer.

"What kind of a girl wets her bed at age ten?" said Aunt Florence, looking disgusted. "I think you must be doing it on purpose."

The more her icy voice droned on, the less Norah listened. Something inside her had turned to stone.

"Norah! I said, would you like me to have you transferred to another family? I'm not at all sure I want to continue to try to get along, when you make absolutely no effort yourself. I'm not even sure that Gavin should be around you. Perhaps you would be better apart."

Norah fastened her own grey eyes upon Aunt Florence's granite ones. "I don't care. Do whatever you like. May I go to my room now?"

Aunt Florence seemed about to say more. Then she took a deep breath and nodded. "Very well. We'll discuss this again later, when we've both cooled down. You'd better go to school this afternoon. Wash your hands for lunch and I'll write you a note."

Norah sat on the window seat of the tower. She struggled through five short minutes of indecision, then she dumped her books out of her schoolbag and began to pack.

XIX
GAVIN

"Are you sure you feel up to going back to school this afternoon, Norah?" Aunt Mary asked anxiously. She adjusted her hat at the hall mirror. "You must still feel shocked from last night—I know I do."

Her mother bristled. "Of course she can go back. There's no point in missing a whole day of schoolwork. Why are you wearing that dreadful hat, Mary? Go and put on your new one." She and her daughter were going to a lunch party.

Before Aunt Mary scuttled upstairs, Norah tried to smile at her. Then she met Aunt Florence's haughty gaze with one just as cold. There! That was the last time she would ever see either of them.

"I'm glad you didn't get burned up, Norah," said Gavin, as they ate alone at one end of the dining room table.

Norah was too distracted to listen. "Aren't you going to finish your sandwich?" When Gavin shook his head, she stuffed the remains of his lunch and three of the apples from the sideboard into her schoolbag.

"What's that for?" asked Gavin.

"Just a... picnic. We're having one after school. But don't tell, or I'll get into trouble."

"I won't. Can I come? Will you have it in your fort? When did you build the fort? Can I help you fix it?"

"No you *can't!* Leave me alone, Gavin! Why do you

always have to bother me? Can't you see I'm trying to think? Go and find Hanny—I'm going to school now."

Gavin's big eyes filled with tears. Slowly he got down from his chair and trudged into the kitchen.

Norah almost cried herself, with frustration. Why did Gavin always have to make her feel so mean? And shouldn't she say goodbye to him? She wouldn't see him again until the war was over and he was sent back to England. It would just upset him, though, if she told him she was running away. He might even tell the Ogilvies.

The front hall was as soundless as an empty church. Norah pulled down her new snowsuit from the closet and struggled into the leggings and jacket. The weather wasn't cold today, but she didn't know where she would be spending the night. She checked her schoolbag one more time: toothbrush, pyjamas, an extra sweater and her shrapnel; the five pounds she'd held onto all this time and, for some reason, the old doll Aunt Mary had given her. She'd also squeezed in her latest library book. That felt like stealing, but she could mail it back from England.

She breathed in one last whiff of furniture polish and roses and said a silent goodbye to the sombre house that always felt too hot. Then she shut the door softly behind her.

It was difficult to walk fast in the bulky snowsuit. Norah decided to inspect the fort and rest there until she calmed down. This was much scarier than skipping school; scarier, in fact, than anything she'd ever done before.

In the sunlight the charred wood of the fort looked sinister. But the damage wasn't as bad as it had appeared to be last night. Norah sat down beside the damp, sooty circle where they'd made the fire. It seemed years ago that they had all danced around the flames.

She tried to think clearly. Where was she going to go? All she knew was that she wanted to go home, to find her way back to England and her parents. The only way she could do that was to return the way she had come: by train to Montreal and from there by ship. First she had to find the train station; that shouldn't be too difficult. She remembered it was a short distance from the university. She could go downtown and ask someone.

But adults might question her and wonder why she wasn't in school. Could she get away with travelling alone on a train? And how was she going to find out what ship to go on? Would she have to stow away on it, like someone in a story?

The load of all the problems that lay ahead overwhelmed her. She had not slept well the night before and the horror of the fire had left her drained. It was unusually warm for November; her snowsuit was a cosy cocoon. Curling up on a heap of dry leaves, Norah slept.

She dreamed about journeys, about walking and walking and walking with no place to reach. As she walked she held a small warm hand that gave her strength. She was in England; she was walking with Gavin. The sense of endless journeying left when they approached their own village. As they hurried up the main street to their house, a huge relief flowed through Norah. She began to run, pulling Gavin along and laughing in anticipation of feelng her parents' arms around her.

But Little Whitebull was demolished. In its place was a pile of burnt and flattened rubble—like the fort, like Grandad's house in Camber.

"Where are you?" Norah cried desperately. "Mum! Dad! Grandad! Where are you?"

"They're gone . . ." cackled an ugly voice. It was a goblin

voice, a bogeyman, a Guy... coming from a leering face with a brush of a moustache and a swastika on its hat. It leaned over her and laughed raucously. "They're *gone,* they're *dead* ... I killed them!"

"*No!*" screamed Norah and woke herself up. She sat up with a jolt and sobbed. It was only a dream, but she couldn't stop crying for a long time.

Now she wanted to reach England all the more, to make sure her family was safe. Why was she wasting time down here? She stood up, brushed off the leaves, picked up her schoolbag and reached out for Gavin's hand.

Her hand closed on air. She thrust it into her pocket angrily. Gavin was still at the Ogilvies', being cosseted and spoilt. She didn't want or need him.

Then her legs trembled so much she had to sit down again, as everyone's words came to her; "Take care of Gavin, take care of Gavin..."

She had *never* taken care of him. From the very beginning of their journey to Canada, she had only wanted to be rid of him. She remembered all the times when he'd given her that hurt, perplexed look; all the times she could have comforted him, but didn't. And the last time, a few hours ago, when she'd made him cry by pushing him away. He was only five, a small, lost boy with no family but her. He was her brother; Aunt Mary and Bernard and Paige didn't have brothers. She thought of Aunt Mary's anguished voice when she had talked about Hugh. She had lost her brother; Norah still had hers.

She remembered the day, years ago, when they'd set Gavin on one side of the kitchen at Little Whitebull and, chortling with proud glee, he'd taken his first wobbly steps straight to Norah. How he used to call "Ora, Ora," when Mum scolded him. But she had only thought of him as a nuisance; someone who claimed her mother's and sisters' attention so completely that she had turned to her father instead.

But he was her brother. He needed Norah and Norah needed him. And she was planning to leave him behind in a strange country with a foolish woman to ruin him.

Norah ran up the hill almost as fast as she had the night before. She tried to catch her breath as she pushed open the front door a crack and peeked in.

Good: the hall clock said just past two. She hadn't slept as long as she thought. And Gavin, as usual, was playing in the hall with the canes and umbrellas that had once belonged to Mr Ogilvie—patting and grooming and talking to them quietly, pretending they were horses.

Norah watched him for a moment. She saw his dreamy, withdrawn expression, his aloneness. What had it been like for him these past two months, shut up in this dull house by himself when Aunt Florence was busy? She wanted to rush up and greet him noisily; she felt as if she hadn't seen him for years.

But she had to be cautious. "Gavin," she whispered.

Gavin dropped a cane, startled.

"Shhh! It's only me. Come on, we're going out." Norah crept into the hall and got his snowsuit.

"Going out? With *you?*" His face was so eager that Norah hugged him.

"Yes. We're running away. But they might try to stop us, so we have to be quiet. What's Hanny doing?"

"Making a pie. She's going to call when it's done so I can have a piece."

Norah could smell it cooking. "Then hurry!" She helped him into his leggings. "I wish we could get more food and your toothbrush, but there isn't time. Do you have Creature?"

Gavin held up his elephant, his eyes shining. "We're having an adventure, aren't we?"

"Right. Come on, now." With her brother's warm hand firmly in hers, Norah led him out the door.

Five hours later, they sat huddled on a hard bench hidden behind a bush in a park close to the train station. A nearby streetlight radiated a faint circle of light.

Norah sat in the light, reading aloud from *Five Children and It*: "' I daresay you have often thought about what you would do if you had three wishes given you.'" When she reached the part where the children couldn't decide what to wish for, she turned the book over impatiently. *Her* wish was so simple, but bringing it about seemed increasingly complicated.

The temperature had dropped and now she was glad of their snowsuits. Gavin's cheeks and nose were cherry-red with cold. "Keep reading, Norah," he begged. "I like that funny Psammead."

"In a minute—I have to think. You go and swing for a while, it will warm you up."

Gavin obeyed easily. He was so contented to be doing something with Norah that he didn't seem to mind the hours they had already spent walking and waiting.

First they'd gone downtown and ventured into the bank to change the five pounds.

"Where did you get this?" the teller asked suspiciously. "It's a large amount for a little girl."

"Our m-mum sent us with it—she's ill," stuttered Norah, feeling a bit ill herself with the huge lie.

The teller still looked suspicious but she finally handed Norah a wad of Canadian dollars.

After that they had asked a boy the way to Union

Station and gone there on a streetcar. Norah was afraid to call more attention to themselves by asking about the train to Montreal. She finally found a schedule on a notice-board; to her dismay, the next train didn't leave until eight-thirty that evening.

They passed the time by buying tea and cheese sandwiches in the station restaurant. The cashier looked at them curiously but she didn't say anything. Then they settled themselves on a long, slippery bench in the echoing station hall. They took off their snowsuits and leaned comfortably against them. The station milled with weekend travellers, but they were all preoccupied with where they were going or whom they were meeting. No one paid any attention to Norah and Gavin until a policeman approached them.

"Are you kids alone?" he asked kindly, with an English accent.

Norah thought fast. "No, our mum's gone to get us some sandwiches. We have to wait a long time for the train."

"Where are you off to, then?"

"Montreal. We're going to visit some friends of Mum's for the weekend."

"War guests, are you?"

Norah nodded.

"You're lucky your mother could come over with you. I have a sister and three nephews back home I wanted to bring to Canada, but it's too late now. Since that ship was torpedoed, they've suspended all evacuation indefinitely. Where are you from? I grew up in Newcastle."

Norah told him. He was so friendly she wanted to pour out everything, but that was impossible. And the longer he chatted, the sooner he would wonder where their mother was. At least Gavin knew enough not to contradict her story.

She became more and more agitated. Then, to her relief, a drunken man shouting on the other side of the station caught the policeman's attention.

"I'll have to check this out. Now don't move from that bench. I'm sure your mother will be back soon."

As soon as he'd left Norah grabbed their things and pulled Gavin outside. "Where are we going?" he asked, as they hid behind a pillar and struggled into their snowsuits.

"I don't know. We'll just have to keep walking until it's time to buy our tickets. If we sit down we look too conspicuous."

So they walked and walked again until their legs ached, peering into store windows and warming up in the lobby of an enormous hotel. When it got dark they were less visible, but the lights of the passing cars glared in their faces and made them jumpy. Finally they found the park and settled on the half-hidden bench.

Now Norah watched Gavin pumping hard, his body a darting shadow in the darkness. It was too cold to stay here much longer; they should probably start back to the station.

She dreaded trying to buy a ticket. What would she say? She was certain they wouldn't sell her one, and perhaps the policeman would be waiting for them.

Something firm and resolute collapsed inside Norah. She had rescued Gavin from the Ogilvies; to carry on from there seemed impossible. She was only ten years old—the grown-ups would thwart her all the way. However much she wanted to, she had known all along they couldn't really go back to England.

They were stuck here; stuck in Canada with no place to go. Just as at the beginning of her dream, they were on a journey with no end in sight.

Gavin jumped off the swing and ran back to Norah. "I'm

much warmer now, but I'm hungry again. Can I have my sandwich from lunch? Norah? Why are you crying?"

Norah's body heaved with sobs and hot tears stung her cold cheeks. "I'm so tired," she wailed. "I'm tired of—of fighting. Why does there have to be a war? I *hate* the war! I just want to go *home*."

Gavin thumped her back. "Let's go then," he said calmly. "Aunt Florence will wonder where we are. I don't think she'd like it if we ran away without telling her. And there's apple pie for dessert."

Norah was so surprised she stopped crying. "I don't mean the *Ogilvies.* I mean home! In Ringden, with Mum and Dad and Grandad. In *England.* Don't you remember?"

"'Course I remember. But I thought Canada was our home now."

Norah stared at him. "Gavin, do you like living at the Ogilvies'?"

"I like Aunt Florence and Aunt Mary and Hanny and all my new toys. But I don't like shopping and going out for tea all the time. I wish I could go to school like you."

"But you came with me when I said we were running away!"

"You said we were going to have an adventure. But we didn't even go on a train and I thought we'd be finished the adventure by dinnertime. I'm tired of it now. Can't we go home? Please?"

Norah gave up. There was nowhere else to go but the Ogilvies'. "All right," she said wearily, drying her wet cheeks with her mitt. "We'll get into a lot of trouble, though. I will, anyway. Probably they'll send me to a different family." She stood up. "But I won't go without you! Would you mind that, if we had to live with someone else?"

"I wouldn't like it," said Gavin gravely, "but I'd go with you. Dad said we had to stick to each other like glue!"

Norah had to smile at his serious expression. "He was right—from now on, we will."

"Come on." Gavin took her hand and pulled her out of the park. "Maybe there'll be some pie left."

People stared at them on the streetcar, but no one asked questions. When they finally reached the Ogilvies' house they found it blazing with lights. A police car was parked outside.

"Uh-oh." Norah paused a minute and gathered up the last shreds of her courage. This was going to be much more difficult than watching the sky for paratroopers. She was so worn out, she wondered if she could make it up the steps. "All right... let's get it over with."

They pushed open the front door and stood in the entrance of the living room, hand in hand. A noisy rush of bodies descended on them. Hanny squealed and Aunt Mary kissed them again and again. Mrs Worsley wept. Mr Worsley kept ruffling Norah's hair repeating, "Well! You're safe! Well, well!" Even Paige and Dulcie were there, jumping up and down and pulling on Norah's arms.

They were glad to see her! thought Norah with tired surprise. Everyone was hugging and kissing her. No one was angry. She felt as slack as a rag doll, as she was passed from arm to arm.

Then she stiffened. Aunt Florence had Gavin enveloped in her embrace. "Oh, my sweetness, are you all right? Are you sure?" She released him gently and turned to face Norah. For a few seconds the two of them stared awkwardly at each other.

"Are you going to send me away?" whispered Norah.

"Send you away?" To Norah's astonishment, Aunt Florence's eyes were swimming in tears. But they were probably only left over from greeting Gavin.

Her strong voice faltered, though, as she continued. "I will *never* send you away, Norah. You're one of the family. I want to apologize for what I said this morning. Will you forgive me? Will you let me have another chance?"

Everyone, including Norah, was silenced by this humility. Aunt Florence put out her hand. Norah hesitated for only an instant, then she took it in her own. She kept hold of the firm grasp as her eyes closed; Aunt Florence caught her before she reached the floor.

PART THREE

XX
BEGINNING AGAIN

Norah turned over and stretched. Her arm was in a warm puddle of sunshine. She sat up and peeked through the half-open curtains. The sun was high; she must have slept most of the morning. But it was Saturday, she remembered, and delicious to lie here doing nothing.

Then she grinned; her bed was dry. A strange tranquility filled her from head to toe. She didn't understand it; shouldn't she be in trouble, after all that had happened yesterday?

She got up to go to the bathroom, then luxuriated in bed again. A tantalizing smell of bacon drifted up the stairs. Norah tensed again, as uncertain about what to do next as on her first day in the house. Perhaps she was going to be punished, in spite of her reception last night.

There was a knock on her door and Aunt Florence strode in, carrying a tray. "Are you awake now? You've had a good long sleep. You're to eat up all of this and spend the next two days in bed. Did you know that you fainted last night?"

Norah couldn't remember. She dug into the scrambled eggs, bacon and toast, while Aunt Florence told her how Dr Morris had come and said she was over-tired and strained. With awe, Norah watched Aunt Florence swish open the curtains and hang up Norah's clothes. She had never come up here before.

"All finished? Good girl. Now, Norah, there are a few

things I want to say about last night—then we'll consider the matter closed. I think you must know what a foolish thing it was to wander around the city on your own, especially with your little brother in your charge. Do you promise never to do such a thing again?"

Norah nodded.

"Very well. Do you recall what I said last night?" Another nod. They both looked embarrassed.

"I meant it. After we discovered you were gone Mary told me, in no uncertain terms"—Aunt Florence grimaced, as if she were still in shock—"that it was my fault you ran away. She was right, Norah. I've been so wrapped up with Gavin, I've paid no attention to *you.* Perhaps we are too much alike, you and I. That doesn't mean we can't try to get along." She paused awkwardly and took the tray over to the table. Then she stood and stared out the window.

Norah looked at her strong back, knowing she should speak but tongue-tied with mixed feelings. Imagine Aunt Mary saying that to her mother!

Was it Aunt Florence's fault? Not entirely, she thought uncomfortably. She had set herself against Aunt Florence from the start. Aunt Florence had been just as pigheaded. Now, though, she was giving in first.

"Norah?" The majestic figure turned around and faced the bed. "What do you think? I'm willing to begin again if you are."

Norah knew how hard it was for her to say that. She smiled apprehensively. "So am I," she whispered.

"Good! You know, my dear . . . until you left . . . I didn't realize how . . . how fond of you I am." She walked over and gave Norah a firm kiss on her forehead. Then she sat down on the bed and said, as if nothing had happened, "Now then, would you like me to read to you?"

With relief they both escaped into the safe world of *Five Children and It.* Norah only half-listened. Aunt Florence had kissed her! She felt as if she hadn't woken up yet.

Gavin wandered in and curled up on the end of the bed; then Aunt Mary came up to collect the tray. It was strange, but pleasant, to have so many people in the room that had been her solitary retreat for so long.

Norah was left alone to rest. She snuggled under the eiderdown and thought hard all afternoon. Last night Aunt Florence had asked for "another chance" It looked as if Norah were being given another chance as well. She could begin all over again, as though she had just come to Canada.

The rest of the weekend was punctuated by trays of food, visitors, books and naps. Norah lazed in bed and made plans. By Sunday evening she was refreshed and strong, with her new resolutions all ready.

She began at breakfast on Monday morning, after Aunt Florence had appeared at the table unexpectedly. "I decided to let Mary sleep in for a change," she explained.

"Gavin is going to school with me today," Norah announced.

"*Am* I?" cried Gavin eagerly.

"But . . ." Aunt Florence started to frown, then she seemed to remember *her* new self and continued in a more controlled tone. "Now, Norah, I agree that, since he's almost six, he's ready for school. But I planned to enroll him at St Martin's. It's a small private school that will suit him much better than Prince Edward. And I was thinking that after Christmas you could go to Brackley Hall with Paige. Wouldn't you like that? I would pay for both, of course."

Norah tried to speak as politely as possible. "Thank you, Aunt Florence, but I think we should both go to the same school so I can keep an eye on him." She looked Aunt Florence in the eye. "I'm sure that's what my parents would want."

This was a conflict conducted on different terms than before—being civilized instead of out of control. Norah sat up straighter, enjoying herself. She knew she was going to win.

Aunt Florence hesitated, then smiled slightly. "Very well, if you think that's best, Norah. But he doesn't need to start now. He can wait till after Christmas."

"Oh, Aunt Florence, don't you think he might start now?" said Norah patiently. "He's missed so much already. I would hate to have to tell Mum and Dad how much he's missed." She put down her orange juice glass and waited.

Aunt Florence gave one last try. "Maybe we should ask Gavin. Would you like to go to school, sweetness? To Norah's school, or to a nice private school?"

"To Norah's!" said Gavin loudly.

"All right," sighed Aunt Florence, "but wouldn't you rather wait until January? Don't forget, we were going to visit Mrs Teagle today. You know how much you like her cat."

"I want to go now!" Gavin was so excited he tipped his chair backwards and almost fell off it.

With an odd, surprised look at Norah, Aunt Florence sighed again. "If that's what you want, then you can. I'll phone Mr Evans and tell him you're coming this morning with Norah."

Norah hadn't told Aunt Florence how worried she was that Gavin would be as estranged as she was at school. There were several other war guests in grade one, however; he wouldn't stand out like her. When she checked on him at recess, Gavin was holding out his cupped palms while another small boy poured something into them. "Hello,

Norah," he called. "Dick's trading these wizard marbles for one of my soldiers." He pocketed the marbles and ran off with Dick after a football.

Norah went to find Bernard by the flagpole. They had a lot to talk about; she hadn't seen him since the night of the fire.

"Where did you go on Friday?" he asked immediately. "Mrs Ogilvie rang our house to see if you were there."

"I'd rather not talk about it," mumbled Norah. Bernard seemed to understand; they discussed Hallowe'en night instead, reviewing all the horrifying details. "Mum was so upset she cried," said Bernard quietly.

"Would you like to come over after school?" Norah asked, when the bell rang. "Paige is going to meet us there after her piano lesson."

"I thought I wasn't allowed to!"

"Don't worry—things have changed."

As the three of them—Norah, Bernard and Gavin—walked home that afternoon, Norah wondered if she were pushing her luck. But she felt strong enough for another battle and took Bernard directly into the den.

"I've brought Bernard home," she said. "Can we ask Hanny for a snack?"

Aunt Florence looked up from her needlepoint; her arm jerked with surprise. "Bernard? Now, Norah . . ." She stopped and took a breath. "Uhhh . . . does your mother know you're here, Bernard?"

"Yes, Mrs Ogilvie," said Bernard, trying to hide behind Norah.

Aunt Florence continued to stare at him and Norah felt sorry for her. "Can we have a snack?" she asked again gently.

"I suppose so . . . go into the kitchen and get something." She still looked bewildered as they left the room.

Aunt Florence never said anything to Norah about inviting Bernard over; but after that, whenever he came, she treated him with stiff politeness. Norah was grateful; she knew that was the best she could do.

Instead of being marooned up in her tower, Norah began to wander almost as freely over the Ogilvies' house as in her own. She even went into Aunt Mary's bedroom sometimes, talking to her as she got dressed to go out. Aunt Mary let her try on her jewellery and her many hats. The only room Norah didn't venture into was Aunt Florence's; that would be going too far.

Norah also began to spend time in the kitchen again and no one objected. "Mary and Hugh used to visit me like this," said Hanny. "I wondered why you stayed away."

"But Aunt Florence said I was bothering you!"

"Oh, *her.* You'll soon learn she doesn't mean half the things she says. If I believed her, I would have been let go a hundred times over. The trouble with that one is she speaks before she thinks. I always just listen politely and do what I want. She knows I will, or I wouldn't stay."

Hanny was right. To win with Aunt Florence, you had to be just as forthright as she was. Her and Norah's personalities still clashed, but their relationship had changed, as if each had a secret respect for the other.

Now Bernard and Paige sometimes played at Norah's house. Gavin often tagged along and got used to being an extra in their games. School made him braver; sometimes when they went to the Worsleys' he would fight back when Daphne and Barbara teased him.

Norah began to feel as proud of Gavin as Aunt Florence was. "He's a very clever little boy," Mrs Ogilvie boasted. "His teacher tells me he's way ahead of the rest of the class."

Norah took him to the library and introduced him to Miss Gleeson. "I didn't know you had a little brother!" the librarian beamed. "Why haven't you brought him before?"

"He was . . . um . . . busy," mumbled Norah, her cheeks red. "He can read very well for his age. Have you any easy books?"

Norah still didn't know what to do about school—how to tackle the problem of her classmates' indifference or Miss Liers's hostility. She wondered if it would be any better if she *did* go to Paige's school; but she knew she couldn't desert Gavin or Bernard. By now she was quite used to being isolated, but she still watched the playground games longingly and wished for more friends. Everyone seemed to have forgotten about her, even Charlie's gang.

Each Tuesday morning Miss Liers took a few minutes to write the war news on the board and ask for contributions. Before, Norah had never offered any. Instead she would stare haughtily into space and think about how much more she knew about the war than the others did.

A few days after Coventry was bombed, she sat in silence while Miss Liers described the damage in sober tones.

"I saw bombs like that on a news-reel—they can flatten a whole town!" said Charlie. He gave a wailing screech and crashed his hand on his desk.

If the Nazis could do so much to large places like Coventry and London, what would they do to Ringden? Norah's chest felt heavy. She looked across at Dulcie and saw that she was pale and silent.

Charlie kept on describing the bombs with gusto, getting more and more lurid. Suddenly Norah couldn't stand it any more.

"Stop!" she cried, turning around to face him. "You don't even know what it's like! What about the *people?* My grandfather's house was smashed by a bomb. He was just lucky he wasn't in it." She shuddered, remembering her dream.

"Norah is right, Charlie," said Miss Liers. "You are so far away from the war, you find it exciting. But war isn't a game —it's a grim, terrible thing." For once, her voice wasn't sarcastic. She looked at Norah with respect for the first time since she'd read aloud the poem that first week of school. "Would you like to tell us more about what it was like? Come and stand at the front and see how much you can remember."

Norah didn't want to be on display in front of the whole class, but she had to do as she was told. She drew courage from glancing at Princess Margaret Rose in the picture at the front of the room, then began slowly with last May and Dunkirk. She told them how thousands of British troops had been rescued from France by small civilian boats, and how she and Molly had stood by the railway tracks for days, waving to the trains of exhausted soldiers coming from the coast.

Her voice grew more confident as she described how the village had prepared for an invasion; she began to enjoy herself and chose her words with relish. As her story became more exciting she spoke louder and faster. The class was as transfixed as when the librarian had told "Alenoushka." Norah related all the details about the dogfights, the parachutes, the Boot and all the other things that had dropped out of the sky. When she reached the part about the crashed plane her words rushed out with a power that seemed to belong to someone else.

Then Charlie thrust up his hand, startling Norah from the spell she was casting. The others scowled at him for interrupting. "Miss Liers, that couldn't be true, could it?"

Miss Liers frowned at him. "Of course it's true, Charlie. Do you think Norah would lie to us? I thought you knew all about the war. Maybe you should start reading the papers, as well as going to the movies. Let Norah finish, please."

Abashed, Charlie kept quiet. Norah talked all the way through the first period, when they were supposed to be having arithmetic. Even Dulcie looked awed, as if the things Norah was describing hadn't happened to her as well. After Norah reached the part about arriving in Toronto she stopped, as drained as if she had experienced the whole journey again.

Miss Liers actually smiled. "Thank you, Norah, that was *very* interesting. We're glad that you and Dulcie are safe in Canada." For once, she didn't remind the class of all the children who weren't.

At recess Norah was surrounded by questioners, just as Dulcie had been on their first day. Charlie even asked her if he could see her shrapnel. When Norah brought it back after lunch, the grade sixes came over to admire it as well.

Norah thought that after that she would be popular again. But although people were friendly to her now, she was still barred from the activities she liked. In this school, the unspoken rule about boys never associating with girls was never broken. When she asked the boys if she could be in their football game, they just muttered, "Girls don't *play* football," and looked embarrassed.

Instead, she sometimes joined the girls' skipping. She learnt a lot of new rhymes: "I love coffee/I love tea", "Dancing Dolly" and "Yoki and the Kaiser". But when she played with the girls she felt guilty for abandoning Bernard. He was still bullied, especially if Norah wasn't with him.

"Can't you leave him alone?" Norah yelled at Charlie, when they had painted a swastika on his bike.

"You don't understand," said Charlie, running away before Norah could argue.

"We should tell Mr Evans!" said Norah, but Bernard wouldn't let her.

"He knows. He's even spoken to Charlie, but that doesn't do any good." Bernard tried to scrape off the black cross on his fender. "Do you think Paige has any paint I can cover this with?"

Norah kicked the frozen ground angrily. There were some things she could not change.

The weather became so cold that part of the school playground was sprayed with hoses and turned into a skating rink. Aunt Mary took Norah and Gavin down to the basement, where she opened a cupboard crammed with skates, skis and hockey sticks. "I'm sure we can find some to fit you," she said. "Look, these must be your size, Norah."

The black, lace-up boots had shiny blades attached. For Gavin there were double-edged skates that fastened to his galoshes. Aunt Mary dusted off her own skates and had all of them sharpened by the knife man. Then she took them skating.

Last winter, when the village pond had frozen over, Norah had longed for skates. She thought she would be able to do it immediately, but at first she skidded and slipped on the hard cold surface. Soon, though, she was able to take tentative glides, holding Aunt Mary's hand. Gavin clomped around happily, stepping more than skating.

To Norah's surprise, Aunt Mary was really good. Her plump figure became graceful as she turned circles, wove backwards and even performed little jumps. "What fun!" she laughed. "I thought I might have forgotten. Do you know that I once won a cup for skating?" She taught Norah how to keep her balance, and by the end of the afternoon Norah had gone all the way around the rink by herself without falling. The cold air blew by her glowing cheeks as she tried speeding up. It felt like flying.

Then Paige and Bernard appeared and started a game of hockey. When it was over, Norah had fallen so much that her knees, elbows and bottom were sore and wet. But she could hardly wait to skate again the next day.

Gavin turned six at the end of November and Aunt Florence held an elaborate party for him. All the children in his class were invited, as well as the Worsleys and the Smiths. Bernard came too—Gavin had asked for him especially. After a hired magician had performed, the older children helped organize Musical Chairs, Pin the Tail on the Donkey and Button, Button, Who's Got the Button. Then they all sat around the dining-room table for cake and ice cream.

Gavin's face was as bright as his six candles. He had received countless toys and books; the biggest was a red tin fire engine he could ride in. But his favourite present was a tiny sweater for Creature that Hanny had knit on toothpicks. Norah was no longer worried about him being too indulged. Gavin, she decided, was so much himself that no one could spoil him.

After most of the guests had gone home, the Ogilvies, Mr and Mrs Worsley and Norah and Paige collapsed in the living room. Barbara and Daphne had taken over Gavin's Meccano set and were teaching him how to use it in his room.

"Let's have a drink," moaned Aunt Florence. "I'd forgotten how exhausting birthday parties are."

The living room was a disaster: paper hats, burst balloons, streamers and candy wrappers littered the rug. "Shall we start to clean up?" Norah asked.

"The cleaning woman will do it tomorrow," said Aunt Florence with relief.

Norah thought of Gavin's party last year. He'd had only two friends in, but they'd made almost as much mess as thirty children today. It had taken Mum all evening to get the house tidy again.

Today Mum would probably be thinking about Gavin turning six. So would Dad and Grandad and Muriel and Tibby. They would be missing him a lot. She wondered if Mum would make a cake anyway, but that would be difficult this year, with rationing. Norah suddenly wanted to be home so much that she picked up a magazine to hide her brimming eyes.

Paige scratched herself under her pink organdy front. "I wish I could change out of this prickly dress," she whispered to Norah. "I'd like to give it to your friend Dulcie. She kept telling me how much she liked it."

"She can't help it," said Norah automatically. She'd blinked away her tears and was now listening intently to the grown-ups, who were sipping their drinks and talking about the blitz.

"First London and Coventry, now Southampton and Bristol," sighed Mr Worsley. "When will it end?"

"When *will* it?" asked Norah desperately, her voice strained and broken.

He answered carefully. "No one knows, Norah. Not for a long time, I'm afraid." He smiled at her. "It's tough, I know—but we're glad you and Gavin will be here for the duration."

"She's a very brave girl, to endure what she has so far," said Aunt Florence. Every time she said something as flattering as this, Norah was surprised.

Paige chuckled. "Be tough, Norah—endure the duration!"

"Very clever," said her father dryly, "but stop showing off."

Norah sighed. "Endure" and "duration" and "tough" were all hard words—and hard to do. Perhaps now she *could* endure. In the past month she'd "adjusted"; she'd even stopped wetting the bed.

Now she was able to write long, uncensored letters home and say honestly that she was all right. But that still didn't mean she wanted to be here.

XXI
TIDINGS OF COMFORT

Norah packed a snowball and threw it at Dulcie's feet. Paige, Barbara and Daphne, in matching tweed coats, tried lying in a row and making snow angels until their mother stopped them. All around the front door of St Peter's Church, children threw polite snowballs that missed their targets or kicked at the ground with impatient feet, unable to play properly in stiff Sunday clothes while surrounded by adults.

Norah edged up to the group that included the two Ogilvies. Maybe if she looked hungry enough, they would get the hint and start for home. Every Sunday Aunt Florence and Aunt Mary talked to the other churchgoers before the service, whispered about them during it and stood around in chattering groups afterwards. It had been the same in Ringden. Grownups seemed to go to church to observe and gossip—and to waste valuable time. Last night it had snowed again. It was almost noon, and Norah still hadn't been set free in it.

"Since this is their first Christmas away from home, we're going to make it as special as possible," Aunt Mary was saying.

"Oh, so are we!" said Mrs Milne eagerly. "We're so worried that Derek and Dulcie and Lucy will be homesick, though they've managed splendidly so far. It's changed our lives, you know, to have children with us."

Aunt Mary said softly, "Yes . . . it's changed ours, too."

Finally the last handshakes were given, the last goodbyes were said and the children were released from waiting. Norah and Gavin ran ahead, kicking up sparkling sprays of snow.

Norah thought about Christmas. No matter how special the Ogilvies tried to make it, she knew Christmas couldn't be the same in Canada. She slowed down, trailing a branch along the sidewalk. While the Ogilvies' household was busy with elaborate Christmas preparations, all she could think of was what her family would be doing at home.

"Will you help me build a snowman after lunch, Norah?" asked Gavin.

Norah nodded. The busier she was, the less time she had to be homesick.

Buying presents was one thing that kept her from brooding. She had helped Hanny pack an enormous food hamper for her family, filled with Christmas pudding, cakes, tins of fruit and fish, and a whole ham. Norah wriggled with excitement as she thought how glad they would be to get it.

"Before you came, the war seemed so far away," said Hanny. "Now it's our war, too."

Aunt Mary had taken them to Woolworth's to buy the rest of their presents. "Hugh and I always did our shopping here when we were your age," she explained. She gave Norah and Gavin a dollar each and left them alone. They spent an hour wandering separately up and down the crowded aisles.

Norah chose a handkerchief for Aunt Mary, "Evening in Paris" perfume for Aunt Florence and a packet of bobby pins for Hanny. Even though Edith was still acting unfriendly, she picked out a purple comb for her. In the toy section she found water pistols for Paige and Bernard and pretend lipstick for Dulcie. Then she remembered Miss Gleeson and got her a bookmark with "This is where I fell asleep" printed on it. Her basket began to be crowded with presents. What a lot of people she knew in Canada!

She couldn't make up her mind about Gavin. He had plenty of cars and planes and soldiers. She turned down the aisle towards the sound of birds, where brightly hued budgies *cheeruped* importantly. Gavin would love one, but they were too expensive. Then she saw a tank of glittering orange goldfish. Five Cents, said the sign. That was perfect.

She found a clerk, who dipped a small net into the tank and scooped out the fish she chose, the brightest and plumpest. He put it with some water into a waxed cardboard carton with a wire handle. She had just enough money left for some food. Norah peeked into the carton and watched the goldfish dart around its temporary home. She would ask Hanny for a jar to use as a bowl and hide it in her wardrobe until Christmas.

When she met Gavin, after paying for her presents first so she could conceal the goldfish in her bag, she discovered he had chosen mothballs for everyone. "It says 'useful' on the package," he explained, sounding out the word carefully. "I like the smell, too."

The next sign of Christmas was a huge party that a wealthy store owner was holding for all the Toronto area war guests. Norah remembered Miss Carmichael telling them about it. She didn't want to feel like an evacuee all over again. "Do I have to go?" she asked.

But Aunt Florence insisted. "And please, Norah, let me buy you a new dress. You'll need one for Christmas dinner anyway, and you simply cannot wear that old Viyella any longer."

"Mum said in her last letter she was cutting down a dress for me out of one of her old ones."

"But it won't get here in time for the party. I want you to look nice—after all, it's a special occasion. And they'll think I'm not taking good care of you if you look shabby."

Norah gave in. "All right," she sighed. Going shopping was a waste of good tobogganing time.

Aunt Florence took her to a fancy store downtown with thick carpets and lots of mirrors. All the salesladies seemed to know who she was. "This way, Mrs Ogilvie," said the lady in charge. "Would you like to sit down?" She took Norah into a changing room and brought dresses in to her.

Norah grew interested in spite of herself. Most of the dresses were too frilly, like the ones Dulcie wore. But there was one she took to immediately. It was red velvet with a simple white collar and cuffs. When she tried it on, the rich weight of it made her feel cosy and secure.

"I like this one," she said, coming out to be inspected. She ran her hands up and down her sides, relishing the thick pile.

"But don't you want to try on the others?"

"No, thank you."

Aunt Florence examined every inch of the dress with the eyes of an experienced shopper. "It certainly looks nice on you—it suits your dark hair." She turned to the woman. "Do you have a hairband that would go with it?"

"Of course, Mrs Ogilvie." The manager bustled away and arrived back breathless with a narrow red band. It matched exactly and made Norah's hair feel neat and out of the way, much more comfortable than awkward bows or scratchy hair-slides.

"Very well, we'll take it. You have good taste, my dear. Now shoes."

Aunt Florence bought Norah black patent strapped shoes and new white socks. Norah peeked at the bill when it was all rung up and gulped. Even in pounds, it was an enormous sum.

"This is awfully expensive, Aunt Florence."

"Nonsense. It's nice to have someone to spend money on."

Norah swallowed her pride and said thank you.

"Oh, Norah, just look at these!" cried Aunt Florence. She held up a pair of red velvet shorts. "Aren't they wonderful? Gavin would look adorable in them and then you'd match. I'll take a pair in size six."

When they got home Gavin took one look at the shorts and shook his head. "I don't like them. Thank you, anyway," he added, politely but firmly.

Aunt Florence was surprised; it was the first time Gavin had rebelled. "Well, maybe they *are* too young for you," she conceded. "I'll return them and you can wear your sailor suit to the party."

Gavin smiled. He liked his sailor suit because it had a whistle.

Aunt Mary dropped them off at the Royal York Hotel, where the party was being held. It was the same towering building where Norah and Gavin had sheltered on the day they ran away; Aunt Mary told them it was the largest hotel in the Empire. A woman conducted them into a huge ballroom milling with dressed-up children. Norah held Gavin's hand as they stood amidst the shrill voices.

"Why, it's Norah and Gavin!" Miss Carmichael rushed up and kissed them. "Don't you both look well! You've put on weight—our Canadian food must be agreeing with you. What a lovely dress, Norah! Are you all settled in now? Do you like your school?"

"Yes, thank you." Norah answered all her questions politely and Gavin began to tell her about grade one. Miss Carmichael was *kind,* Norah realized. She had been kind at the residence too, but Norah had been too miserable to notice. That confusing week seemed a long time ago.

"You're losing some of your accent, Gavin," said Miss Carmichael. "By the time you go back to England you'll sound like a Canadian! Yours is changing too, Norah."

Surely it wasn't. Norah didn't want to lose her accent. It wasn't fair that it could happen without her consent.

Dulcie and Lucy found them and they all made their way to the food. "Derek wouldn't come," said Dulcie. "He says he's too old for a children's party and that he's a Canadian now, not a war guest. I love your dress, Norah."

Norah was confused. She didn't want to be a Canadian *or* a war guest; she just wanted to be herself. But the long tables of food distracted her. They were piled with Christmas cake, punch, cookies and dishes of candy. Norah had to stop Gavin from stuffing his pockets. She recognized some children from the ss *Zandwort* and they stood in a circle and compared their new families.

"We have a dog!" boasted Johnnie.

"I live with my aunt and uncle in a small town outside Toronto," said Margery. "I have my own chickens and I sell the eggs."

For a second Norah envied her; it would have been nice to have been sent somewhere that was more like home. But then she wouldn't be with the Ogilvies. That would seem strange, she was so used to them now.

Seeing some of the children from the ship made her wonder how Jamie was; she'd forgotten all about him.

"Aren't you excited about Christmas, Norah?" Dulcie asked her. "We're going to a pantomime at the Royal Alexandra Theatre. Aunt Dorothy is going to ask you, too." Norah didn't want to disillusion Dulcie by telling her that Canadian Christmas wasn't going to be the same.

A man called for silence and introduced their host. Everyone cheered and clapped and one of the older British girls gave a short speech of thanks. "We are all touched and grateful at how the Canadians have welcomed us into their homes," she said. "Let's show our appreciation, everyone."

There was more clapping and one of the adults began to sing "There'll always be an England." Norah groaned, but halfway through the song she joined in. Everything at this party was as it had been at the beginning: all of them crowded into a room with speeches and singing. But it didn't bother her any more; somehow it didn't seem important enough to worry about.

"It wasn't too bad," she admitted to Aunt Florence on the way home. But she was glad it was over.

"It was super!" said Gavin through a mouthful of fudge. "I'm glad we're war guests."

"I'm not!" blurted out Norah, forgetting to be grateful.

Aunt Florence glanced at her. "Sending you away must have been a terrible decision for your parents to make. But since they did, I'm happy it was our home you came to."

At school everyone was getting so excited about the holidays that for the first time Miss Liers had trouble keeping order. She tried to get them to sing a carol every morning, but they kept changing the words to "While shepherds washed their socks by night" and "Good King Wenceslas looked out/In his pink pyjamas."

"That's enough! We won't have *any* singing, if you're going to act so silly!" She slammed down the piano lid. Norah shared in the suppressed giggles of the class. Poor Miss Liers—she never seemed to want to have any fun.

One afternoon, when Norah went as usual to pick up Gavin at his classroom, some other British children were standing around the grade one and two cloakroom, looking doleful. Lucy was crying and Dulcie was trying to comfort her. "We didn't get the *presents*..." she wailed.

"What happened?" Norah asked. Gavin and Lucy tried to explain.

After lunch a film crew had arrived at Prince Edward School to make a movie of all the kindergarten to grade two war guests. They were going to send it to England so their parents could see their children having a happy Christmas in Canada.

"He took us into the gym and there was a huge Christmas tree," sniffed Lucy. "There were all sorts of presents underneath."

"The man said they were just empty boxes," said Gavin solemnly. "He said we had to open them and pretend they were presents, because it was just a game for the movie."

"But they weren't empty at all!" said Lucy. "There were dolls and games and I got a music box that played 'Somewhere over the Rainbow'." She began to cry again. "But at the end of the movie we had to give them back. He said all the toys belonged to his children!"

"Never mind," said Dulcie. "Soon it will really be Christmas and you'll have presents you can keep."

Norah wondered if her parents would see the movie. She had never known that being evacuees would involve so much attention—applauding crowds, newspaper photographs, broadcasts from the princesses and now a movie.

The next week there was another radio message, one far more personal than the one from Princess Elizabeth. "I have a wonderful surprise for you, Norah and Gavin," bubbled Aunt Mary. "The CBC is sending messages to Canada from your parents. They can't give us an exact time, but after school today you might hear their voices!"

Norah couldn't believe it, not until they all crowded around the radio that afternoon. Out of the shiny wooden case came faint British voices, full of longing: "Keep your chin up, Tim... We miss you, Kathleen and David... Happy Christmas, Margaret..." Before each message, the announcer said the family's name.

As the broadcast went on, Norah's throat constricted with fear. She thought of her terrible dream. Ever since she'd had it, she had waited even more avidly than before for letters from her family to make sure that they were all right. But she hadn't had one for two weeks. If she didn't hear her parents' voices now, the worst might have happened.

But then the announcer said, "And now we have a message for Norah and Gavin Stoakes, who are staying with the Ogilvies in Toronto."

Mum's light voice filled the quiet room. "Hello, Norah and Gavin. We want you to know that we miss you and love you." She wavered at the end.

"Dad here. Have a very happy Christmas. Everyone is fine and Grandad and the girls send their love."

That was all.

Gavin had frozen as soon as he heard his mother. When the message was over his mouth hung open for a second; then he began to babble. "That was Muv and Dad! Did you hear that, Norah? Did you, Aunt Florence? That was my *muv!*" He looked at Aunt Florence doubtfully and pulled Creature out of his pocket. On his face was the same bewildered expression he'd had when he first left home.

"You poor little boy . . ." began Aunt Mary, but her mother gave her a sharp glance.

"I did hear them, Gavin," she said. "Didn't they sound close? Now you come with me and we'll have a nice story about Pooh." She led him out of the room.

They had sounded *too* close, thought Norah. It made it all the harder to accept that they were so far away. How could their voices come all the way across the ocean? She wondered where they'd gone to send their messages—to London? Mum would have got all dressed up in her grey suit and Dad would pretend he wasn't nervous. And Grandad would bluster about being left behind.

"O-oh tidings of co-omfort and joy," sang a choir at the end of the broadcast. It *had* been a kind of comfort, to hear their familiar voices. At least she knew they were safe. But it wasn't a joy. She would only feel joy if she could be with them for Christmas.

"Are you all right, Norah?" asked Aunt Mary. She took out the cribbage board. "Shall we have a game?"

Norah was good at cribbage now. She let herself think only of her peg drawing ahead of Aunt Mary's.

On Christmas Eve afternoon Norah helped Aunt Mary balance Christmas cards on top of picture frames. They were waiting for the "Drummond clan," as Aunt Florence called it, to arrive; some of the Montreal cousins were driving down to stay for three days. Edith had spent the whole morning complaining and making up beds in the spare rooms. Three great-nieces were to sleep on cots and the extra bed in Norah's tower. She tried not to worry about what they would be like.

She had never seen so many cards. At home her parents got just enough to fill the mantlepiece, but dozens and dozens had arrived at the Ogilvies.

"You must know a lot of people," she said to Aunt Mary.

"Well, the Drummonds and Ogilvies are both very large families and since Mother is the oldest, all the friends of the family send cards to her. We're never able to get them all up.

And the trouble with getting so many is the number we have to send."

Norah had seen Aunt Florence's special notebook, with long lists of names and ticks for sending and receiving cards. Some names got crossed off, and some added; it was like an elaborate game.

She had received five Christmas cards herself. There was one from her principal and joint ones to her and Gavin from Joey's mother and Mrs Curteis. Another was from Molly. She said she was sorry Norah had been evacuated too, but she hoped she was having a good time in Canada. "Wales is very wet," she wrote. "Sometimes I get homesick, but Mother and Dad are coming here for Christmas."

The last card had an English robin on the front. It said:

> Dear Norah,
>
> The dogfights have stopped so I guess the Battle of Britain is over. Now there are bombs in London instead. We don't have the Sky-watchers any more. I have the most shrapnel in the village. When are you coming back?
>
> Your friend,
>
> Tom

Both of these cards were so unsettling that Norah put them on her windowsill without reading them again. Molly and Tom and her other friends at home seemed like people in another life.

"There!" Aunt Mary stepped down from her stool. "I think we're finally ready."

Norah followed her glance around the living room. Every picture had cards stuck on top and large bunches of holly stood in silver bowls on the tables. In one corner was the largest Christmas tree Norah had ever seen, making the room smell like a forest.

"Turn the lights on, Norah," said Aunt Mary. "They should be here any moment. I'll go and help Hanny get things ready."

Norah plugged in the tree. She and Gavin had helped decorate it with fragile glass balls, crocheted snowflakes and lights that bubbled. As the lights heated up, the balls swayed gently. On the top branch perched an angel with gauzy wings.

It was certainly a beautiful tree . . . but Norah thought of another one, the little tree that Dad cut down in Stumble Wood each year and set on a table in the front room. There were no strings of lights, but the tinsel on it sparkled in the light coming through the window. She remembered making paper chains; opening a new package of coloured paper that sometimes included a few silver or even gold strips and the whole family sitting around the kitchen table pasting the strips into circles. They hung the chains in garlands from corner to corner in all the rooms; Dad's head would brush against them. Last of all they hung the mistletoe from the front door and everyone who visited was trapped under it and kissed, accompanied by shrieks of laughter . . .

Norah blinked hard and looked at the Ogilvies' tree again. Presents were piled so high under it that its lower branches were hidden. More were beside it against the wall. Many of the presents had her and Gavin's names on them. One large parcel was wrapped in brown paper and string. It looked plain beside the fancy paper of the rest, but it said "To Norah from Mum and Dad". She was going to open that one first.

A faint stirring of excitement rose in Norah. She bent to

rattle her parents' present. Then the door knocker sounded and she quickly dropped the parcel.

"Merry Christmas!" cried voices in the hall. "Aunt Florence! Aunt Mary! And who's this cute kid? You must be Gavin."

A crowd of people swarmed into the living room, bearing even more presents. Norah stepped back as they kept pouring in. All of them had loud ringing voices and a purposeful bearing. A whole roomful of people related to the Ogilvies was too much to take in.

"And this is Norah, our other war guest," said Aunt Florence. She looked proud and put her arm across Norah's shoulder as she introduced her. Norah drew strength from its warmth as she said "How do you do" again and again.

After they had all sat down with their drinks, she began to sort them out. There were five adults and five children. Two little boys about Gavin's age would be sleeping in his room.

The three girls brought their ginger ale over to sit beside Norah. The eldest was Florence—Flo, she corrected quickly. She was fourteen and her sister Janet was eleven. The other girl, Clare, was twelve. They chatted with an assurance that made Norah feel like a stranger again. After all, they were really family, not just guests.

Janet looked the nicest of the girls; she had a plain, broad face and laughed a lot. "I'm so excited, I think I might be sick!" she told Norah. "I usually am at Christmas."

"Please spare us this year," said Flo. She tossed back her long hair, looking sophisticated. Clare was complaining about having to come. "We have to every year," she explained. "It's a tradition. But I wanted to go skiing with my friends in Montreal."

Beside her, her mother gave her a warning look and began

to ask Norah the usual questions. "I bet you get tired of telling people how you like Canada," whispered Janet. Norah grinned and moved closer to her on the chesterfield.

"Have you been to Gairloch yet?" asked Janet.

"Oh, yes!" said Norah eagerly. She had forgotten about Gairloch. "I liked it there."

"Wait till you see it in the summer! It's my favourite place in the whole world. We have lots of fun sleeping over the boathouse. We sneak out at night and go skinny dipping, and catch frogs and put them in the Boys' Dorm."

All of this sounded scary but intriguing. Norah recalled the peace of the rippling lake, the screen of trees and the friendly old cottage. Next summer she would be able to spend three months there. Next summer…

Gavin and the two younger cousins seemed to have turned into one very noisy boy, racing cars up and down the hall floor. "Quiet, you three!" called a mother. "Go and wash your hands for dinner."

The clan trooped into the dining-room. Dinner was modest in anticipation of tomorrow's feast: tourtière and salad. Before dessert, Norah jumped as everyone started chanting at once: "*You* scream, *I* scream, we *all* scream for ice cream!" Hanny marched in with a glass bowlful of it.

Norah ate hers silently, feeling left out again. What other strange rituals did this family have?

After dinner they stood around the piano and sang carols while an uncle played. Then Aunt Florence read part of *A Christmas Carol* aloud. By now the little boys were nodding. All seven children, despite Flo's protests, were sent to get ready for bed.

At home Norah laid one of Dad's socks across the end of her bed, but here they hung specially knitted, patterned stockings on hooks under the mantel. Aunt Mary had found hers and Hugh's for Norah and Gavin, and the cousins brought their own. Gavin had stopped saying "Father Christmas" ever since he'd been taken to the Santa Claus parade in November. Aunt Florence let him be the one to put out the milk and cookies on the hearth.

"Now off to bed!" she smiled. "Santa won't come until you're asleep."

"Will he find me here?" asked Gavin anxiously. "Will he think I'm still in England?"

Aunt Florence kissed him. "He'll find you—I told him where you were." Gavin stared at her with awe, then went up with the others to bed.

Flo and Janet and Clare talked and laughed and tossed on their narrow beds for a long time. At first Norah didn't like sharing her room with three strangers, especially when they told her they always slept up here at Christmas. She wanted to let them know it was *her* room now, but she couldn't find the right words.

"How can you bear living with Aunt Florence?" asked Flo. "She's so bossy, she thinks she's the Queen!" Flo got up, stuffed her pillow under the top of her nightgown and tied it in place with a belt. Then she sauntered across the room, bowing left and right. "You may kiss my hand," she said haughtily.

For a second Norah was shocked. Then she laughed so hard they had to pat her on the back. How wonderful to be able to be so wicked, to make fun of Aunt Florence with someone else who knew her! Norah began to talk as easily with the cousins as if she were really related to them. She fell asleep in the middle of telling a joke.

Something in the room made Norah stir. She turned over and felt a weight on her feet.

Of course—her filled stocking. Aunt Florence or Aunt Mary—or Santa Claus, she smiled—must have crept in and put it there. It felt exactly the same as her stocking at home. It was one of the most familiar feelings she knew, but she always forgot about it until Christmas. Every year, for as long as she could remember, she had woken up in the early morning dimness and felt that delectable weight on her feet. She never let herself touch it until it was really morning; she always fell back immediately to sleep.

But now she lay awake. The thrill of the stocking was the same—but nothing else was. It never would be again. She was far away from her own family in a strange country, and she would probably be here for a long time.

But she had ways to get through it. A family she was finally feeling a part of, with a new, unexpected set of "cousins". And Paige's family, and Bernard's. Perhaps it took three borrowed families to make up for one real one. There was Gairloch to look forward to in the summer. And most important of all, Gavin to take care of.

Gavin's goldfish! Norah slipped out of bed and padded to her wardrobe, trying not to wake the others. The goldfish was swimming friskily around its bowl. She picked it up carefully. She would take it down to Gavin's room and put it where he'd see it first thing in the morning.

Norah tiptoed down the stairs and into his room. At first she couldn't find him amidst the visitors. He was slumbering peacefully, Creature by his cheek. She placed the bowl on the table beside his bed and slipped under it the card she had prepared: "A very Happy Christmas to Gavin from Norah." She watched his face for a few seconds. Whatever else happened during their time in Canada, she was going to make sure Gavin kept on being as happy as he could be.

She was still wide awake. It was exciting to be the only one in the slumbering household. She decided to sneak down and peek at the tree again. The living room was dark and chilly, but after she plugged in the tree it came alive. In the darkness the lights glowed even more gloriously than they had in the daytime. Norah stood in front of the tree with her hands out, watching them change colour.

Then she gasped. Propped against a chair by the tree was a shiny new bicycle. Holding her breath with suspense, she read the card tied to its handlebars: "Merry Christmas to Norah with love from Aunt Florence."

It was a Hurricane, like Paige's—maroon with gold striping. It even had a dynamo set and a large wicker basket. She ran her hands over the smooth chrome and the leather seat, not quite sure whether to believe it was real. When they played horses, she would *call* it "Hurricane", to remind her of the planes.

A bicycle meant freedom. It meant Aunt Florence trusted her and knew her well enough to guess what she wanted the most. Norah longed to climb onto it, to continue to caress it; but she shouldn't be here, seeing her present before morning. Quickly she unplugged the tree and fled up to bed. She shivered and squirmed under the covers to get warm again, giggling to herself. A bicycle!

Someone crunched by in the snowy street outside. A man and woman's voices sang softly as they passed: "Where the snow lay round about / Deep and crisp and even."

Norah sat up and pulled the curtains open. She was suddenly filled to the brim with Christmas, with the magic feeling that came every year. Christmas was the same, after all. If Christmas carried on in Canada as it did at home, maybe other good things would stay the same as well.

Norah bounced down again into her cosy bed, making

the bell on her stocking jingle. She lay on her back and watched the dim, pewter-coloured clouds outside. Her breathing was light and easy, as if a heavy weight had rolled away. All that fell out of the sky was soft white snow.

AFTERWORD

During World War II around 15,000 British children were evacuated overseas. Nearly 8,000 of them came to Canada; most were privately sponsored but 1,500 were assisted by the Children's Overseas Reception Board. Of these government-sponsored children about one third, like Norah and Gavin, went to the homes of complete strangers.

The response of Canadians to the plight of British children was overwhelming; probably many more children would have been brought over if the tragic sinking of *The City of Benares* had not brought an end to evacuation plans. A fascinating account of Canada's involvement is given in the late Geoffrey Bilson's *The Guest Children*, the only nonfiction book so far devoted entirely to the subject.

My book, however, is fiction. There is no doubt that many of the children who came to Canada enjoyed the adventure and found warm, welcoming homes. I tried to imagine a child who didn't. My depiction of the events of the war is as true as possible for someone who was born just after it. The major places, too, are real. But most of the details, such as Norah's village, the ship, her school, her local library and, especially, the characters, are fictional creations.

I would not have been able to write this story without the help of many people. Thank you to Bryan Bacon; Auriol Hastie; Jacquetta, Shaun and the late Pat Jackson; Kay and Sandy Pearson; Kathleen Tankard; and Alan Woodland for sharing with me their experiences of the war; to David Conn for his invaluable advice about the Battle of Britain; to Sarah Ellis and Jean Little for reading the manuscript; to Patrick Dunn for procuring books from all over the continent; to David Kilgour for his sleuthing; and to Vicki Lazier and Christine McMeans for remembering a family song. Above all I would like to thank Alice Kane, from whom I first heard "Alenoushka and her Brother", and whose story of telling it to evacuated children inspired this book.

LOOKING AT THE MOON

For Betty Anne and Ron

I whispered, "I am too young,"
And then, "I am old enough";
Wherefore I threw a penny
To find out if I might love.

O love is the crooked thing,
There is nobody wise enough
To find out all that is in it,
For he would be thinking of love
Till the stars had run away
And the shadows eaten the moon.
Ah, penny, brown penny, brown penny,
One cannot begin it too soon.

W.B. Yeats

SORTING OUT THE DRUMMONDS

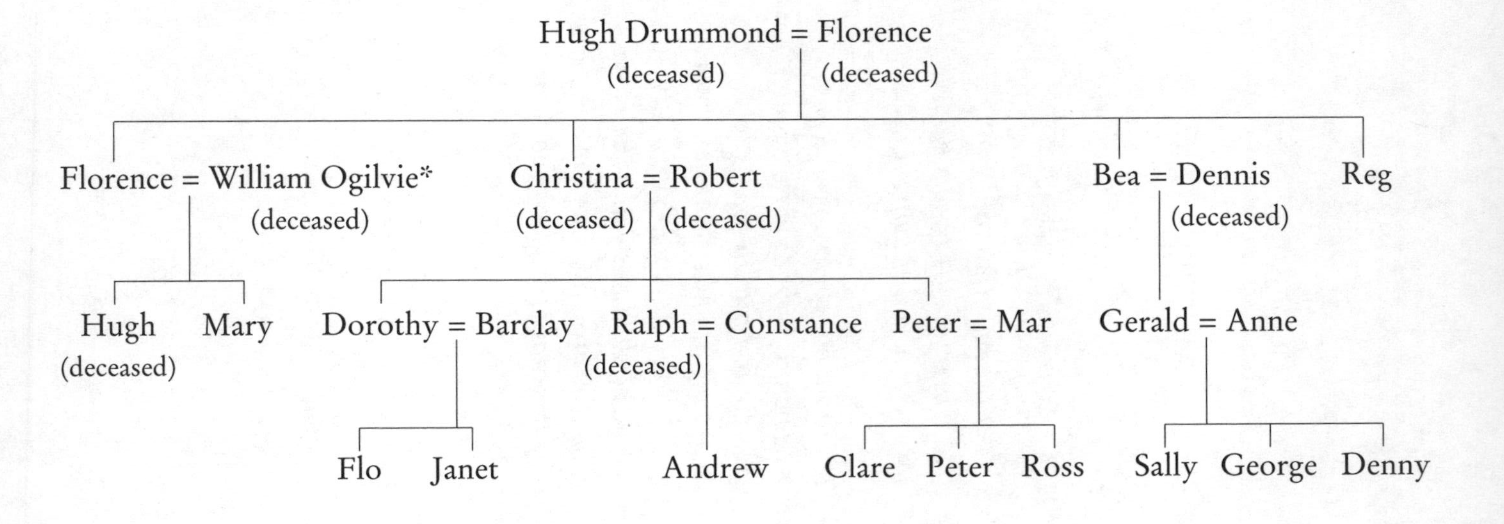

*Brother of "Aunt Catherine"

CONTENTS

I

RETURN TO GAIRLOCH

I look so ugly!

Norah peered over her brother's head at the photograph, while Aunt Mary held open the Toronto newspaper and read aloud from the "Personal Notes" for August 2, 1943:

> Mrs Wm. Ogilvie, her daughter Miss Mary Ogilvie, and their young war guests, Norah and Gavin Stoakes, have just returned from a trip to Vancouver. They will be spending the month of August at "Gairloch," their summer home in Muskoka.

In the picture above the caption Aunt Florence sat stiffly on the chesterfield, looking as majestic as usual. Gavin was perched on its right arm and Aunt Mary smiled timidly on the far left. Between the two women scowled Norah, her face all nose, and her arms and legs as skinny as toothpicks.

"What does 'Wim' mean?" asked Gavin.

Aunt Florence laughed. "William, pet. It's an abbreviation." She took the paper from her daughter to examine it more closely. "Must you always frown, Norah? At least your new dress looks presentable. We'll buy two copies so we can send one to your parents. Won't that be nice?"

Norah shrugged. She ran out of Ford's Bay Store, where they had picked up the newspaper while they waited for the launch. Standing on the dock, she hooded her eyes with both hands and gazed hungrily out at the lake.

At last they'd arrived! The hot, hundred-mile drive from Toronto had seemed endless. Norah had smouldered with frustration while they wasted a whole hour in Orillia, having lunch with friends of the family. During the meal she'd made so many hints about the time that Aunt Florence had marched her out to the car and made her wait there without dessert.

After Orillia Gavin had slept, but Norah had squirmed in the back seat, while Aunt Florence nattered to her daughter about their friends' connections. "Let's see now...Alma Bartlett married Harry Stone . . . wasn't he the brother of William Stone?" For all of July, during their trip to British Columbia, Norah had been subjected to the same boring gossip. *Who cares?* she wanted to scream.

But now she watched the dancing waves and sniffed in the balsamy smell that was always her first sensation of being back in Muskoka. A breeze lifted her sticky hair. She knelt on the dock and dipped her hands in the clear water. She splashed it into her face, then took a drink. All summer she had been waiting to feel and taste the lake again.

And in a very short while she would be at Gairloch itself! She hadn't been there since last October; now that there was gas rationing, and you couldn't buy new tires, they no longer came up in May. Norah still hadn't forgiven Aunt Florence for cheating her out of a whole month on the island. And a month spent almost entirely in Aunt Florence's company had been too much to bear.

Norah was used to her guardian after living with her for almost three years. After a rough beginning they had reached a sort of truce. But lately Aunt Florence's fussiness had driven her wild. Kind Aunt Mary understood that Norah was growing up, but Aunt Florence still treated her like a child.

"I'm thirteen!" she had protested, when Aunt Florence had brought home the "presentable" dress before their journey—impossibly babyish, with puffed sleeves and a sash. "I'm a teen-ager now—why can't I pick my *own* clothes?"

"A teen-ager!" Aunt Florence had sniffed. "I don't hold with these newfangled notions. There's no such thing as a teen-ager. In our family you are a child until you leave home and then you're an adult. I don't want to hear that word again."

And all Norah could respond was "Yes, Aunt Florence," as sulkily as she dared. Whenever she tried to explain *her* side of things, Aunt Florence just said "Sauce!" and closed the conversation. Norah remembered having loud, satisfying arguments with her mother. But her mother was in England and Norah hadn't seen her since she and Gavin had been sent to Canada to be safe from the war. With Aunt Florence she was supposed to behave like a polite guest and keep her mouth shut.

At last the launch curved around the headland, and Norah saw her "cousins" Janet and Flo in it, waving. She shouted and waved back and jumped away her car stiffness. Now she had five whole weeks of freedom ahead of her, when she could have as little as possible to do with bossy adults. She glanced down at the comfortable shorts she was only allowed to wear up north. Maybe she didn't *really* want to be a teen-ager, not yet...

"Norah, Norah!" Janet was leaning over the bow screaming her name. The spray flew into her mouth, making her choke. Flo pulled her back and waved.

All summer Aunt Florence had nagged at Norah to smile more often. Now she grinned so hugely her cheeks felt as if they were cracking. There had been "cousins" in Vancouver, but they were all boys and not very friendly. Flo and Janet were like real cousins. Sometimes Flo seemed distant—she was seventeen—but Janet was only a year older than Norah.

As soon as the launch putted up beside the dock, Janet leaped out and grabbed Norah, whirling her around. "Oh, *Norah,* you've finally come! It's been so boring without you!"

"Hi, kiddo," smiled Flo, tying up the boat efficiently. "Thank goodness you're here—now I can get this pesky sister out of my way."

"Your hair's longer!" cried Janet. "I like it. Do you like mine? I put it in pincurls now." Janet's hair was a blonde fuzz that emphasized her fat cheeks. She hugged Norah again, then controlled her excitement as the aunts and Gavin, loaded down with bags of groceries, came out of the store.

"Hello Janet, hello Florence." The cousins were kissed and exclaimed over. Gavin beamed up at everyone, his eyes the same bright blue as the water.

"You might have helped us carry these, Norah," said Aunt Florence. Norah ignored her as they all found places in the long boat. She ran her hands over its mahogany sides and leather seats. The launch was called *Florence*—not after Aunt Florence but after her mother. But Norah thought it suited her guardian to have the same name as the luxurious boat, whose luminous wood, thick glass windscreen and shiny brass all glittered with importance.

She watched carefully as Flo turned the key to start the ignition. Only the older teen-agers were allowed to drive the *Florence,* but you could run the smaller launch by yourself when you turned thirteen. She hoped the grown-ups would remember that before she had to remind them.

"Isn't it great to be back?" whispered Gavin. He leaned against Norah and the two of them threw their faces back to drink in the spray, keeping watch for their first glimpse of the island.

All of the Drummond clan were on the dock to greet them. Aunt Florence stepped out regally and accepted the homage of her sisters, brother, in-laws, nieces and nephews as if she were their ruling monarch—which, being the eldest, she was. Norah barely noticed which of the crowd of grown-ups was kissing her. She was too busy taking in the white dock, the grey boathouse with its fancy railing and, best of all, the circular cottage waiting above.

"*Bosley!* Look, Norah, he remembers me! Wave, Boz!" Uncle Reg's black-and-white springer spaniel had bounded onto the dock and leapt at Gavin. Then he lifted one of his paws in greeting while everyone laughed.

Norah kicked off her shoes, wriggled through the excited group and ran up to the cottage. The stone steps were cool and rough under her tender feet. She dashed into the kitchen.

"Hanny! We're back!"

Hanny, Aunt Florence's cook in the city, turned around from the stove and opened her arms. Norah ran into them and their noses collided. They both laughed.

"Norah, what a treat to see you again! Did you have a grand trip? I got all your postcards, and Gavin's too—where is he?"

"Down at the dock, still being kissed," grinned Norah. She circled the spacious kitchen, grabbed a cookie off a plate and plopped herself on top of the old pine table, munching noisily.

"Not before dinner and no sitting on my clean table," said Hanny automatically, but her lined face still smiled. "Oh *my,* I've missed you all this month—even Mrs O! The family seems rudderless without her here."

"How is Mr Hancock?" asked Norah politely. Hanny's husband was retired, but he always came up with her in the summers to help out.

"Having a nice, lazy time as usual. He gads about fetching mail or taking your uncles fishing, while I slave away in a hot kitchen. Though I must say your aunts are very helpful." Hanny pushed her untidy hair under its net and turned back to the stove. "Now, Norah, it's lovely to see you but we'll have to talk later. You're all eating together this evening—all twenty of you!—and I'm not nearly ready. You'd better skedaddle—unless you'd like to peel some carrots."

Norah left quickly in case Hanny meant it. Before the family came in she made a swift inspection of the rest of the cottage: up the stairs and down the slippery hall, peeking into each of the huge bedrooms, then through the sunny dining room into the living room.

Nothing had changed; nothing ever did. Old photographs dotted the panelled walls. Cups from regattas, faded rugs and comfortable wicker furniture filled the dim space. A faint smell of wood smoke came from the massive stone fireplace. In an alcove beside it was the same wooden puzzle that had been there for years, its pieces scattered on a small table. Above it was Aunt Florence's mother's collection of china cats, and the knot board where all the children, including Norah, had learned to tie knots.

Norah ended her tour on the verandah, her favourite part of the cottage. She ran all around its wide circumference, then leaned against one of its thick cedar posts and watched the clan parade up the steps—as if she, not Aunt Florence, were the ruler of Gairloch.

Surely, the black cloud of angry misery that had hung over her almost constantly since she had turned thirteen would now dissolve.

II
THE COUSINS

The long evening meal was over, the younger children had gone to bed, and the two generations of aunts and uncles, whom Flo had long ago christened "the Elders," were relaxing in the living room.

Norah sat on the rug opposite Janet, her calm mood already vanished. She was trying to concentrate on a game of slapjack, but inside she seethed at what Aunt Mar, her least favourite Elder, had just said to her in the kitchen.

"Look how you've grown, Norah! You'd better ask Aunt Florence to buy you a brassiere before school starts."

How dare she make personal remarks like that! At least the two of them had been alone, bringing out the dessert plates.

Norah tugged angrily at the skirt Aunt Florence had made her change into. The Elders changed for dinner every night, but the children only had to when they had what the younger cousins called a Big Dinner together.

It wasn't dark yet and Norah hadn't even had time to explore. She kept glancing out at the beckoning evening. Finally she couldn't bear to be inside a moment longer.

"I'm going for a walk," she whispered to Janet. She slipped out of the room and ran down to the boathouse to change. Comfortable again in slacks, an old shirt and bare feet, Norah strode along the shoreline path that circled the island. A chipmunk skittered out of her way and soft pine needles crunched under her feet.

Soon she reached the tiny log cabin that was the children's playhouse. No one seemed to have used it since she and Janet, with Bob and Alec—cousins on the Ogilvie side—had called themselves the Hornets and pretended the playhouse was a gangsters' hideaway. But this summer Bob and Alec hadn't come.

Four yellow-and-black striped masks hung on nails inside the door. Norah closed it quickly. It seemed much longer than a year ago that they had played that silly game.

Beyond the playhouse was the babies' beach. Norah rolled up her pant legs and paddled, her feet stirring up silt. The bay was so shallow that it looked brown, every ripple of sand showing through its crystal surface.

Her next stop was the gazebo perched on a rocky point at the far end of the island. An empty cup and saucer had been abandoned on the bench inside. Norah knew she should take them back to the kitchen, but that would slow her down.

She passed the windmill which pumped up water for the tank behind the cottage. Then she cut through the woods in the middle of the island, weaving through tree trunks and ferns until she reached a clearing. Here stood two extra cabins for overflowing family and guests. Behind them was Norah's favourite place on the island, the high rocky promontory that overlooked it all. Her feet reached for the familiar footholds as she scrabbled up the rock to the level platform on top. There she collapsed, panting and sweaty.

She ran her hands over the streaky pink rock and gazed down at the massed green foliage beneath her. Beyond it stretched the lake. Clumps of land—other islands and long fingers of mainland—broke up its flat expanse.

Vast as it was, this lake was the smallest of three huge ones that were joined together by narrow ribbons of water.

But their lake was the deepest, Norah thought with satisfaction, and the most beautiful. She never tired of watching its colour change from silver to blue to green. Now its surface reflected the pink-tinged sky. The slanting light picked out each rock, tree and wave.

Norah let out a relieved breath—finally she was alone.

Her first encounter with the Drummond clan each summer was always overwhelming. Ten adults and eight children were here this month and they were all related. Norah had heard the expression "blood is thicker than water"; Ogilvie and Drummond blood seemed thicker than most. Over the summers she had grown used to the family's established rituals, jokes and conflicts. She knew as well as all the cousins that Aunt Bea was shrill and giddy because she resented Aunt Florence being the eldest, and that Uncle Reg played practical jokes on his two sisters whenever he had the chance.

But although the family was always warm towards their two war guests, Norah often felt as though they belonged to an exclusive club she and Gavin could never join. Every once in a while the family shared something that excluded them. This evening, for example, they had all started talking about Andrew, an unknown cousin who was supposed to arrive tomorrow. Andrew's funny expressions when he was four, the time he ran away and hid under the canoe when he was eight, the plays he made up . . . all through dinner they had discussed him.

But Aunt Mar's rude comment had been much worse than the chatter about Andrew. Norah knew she needed a brassiere; she just couldn't bring herself to ask Aunt Florence for one. And anyway, shouldn't Aunt Florence notice for herself and suggest it?

It was difficult to believe that the two mounds on her chest, that had appeared almost overnight, really belonged to *her.* This last year she was sure her nose had grown as well. It seemed to fill up her whole face like a beak.

Dad had a nose like that—but it didn't matter on a man. Thinking of Mum and Dad produced the usual small ache, like prodding a sore spot. When she and Gavin finally went back to England, would her parents recognize this new person with a beaky nose and breasts like a woman's?

One day in the spring, as she was waiting nervously to attend her first mixed party, Norah had asked Aunt Florence if she was pretty. She knew Aunt Florence would tell her the truth; she didn't believe in false flattery.

"You are when you smile," was the brisk reply.

That meant she *wasn't* pretty, for if she always had to smile to enhance her looks, she couldn't be. It was also an infuriating way for Aunt Florence to get in some advice, instead of just answering the question.

Now she scraped away lichen from the rock. Why wasn't the magic of Gairloch making her troubles disappear, the way it usually did?

Tired of her own thoughts, Norah slithered back down the rock. She would go and check on Gavin. All of the boys except the two youngest ones slept in half of the old servants' quarters behind the cottage. The Hancocks slept in the other half. Norah poked her head into the large room that the family called the "Boys' Dorm." With Bob and Alec away, only three small boys, Peter, Ross and Gavin, occupied cots. All three were fast asleep.

Norah went in and bent over Gavin. As usual he clutched "Creature," his toy elephant, in his fist. She covered him up more closely. Even though the gentle little boy was everyone's favourite, the family accepted that Norah was the one who was really responsible for him. She had never forgotten how she had neglected that responsibility when she'd first come to Canada. Now her love for Gavin was the most constant element in her life here.

She heard laughter coming from the water's edge; the others must have already gone to bed. Norah wished she could go straight down to the boathouse, where all the girls slept, but one of the family rituals was saying good-night.

Aunt Anne and Uncle Gerald, who stayed in one of the cabins with their two youngest children, had already retired. The rest of the Elders were playing bridge.

"I'm going to bed now," Norah announced.

"I was just going to call you," said Aunt Florence. "What were you doing out there all by yourself? Janet was upset you left so abruptly."

Norah shrugged. On the first night back at Gairloch you were expected to kiss everyone. Dutifully she made her rounds. "Good-night Aunt Florence... Aunt Mary... Aunt Catherine... Aunt Bea... Aunt Dorothy... Uncle Barclay... Uncle Reg . . . Aunt Mar." Whew! Eight kisses, some on papery cheeks or rough skin that needed a shave.

She fled to the toilet, then down to the dock. The boathouse was built directly over the lake. On this side of the island the water was so deep that the boats could be driven right into their slips, like putting a car in the garage. Before she went up the stairs, Norah paused to admire the family's fleet. Inside, the *Florence* bobbed beside the smaller launch—the *Putt-Putt*—and the heavy old rowboat. The sailboat was moored outside and the canoe was overturned against a wall.

She looked for her mug and toothbrush on the shelf built under the window. It was in the same place it had been last Thanksgiving. Norah brushed her teeth vigorously and cleaned the brush in the lake. Ignoring the bar of soap beside the mug, she splashed her face and dried herself with the fresh towel waiting for her on her hook.

She stood for a moment, listening to the haunting wail of a loon. A few stars had already appeared and the fat moon made a silver trail on the water. Norah drank in a gulp of cool night air, then climbed up the stairs to the "Girls' Dorm."

The familiar space seemed to welcome her. Everything was the same: the messy clutter of clothes and bathing suits, the dark wooden walls, the nails to hang their things on and the faded gingham curtains they always left open.

"Where have *you* been?" Clare asked her. "Moon-gazing? Maybe our Norah has been having romantic thoughts."

Norah pulled off her clothes and got into her pyjamas without answering. Clare was so impossible, no one took her seriously. She was sitting on the edge of her bed, plucking at her ukelele and yowling "You Are My Sunshine" out of tune.

"*Please* stop, Clare," begged Sally. "I'm trying to go to sleep."

Clare's pretty, pouty face looked up. "Then go back to the cabin with your parents and little brothers," she said rudely. "If you want to be out here with the *big* girls, you have to put up with us." She began again, even louder.

Abashed, Sally sank down into her pillow. She was only seven and in awe of her older cousins. But Flo reached over and snatched away Clare's ukelele.

"You're too noisy," she said calmly. Ignoring Clare's protests, she blew out the lamp. "Get into bed, everyone, and keep quiet so Sally can go to sleep."

The five girls lay in bed for a few silent moments. The loon warbled again and something, a frog or a fish, splashed briefly. Waves lapped soothingly against the sides of the boathouse. Norah snuggled farther into her narrow but cosy bed, feeling as usual as if she were *on* a boat. She began to think of the treats that waited for her tomorrow . . . the first of a long string of days when there was nothing she *had* to do.

Then, as usual, they all began talking again, as revived and wide-awake as if they had had hours of sleep. Only Sally dozed. The others sat up in bed, their faces white ovals in the moonlight.

First Flo, Janet and Clare finished telling Norah everything she had missed in July: the Port Clarkson Regatta, the *Ahmic* steamship accident, and how Uncle Gerald had seen a bear swimming from one island to another.

"Aunt Bea tried to organize us like Aunt Florence," giggled Janet.

"We had to recite *poetry* every night," complained Clare. "It was terrible."

"I hate to admit it, but it's a relief to have Aunt Florence back," said Flo. "Now it's your turn, Norah. Tell us all about your trip!"

Norah began with the only good part—the train. They had slept in narrow bunks with straps to hold them in; the train rocked them to sleep every night like a noisy cradle. "The meals were *wonderful*, and really fancy, just like in a restaurant. There were white tablecloths and finger bowls and we had roast beef and trout and things like that."

She couldn't find words to describe her astonishment at how huge Canada was; the train seemed to go on forever, unfolding mile after mile of empty country. She remembered her first awestruck glimpse of the Rockies, their sharp peaks outlined against a hard blue sky.

Nor could she explain how being on the train had made her realize that, in a way that hadn't been true when she had first come to this country, the war seemed to have finally touched Canada. Every day she and Gavin walked the length of the whole train, through crowded cars full of soldiers and solitary, worried-looking women who soothed crying children.

She went on to describe Vancouver with its rounded mountains rising straight up from the sea; and the Ogilvie cousins whom the Drummonds had never met.

"Vancouver was sort of like England," said Norah. "But there was nothing to do there except visit a lot of boring relatives. Do you know they even had black-outs? After Pearl Harbor, because they're so close to Japan."

Clare interrupted her. "Did *you* know that I have a boy friend, Norah? Now that I'm fifteen, I'm finally allowed to date. His name's John and he's planning to join the RCAF. He's—"

"Spare us the details," Flo broke in. "We're already so tired of hearing about him."

"But *Norah* hasn't heard," persisted Clare. She continued to go on about how dreamy her new boy friend was until Flo interrupted her again.

"You don't even know what loving someone is," she said quietly. "Wait until he *does* join up. Like Ned..."

"Who's Ned?" Norah asked, because she knew Flo wanted her to.

"He's *my* boy friend, and he's in the army and stationed overseas. I write to him three times a week."

"She also writes to two other boys," said Janet. "She uses so much paper that Mother makes her buy her own."

"Well, it's important," said Flo. "They need to be cheered up."

Norah turned over impatiently. Flo seemed much more grown-up this summer, as if she had already entered the strange adult world that was still closed to the rest of them. And she wished all of them would stop going on about *boys.*

They were just like her friend Dulcie. This past year Dulcie had "discovered" boys. She was always moaning about being too young to go to dances, and she didn't understand when Norah said she wasn't interested. At least Janet wasn't like that yet.

But then Janet disappointed her too.

"What do you think of Frankie, Norah?" she asked. "I think he's the greatest thing since canned peas."

Flo roared with laughter. "Sorry, Janet," she choked, seeing her sister's hurt face. "But when you try to use expressions like that you sound so—"

"I don't want to hear how I sound," interrupted Janet huffily. "I was asking Norah a question. What do you think of Frankie?"

Norah knew she meant Frank Sinatra. "He's okay, I guess," she sighed. She didn't mind the mellow voice which seemed to be on the radio every time it was turned on. But she was tired of him. Her other city friend, Paige, had every one of his records and played them until Norah wanted to scream. At least they didn't have a phonograph in the boathouse.

The conversation turned to a comparison of their school years in Montreal and Toronto. They had a lot to catch up on since last summer.

"Stop *talking,*" moaned Sally, turning over and going back to sleep. Norah herself was drifting through whole patches of conversation. Then Janet asked her a question. "Have you ever met Andrew, Norah? I can't remember if you were here the last time he came."

"No, I haven't. Who *is* this Andrew, anyway?" she added irritably.

"He's the only son of Uncle Ralph and Aunt Constance," explained Flo. "Uncle Ralph was my mother's and Clare's father's brother—he died about five years ago. They used to come to Gairloch every summer but then Aunt Constance married again and Andrew had to move to Winnipeg. He's been back a few times for a visit. And tomorrow he'll be here again! He's transferring to the University of Toronto this fall."

"He's *dreamy,*" said Clare. "He visited us in Montreal last year and all my friends were envious. If he wasn't my cousin I'd have a huge crush on him."

"He's the best person in the family," said Flo. "We were really close when we were kids."

"The last time he came he taught me how to dive," said Janet. "Wait till you see how handsome he is, Norah!"

Norah pretended she was already asleep. What a bore this Andrew sounded! And what a bore the cousins were going to be, if all they wanted to talk about were boys and singers.

And yet, since she was now a teen-ager too, shouldn't she be more interested in those things? She didn't want to be as childish as Sally or as grown-up as Flo. But it wasn't much fun to flounder in between.

III

A STRANGE STORY

The jubilant clamour of birds, much louder than in the city, woke Norah early. She peeked out of the window at the fresh morning and decided to go for her first swim of the summer.

A few minutes later she was balancing on the edge of the diving board, fastening the strap of her bathing cap and admiring how the ripples broke up the sunlight into a sparkling web. Then she bounced up and down, pointed her arms straight up and plummeted into the lake.

She struggled up through the icy depths and spat out air and water. For a few minutes she thrust vigorously away from land. Once she was used to the temperature, she swam back slowly, staring at the way her limbs looked green below the surface of the water. She ducked her head under and twisted and somersaulted like an otter. Swimming at an indoor pool in the winter could never match this.

Seizing her towel, Norah scrubbed warmth back into her tingling skin. This afternoon the water would be warmer; she wondered if she could still make it to Little Island and back. When she'd first come to Canada, she'd barely been able to swim. The sea at Grandad's, where she'd spent almost every summer in England, had been too rough to do much but paddle. But now she was as good as Bob and Alec. She sighed, missing them. She wouldn't be able to have races with Janet and Clare, who were both good swimmers but lazy.

"I bet it was cold," yawned Flo, as Norah rushed back into the Girls' Dorm to change.

Norah grinned as she tugged off her bathing suit and flung on her clothes. "Not for me! Maybe for sissy Canadians..." Everyone leapt out of bed and began a pillow fight. This was more like old times: larking around, not mooning about boys.

When the breakfast gong sounded, Norah left the others to get dressed. She sped up the hill to the cottage and was the first one to sit down at the children's table.

"Hungry, are you?" Hanny came out from the kitchen, set a bowl of oatmeal in front of Norah and sat down beside her with her cup of tea. "I've missed my good eater. The other girls are always on diets, except for Janet. And she should be!"

Norah began to tell Hanny about the trip to Vancouver. Their peaceful conversation was interrupted by Aunt Dorothy hurrying in. Meals at Gairloch were usually in shifts. The children ate first and the adults wandered in as they were finishing; all except Aunt Florence and old Aunt Catherine, who had breakfast in bed. Each of the other aunts took turns coming down early to help Hanny.

In a few minutes the long table was crowded with eight children. Sunlight streamed through the windows that spanned three walls of the dining room. Norah helped herself to a fourth piece of toast and spread it thickly with Hanny's "Muskoka Jam"—a delicious combination of wild blueberries and raspberries. Since food was rationed in Canada now, they had bacon once a week instead of every morning and were only allowed to put butter on one piece of toast. Norah preferred jam anyway; the butter tasted weird because Hanny stretched it with gelatin and evaporated milk.

She knew it was much worse in England. Her parents

wrote that they ate tasteless grey government bread, only got a meagre amount of meat and butter each week, and never saw oranges or bananas. Even though the Ogilvies regularly sent food and clothing parcels to her family, Norah often felt guilty, knowing she was so much better fed and dressed.

Lately she'd been feeling guilty for another reason. It wasn't just the war that made her real family different. Her Canadian family was *wealthy*. Norah had never known, before she came here, anyone who had an enormous house in the city, one just as big for the holidays, and a boathouse that would hold her own house in England. Or a private telephone and a refrigerator and a car, and new, store-bought clothes as soon as you outgrew your old ones. Gavin had so many toys he regularly gave them away to "Bundles for Britain." Norah had a fancy bicycle, skates and a toboggan, a closet full of expensive dresses and a whole bookcase full of her own books.

Of course not everyone in Canada had this plenty. Her friend Bernard wore patched clothes and lived in a cramped apartment. And she'd heard people on the train to Vancouver complain about not having homes at all.

It wasn't right, that some people had too much and some not enough. The trouble was—and this always made Norah squirm—she *enjoyed* the luxuries she now had: the food, the books, her own room and above all, Gairloch.

Norah sighed and took another piece of toast. What was the point of feeling guilty for something that wasn't her fault? She hadn't wanted to come to Canada in the first place; but since she was here, she decided, she might as well appreciate all of this while she still had it.

"What time is Andrew coming?" Janet asked her mother.

"Late afternoon," said Aunt Dorothy. "Some of you can go in the launch when Mr Hancock picks him up at the train."

"Is he going to sleep in the Boys' Dorm?" asked Peter. "There's lots of room."

"No, Peter, Andrew's too old to sleep with you. Florence said he could use the other cabin, since no one's there this month. And you little boys are not to disturb him. We want him to have a good rest before he starts classes."

Hanny brought Aunt Dorothy her tea. "I've made his favourite dessert for tonight. He was always fond of my snow pudding. It'll be just like the old days to have Andrew here again."

"Remember when he swam all the way around the island?" said Clare.

"He was the first person to do it since Hugh," said Flo proudly.

Norah glanced at Gavin, who was eating quietly. Once again the two of them were being left out. Everyone talked about this Andrew as if he were some kind of hero.

Aunt Anne and Uncle Gerald came into the cottage with the two youngest cousins, George and Denny.

"Mummy," said Sally immediately, as Aunt Anne tied on her brothers' bibs. "Can I sleep in the Boys' Dorm instead of the boathouse?"

Aunt Anne looked worried. "But why, Sally? You begged and begged to sleep with the girls instead of us, and you've only been out there for one night—don't you like it?"

"No," said Sally bluntly. "They're too noisy—especially Clare. They keep me awake and all they talk about is *love.* Why can't I sleep with Gavin and Peter and Ross?"

Gavin smiled at her; Sally was his best friend in the summers. "Please, can she, Aunt Anne?" he asked shyly. "*We* won't keep her awake, I promise."

"Well, perhaps it makes more sense to have all the younger ones together," said Aunt Anne. "But it's never been done before—the boys and girls have always slept separately. Why don't you just come back to the cabin, Sally?"

"No!" protested Sally. "You said I was old enough to sleep on my own! But I'd rather be with my *friends.*"

"I suppose it would be all right," said her mother. "I'll have to ask Aunt Florence, then we'll see."

Norah sighed; all this fuss over a simple change in routine. Of course Sally should sleep with the younger cousins. It seemed so ridiculous to have to get Aunt Florence's approval, but Aunt Anne, the youngest and most timid in-law, had always been frightened of her.

Norah turned to Aunt Anne's husband, placidly eating his porridge. "Uncle Gerald, could you test me on the boat so I can use it by myself?"

"Glad to," he murmured through a mouthful. "Why don't you meet me on the dock in an hour?"

"Why, Norah, I'd forgotten you were thirteen!" Aunt Dorothy gazed at Norah, and at her daughters and Clare, with misty eyes. "You're all growing up much too fast."

More Elders began to fill the dining room. They all kissed their own children.

"How's my princess?" asked Uncle Barclay, leaning over Janet. She pulled on his moustache and giggled. Norah bent her head to hide her envy. In Canada she had plenty of mothers—almost too many—but no one could match the close relationship she'd had with her father.

Then Aunt Mary came in and kissed her and Gavin. This is the *kissiest* family, Norah thought impatiently.

"Norah, could you take up Miss Ogilvie's breakfast?" Hanny asked.

Glad to escape, she carefully ascended the stairs with the heavy tray. "Aunt Catherine," she said softly when she reached her door.

"Come in, dear," called a deep, hoarse voice. Aunt Catherine, the oldest person at Gairloch, was sitting up in bed with a book.

"It's Norah this morning—how pleasant! Sit down and talk to me while I eat."

Norah sat cross-legged on the bedspread, leaning against the white iron footboard. Tiny Aunt Catherine always looked so comical in bed. She wore round glasses and a pink nightcap, and her sharp eyes peered out from its flounces as if she were Red Riding Hood's grandmother.

Aunt Catherine was Norah's next favourite after Aunt Mary. She and Norah were both outsiders; the old woman was Aunt Florence's late husband's elder sister, so she wasn't related to the rest of the family. She had never married and Norah thought she'd had a much more interesting life than any of the other aunts. She had grown up in Glasgow and taught for years in a Scottish girls' school. After she'd retired she had travelled all over the world before she settled with her niece in Ottawa. She was the only grown-up Norah had ever met who confided in her as if there were no age difference between them.

Aunt Catherine still had traces of a British accent; that was another bond between them. Unlike Gavin, Norah had never completely lost her accent—she held onto it on purpose, determined not to lose that last link with home.

"Well, Norah, are you glad to be back?" the old woman asked.

"Oh, *yes!* I hated missing July!"

"I don't blame you. But I think it was a good idea of Florence's to show you and Gavin some of the rest of Canada. You don't want to go back to England only knowing Ontario. Did you read any good books while you were away?"

Aunt Catherine always asked *important* questions, not

"Did you have a good time?" like all the others. Norah chatted to her about *The Three Musketeers.* Immersing herself in it last month had been the only way she could escape from Aunt Florence.

"I have a book here you might like," said Aunt Catherine. "I think you're old enough for it now. I loved it when I was your age, perhaps because the heroine's name is Catherine! It's called *Wuthering Heights.* Look in my bookcase—that green volume on the right."

Norah found *Wuthering Heights* and brought it back to the bed, examining it doubtfully. The print was small and the cover plain. She flipped through the pages and her eyes caught the words "Whatever our souls are made of, his and mine are the same..."

"This isn't about love or anything like that, is it?" she asked suspiciously.

"Oh, Norah," laughed Aunt Catherine. "You are a one. It's *all* about love. Put it back and wait until next summer."

"I have a new Angela Brazil book to read, anyhow," said Norah. "Aunt Mary bought it for me. And there are lots of Agatha Christies in the living room."

"Then you'll be fine. Doesn't it make you feel *safe* to know you have enough to read? If I didn't always have a book waiting, I'd panic."

She put down her teacup and looked out the window. "What a perfect day for Andrew to arrive. Have you ever met him?"

Norah shook her head impatiently. Even Aunt Catherine was going to spoil her first day back with talk about this intruder.

Gavin appeared at the door. "Norah, Aunt Florence would like to see you." He must have already taken up her tray and had his usual morning visit with her.

Norah frowned. What could Aunt Florence want? It was almost time to meet Uncle Gerald at the dock. She left Gavin in her place, earnestly telling Aunt Catherine how Creature had nearly been left behind in Vancouver.

Aunt Florence's room was at the end of the long hall that had seven bedrooms off it. Norah knocked at her door.

"Come in, Norah." She was dressed perfectly and elegantly as usual, even though she was still in bed; her pink satin nightgown and matching dressing gown added to her queenly air. Every silver curl of her hair was in place.

Norah went over and pecked her cheek. Then she glanced meaningfully at the blue and green brightness beyond the window.

"Yes, I know you want to get outside, but it won't go away. Sit down, please, Norah. I promise I won't keep you long, but there's something I have to tell you."

Norah tried to control her sigh. She pulled over a chair—you never sat on Aunt Florence's bed—and waited. Then her heart lurched: had something happened at home?

"Is it—is it bad news?" she whispered.

"Oh *no*, Norah dear—I'm so sorry if I scared you!" Aunt Florence leaned over and patted her knee. "No bad news, nothing at all like that. This is something your mother wanted me to tell you and I'm afraid I've put it off. It's a matter that really only your mother *should* talk to you about. But she didn't want to do it in a letter, so she wrote and asked me to. I should have brought it up earlier but I keep forgetting how fast you're growing..."

Norah scuffed her feet. Uncle Gerald was probably waiting for her by now. What was her guardian going on about in such a roundabout way?

"What it is..." Aunt Florence looked hopeful. "Perhaps

Flo and the others have already mentioned it, or you've read about it in one of the magazines you girls read."

Mentioned *what?* Norah never read the boring magazines that Clare always had around. She shook her head.

"Well, then, I'll have to explain. It's something that happens to you when you're around thirteen—although Mary didn't get it until she was fifteen. It happens to everyone every woman, that is—and we just have to put up with it." Aunt Florence took a deep breath and then her rich voice took on a storytelling quality. "Every girl and every woman has a little room inside of her. As the month goes by the little room gets untidy, and then a little visitor comes and sweeps it out clean. Then it becomes untidy again until the visitor comes again the next month. Now when *your* little visitor comes—and it might not even be this summer, but it will probably be this year—you *will* come and tell me so I can get you equipped, all right? I've brought all you need with me, just in case."

Norah just gaped at her. Then, because Aunt Florence seemed to expect an answer, she nodded.

"*That's* all right, then. I'll write to your mother and tell her I've prepared you. Run along now—you can take my tray with you."

Norah carried the tray down to the kitchen, then escaped outside. Aunt Florence was *nuts!* What on earth had she been talking about? Perhaps this was some weird Ogilvie or Drummond or Canadian fairy tale. Really, this family was very *odd* sometimes.

She forgot Aunt Florence's strange talk in her glee at being pronounced an expert boat-handler by Uncle Gerald. He went out with Norah in the *Putt-Putt* and made sure she knew how to start and stop the engine and how to fill it with gas. Then he reviewed the safety rules and watched as she drove the boat around Little Island all by herself.

"Well done!" he smiled. Norah asked permission to go out alone again and she spent a blissful half-hour driving to Ford's Bay and back. Whenever she passed another boat, she carefully took one hand off the steering wheel and waved.

Then she went out again with Janet and Bosley. The spaniel's ears streamed backwards as he perched happily on the bow. They landed on Little Island and explored every inch of it. Then they flopped down on the narrow shore, their heads resting on a mossy log and their feet in the water. Bosley leapt around them, chasing dragonflies.

"We should have brought a picnic," complained Janet. "I can't last much longer without something to eat. Norah . . . do you think I'm fat?"

Norah turned her head and examined her friend. She couldn't say Janet *wasn't* fat—she was fatter than ever. But she didn't want to hurt her feelings.

"Well . . ." she began.

"I'm fat," sighed Janet. "You're so lucky, Norah. You eat as much as I do and you *never* gain weight."

"But I'm too *thin,*" said Norah. She squinted at a gull soaring against the dazzling blue sky. Fat or thin—what did it matter on such a glorious day? The sun seeped into every pore on her body. Apart from feeling hungry herself, there was nothing she wanted to do except lie here in perfect peace. *This* was what she'd been waiting for all July.

"In a few hours Andrew will be here!" said Janet. "You'll really like him, Norah."

Andrew again! Norah scowled. "How do you *know* I will?"

"Everybody likes Andrew."

When Norah didn't reply, Janet changed the subject. "Don't you have a crush on anyone? Like a movie star or someone? You can share Frankie if you want," she added generously.

"No, I don't!" said Norah crossly. "I don't have to have a crush, you know. It's not a *rule.*"

"Well, you don't have to get so mad." Janet sat up and splashed water over her sunburnt legs. "Sometimes I really feel the gap in our ages, Norah. Fourteen is a *lot* different from thirteen."

Norah jumped up and tramped into the trees. She and Janet often quarrelled and it never lasted long, but she wished they hadn't on their first day. She found the tree fort that they had made with Bob and Alec last summer and climbed up to the platform.

I am a lonely shipwrecked sailor, she told herself. My throat is parched and all I have to eat is a few berries...

But she couldn't make it real. That comforting imaginary world of pilots and cowboys and shipwrecked sailors, which she had been able to step into easily for years, suddenly seemed closed to her.

Her stomach rumbled and she started to descend, but the foothold they had nailed to the tree trunk crumbled under her foot. "Oh, *swell,*" groaned Norah, pulling herself up to the platform again.

"Help!" she called in mock anguish. "Help me, fair sir! I'm stuck in this tree and a dragon is coming!"

Janet rushed through the woods and they couldn't stop laughing as she helped Norah down, Bosley barking and jumping around them. All the way back to Gairloch they made each other start up again, as they kept on pretending to pretend.

After lunch Norah read for a while on her rock, until she got too hot. Then she wandered down to feel the water, wondering whether an hour had passed since she had eaten and it would be safe to swim without getting cramps.

Aunt Mary was standing on the dock, all dressed up in a print dress and a yellow straw hat. Her hair, usually rolled into a tight knot, was in loose waves around her face. "Oh, Norah, I was looking for you. Gerald told me you passed your test with flying colours. Would you take me over to the mainland? Mr Hancock has to pick up Andrew later and I need to go to Port Schofield."

"Sure!" They settled themselves in the *Putt-Putt* and Norah, flushed with importance, backed it carefully out of its slip. Flo and Janet and Clare were always driving the Elders somewhere; now she could too.

Aunt Mary sat in the bow beside her, clutching her hat. Her cheeks were pink and she looked unusually animated.

"Why are you going to Port Schofield?" Norah asked. "Should I wait for you? Then I could take you back."

"Um... I think it would be best if I went alone, Norah. I have an appointment that might take a long time, and you'll want to be there when Andrew arrives. I'll be finished before dinner—could you come and pick me up at five-thirty?"

She waved goodbye from the dock and hurried away. Norah wondered why she didn't carry her usual shopping basket.

On the way back she went as fast as she dared, bouncing the launch on the waves and getting drenched. She slowed down sedately when she was within view of the island. Gavin, Sally, Peter and Ross were sitting in a row on the dock, each dangling a line in the water.

"Look at all the bass we've caught, Norah!" Gavin showed her a pail full of flopping silver fish.

Norah fetched a fishing pole from the boathouse and joined them. They caught four more bass, cleaned them in the lake and took them up to Hanny to put in the icehouse. Then they all went swimming. The water was so warm now that they stayed in until the tips of their fingers became wrinkled.

"This summer we're being detectives," Gavin told Norah as they baked on their towels in the burning sun. "We have an agency called 'The Fearless Four.'"

"We'll solve *anything*," said Sally. "No case is too difficult."

"Peter and I got a fingerprinting set for Christmas last year," said Ross.

"And I borrowed Aunt Florence's magnifying glass," said Gavin.

"So what case are you solving right now?" asked Norah lazily.

"We haven't actually *begun* yet," Gavin told her. "We're getting prepared, though. Tonight we're going to take everyone's fingerprints, so we'll have them on record."

"Our headquarters are in the playhouse," said Peter. "No one else seems to be using it this year," he added defensively. Last summer the younger cousins had been banned from the playhouse by the Hornets.

Gavin looked worried. "Is that all right, Norah? We've already moved some stuff in there."

"Go ahead and use it," Norah told them.

"Thanks!" said Sally. "If you want anything solved, just come and see us there."

Norah promised she would. She'd never thought of playing detective herself. Now it was too late.

At two-thirty Mr Hancock, Flo and Janet took off in the *Florence* to pick up Andrew in Port Clarkson. Two hours later most of the clan were on the dock waiting for them to come back. Norah hadn't intended to meet him with the others, but curiosity kept her there.

"He's here! Andrew! Andrew!" screamed Clare, waving both arms.

"For heaven's sake, Clare, control yourself!" Aunt Mar told her daughter. But Clare shrieked even louder when the launch drew up to the dock. A tall boy stepped out, laughing as he pushed away Clare's attacking arms.

"My dear boy, how wonderful to have you back with us." Everyone let Aunt Florence greet him next, then they all descended upon him. Andrew didn't seem to mind. He shook hands with his uncles and kissed his aunts' cheeks, his deep laugh rising above the babble.

He acts like he's a prince or someone, Norah thought.

"You've never met our war guests, have you?" said Aunt Florence. Norah scanned Andrew's face warily as she and Gavin were introduced. He had slicked-back, wavy brown hair, a wide mouth and long grey eyes that curled up at the edges and made him look as if he were always smiling. Norah frowned. Anyone this good-looking was bound to be conceited.

Andrew focused his smile on her and said quietly, "How are you, Norah? I've heard a lot about you. Do you feel like a Canadian now that you've been here for so long?"

How dare he ask something so personal! He'd only just met her! And he acted so condescending, as if he felt sorry for her. Norah didn't answer. She moved away as Andrew, hemmed in by his relatives, was practically carried up to the cottage.

Norah stayed down at the dock with her book until it was time to pick up Aunt Mary, trying not to hear the whoops of laughter from above. Her first day back had turned sour. And the rest of the summer was going to be terrible if all this fuss over Andrew continued. But maybe he wouldn't stay long.

"Has he come?" asked Aunt Mary as soon as Norah landed at the Port Schofield dock. Norah nodded curtly.

"Isn't he nice? Do you like him? I think there's something really special about Andrew."

Norah kept her face straight ahead, trying to conceal her scowl.

IV
ANDREW

After the children's dinner Norah took out the canoe. The steady pull of the paddle soothed her jangled feelings and she pretended she was the only person on the lake. But just as she came back around the corner of Little Island she heard Gavin calling her. Every evening the whole family had to gather in the living room for games and reading aloud.

Gavin waited while Norah lifted up the canoe. "Did you know Andrew once caught a lake trout that was as big as *Denny?*" he told her.

"That's impossible," snapped Norah.

She lingered in the doorway of the living room, looking for Andrew so she could sit as far away from him as possible. He was on one side of the fireplace, Denny on his lap and the rest of the cousins as close to him as they could get. Gavin skipped over to join them.

Aunt Bea leaned towards Andrew, an eager look on her foolish face. "Now tell us about your mother. Is she over that dreadful flu?"

"It wasn't flu, it was a cold," said Aunt Florence.

"It was flu!" cried Aunt Bea, her hair falling out of its pins. "She told us in her last letter!"

"It was a cold," Aunt Florence repeated firmly. "You know you never read letters properly, Bea—you must make up things you *think* you've read."

"I certainly do not!"

"Now, now, you two," interrupted Uncle Reg. "Why don't you ask Andrew? Surely *he* knows."

Andrew had been throwing amused glances at Flo. "I think it was . . . a kind of flu-y cold," he said carefully. "And she's fine now."

"Do you want to come sailing with Gerald and me tomorrow, Andrew?" Flo asked him.

"Sure! I wonder if I remember how. But you two are such experts, you can show me what to do."

"Can I come?" Clare asked.

"And me?" said Janet and Peter at the same time.

"We'll let Andrew get used to the boat again, then you can each have a turn," said Uncle Gerald.

Andrew glanced all the way across the room at Norah, who had been staring at him. She quickly lowered her eyes.

"Do you like sailing, Norah?"

"Not much," she shrugged.

"But you *love* sailing!" Gavin gave his sister a puzzled look, then said to Andrew, "I like sailing and I don't take up very much room."

Andrew laughed. "Then you can be our first passenger."

"Tell us about university," said Uncle Gerald. "You're taking COTC classes along with your regular engineering course, right? How soon can you be an officer?"

"In a few years," said Andrew.

"I certainly envy you. If it wasn't for these darned eyes . . ."

"It must have been frustrating for you, being turned down," said Andrew quietly.

"Well I'm certainly kept busy. It was difficult to take this month off."

"Did you know Gerald left his law firm to be an aircraft assembly inspector, Andrew?" said Aunt Bea proudly.

"But it's not the real thing," said Uncle Gerald. He fingered the small button he always wore on his lapel. "And even if they gave me this, people don't realize that I was turned down. You should hear some of the comments I get, from complete strangers!"

Norah had never seen his placid face look so agitated. Aunt Anne took his arm. "Never mind about them. *We* know you would be fighting if you could."

"If I was young, I wouldn't go on any officer training scheme," said Uncle Barclay gruffly. "I'd join up now! After all, with the Russian victory and the Americans finally in on it, the tide's beginning to turn. You may not even get over there, Andrew."

Aunt Dorothy gave her husband a horrified look. "Oh no, Barclay! Andrew's only nineteen—he's too young to go now." She shuddered. "It will be a blessing if he doesn't have to at all—and I'm glad you couldn't, Gerald."

"I was nineteen," Uncle Barclay reminded her.

The colour had left Andrew's cheeks, and a muscle twitched in one of them. "Perhaps you're right, Uncle Barclay," he said slowly. "But Mother is determined that I become an officer."

"She's perfectly right," said Aunt Florence briskly. "There's no reason you should join up as a common soldier. But let's have no more depressing talk about the war. Tell us what your family has been up to, Andrew."

Norah had joined Janet in a game of cribbage. She tried to shut her ears to Andrew, but he was such a good storyteller she couldn't help listening. He was describing his mother's new volunteer work driving an ambulance. Every time Norah stole a glance at him she noticed how his long hands gesticulated every word: pointing, turning and slicing through the air as if he were conducting music.

"You're not paying attention, Norah!" complained Janet. "I said go!"

Before the younger children were sent to bed, Aunt Florence took out her book. This week it was *The Wind in the Willows.* Norah had to admit that Aunt Florence was the best reader she'd ever heard. She sank into the story with relief. Andrew was also listening intently, a delighted smile on his face.

"Bravo for Toad!" he cried at the end of the chapter. "I remember you reading that when I was about six, Aunt Florence."

Andrew got down on the floor, held up his arms as if clutching a steering wheel, and stuck his legs straight out in front of him. "Poop-poop!" he muttered faintly. "Poop-poop!" The younger cousins collapsed with giggles.

"My dear boy," said Aunt Florence. "I'd forgotten what a good actor you are."

"Are you doing many plays?" Aunt Catherine asked.

"As many as I can!" said Andrew. "I was Prince Henry in our college production of *Henry IV* this year."

He stood up and looked at them silently for a second, his graceful body suddenly regal. His cheek twitched again and, when he spoke, his words were both disdainful and wistful:

> Yet herein will I imitate the sun,
> Who doth permit the base contagious clouds
> To smother up his beauty from the world,
> That, when he please again to be himself,
> Being wanted, he may be more wonder'd at...

He stopped abruptly, his face flushed. All the family applauded at how easily he had changed from being a conceited toad to a courtly prince.

All except Norah. *Show-off,* she muttered under her breath.

"Haven't they come back from sailing yet?" Janet asked the next morning. She and Clare and Norah were doing their laundry together at the back of the cottage.

Norah didn't answer. She concentrated on scrubbing her blouse against the ripply metal of the scrub-board. This was the only part of being at Gairloch that she disliked. Each of the older girls had to do her own laundry, which meant heating up water, rubbing until your hands ached, and wringing out each piece of clothing to hang up in the sun.

"It's my turn to go in the boat next," said Clare. She shaded her eyes as she gazed out over the lake, then turned to Janet. "Wasn't it awful when your dad said Andrew should be a soldier right now?"

"He couldn't help it," retorted Janet. "That's just the way Dad is. All he ever talks about is the First World War and this one."

"I think Uncle Barclay was right," said Norah. The other two stopped washing and looked at her with astonishment.

"What do you mean?" said Clare coldly.

"I mean, I think Andrew *should* join up now. He's probably just trying to avoid it by going to university. I think he's a coward."

"He's not!" Clare flicked some of her soapy water at Norah. "You have no right to say that about one of our relatives!"

Resisting the urge to dump her whole pail of dirty water over Clare, Norah bent her head down and resumed scrubbing. "I can say what I want," she muttered. "He's not *my* relative. You all treat Andrew as if he was royalty or something."

"Why—you—" But then Clare spotted the sail and ran down the steps.

"You haven't finished your laundry!" Janet called after her. "Now I'll have to do it for her," she grumbled.

Norah could have cried with frustration at being forced into a stupid confrontation with Clare. But she prided herself on *never* crying; she had done too much of it in her first few months in Canada.

Why had she said that about Andrew? The words had rushed out before she'd known if she meant them.

"You're wrong about Andrew," mumbled Janet through a mouthful of clothes-pins. "Why did you say such a mean thing? He hasn't done anything to you. And he's so nice!"

"I don't know," said Norah miserably. "I just—don't—*like* him!" Then she ran away too, leaving Janet to hang up all the clothes by herself.

Norah headed towards her rock, but on the way she almost collided with Flo.

"I was just looking for you, Norah," said the older girl. "Andrew and I picked up the mail. Here's a letter from England for you!"

Norah clutched the letter as she ran up to her lookout. As always, she took a steadying breath before daring to open it. Bad news usually comes in a telegram, not in a letter, she reminded herself. The envelope was a mess; it had been ripped open and resealed by the censor, and the layers of labels showed how many times it had been used. She squinted in the glaring sun and read.

Dear Norah and Gavin,

Congratulations to both of you on your excellent marks in school! Dad and I are so proud of you. We can't believe you are old enough to be going into "grade four" and "grade eight" this fall. When you are back in England you'll find it strange to say "form" instead of grade.

I must tell you all about Muriel's wedding. Of course we couldn't do anything fancy, but we had a very good time all the same. Muriel and Barry were only able to get a few days' leave, but Barry's mother came all the way from Devon and Tibby managed to get down from Reading for the day to be bridesmaid. After the church ceremony we had a small celebration at the house for just the family. I saved my sugar rations for weeks and the hens have been laying well, so I was able to make a small cake. You never would have guessed I used marge instead of butter. Of course I couldn't ice it, but Tibby put a bunch of sweet peas on top and they looked lovely. Grandad somehow managed to get a bottle of wine and we all drank a toast to the two of you as well as to the bride and groom. Muriel looked beautiful in her pink suit. She cut it out of that old coat of mine. Barry was very handsome in his uniform. He's such a nice boy, I'm sure you'll like him. Muriel promises to send you a snap of him soon.

After our little party we all went off to the dance in the village hall. A lot of American GIS were there and they had everyone doing the jitterbug! Even Dad and I tried it but it wore us out. Grandad *wanted* to try but I wouldn't let him. As usual he forgets his age.

Yesterday, while I was waiting in the fish queue, I stood next to Mrs Brown. She said she's having a hard time keeping Joey away from the Americans when they come into the village. He and all the other children run up to them asking "Any gum, chum?" Usually they get some! The village is divided in its feelings about the Americans. Some people, including Grandad, think they're too boastful, but Dad and I find them pleasant and friendly. And after all, look what they're doing for us!

Our pig club has a new pig! So I'm saving scraps for it and Grandad takes them to the pig every evening. He stays and talks to it as if it's a person! It's getting nice and plump and I'm sure it will be as delicious as the last one.

I wrote to Mrs Ogilvie to thank her for her last parcel, but I'd like to thank both of you as well. I'm sure you helped to pick out the things. You've no idea how grateful we are. The soap was especially appreciated—it's so hard to find. What kind people they are.

Norah, I also wrote to Mrs Ogilvie and asked her to tell you about a very important matter. I hope she does so soon. It's too personal for a letter.

By the time you get this you will be back from your trip across Canada and enjoying Gairloch again. What lucky children you are! Dad says he hopes you each kept a journal. We are looking forward to hearing about it and so is everyone else in the village. Even after three years, someone asks about you every day.

I must stop this now and dig up some potatoes for dinner. Muriel has introduced me to slacks! They're so comfortable around the house and do save on stockings.

We all send our very best wishes and hope as usual that it won't be too long before you come back to us.

Love from us all,
Mum

Norah thumped the letter so hard against the ground that she grazed her fist.

Their school marks were such old news; why did the mail have to take so long each way? What did Mum ask Aunt Florence to tell her? Surely not the crazy story she *had* told her. Why hadn't she thought of keeping a journal?

Why did Muriel have to *change*? Norah had completely forgotten that her oldest sister was getting married.

Poor Mum, scrimping so much just to make a cake. Norah could always sense the weariness behind her cheerful words.

What if something had happened to them that they weren't telling her about? Why should she and Gavin be safe in Canada when her family was always in danger?

If only she could *be* there, playing cricket with Dad and helping Mum with the chickens. If only she could tell them how much she loved them, but somehow she never could say that in her own letters.

Gradually Norah got control of her racing emotions. After all, she should be used to these letters by now.

She would read the letter to Gavin and answer it tonight; she always liked to get that done before Aunt Florence reminded her, so that she could say smugly, "I've already written it." But it was going to be especially hard to be cheerful in this one. She couldn't say, "Dear Mum, Dad and Grandad… At first it was wonderful to get back to Gairloch but a boy has come who has spoiled everything."

Late that afternoon Andrew came up the verandah steps as Norah and Gavin were sitting on them and talking about the letter. "Is your family well?" he asked.

"Uh huh," said Gavin. "My big sister got married!"

"You must miss them very much," said Andrew quietly.

Mr Hancock came out to the verandah and sounded the dinner gong. "Come on, Gavin," Norah said, taking his hand. "Let's go in."

But Gavin called back, "Hey, Andrew—any gum, chum?"

V
ON THE LAKE

Norah sat reading her Agatha Christie mystery on the verandah, curled up in an ancient chair with a canopy over it—the family called it a "glider." Besides her rock, the glider was her next favourite retreat at Gairloch. The verandah was like another room, a neutral zone between the cottage and outdoors. Swinging gently on the creaking chains, she could keep an ear open to whatever was going on inside, and watch all the comings and goings without being too suffocated by the clan. The lacy screen of trees beyond the verandah always made her feel secure, as if she were in an airy cave.

But this afternoon she couldn't concentrate on *The Murder of Roger Ackroyd.* The verandah was dotted with other members of the family. From around one corner drifted the usual flow of gossip.

"But what was *her* name?" Aunt Dorothy was asking.

"Wasn't she a Ferguson? The Manitoba Fergusons, not the Ontario ones. Her mother would have been a Baxter," pronounced Aunt Florence. The aunts seemed to know the last names of everyone in all of Canada.

The strains of one of Uncle Reg's Gilbert and Sullivan records floated from around the other corner: " . . . and his *sisters* and his *cousins* and his *sisters* and his *cousins* and his *aunts!*" Uncle Reg would be stretched out as usual on a chaise longue, close enough to his phonograph to reach over and wind it up.

Aunt Catherine was sitting in a rocking chair not far from Norah, her tiny foot bobbing to the music and her nose in a book. She'd given Norah a friendly wave when she first sat down, but *she* understood that people didn't want to be disturbed when they were reading.

Norah had watched Aunt Bea and Aunt Mar set out for the gazebo, carrying a basket, a kettle and a spirit-lamp. She knew Aunt Anne was at the babies' beach with George and Denny. Now she saw Aunt Mary, again dressed up, descend the steps to the dock. Flo came out of the Girls' Dorm and they both got into the *Putt-Putt* and drove away. Once again Aunt Mary had no shopping bag.

Norah watched the launch disappear, then looked for the sail. By now Andrew and Uncle Gerald, or he and Flo, had taken all the cousins out in the sailboat—everyone but Norah.

Gavin was right—she loved sailing. Two summers ago she and Janet rigged up the rowboat with an improvised sail made out of an old sheet and pretended it was the *Swallow*, from one of Norah's favourite books. But the rowboat was too heavy to move very fast without oars.

They were only allowed to go out in the sailboat when Uncle Gerald or Uncle Peter, Clare's father, was here. But the two youngest uncles were never able to come to Gairloch for long and the other two didn't like sailing.

Now Norah watched Andrew and Uncle Gerald tack as they approached the dock. Gavin and Sally were crouched between them. Norah wanted to be in the boat so much she could feel the jibsheet between her hands.

But she wouldn't ask—not Andrew. She swung the glider violently until its creaking almost drowned out Uncle Reg's record.

"Norah!" Gavin had rushed up the hill to the verandah.

He always knew where to find his sister. He climbed into the glider beside her, his cheeks flushed and his fair hair in a tangle. "Did you see me out there? It was swell! We went really fast and I leaned right over the water—that's called 'hiking.' Sally almost forgot to duck when Uncle Gerald gybed. Do you know what gybing is?"

"Of course I do," sighed Norah.

"Andrew sent me to find you," continued Gavin. "He wants to know if you want a turn next. This will be their last sail today."

Despite the reluctance in her mind, Norah's feet seemed to stroll down to the dock on their own. She tried not to let her face show how much she wanted to get into the boat.

"There you are, Norah!" Andrew was sitting in the stern. "You're certainly hard to find. Every time we tried to give you a turn you'd disappeared."

"Want to come now?" Uncle Gerald asked her.

"Yes, please." Norah looked only at Uncle Gerald as she answered. With him along, she could ignore Andrew. She put on a life-jacket and stepped into the *Christina.* The boat's canvas sails crackled in the breeze, as if it were impatient at having to stand still.

"Gerald!" Aunt Anne came hurrying down the steps, Denny in her arms. "Will you come and cope with George? I've left him screaming in the cabin. He says you promised to take him fishing right after lunch and he *won't* mind me. You have to come."

Uncle Gerald frowned. "But we were just about to take Norah for a sail. Can't he wait an hour?"

"You know how worked up he gets. Please, Gerald—I can't do a thing with him!"

"Georgie's screamin' real loud," said Denny with satisfaction. They could all hear the faint, enraged cry: "*Daddy . . .*"

"All right . . ." Uncle Gerald stepped out of the boat. "Norah's used to sailing, Andrew, and you're doing fine. I think the two of you will be all right on your own." He hurried up to the cabin.

"Let's get going!" said Andrew. He handed Norah the jibsheet and took hold of the mainsheet and the tiller. "Cast us off, Gavin."

Norah thought of leaping from the boat but it was too late. Gavin untied the painter and she had to catch it. Then he pushed away the bow and in an instant she was out on the lake, trapped with Andrew.

Frantically Norah tried to remember her duties as crew: pulling in the fluttering jibsail and setting it to the same angle as the mainsail. She clutched the rope so tightly, her bones showed through her knuckles. If she had to be in the boat with Andrew, at least she would show him she knew how to sail.

They were going to be too busy to have a conversation. Andrew's only words came every few minutes: "Ready about . . . tacking." At first the two of them moved awkwardly, stumbling over each other's legs; but soon they synchronized their movements and shifted from one side of the boat to the other as one person. The *Christina* skimmed the water like a gull, the wake curling behind. No motor noise jarred the ride, just the vibration of the wind against the taut sails. Norah gazed up the mast, which seemed to pierce the bright sky. Then they hiked out to flatten the boat and she leaned far over the water, her hair whipping backwards and spray flying into her mouth. She let her mind fill with the joy of sailing, and pretended there was no one in the boat but her.

Finally Andrew, shaking the water out of his hair, grinned at her. "I hate to end this, but I think we'll have to go back. I missed lunch and I'm ravenous! Get ready to gybe." He reversed the tiller and hauled in the mainsheet. "Boom over..."

Norah ducked her head as the boom swung across. Now the two sails billowed out on either side and the *Christina* became a sedate swan swimming for shore.

Andrew pulled up the centreboard and told Norah to move back. She perched on one side so she'd be as far away from him as possible. She tried to keep watching the jib, but there wasn't much need to concentrate on it now that they were moving more slowly.

Andrew stretched out his long legs and leaned against the stern. "You're a good sailor, Norah. Did you learn in England?"

Why did he always have to look right into her face when he talked to her? Norah's words came out in hard, painful chunks. "Oh, no. *My* family doesn't own any boats. I learned here. Uncle Gerald taught me. And Uncle Peter."

"I learned at Gairloch, too. My dad taught me—my first dad, that is. But my stepfather doesn't like sailing. He gets seasick!"

Norah wondered if he liked his stepfather and how he had felt when his mother married again. But if she asked him that he might ask *her* more questions.

It was so difficult to remain aloof when they were sharing something so enjoyable. Norah trailed one hand in the warm water. Perhaps—just for this trip—she would let herself forget about how much he bothered her.

"Your little brother is a real character," chuckled Andrew. "He told us that his elephant—what does he call it—Creature?—should have a life-jacket too, in case he fell in. He must have been very young when he left England."

"He was five," said Norah. "That's the youngest age you

could come over on the overseas evacuation plan." For a surprised second she wondered if her parents would have sent her alone if Gavin had been only four.

"At least you had each other," said Andrew, as if he were reading her thoughts. "And did you really not know who you'd be living with? Aunt Florence said you were *assigned* to her!"

"No, we didn't know. We waited for a week at the university before we found out."

"I'm not sure *I'd* like to have Aunt Florence as my guardian," said Andrew. "Aunt Mary is a peach, but Aunt Florence has always reminded me of the Queen of Hearts in *Alice*—'Off with her head!' She read *Alice* to us the last summer I was here with my parents. That book sometimes reminds me of this whole family. A bit mad, don't you think?"

Norah nodded vigorously, remembering Aunt Florence's odd story about the little visitor. "Sometimes I just don't understand them! And Aunt Florence *is* hard to live with. She's so fussy!" Then, remembering as always that she was a guest in this country, Norah added dutifully, "But it was very kind of her to take us in. And sometimes she's funny. Last winter she took up tap dancing! They had lessons on the radio and she thought it would be good for her figure. Gavin and I used to spy on her. She looked *so* silly, bouncing around the dining room. But she gave up after two lessons—she said it was bad for her heart."

Andrew threw back his head and crowed with laughter. "Aunt Florence probably has a better heart than *I* have! She can be ridiculous, but there's something magnificent about her, too. I think my grandmother was terrified of her. Did you know this boat was named after her?"

"After who?"

"My grandmother. Christina. She was Aunt Florence's

younger sister, but she and my grandfather are both dead. She was my father's mother—and Aunt Dorothy's and Uncle Peter's."

"Oh." Sorting out the Drummonds was like doing a hard puzzle.

Andrew sighed. "My grandparents were easy to take, but I think my mother was glad to get away from the rest of the family when she married again. Yet there's something endearing about all of them, too. When I'm here I feel so... *safe.* As if nothing has changed and nothing else in the world—the war especially—exists. I guess that's why I have to come back once in a while. And of course the best part is this incredible lake—just look at it!"

Andrew let go of the tiller and flung his arms dramatically. The boom swung over without warning, the boat heeled—and Norah was tipped backwards into the water.

She heard herself yelp before she went under. But she bobbed up immediately like a cork, spluttering out a huge mouthful of the lake. The *Christina* was making a wide circle ahead of her as it turned back.

When the boat drew up beside her, Andrew leaned over and grabbed the back of her life-jacket. He fished her out, dripping and giggling. "Norah, are you all right? What a *stupid* thing to do—I'm so sorry!"

"I'm okay," gasped Norah. "I fell off before the boom could hit me. It was just such a surprise! But the water isn't cold at all. At least you righted the boat before it capsized."

"You're shivering! Here, take this off." Andrew helped her undo her sopping life-jacket, and rubbed her arms and legs. Then he took off his shirt and wrapped it tightly around her, his face full of concern. "Don't tell anyone about this, promise? Think of what Aunt Florence would say, nearly drowning her war guest! I still can't believe I did something so idiotic. Don't worry about the jib any more. Just sit up on the side and get some sun. We're almost there—I can see the dock. I only hope no one saw *us!*"

Norah kept shaking, but it wasn't from being cold. She turned away from Andrew so he couldn't see her face and struggled to get herself under control. With awe, she hugged his protecting shirt around her, still feeling the touch of his warm hands on her skin.

VI
SECRETS

Norah left Andrew without a word. Up in the boathouse she peeled off her wet clothes and put on dry ones, then hurried out again in a daze, not knowing where she was going.

"Can you help me?" Flo's words startled Norah. She was plodding down the steps, weighed down by Uncle Reg's phonograph. Norah ran up and grabbed one end of it.

"Where are you taking this?" she asked.

"To the boathouse!" said Flo triumphantly. "It's for us! The Elders have a new one—Mr Hancock just picked it up in Port Clarkson. Uncle Reg says this one sounds tinny, but I don't care. Now we can have music!"

Flo began setting up the phonograph on Sally's empty bed—the little girl had got her way and now slept in the Boys' Dorm. Janet and Clare rushed in, their arms full of records. "Where is it?" asked Clare. "Dibs on choosing first! I wondered when I'd get to play these—Uncle Reg was always hogging it."

She dropped her pile of records on the bed and flipped through them. "Put on this one—it's number one on the hit parade."

Frank Sinatra's smooth voice filled the space. The sound *was* tinny and the needle scratched, but having music made the boathouse even cosier. Each of the girls curled up on her bed and hummed along.

"You'll never know just how much I care..."

That's *me!* thought Norah. Turning to the wall to hide her blushing cheeks she mouthed, "I love you." The revelation was still a shock—like bursting out of her old skin and finding a fragile new one underneath.

Every Saturday in the city Norah went to the movies with her friends. Now she felt as if *she* were in a movie: like *Casablanca* or *Gone with the Wind.*

Her feelings had to be a secret; even—especially—from Andrew. She didn't know how she would handle it if he knew. For now she just wanted to think about him as much as possible.

The song ended and Clare beat Janet to the turntable and started it again. Flo jumped up and grabbed her brush. "How I wish I could *do* something!" she grumbled, dragging the bristles through her long hair.

"What do you mean?" asked Janet.

"I wish I could leave school and get a job in an airplane factory or something—but Mother and Dad won't let me. It's so unfair. All my male friends are over there helping to fight and I'm stuck at home learning *algebra.*"

"The war's so boring," yawned Clare. "How can you be interested in it?"

"I don't see why I can't contribute," said Flo. "Like Norah's older sisters—they're in the British army, right, Norah? As soon as I'm eighteen I'm going to join the RCAF, if I can talk Mother and Dad into it. But that's a whole year away. Lucky Andrew—at least he's starting his officer training this fall."

"Is Andrew staying for the rest of summer?" asked Norah. She dropped his name into the conversation as casually as she could, amazed that it didn't ring out like a gong to the others the way it did to her.

"I think he's staying until university starts," said Janet. "So he'll probably drive back to Toronto with you."

"Too bad for Norah," said Clare. "You'll just have to put up with him."

"Don't you like Andrew?" Flo asked her with surprise.

Norah flushed so hotly she was sure Flo guessed her secret. But Clare saved her. "Norah's too much of a tomboy to like boys. When we're all engaged she'll still be climbing trees."

"Don't be mean, Clare," said Flo. "There's no reason Norah has to be interested in boys. She's only thirteen—give her time." She smiled at Norah, and Norah was so relieved she smiled back. Let them all go on thinking she didn't like Andrew.

The record ended and the rasp of the needle filled the room. Janet put on "That Old Black Magic" and Norah lay back dreamily. She had never really listened to the song; now every word seemed to be speaking to her alone.

"Norah, wait!" called Janet the next morning. "I thought we were going out in the canoe!"

But Norah had already fled to her rock. She lay on her stomach and peered down at the cabins. In front of the larger one Aunt Anne was shaking out a rug, shooing away George and Denny, who were playing with toy cars on the front steps.

Andrew's cabin looked unoccupied. But he must be in there because he hadn't been to breakfast yet. If he came out, could she call him and wave casually? She knew she couldn't. Right now she just wanted to study him—to learn him by heart.

But in that case she'd better hide, in case he looked up and saw her here. At the back of Andrew's cabin were some low-lying bushes. Norah waited until Aunt Anne went inside, taking the little boys with her. Then she slipped off the rock and ran down to hide in the bushes.

Whew! Her heart thudded as she crouched in the damp dirt. The branches poked into her back, and she wanted to sneeze from the dry leafy smell. Immediately, she wished she hadn't come; it would be so humiliating if Andrew discovered her. But now that she was here, it was safer to stay hidden until he came out.

She didn't have long to wait. The screen door creaked and slammed and she peeked out to see Andrew stroll out of the cabin and up the hill to the main cottage. When he was far enough away, she dashed back up to her rock and watched his progress.

He wore a white shirt that emphasized his tan, and khaki shorts. His hair glistened in the sun. Norah sighed, thinking of all the days she had wasted avoiding him when she could have been feasting her eyes like this. Andrew went in the kitchen door—Norah could hear him greeting Hanny before it closed.

For the next few days she tracked Andrew as much as possible, feeling as daring and resourceful as when she had been ten, watching for enemy paratroopers during the Battle of Britain. Janet complained because she couldn't find her. "What are you *doing* by yourself so much?"

"Oh . . . reading." Norah carried a book as an alibi and often needed it while she waited for Andrew to emerge from the cabin or return from the mainland. The lake was too calm for sailing and he spent some time off the island—she'd heard him say he was visiting friends.

"Reading . . ." sighed Janet. "I wish you'd do something with *me,* Norah. Clare's always reading too—movie magazines. Or she's visiting her friend Louise on Cliff Island. And

Flo spends all her time writing letters. I'm so *bored!* Gairloch used to be a lot more fun than it has been this summer. I thought that would change when you came."

Norah squirmed at her foster cousin's forlorn expression. "Okay—let's go out in the rowboat." They rowed out to the middle of the lake and spent an hour diving off the boat. But all the time, Norah wondered what Andrew was up to.

Every night in bed, and during her solitary vigils during the day, Norah made up elaborate stories about her and Andrew. Sometimes she didn't have on her life-jacket when she had fallen out of the boat and he rescued her just before she drowned. Sometimes she rescued *him,* pulling him to shore and applying mouth-to-mouth resuscitation.

"You are the one," he would say when his eyes finally opened. "The special person I've been waiting for all my life." Because of Norah's age they had to keep their love hidden. Andrew would meet Norah secretly in Toronto during his time at university. Then he would go away to war carrying her picture in his pocket. He would be a hero and win many medals. After the war, when she was eighteen, he would return and marry her. (This part needed adjusting because Norah didn't want the war to go on that long.) *They would live in England, in the same village as her parents. Aunt Florence would be furious that Norah had married so young, but there was nothing she could do . . .*

She picked up a sharp stone and began scratching initials in the rock: N.S. + A.D.

"Ugh!" A wet nose was poking the back of her neck. Then Bosley slobbered all over her face. Gavin was climbing up the rock behind him.

"What are you doing, Norah?"

Quickly Norah moved so she was sitting on top of the initials. She smiled at her brother.

"Nothing much. How's the detective agency?"

"Okay . . . but we haven't got any *cases.* Uncle Reg hired us to find his glasses but that was too easy—they were on the verandah, where he always leaves them."

Norah gazed out at the lake and saw Janet returning in the *Putt-Putt* with Aunt Mary. "I know what you can investigate," she said.

"What?"

"You can find out why Aunt Mary has gone into Port Schofield almost every day since we got here."

"I heard Aunt Florence ask her that—she's getting a dress made. There's a lady there who sews."

"That's what she says, but I don't think that's *all* she does. On Friday I got there early to pick her up and I saw her coming from that big hotel across from the marina—running! Then she went over the bridge and came out from the direction of the dressmaker's as if she'd been there all along. And yesterday I saw her coming *out* of the hotel when I drove the boat by it—she had her head down and didn't see me."

"Wow!" said Gavin. "I wonder what she was doing there? See you later, Norah!" Gavin sped off to tell his gang.

Norah went back to her scratching, glad she had given him something to do. She felt vaguely curious about Aunt Mary, but she was sure there was some boring explanation. Aunt Mary was too ordinary to be involved in a real mystery.

All of her senses were alert when she spotted Andrew come out of his cabin, walk to the lake and dive into the water, swimming vigorously to Little Island.

Norah wiped back her sticky hair and sighed. She felt dopey, as if she couldn't wake up. A swim would refresh her; but she couldn't go down while he was still there.

A few times since their sail Andrew had tried to talk to

Norah. She mumbled her answers, too shy about her new feelings to have a conversation. He seemed to realize she didn't want to talk, and, although he sometimes gave her a quizzical look, he left her alone. That was the way she wanted it; for the time being, anyhow.

Before the children's dinner that evening Norah sat in the living room with her book. She was actually reading it; Andrew and Flo had left the island to go to a dance at Bala.

"And what are you doing in a corner all by yourself?" Uncle Barclay had come into the room without her noticing; he was pinning up little flags onto a huge world map he'd hung on the wall near the piano.

Norah shrugged. "Just reading." She went over to examine his map. Most of the countries bristled with markers, according to some complicated scheme of Uncle Barclay's that she didn't understand.

"What's that place?" she asked politely, pointing to a small green island that he was covering with flags.

"Sicily," said Uncle Barclay with satisfaction. "We're making great advances there—it's very encouraging."

"Do you think we'll *win* the war?" Norah asked him, still staring at the flags dotted all over the map. She hadn't realized how much of the world it now affected.

"Of course we'll win! It's looking better all the time—the Axis can't hold out forever."

Uncle Barclay knew more about the war than anyone else; perhaps he could help her make her daydreaming more accurate. "How long do you think it will be before Andrew is in it?" she asked carefully, thrilling as usual at pronouncing his name.

"Well, he just might get in at the end of it. Then again, he could miss it entirely. That's what I don't understand. If *I* was younger and could help fight that brute . . ." Uncle Barclay snorted, then looked at her kindly. "The only bad thing about the Allies winning is that then you and Gavin will have to go back to England. Flo and Janet will certainly miss you. So will we all," he added gruffly. "But you'll be glad to see your family. Aunt Florence told us how homesick you were at first—you must still miss them."

Norah gave him a smile in exchange for his own awkward one. Uncle Barclay was much stiffer than clownish Uncle Reg, but he was nice in his own way. Guiltily she realized that, this week especially, her thoughts had never been farther from England. If someone told her she could go home tomorrow she wasn't sure she'd want to—not if it meant leaving Andrew.

That night she couldn't sleep. She crept past her inert roommates to go out and sit on the dock. The smaller launch was still gone; Andrew and Flo hadn't come back yet.

Someone coughed and Norah jerked her head around. To her surprise she saw Aunt Mary standing on the far end of the dock, her cigarette a tiny glow in the darkness. She came over and sat beside Norah.

"What are you doing up?" she smiled. "Couldn't you sleep either?"

Norah shook her head. For a few comfortable moments they gazed at the moon. One side of it was caved in, as if someone had taken a bite out of it. Strands of mist rose from the lake like steam. In the distance a dog barked, then was silent.

"It's so quiet up here this summer," said Aunt Mary. "I guess some people have shut up their cottages until after the war. I have an idea." Aunt Mary jumped up, sounding as young as Norah. "Let's take the canoe to Little Island!"

"Now?" Norah could hardly believe what she was hearing. Timid Aunt Mary suggesting such an adventure?

"Why not? Go and get a sweater—it will be cool on the water."

In a few minutes they were in the canoe. At first their dripping paddles made the only sound. Then, by an unspoken agreement, they both began Indian paddling, turning and sliding their blades so they didn't break the surface; then there was no sound at all. In the darkness the shoreline seemed to slip by much faster than it did in daylight. Two summers ago, when she'd first learned how to paddle, Norah had spent hours in this canoe with Aunt Mary.

Little Island made a dark shadow in the water ahead of them. "Shall we get out?" Norah asked shyly. Her voice seemed to boom out in the quiet. Tonight Aunt Mary was a stranger; Norah couldn't predict what she'd want to do next.

"Yes, land over there. I want to show you something." They pulled the canoe up onto the same logs where Norah and Janet had sunbathed last week. Then they stole through the woods to the centre of the island, Aunt Mary's flashlight beaming their way. Norah took her hand, feeling as if she were in a dream.

"Here we are!" The flashlight picked out a clump of six birches that formed a circle. Aunt Mary sat down in the middle and laughed softly. "Come in, Norah! I haven't been here for years and years. This was my special place when I was young. Whenever Mother was upset with me, I would take refuge over here."

"*We* used to pretend this was a teepee," Norah told her, cross-legged beside her on the rocky ground. It didn't feel quite right for one of the Elders to be in the circle now, even if she had come here as a girl. And it was odd to be sitting here in the middle of the night in her pyjamas. She waited;

Aunt Mary seemed lit up with importance, as if she were going to tell Norah something.

"I had a difficult time as a girl, Norah," she said slowly. "What with my brother's death, then Father's, and Mother being so . . . well, you know how she is. And then . . . I met someone I liked very much. So much that I wanted to marry him."

Norah's ears stretched. Hanny had once told her that Aunt Mary had a Secret Sorrow. Now she was finally going to hear about it!

"Why didn't you?" she asked softly, trying not to stem the flow of confidence.

"For a number of reasons . . ." Aunt Mary's voice grew tender. "His name was Thomas and he was a stockbroker in Toronto. I met him at a church meeting and he began coming over for Sunday dinners. I think Mother liked him; he was respectable enough, even for her. But then he found out he was going to be transferred to Regina."

So Aunt Mary had once been in love too! "Did he *ask* you to marry him?"

"Yes, he did. It took me a week to decide. But finally, after talking it over with Mother, I said no. I just couldn't leave her alone, you see—not after the losses she'd already had. I even asked Thomas if she could come with us, but he was very reluctant to have her. I don't blame him, and Mother didn't want to leave Toronto anyway."

"But that's terrible!" cried Norah. "You gave up the man you loved for *Aunt Florence*? How could you? She ruined your life!"

Aunt Mary patted Norah's hand. "It seemed the right thing to do at the time. And I haven't suffered *that* much, you know. I did then, but I got over it and I think I have a very pleasant life—certainly more pleasant than most people in the world. Think of how much some of them must be suffering in the war this very moment, while we're enjoying this beautiful place."

Sometimes Aunt Mary was too good to be true. Norah crumpled a strip of birchbark and flung it across the clearing. "Think of *you!* Think of Thomas! It's *terrible* that you gave him up!"

"Well, it was all a long time ago and it's over now. And who knows? Maybe I wouldn't have had such a happy life with Thomas. When you grow up you'll find that you have to learn to live with your own decisions." Her voice had a sad, dreamy quality to it, but then she looked up at Norah and laughed. "Well! I don't know why I'm telling you about it. It's just such a restless kind of night. For some reason it made me think of him and I couldn't sleep."

As they paddled back, Norah seethed with the injustice of Aunt Mary's decision. But she had to admit that Aunt Mary herself didn't seem to be upset about it; in fact she was curiously happy and excited. They kissed good-night, grinning at the secret of their shared expedition.

I'll never give up Andrew for *anyone,* Norah thought sleepily as she crawled back into her warm bed. She tried to stay awake long enough to hear him come in, but when she turned over again it was morning.

VII
AN ACCIDENT

The whole family was assembled on the dock the next afternoon. Norah lay on her stomach, basking after her fifth swim. Lazily she watched Aunt Florence and Aunt Catherine taking what they called their "constitutional."

Aunt Catherine was amazingly spry for someone in her eighties. Her wiry body moved through the water as easily as Norah herself, as she performed her usual ten strokes out and ten strokes in. Bosley accompanied her all the way.

Aunt Florence didn't really swim. Her figure was encased in a ballooning flowered bathing suit she called her "swimming costume" and her head was wrapped in a kind of turban. She let herself awkwardly down the ladder, then heaved herself in, flopping about and spewing water like a whale. Then she emerged, as proud as if she had swum a marathon. All the children suppressed giggles behind their towels.

Denny jumped in again and again, buoyed up by his life-jacket. George was having a swimming lesson. Uncle Gerald stood at the edge of the dock and held him up by a rope tied around his middle. "Thatta boy! You're doing fine!" he called. The little boy splashed and kicked valiantly. All the other cousins bobbed around him.

Aunt Mary sat in the shade under the roofed part of the dock, deep in a new book called *The Robe.* Uncle Reg sat in the sun, a knotted white handkerchief draped on top of his bald head. He squinted at his needlepoint. This summer he'd asked Aunt Florence to teach him. His sisters teased him but he retorted that he didn't see why a man couldn't be as good at needlepoint as a woman. Now he and Aunt Florence were having a competition to see who could finish a cushion cover first.

Aunt Bea and Aunt Dorothy came down from the changing room that was next to the Girls' Dorm. They sat beside Norah, dangling their feet in the lake and fanning themselves. "I always hate the first plunge," said Aunt Bea. "The only problem with this side of the island is that there's no shore. When I was little I thought there was a sea monster down there!"

Uncle Reg chuckled. "That's because once I dived underneath and grabbed your ankle—do you remember?"

"Of course I do!" bristled Aunt Bea. "It was very naughty and Father was right to punish you."

Norah listened to the two of them bickering as if they were children again. It was so hard to believe that any of the Elders *had* been young.

While everyone was resting after lunch she had made a secret inspection of the cottage walls for pictures of Andrew. She recognized him in several family groups: a solemn page boy in a kilt at Uncle Gerald's wedding; squeezed between Flo and Clare at a picnic. He didn't look much different when he was Norah's age, though his hair had been lighter and his face not as lean.

If he *were* her age she could be his friend as easily as she was friends with Bernard in the city. Then she wouldn't catch her breath every time she looked at him. Friendship would be much more restful; but there was nothing she could do to stop her love. It *ran* her, as if she were a puppet dangling on its strings.

When she'd found all the pictures of Andrew, Norah

turned to a photograph that had been pointed out to her again and again: the first generation of Elders as children, sitting on the steps of the newly built Gairloch. Three sisters and a brother, the girls in white dresses and black stockings. As usual she felt sorry for them, dressed so uncomfortably in the summer. Thirteen-year-old Aunt Florence looked as haughty and confident as she did now. *She* didn't seem to have found it confusing to be a teen-ager. Beside her, in order of age, sat Christina, Bea (pouting) and little Reg, who was smiling mischievously.

On the wall beside Aunt Florence's chair hung a picture of her son, Hugh, who had been killed in World War I. He was standing alone on the verandah, dressed in his uniform. His open, eager face laughed at the camera, as if he could never die.

Norah glanced at a few recent photographs that included her and Gavin. After they left Canada their likenesses would still be hanging here, as if they were really part of the family.

All of the Drummonds, dead and alive, stared at Norah, until she suddenly felt oppressed and fled out to the sunshine.

Now she lifted her head from her towel and watched Andrew and Uncle Gerald race to Little Island and back. When Andrew won, she lowered her face to hide her proud grin. He climbed out and stood over her, puffing and dripping. Norah stiffened and stared at his feet. His long toes were as elegant as his fingers. He dived back into the lake without speaking to her.

Norah flipped over and sighed. It wasn't *enough.* She was no longer content with simply watching Andrew. Now she wished he would talk to her as easily as he had that day in the boat, but her shyness had made him stop paying attention to her. She had to do something to get that attention back.

"Watch me, Norah!" cried Janet. She was poised on the

balcony of the boathouse. Then she cannon-balled into the lake; the aunts shrieked in mock alarm as they got splashed.

Norah ran up the stairs to the dorm and climbed out the window to the balcony. For a few seconds she balanced on the railing, curling her toes around it and trying to will Andrew to look at her. She called down to Janet. "Watch *me!* I'm going to dive!"

She had never dived before. It was safe enough—the water was so deep, there was no danger of hitting bottom. But the lake was an awfully long way below. When Andrew finally glanced up, Norah crouched and sprang.

The lake rushed up at her, then roared in her ears as she shot into its green depths. She struggled up through the watery silence, whooshed out the air from her aching lungs and struck out for the dock. She'd done it!

The family applauded. "Did you see my *sister?*" Gavin asked Ross.

"You're so brave!" said Janet, helping her up the ladder. "I'll never get up the nerve to dive."

"Good for you, Norah," smiled Andrew. "I was much older the first time I did that." His praise rang in her ears for the rest of the day.

Then Norah had a much more daring idea than diving off the boathouse. The next morning, after rehearsing the whole scene several times in her head, she walked casually by Andrew's cabin when she knew he was still there. Then she stumbled deliberately. *"Ow!"*

Andrew rushed out. "What's the matter?"

"My ankle," moaned Norah. "I think I twisted it or something. I was just on my way to visit Aunt Anne," she added quickly, so he wouldn't wonder what she'd been doing outside his cabin.

"Let me see." Andrew took Norah's ankle in his hand. He turned it gently in different directions. "Does this hurt?"

"A little—not *too* much." Norah's cheeks flamed. This presence was working too easily; there was something shameful about it.

"Can you stand?" Andrew helped her up and Norah was so overcome with the thrill of having his arms around her that she trembled convincingly.

"It's—it's all right now. I think I can walk on it." She pretended to limp a few steps.

"Come in and rest it for a few minutes. If it doesn't get any better I'll go up and get Aunt Dorothy—she used to be a nurse, you know."

Go *in,* to Andrew's own place? Norah grimaced, not with pain but with excitement, as Andrew helped her through the door and onto a couch.

"Do you want some tea? I've been making my own breakfast in here. It's more peaceful than having it with the Elders. All of them first thing in the morning are too much to take. And Hanny usually gives me leftovers, anyway."

Andrew calling the grown-ups the Elders, as he had in the boat, made Norah feel slightly more at ease. She accepted his offer of tea gratefully; she hadn't had any for ages. Even though children over twelve were allowed tea coupons, Aunt Florence insisted on keeping Norah's for herself and Aunt Mary.

"Toast too?"

"No thanks—I've *had* breakfast."

Andrew toasted bread for himself over the tiny wood stove. Norah looked around the cabin, trying to calm down and savour these precious moments alone with him. She'd been in this cabin a few times before, when various relatives had overflowed from the cottage out here. It was only one room containing two narrow couches, a table and chairs, and a shabby rug. Now a large glossy photograph of a handsome man was pinned to one wall.

"Who's that?" Norah dared to ask.

"Laurence Olivier—my inspiration," said Andrew. "Didn't you ever see him in *Wuthering Heights?* I guess not, you would have been too young. He's a brilliant actor."

"I thought that was a book."

"The movie was *from* the book."

Norah resolved to borrow it from Aunt Catherine right away. "Do you think you'll ever be an actor yourself?" she asked timidly. "Aunt Catherine told me she thinks you should be. She said you were a natural and she should know—she's seen lots of plays."

"Good old Aunt Catherine," said Andrew. "She's always taken my acting seriously. Too bad she's the only one." The muscle jumped in his cheek and his blue-grey eyes looked sad.

"But everyone thinks you're a *wonderful* actor!" cried Norah, forgetting her shyness. "You heard what Aunt Florence said on your first night."

"Yes—as long as it's just a hobby. I'll tell you something, Norah. I *do* want to be an actor. More than anything in the world. But *they*—all the Elders and especially my mother and stepfather—think I should be an engineer, like my father. That's what I've been taking at university and what I'll continue taking at U of T along with the COTC course. You wouldn't believe how boring it is. But they don't need actors in the war," he added dryly.

"Can't you become an actor *after* the war?" asked Norah.

"I suppose so. Maybe I'll have the guts to do it by then. You see, it's not just because it's a good lead-in to officer training that they had me take engineering. It's because it's practical and will give me the kind of career every other man in this family has always had—something that will make me lots of money, that will *establish* me…"

He waved his piece of toast in time to the rise and fall of his words. The bitterness in his voice made Norah uncomfortable. This wasn't how she wanted him to be; he was supposed to be confident and cheerful. "I don't see why you can't be an actor if you want to be," she said impatiently.

She was relieved when Andrew smiled. "You're perfectly right. And I shouldn't be boring you with my problems. I don't know why I'm telling you all this—probably because you're *not* part of the family." He glanced at his watch. "Now… how's the ankle?"

Norah had completely forgotten she was supposed to have twisted her ankle. "Oh!" she said with surprise. "I guess it's going to be all right." She stood up, put her weight on it, and limped around the room. "Yes, I'm sure it will be. The more I walk on it the better it feels."

"Good." Andrew was gathering up a tennis racquet and a white sweater. He wanted her to go.

"I'm meeting some friends at eleven," he said. "Be sure to get someone to look at your ankle if it bothers you."

"I will." Norah hobbled out of the cabin and up the hill, trying to remember which foot she was supposed to be favouring. She turned back to wave but Andrew was already hurrying to the dock.

Still, he'd asked her in! And he'd confided in her! For the rest of the day Norah moved around in a cloud of happiness, and that evening it was crowned when Andrew asked her in a concerned voice, "Is your ankle better, Norah?"

"Yes, thanks," she said in a croak, as his eyes focused on hers.

"What happened to your ankle, Norah?" demanded Aunt Florence. "Why didn't you tell me?"

"I just twisted it a bit. It's fine now. It doesn't even hurt."

Aunt Florence looked so suspicious that Norah retreated from the room. She still felt guilty about her trick—but it had worked! Surely, from now on, Andrew would pay more attention to her. And, after all, she'd only been in love with him for four days—though it seemed like years. It was natural that he'd take that long to really notice her.

World-famous actor Andrew Drummond says he wouldn't have persisted with his career if it had not been for the encouragement of his beloved wife, Norah. Often compared to Laurence Olivier, this handsome star says he has his wife in mind every time he plays a love scene . . .

VIII
BEING DETECTIVES

"Norah, we'd like to have a meeting with you."

The Fearless Four stood solemnly on the verandah. "Could you please come to our headquarters?" added Gavin.

Norah left the glider and followed them along the path to the playhouse. Above the door was pinned a sign—FEARLESS FOUR DETECTIVE AGENCY—NO CASE TOO DIFFICULT. Inside, all the evidence of the Hornets had been cleared away. Now a pair of toy handcuffs and a magnifying glass sat on a low table. Leaning against the wall was a chart covered with all the family's fingerprints. A complete set of Sherlock Holmes books stood on a rickety shelf; Creature was perched on top, as if he were guarding all this.

Norah was struck by how small the room was; her arms and legs seemed to fill the whole space. She sat on the floor with the others around the table. "Does Aunt Florence know you have these books out here?" she asked, reaching up to touch one of the red leather bindings.

"Well . . . not exactly," said Gavin, always truthful. "She said I could borrow them, but she thinks they're in the Boys' Dorm. We'll put them back at the end of the summer. Listen, Norah—we need your help."

"What for?"

"We just can't crack this case," said Peter solemnly. He pushed up the thick glasses that were always sliding down his nose.

"*What* case?"

"Aunt Mary's," said Sally impatiently. "We've got a lot of clues but now we're stuck."

Gavin handed Norah his notebook. A pencil was tied by a bedraggled string to a hole in the cover. She opened it to the first page, which was headed "Clues—The Case of the Mysterious Visits."

1. Aunt Mary has gone to Port Schofield five or six times since the beginning of August.
2. She says she is going to town to get a dress fitted but Norah Stoakes (friend of the agency) says she saw her coming out of Eden House Resort.
3. Aunt Mary acts as if she is up to something. She is dixtacted and sings to herself.

Norah smiled at "friend of the agency." "What does 'dixtacted' mean?" she asked them.

"You know—kind of absent-minded, as if she's always thinking of something else," said Gavin.

"Oh—*distracted.* You're right, she has been acting different. You've been very observant."

The Fearless Four beamed at her praise. "But now we're stuck," said Peter.

Ross, never able to sit still for long, climbed on a stool and began swinging from the top of the doorway. "We're stuck because we can't *trail* her," he said. "We aren't allowed to take the boat out alone until we're thirteen."

"So, Norah . . ." Ross dropped with a thud and all four looked at her expectantly.

"So you want *me* to take you in the boat and drop you off so you can follow her," said Norah. "But what if she sees you?"

"We'll be very, very careful," said Gavin. "We know how to track people quietly. We've been practising on the aunts—we followed them all the way to the gazebo and back without getting caught."

Norah reflected on how good she was at tracking Andrew. In spite of a reluctance to invade Aunt Mary's privacy, she felt a twinge of excitement, as if she were their age again. Maybe she could do more than just take them over in the boat. It would be almost a relief to have a holiday from her feelings for Andrew. She picked up a Captain Wonder comic from the floor and flipped through it while she decided.

"Okay," she said finally. She hushed their eager voices. "I think I'd better help you track her, though. You'll need someone to help make up an excuse if you're caught. And five of us will attract too much attention. I'll take Gavin and one other."

"Me! Me!"

"Sally," said Gavin at once. "She's the best at tracking." The other boys looked disappointed but accepted his decision. It had always surprised Norah how they let Gavin lead them, even though Peter was a year older. Somehow his gentle manner carried a lot of authority.

"I'll have to get permission," said Norah. "It'll be tricky because we won't know she's going until the last moment and she might take the *Putt-Putt*. And remember, Aunt Mary may not be up to *anything*—there could be some logical explanation." She knew from their eager faces that they didn't believe that, and all at once she didn't want to believe it either. "I'll be your Chief Detective," she continued. "You'll have to do exactly what I say." Then she added, a bit sheepishly, "Can I borrow a few of these comics?"

For the rest of that day they all observed Aunt Mary's movements. But she didn't appear on the dock in her hat until the next afternoon, when Mr Hancock drove her away in the *Florence.* Gavin dashed up to tell Norah and Norah tried to appear nonchalant as she looked for an Elder. She found Aunt Anne in the kitchen, helping Hanny roll out piecrust.

"May I please take Gavin and Sally to Port Schofield in the *Putt-Putt?*" she asked.

As usual Aunt Anne looked uncertain. "Why do you want to go there?"

"To buy some comics and have ice cream."

"I wonder . . . I suppose it's all right. But make sure they wear life-jackets. How long are you going to be?"

"We'll be back by five," promised Norah. She skipped out before she could be questioned further.

Gavin and Sally looked solemn as they sat side by side in the bow of the *Putt-Putt,* muffled in fat orange life-jackets.

"I think we should moor at the hotel, not in town," said Norah. "After all, we're assuming that's where she is." She slowed down the boat and turned in to the hotel dock. A few guests sitting in wooden chairs along the shore glanced up at them. Not at all sure if they were allowed to use the dock, Norah tied up the painter quickly and hissed at the others. "Quick! Take off your life-jackets and follow me." The three detectives strolled across the lawn as if they were guests too. They hurried up the long path and retreated under a clump of trees for a conference.

"So far, so good," said Gavin, his eyes dancing. "Stop laughing, Sally!" He pulled out his notebook and began to scribble while Norah examined the hotel.

How were they ever going to find Aunt Mary? The huge three-storey building in front of them must contain hundreds of people.

"What are you writing, Gavin?" asked Sally.

"The colours of those chairs and where this hiding place is," he told her.

"That's not important," said Norah. "You don't have to write everything down, just what's relevant."

"But you never know what *could* be relevant," said Gavin, continuing to scribble.

Norah kept staring at the hotel, thinking hard. "Let's walk all the way around the outside," she suggested. "Maybe we'll spot her on the verandah. Now remember, look as if you're staying here. If she spots us we'll say . . . Oh, yikes, what *will* we say?"

"We could say that we're visiting Mummy's friend," said Sally. "You know, Mrs Abercrombie. She's staying here all month. She was on the island last week with her daughter. *Enid,*" she added with disgust.

Norah looked at Sally with exasperation. "But why didn't you say so earlier? It's a perfect excuse. You could say I brought you over to play with Enid!"

"Ugh!" said Sally. "She's so babyish, isn't she, Gavin?" Gavin nodded.

"Still, that's our alibi—don't forget! Let's just hope we don't have to use it."

They began circling the lawn underneath the verandah, pulling their sun hats down over their faces. A group of well-dressed people were playing croquet. "There she is!" whispered Sally.

"Aunt Mary?" breathed Norah.

"No—Enid. And her mother." A small girl in a frilly dress was standing on the edge of the group, licking an ice cream cone while her mother bent over her and wiped her chin.

"Don't let them see us!" Norah grabbed each of them by the hand and headed back around the corner.

"I'm hungry!" complained Sally. "Couldn't we get some ice cream too?"

"Not yet," said Norah. She looked at her watch. "If we haven't found Aunt Mary by four-thirty we'll take the boat into town and get some."

They strolled back and forth aimlessly, avoiding the croquet game. Norah was just beginning to get up the courage to venture into the hotel itself when Gavin called "*Look!*"

"Shhh!" Norah pressed her hand over his mouth as a woman turned around at his voice. "Stay calm—sit down on the grass and don't turn your head. Did you really see her?"

Gavin nodded and leaned over to whisper into her ear. "She's out on the lake! In a boat! Left of the boathouse—I saw her yellow hat."

Carefully Norah raised her eyes. Sure enough, Aunt Mary was in the bow of a red canoe, her back to them. And someone was with her—a stocky man who steered awkwardly, making the canoe go in a wavering line.

"Good for you, Gavin! Okay, be as quiet as mice—we'll follow the canoe from the shore."

They ran lightly down to the lake and slunk along the shoreline behind the screen of trees. The canoe was far enough out that they wouldn't be seen. Soon it rounded a promontory ahead of them.

"Be *very* quiet," warned Norah. "We don't know how close it'll be to the shore on the other side." They got on their stomachs and slithered over the rocks until they could peek over.

The canoe had turned in to a tiny cove below them. The man hauled it up on the beach, then held out his hand to Aunt Mary. They sat on some rocks, Aunt Mary drawing her legs up under her dress.

Before Norah could stop them, Gavin and Sally had crept

through the bushes to get closer. She joined them reluctantly. Suddenly it felt wrong to spy on Aunt Mary like this. Whoever this man was, it wasn't their business. She imagined her guardian's hurt face if she caught them.

"Let's go," she whispered to the others when she reached them. "We've seen enough."

"Not yet," entreated Gavin, digging out his notebook. "I need to describe him."

Norah fidgeted while he looked and scribbled. Aunt Mary and the stranger were talking intently to each other, their voices too far away to be heard. But Aunt Mary's frequent laughter floated up to them. The man looked as old as she was; he took off his hat and his white hair caught the light. At least they were both facing the lake, not the trees.

After what seemed like an eternity, the couple got into the canoe again and the three detectives trailed them back to the hotel dock. They hid behind the boathouse as the canoe arrived. Now they could hear every word.

"Just look at the time! I must get back to town before Mr Hancock comes. Goodbye, Tom. I've had a lovely afternoon."

"Goodbye, then, Mary. I'll see you on Friday at three." The man lifted his hat as Aunt Mary hurried past the boathouse.

"Who *is* he?" whispered Sally.

"Not yet!" hissed Norah. "No talking until we get out of here. Wait until he's gone too." The man finished tying up the canoe and went up the path. When he reached the hotel, they got into their own boat.

Gavin whipped out his notebook, but Norah clapped her hand over his. "Don't write anything!" she ordered. "As soon as we get back to Gairloch we'll have a meeting."

"But aren't we going to have any ice cream?" asked Sally.

"No!" said Norah fiercely. "We're going straight back before Mr Hancock comes. But you can say you had ice cream if your mother asks you what you did."

"That's not fair—" began Sally, but the engine revved and Norah drove back to the island as fast as she could.

"This case didn't turn out to be very interesting," said Gavin, back in the playhouse. An indignant Peter and Ross had been shooed out of it. "All she does is visit that man. But wasn't it exciting when we were following the canoe?"

"Is he her *boy friend?*" giggled Sally. "Aunt Mary's too old to have a boy friend!"

Norah's thoughts raced. "Of course she is," she agreed. "He's probably just a friend of the family."

"So why does she keep it a secret?" persisted Sally.

"Uhh… maybe he's someone Aunt Florence doesn't like. You know how many people she disapproves of."

"Like Bernard," said Gavin. "Bernard is our friend in Toronto," he explained to Sally. "When Norah first knew him she had to meet him secretly—even I didn't know. She doesn't have to do that any more, but Aunt Florence still doesn't like him much. She's always telling me how 'unsuitable' Bernard is because his mother's a cleaning woman."

"And if you'd *known* that I was meeting him, you wouldn't have told Aunt Florence, would you?" Norah asked him.

"Of course not!"

"Well, this is the same situation. Aunt Mary obviously wants to keep her visits a secret—but now *we* know. So we have to keep it a secret too. Do you understand? We can't tell anyone, or we'll get her into trouble with Aunt Florence. I don't even want you to write it down in your casebook, Gavin."

"But—" Gavin looked deflated, but then he sighed and said, "Okay, Norah, I won't."

"But can't we tell Peter and Ross?" asked Sally. "They're waiting to hear what happened!"

Norah knew they'd tell them anyway. "All right . . . but no one else! You've solved the case and you did it very well, but we found out something we shouldn't have known—and we don't want to hurt Aunt Mary, right?"

They nodded solemnly. Norah made them each say cross-my-heart-and-hope-to-die. Then she left them and climbed up to her rock.

She stretched out on her stomach, trying to absorb all they'd seen. Aunt Mary's secret was probably safe. To the Fearless Four, everyone except herself was an Elder and therefore not to be trusted.

But what did the secret mean? Of course the man *was* Aunt Mary's "boy friend." Norah had known that at once from the tender way they had looked at each other. Now she recognized in Aunt Mary the same symptoms she possessed herself.

Most important of all—his name was Tom! That meant he was *Thomas,* Aunt Mary's long-ago love, who had somehow come back into her life. He must be visiting from the prairies, just so he could see Aunt Mary.

No wonder she'd wanted to talk about Thomas with Norah that night! It was the same reason that Norah was always trying to casually introduce Andrew's name into conversations. Norah wished Aunt Mary had told her she was seeing him again, but she was probably afraid to reveal that even to Norah.

She glanced at Aunt Mary all evening and pressed up against her when Aunt Florence was reading. Aunt Mary smiled and squeezed her shoulder.

Surely she would soon have the courage to tell her mother—and this time she wouldn't give in. Then she would marry Tom and live happily ever after—just like all the songs and movies.

Norah's own love was far more insecure, especially since so much of it had to wait until she was older. She gazed at Andrew, who looked lost in a daydream as he stared at the fire. It was wonderful that she could talk to him again, but even that was no longer enough. He thought of her the same way he thought of Janet or Flo.

She knew what she had to do. She had to *tell* him, to reveal her feelings. Then he would realize that he loved her too and he would wait for her until she was old enough to marry him.

None of the songs or movies said how loving someone required all these difficult tasks.

IX
STORMY WEATHER

Norah and Janet sat together on the dock, listening to Clare's mother rant at her. Her furious voice drifted out of the open window of the Girls' Dorm. She had appeared there after breakfast and grimly ordered everyone out so she and Clare could have a "talk."

"You are completely irresponsible, Clare! How could you possibly forget them?"

"I just did," said Clare sullenly. "I didn't want to take them anyway—they talked me into it. They should have noticed when I was leaving."

Yesterday Clare had taken her brothers with her when she drove the *Putt-Putt* to visit her friend Louise on Cliff Island. The little boys had gone off to play on the rocks and Clare, forgetting all about them, had returned alone. Louise's father had had to bring back Peter and Ross, tearful and scared; Ross had scraped his knee badly.

Clare's mother, who'd been visiting some friends on one of the other lakes for a few days, had arrived back very late herself and only heard about the mishap this morning.

Norah and Janet glanced at each other uneasily as Aunt Mar's voice grew more shrill. They shouldn't be eavesdropping, but they couldn't resist hearing Clare get into trouble.

"Clare Drummond, you are fifteen years old, not a child! If your father was here he'd be very disappointed in you.

Why can't you be more like Norah? She takes such good care of Gavin."

"Oh, *Norah,*" said Clare scornfully. "I'm sick of hearing about perfect Norah. Just because she's a war guest she gets treated differently. Not like me. This family is so mean to me . . . ," she howled.

Janet rolled her eyes. "What a baby," she whispered. "Don't worry, Norah, she didn't mean it."

Norah knew she did, but she tried to tell herself she didn't care.

"You're grounded for a week," Aunt Mar was saying. "That means not leaving the island at all—not by yourself or with anyone else."

"That's not *fair!* I didn't mean to leave them, I just forgot!" But her mother was already gone, not even noticing Norah and Janet as she marched past them up the steps.

"Well, I'm not going to stay out here all morning," said Janet. "I was in the middle of painting my toenails."

They ventured into the boathouse again, pretending to ignore Clare, crumpled up on her bed and sobbing into her pillow. "Everyone picks on me," she wailed. "It's not *fair* . . ."

Janet put on "In the Blue of the Evening" and hummed along.

"Turn that off! I don't feel like listening to records!" Clare hurled her pillow towards Janet and it landed on the record, sending the needle screeching across it.

"*Now* look what you've done! You've ruined it!" Janet snatched up the record, examined the ugly scratch, then threw it down and dashed out the door.

"That was really mean," said Norah. "It was her favourite."

"Oh you shut up! It's none of your business, Norah Stoakes—you're not part of this family. You should be grateful that we took you in. And another thing, Norah—I've noticed how you follow Andrew around. You may as well give up. You're not nearly good enough for him. Anyway, you're only thirteen—it looks ridiculous for someone your age to go mooning after a nineteen-year-old."

Norah was speechless. She almost jumped on Clare and pulled her hair. Last summer she would have. But now she just wanted to get away from her.

"You—you are *despicable!*" she hissed. She ran out even faster than Janet had and didn't stop until she collapsed on her rock.

Clare knew about Andrew! Would she tell Janet and Flo? Worse, would she tell Andrew? Did *everyone* know? Were they all laughing at her?

Norah sat up and hugged her knees against her sweaty blouse. If only it were last summer, when her life at Gairloch was so simple. She almost wished she could cast off her feelings for Andrew. But she couldn't—it was as if she had an incurable disease.

And she hardly even saw Andrew these days, which made her long for him all the more. He'd been spending all his time with a family on the mainland. Janet told her they were the brothers and sister of a boy he'd been very close to who was now in the air force. Jamie and Lois and Dick Mitchell, his friends were called. Norah smouldered with jealousy every time she heard their names.

Two hours later Norah sat listlessly on the dock with her fishing rod. She'd had a long swim but she was already hot again. Thunder rumbled in the distance; a storm was holding its breath but couldn't let it out.

"Any luck, Norah?" Aunt Catherine stood behind her, holding her knitting and fanning her face with her hand. "I thought I'd come down and sit by the water to see if I could catch a breeze. I certainly wish the weather would break. Just listen to those cicadas buzz! They're always especially loud before a storm."

Norah didn't tell her that her hook wasn't even baited. She tried to smile at Aunt Catherine but could only manage a shrug.

Aunt Catherine pulled one of the heavy wooden chairs up beside her. "You look rather seedy, Norah. I hope you're not coming down with anything. Do you feel all right?"

"Mmmm," said Norah, trying to control her irritation. It wasn't like Aunt Catherine to be this nosy.

"Everyone seems to be under the weather today," continued the old lady. "'Under the weather'—that's a very appropriate phrase when you think of it, as if the weather held us all squirming under its thumb. Mar is upset with Clare—and I must say, that child gets more impossible all the time. Dorothy told Mar that she shouldn't have been away so long—now Mar isn't speaking to her. Florence and Bea are having the most absurd argument over how to pronounce 'forsythia.' And Mary seems to be off on a cloud. She forgot it was her turn to help with the children's breakfast, which is quite uncharacteristic. What a family... Sometimes I'm glad I'm not really part of it. Aren't you?"

Norah nodded. At least Aunt Catherine was once again confiding in her like an equal.

"I don't think Andrew's been very happy lately either," mused Aunt Catherine. "Poor lad. I'm so very fond of him and I can't abide the idea of him going off to this monstrous war."

Norah's skin prickled with alertness. "But that won't be for a few years, not until he finishes university," she said. "Maybe the war will be over by then."

"Let's hope so. If it isn't, he's going to be doing something that's against his nature—I feel sorry for boys like him."

"What do you mean?"

"I mean he's not cut out to be a soldier. They all want him to be like the other men in the family—like Hugh. Now Hugh was a dear, but he was a completely different sort from Andrew."

Norah was puzzled. "But he *must* want to be a soldier. He *should* join the war." She shuddered. "Not until he has to, of course."

"Should he?" Aunt Catherine's lined face looked tired. "I lost a father, a brother and a nephew—Hugh—in wars, Norah. It's a wicked waste."

"But we have to beat Hitler!"

"I don't know how to answer that, Norah. Yes, we have to beat him. But what a price we're paying! Not just our side —think of what the German people are enduring. We're bombing them just as heavily as they've been bombing Britain." She broke off a piece of wool angrily. "It's all so *senseless!* Do you know what we called the *last* war? 'The war to end all wars.' *Huh!*"

Then she sighed. "Poor Andrew. He was born at the wrong time. Let's just hope your little brother will be luckier."

Norah couldn't bear to think of Gavin fighting in a war. But if he did, he'd be doing it because he had no choice. Like Andrew. Surely Aunt Catherine was wrong. Andrew *must* want to fight Hitler. If he didn't, he'd be a coward—wouldn't he?

"I shouldn't burden you with all these sombre thoughts, Norah. Are you sure there's nothing troubling you?" Aunt Catherine peered at her and Norah looked away. "Lately you haven't seemed yourself."

"I'm all right," mumbled Norah. It was tempting to tell Aunt Catherine about her feelings for Andrew, but after all she *was* an Elder. And she wouldn't understand, anyway. She'd never married and she'd probably never even been in love.

"Ah, well," said Aunt Catherine, pulling out her knitting. "It's just being thirteen. *I'd* never want to be thirteen again—a miserable, muddled age."

Surprisingly, this cheered Norah. She wouldn't always *be* thirteen, she thought suddenly—there was a light at the end of the tunnel. One day she'd be eighty-three and looking back on herself as calmly as Aunt Catherine was doing. But the thought of being as old as Aunt Catherine was too slippery to hang on to.

That evening the air outside still crackled with impending fury. Inside, the atmosphere was the same: a cloud of discord hung over the family.

During the children's dinner, Norah sat as far away from Clare as she could and tried not to look at her. Janet, on the other hand, glared at her cousin all through the meal. Clare made spiteful comments to her brothers for getting her into trouble. After both meals were over, the family sat woodenly in the living room, someone occasionally making a stiff remark about the weather.

Aunt Mar and Aunt Dorothy were glaring at each other as much as their daughters. "Why aren't you girls doing your knitting?" complained Aunt Dorothy, holding up a long grey sock to measure it. "I thought you were each going to make a scarf for a soldier this summer. Don't forget, not everyone leads the comfortable life you do. There's a war on, you know."

"There's a war on, moron," whispered Clare.

"Don't you be rude to my mother!" Janet hissed back.

Aunt Catherine suggested a game of rummy and four of

the Elders gathered around a table. For a while the only sound was the ripple and snap of cards being shuffled.

"A run of five!" gloated Uncle Reg. "Your turn, Florence."

"For*sigh*thia," said Aunt Florence quietly.

"For*sith*ia!" retorted her sister.

"It was named after a Mr Forsythe—therefore it is pronounced the same way as his name," sniffed Aunt Florence.

Aunt Bea didn't even look up from her cards as she muttered, "Madge Allwood, who was the best gardener in Montreal, *always* said 'Forsithia.'"

"Really, Bea." Aunt Florence threw down her cards in disgust. "If you won't see reason I refuse to go on playing."

"Now what on earth does how a flower's name is pronounced have to do with a game of cards?" Uncle Reg asked.

Aunt Florence bridled. "It's not a flower, it's a shrub. And what do *you* know about gardening, Reg? It's not your quarrel—kindly stay out of it."

"I don't see why there has to be a quarrel at all," said Andrew quietly, looking up from his book.

Norah, hiding behind *her* book, was surprised to see the aunts look ashamed.

"You're perfectly right, Andrew," said Aunt Florence briskly. "Let's talk about *you.*" She gazed at him fondly. "It's going to be such a treat to have you in Toronto this year. I do wish you'd live with us, but I know you boys need your freedom. What are you taking in first term?"

As Andrew recited the names of his engineering courses Norah wriggled with excitement. She had forgotten that Andrew would be living in the same city. Surely he'd come over for meals.

"Hugh would have liked to take engineering," sighed Aunt Florence. "You are so much like him, my dear. My poor Hugh..."

Aunt Bea cut in abruptly. "How's your friend Jack doing, Andrew? What mischief you two boys both got up to! You used to spend the whole summer pretending you were savages and smearing yourselves with paint—without any clothes on, if I remember!" She giggled. "Do you hear from him much?"

"I've had a few letters," said Andrew guardedly. "And of course the Mitchells hear from him. He's all right—he hasn't seen much action yet."

"It must make you want to be in on it, when your best friend is," said Uncle Barclay. "Too bad he's older than you—you could have joined up together."

"But Andrew is going to join the army, not the air force," said Aunt Florence proudly. "All the Drummonds and Ogilvies have been army men. You're going to try to get into Hugh's old regiment, aren't you, dear? He would have been so proud of you."

"Florence!" Everyone froze at the hysterical edge in Aunt Bea's voice. "I've always wanted to say this and now I'm going to. You dwell too much on that sainted son of yours. He's gone—why can't you accept it? No one ever talks about *my* son, and he's alive and prospering. I am tired of always hearing about perfect Hugh, and I'm sure Andrew is as well."

In the shocked silence the thunder rolled more ominously. Gerald ducked his head at his mother's words. Aunt Florence drew herself upright, took a deep breath and began to explode just as the storm did.

"How *dare* you . . ." she began.

CRA-AAA-CK! Sally screamed and ran to her mother as the thunder crashed and the clouds emptied onto the roof with a deafening rattle.

Aunt Anne hustled out all the younger children. The older cousins exchanged looks and fled as well. They huddled on the verandah and watched the teeming rain, listening to Aunt Florence's rage compete with the storm. Aunt Bea, Uncle Reg and Aunt Mar's voices soon joined the fray.

"What's *wrong* with this family?" Flo's face was angry and pale. "They're so petty! Don't they realize there are more important things to worry about?"

"I wish they'd stop," said Janet, close to tears. "I hate it when they go on like this."

Flo put her arm around her sister. "Let's just forget about them. *We'll* never be like that. Come on—we'll run to the boathouse and I'll teach you all how to play bridge. Do you want to come, Andrew?"

Andrew had been staring into the storm silently, the flashes of lightning illuminating his twitching face. "Thanks, Flo, but I think I'll have an early night." He ran off into the rain.

"Coming, Norah?" The prospect of getting soaked made Janet giggle.

"I think I'll just stay on the verandah for a while." She watched the others dash shrieking down the steps.

Norah went along the verandah to the side door. She slipped into the hall off the kitchen and found what she was looking for—a long rubber raincoat. While she was slithering into it she spied Hanny washing the dishes with a grim look on her face. Her husband sat at the table, pulling on his pipe. They must be able to hear everything that was being shouted in the living room.

The coat came down to her feet and its sleeves flopped below her hands, but at least it would keep her dry. Pulling the hood over her head, she ventured into the storm.

The rain streamed off her as she groped her way down the hill to Andrew's cabin. The clammy coat made her perspire, but her bare feet were cold against the wet rocks.

Norah circled the cabin restlessly, longing to knock on Andrew's door and have another talk. Then she could *tell* him. But she didn't have the nerve. The hood of the coat blocked her vision; she flung it back and let the driving rain sluice over her head. Leaning against the wall underneath Andrew's window, she tipped back her head and caught the heavy drops in her mouth.

Finally the rain settled into a steady shower and the thunder and lightening grew fainter. Then Norah heard another sound. The sound of someone crying—crying with such desperate gulps that Norah trembled.

It was Andrew—who else could it be? Through his open window she listened to his wrenching sobs, his deep voice gasping for air.

The only time Norah had seen a man cry was when her father had said goodbye to her and Gavin in England. That had been a few controlled tears. This was as violent as the storm had been.

She took a chance and heaved herself up by the windowsill to look into the room. Her aching arms would just let her up for a second. It was long enough to glimpse Andrew sprawled on the couch, his head in his arms and his shoulders shuddering.

Norah slid out of the heavy coat, rolled it up into a ball under her arm and sped away into the night. When she reached the dock she peeled off the rest of her wet clothes and jumped into the lake. The water tingled against her bare skin and her body felt as liquid as the lake and the rain.

Janet poked out her head. "Norah's skinny-dipping!"

In an instant she and Flo and Clare had joined her in the black lake. They whooped and splashed and Norah tried to drown the shock of Andrew's misery.

X
A VISITOR

All the next day the cleansing rain fell on the island. When Norah went up to breakfast, Aunt Dorothy and Aunt Mar were setting the children's table together, singing "Pack Up Your Troubles" and tittering like girls. The rest of the Elders, looking as shamefaced as children who had misbehaved, pussyfooted around each other with careful politeness.

"Aunt Florence told me never to mention that shrub word again," said Gavin solemnly, as he joined Norah on the verandah. "She says when we get back to the city she'll check with the university and then she'll know she's right—but she wants the arguing to stop."

Norah shrugged as she swung in the glider.

"Are you in a bad mood?" Gavin asked her. Bosley galloped up the stairs and shook a fountain over both of them.

She shrugged again, but because it was Gavin, managed a small smile.

"Would you like to have Creature for a while?" Gavin pulled the small stuffed elephant out of his raincoat pocket and handed him over.

Norah took Creature gingerly. His wool body was grimy and one ear was missing. He stank.

"Thanks, Gavin. Why does he smell so awful?"

"He got into the fish guts when we were cleaning some bass."

"Pee-yew! Why don't you wash him?"

"No!" said Gavin with alarm. "Haney says that too, but he might come apart—he almost did the last time he had a bath. You can keep him until tonight. I have to go now, we're having an important meeting. Come on, Boz!" He and the dog ran off to join the other members of the Fearless Four.

Norah set Creature on the verandah railing to air out. Everyone but her was feeling better. But what about Andrew? He hadn't appeared yet, and she was too tired to go check on him. Tired and sluggish, as if she'd been awake all night, even though she'd fallen asleep instantly after their swim. And her stomach felt bloated. Maybe she should go in and ask Hanny for some Castoria, but the thought of that disgusting liquid made her want to gag.

Why had Andrew been crying? Norah swung her chair violently. Was it because the family had been comparing him to Hugh? But he must be used to that. It could have been because of what he had told her—that he would rather be an actor than an engineer. She clenched her fists—they should let him do what he wanted.

Or perhaps he was crying because he didn't want to be in the war. Maybe Aunt Catherine was right and Andrew didn't want to fight. Maybe he *was* afraid.

Norah herself was frightened of the war. Every so often she had a terrible nightmare that her family's house was being bombed to rubble. In the daytime it was easy to reassure herself. She and Gavin had been evacuated overseas to get away from bombs and the threat of an invasion, but now both dangers were more remote. She knew from school and the news that Hitler no longer threatened to invade Britain, and the terrible bombing it had received when she'd first lived in Canada had let up considerably. But her night-time self didn't seem to have absorbed that yet.

Andrew, however, was not supposed to be afraid—he was

perfect! If he no longer fit into the neat category of a hero, she would have to alter her fantasies. Now there seemed to be parts of him she didn't know at all.

She still loved him. If only she had the courage to tell him, it would help him be brave, the way Flo's letters to her boy friends did.

Andrew Drummond, the youngest ever recipient of the Victoria Cross, said in a recent interview that he got over his initial fear of fighting through the inspiration of his beloved fiancée, Norah.

But today her fantasies couldn't console her. She curled up on the seat of the glider and listened to the rain increase its drumming. Janet and Clare were playing ping-pong on the table at the far end of the verandah. The monotonous click of the ball, and their giggles when one of them missed, made Norah scowl. How could Janet forgive Clare so easily? But the two of them were cousins; that gave them a bond Norah would never have.

"And what is young Norah doing out here all by herself? I've just made a fire in the living room—wouldn't you be warmer in there?" Hanny's placid, plump husband stood beside her, his clothes covered with pieces of bark.

"I like it better here," said Norah, sitting up again. "Thanks anyway."

"You're a funny one," smiled Mr Hancock. "Suit yourself." He ambled around the corner and Norah resumed her curled-up position. She could hear talking in the living room; Uncle Reg and Uncle Barclay were playing checkers.

Usually she liked lazy wet days at Gairloch. She could go in and work on the puzzle; she'd never managed to finish it in one summer. But she felt trapped in a sticky web of inertia. She stayed half-asleep in her chair for an hour, until her cramping stomach forced her inside to the bathroom.

Fifteen minutes later, Norah lay on a folded towel on her bed, shaking so much that her teeth clacked. She pulled her blanket tighter around her shoulders.

Something was wrong with her! Somehow she had injured herself inside—or she was terribly sick.

She had to tell someone, and soon. But who? There were too many possible people: Aunt Mary, Aunt Florence, Aunt Catherine or Hanny. They would all be kind and concerned. But it would be so embarrassing to say *where* she was hurt. And how could she make it up to the cottage?

There was only one person she wanted. "*Mum . . .*" whispered Norah, sitting up and rocking back and forth. "Oh, Mum . . ."

"Norah!" Flo was shaking her shoulder. "Norah, what on earth is the matter? You look terrified!"

"I want my m-*mother*," croaked Norah. "I *need* her, and she's so far away . . ."

Flo sat on the bed and hugged Norah. "You poor thing. But why are you so homesick all of a sudden? What's happened?"

"Oh, Flo . . ." Norah looked up at the older girl desperately. "Something's wrong with me! I'm *bleeding* . . ."

Slowly she choked out where. To her astonishment Flo began to smile.

"Norah, it's all right! It's perfectly natural, what's happened to you. Didn't you know? Hasn't Aunt Florence told you?"

"Told me what?" Relief flooded through Norah at Flo's matter-of-factness. At least she wasn't going to die. But what was she talking about?

"I guess I'll have to tell you then. Listen, Norah." The older girl flushed. "You know that babies grow inside a woman's stomach, don't you?"

Norah nodded, a dim memory in her head of her mother,

huge with Gavin, leaning over her in the tub and telling her she had a baby inside her.

"Well, when you start to grow up you make a kind of lining inside yourself for the baby to live in."

"What baby?" This was getting more confusing every moment.

"No baby yet. But your body doesn't know it's not time for one. So the lining comes—well, it comes out—and it's made of tissues and stuff that looks like blood. It lasts a few days, then it stops. Oh dear. I don't think I'm explaining this very well. I wish I could remember what Mother said when she told me—it made sense then."

Light dawned. "You mean—the visitor? The little man who sweeps you out?"

"What?"

Shyly Norah told Flo what Aunt Florence had said.

"No wonder you didn't understand! What a stupid way to tell you. That must be why some women call it their 'little visitor.' I call it 'the curse.'"

"The curse! That sounds horrible!"

Flo shrugged. "It does, I guess. I never really thought about it, it's just what my friends and I say. I guess because it's such a nuisance, putting up with it every month. But you get used to it."

Norah was still digesting her earlier words—that this was normal and would only last a few days. Would she have to stay in bed all that time? she wondered.

Then she realized what Flo had just said. "What do you mean, once a month?" she asked suspiciously. "This isn't going to keep on happening, is it?"

Flo looked apologetic. "Uhhh, yes, I'm afraid so, Norah. Once every month until you're about fifty. Then you stop. And you don't do it if you're pregnant, of course."

Norah looked at her with horror. "Once a month until I'm fifty! That's forever!" She sat up straighter, pushed back her hair and said haughtily, "I'm not going to have anything to do with this curse! I won't *do* it!"

Flo laughed so hard she wiped tears from her face. "Norah, you are so funny! You *have* to do it—you don't have a choice. It just—it just happens."

Norah was filled with an enormous lassitude. Something inside her said that Flo was right; mysterious ads in magazines and whispered remarks at school suddenly made sense. She listened dully while the other girl, embarrassed again, started mumbling about sanitary belts and something called Kotex. In the middle of it Janet burst in.

"What's up?"

"Oh, nothing drastic . . ." said Flo. "Norah just got the curse and I'm telling her about it."

"Lucky you!" said Janet passionately. She gazed at Norah with clear admiration. "I wish *I* would start. I'm so slow. Mother says she didn't get it until she was fifteen—she thinks you start younger in each generation. But now I'm *fourteen* . . ."

"Why would you ever want to?" asked Norah with astonishment.

"Because then I'll be a grown-up. Because getting the curse means you're a woman and can have babies—when you're older, of course, and when . . . well . . ." She blushed, and so did Norah.

"Did you two *know* about babies?" said Flo. "If there's something you don't understand, you can ask me." She looked important and they both realized that she knew things that they didn't.

"No thanks," said Janet stiffly. "I'll ask *Mother* if I want to find out anything."

Flo lost her secretive look. "That's probably the best. And Norah can ask her mother when she gets back to England."

Norah thought she knew what Flo was hinting at, but she was quite willing to let the details wait until she was older.

It was bad enough having to deal with this . . . this *curse.* Although Janet's envy made her feel rather proud. She, a year younger, had begun first!

"Has Clare started?" she asked them.

"Clare started at twelve," said Flo. "That's why it makes me mad that no one told you properly—you could have been even earlier!"

Norah sighed and looked at Flo helplessly. "Umm—I need to get some of that Kotex soon, Flo."

"Of course you do—but I don't think I'm the one who should help you. I'll get one of the aunts. Who do you want?"

At first Norah started to say Aunt Mary, but she knew how embarrassed she would be. Aunt Florence would be calm and efficient, and besides, she was the one who'd brought it up in the first place.

"Aunt Florence, I guess." Flo ran up to the cottage.

"Why didn't you *tell* me?" Norah asked Janet. "If you knew all along, you could have said something."

Janet's fat cheeks turned pink. "I'm sorry . . . I guess I thought you knew. I thought everyone our age knew. Anyway, your mother tells you. Oh, Norah, I'm sorry! I mean, I thought Aunt Florence would have told you."

"She tried," said Norah wearily.

Aunt Florence marched up the boathouse stairs, a package under her arm. "Out you go, Janet. Now, Norah, I have exactly what you need. Aren't you glad I informed you just in time? There's nothing to worry about, it's all perfectly natural . . ." Her briskness put the whole traumatic morning into perspective. Norah sighed and submitted herself to this new feminine ritual.

"You won't tell anyone but Aunt Mary, will you?" Norah had a vision of Aunt Florence announcing it at dinner to the whole clan.

"Of course not—it's not something you talk about." Her guardian gave her an odd, sad look. "Hmm . . . when we get back to Toronto, Norah, I'm going to take you shopping for a brassiere." She kissed the top of Norah's head. "You're growing up, my dear. I don't know if I like that or not."

XI

A TRIP TO TOWN

For the next day or so, Norah spent so much time reading in her glider that she felt as if she were planted there. To her relief no one seemed to notice she was any different, and when Aunt Florence and Flo and Janet gave her special smiles she was comforted.

"You don't need to rest all the time," Aunt Florence told her. "You're not ill."

But although Norah felt perfectly all right, the shock of what had happened to her made her want to pretend to be an invalid. And, anyway, she couldn't go swimming—that was the worst part.

"What are you up to, Norah?" Andrew's voice startled her from her book. She'd finally borrowed *Wuthering Heights* and was immersed in the turbulent saga of Catherine and Heathcliff.

She shrugged and smiled shyly. "Did you have a good time?" She knew he'd been on a canoe trip with the Mitchells.

"Wonderful! We almost dumped all our food overboard, though." He was so cheerful that his wretched sobbing seemed like something she had dreamt.

"I need to go to Brockburst," Andrew continued. "Hanny asked me to pick up her cooking pot—it's having a hole mended. Mr Hancock has taken all the aunts to see the gardens at Beaumaris and everyone else seems to have disappeared this afternoon. Do you want to come?"

"Oh, yes please!" Trying to control the excitement in her voice, Norah added, "Do you think I need to tell someone?"

"You can tell Hanny. Why don't you meet me on the dock in ten minutes?"

Norah forgot about being an invalid. She ran into the kitchen to tell Hanny, then raced down to the Girls' Dorm with all the energy of her former self. The others had rowed over to Little Island for a picnic. Thank goodness none of them was here to see her leave alone with Andrew—especially Clare.

A few minutes later Norah sat in the *Putt-Putt* opposite Andrew, gloating over her good fortune. Not only did she have him to herself for the rest of the afternoon, she hadn't been to Brockhurst yet this year. She had changed into a skirt and borrowed, without asking, Clare's straw hat. In her lap she held a purse Flo had given her. Since she was now officially a teen-ager, she might as well act the part.

To her surprise, Andrew headed towards Ford's Bay and moored the boat there.

"Aren't we going by water?" asked Norah.

"Aunt Florence told me this morning that I could take her car."

"Do you know how to *drive?*" blurted out Norah, then flushed when Andrew laughed.

"Don't worry—I'm an expert. Climb in, Miss Stoakes, and I'll show you."

Norah started to rush into the car, then restrained herself and drew up each leg gracefully after she sat down. Just last week Clare had read aloud an article about how to get in and out of a car in a ladylike manner.

She leaned back and let the breeze ruffle her hair as Andrew sped up the dusty road. Tongue-tied with the bliss of sitting next to him, Norah gazed out the window as they passed through Glen Orchard and Bala, catching glimpses of the blue water through the firs. Andrew, as silent as her, concentrated on driving.

At last they arrived in Brockhurst. Andrew parked carefully at the edge of town and they headed towards the hardware store where the pot was being soldered. The man looked surprised to see them.

"Haven't had a chance to do it yet," he muttered. "You'd be best to come back tomorrow."

"I'm afraid we can't," said Andrew politely. "We don't mind waiting—could you have it done by four?" Grudgingly, the man agreed.

"Let's look around," suggested Andrew. "Then I'll buy you a milkshake."

Norah hung her purse over her arm and adjusted her hat, trying to look as if she were Andrew's girl friend. Brockhurst was crowded with tourists who had come up by train from Toronto. Norah and Andrew joined them, meandering in and out of stores and admiring the stately Opera House. They wandered down to the wharf and watched all the boats arriving and departing in the bay.

"Ready for a cold drink?" Andrew asked finally. "It's getting awfully hot."

"Yes, please," said Norah. She wanted to impress him with her brilliant conversation, but she could hardly manage those two words.

As they turned up Beach Road they saw a group of soldiers marching towards them, and stood on the side to let them pass: a long column of men with closely cropped hair, wearing uniforms that looked like pyjamas. Some of them carried shovels or rakes and one had a football under his arm.

"Who are they?" whispered Norah.

Andrew was staring at the men intently. "They're German prisoners of war," he whispered back.

"You mean—they're *Nazis?*"

"That's right. In fact, the Brockhurst camp is full of top-ranking ones."

Now Norah stared even harder, her legs trembling. Nazis in Canada? The men held up their heads proudly as they passed. Norah stepped closer to Andrew.

She simply couldn't believe it. They looked like any other men, not like monsters or villains—like the Enemy.

"Strange, isn't it?" said Andrew as the last of the men passed and they continued back into town. "I've seen them before. They mark off an area in the bay with barbed wire where they swim." The muscle twitched in his cheek. "That's who I'll be fighting one day, Norah. They seem so ordinary, don't they?"

"But they must have done terrible things," said Norah in a small voice.

"No doubt they have." Andrew sighed, then picked up a rock and heaved it into the bushes. "But let's not worry about that on such a gorgeous day. Weren't we thinking about milkshakes? And look who's coming!"

Heading towards them were three teen-agers: a very pretty girl about Andrew's age and two younger boys. They were laughing loudly and shoving each other.

"Look who's here—it's the Great Andrew of Drummond!" cried one of the boys.

"Hello there, Mitchells! Norah, these are my crazy friends—Lois and Jamie and Dick Mitchell. This is Norah, my aunt's war guest. I don't know if I should be introducing you to these nutcases, Norah. I'm sure they're a bad influence. Would you all care to join us for a milkshake?" The four of them were obviously good friends. They continued to tease and fool around as they walked back into town.

Norah lagged a little behind, furious that her time alone

with Andrew had ended. When they got to the ice cream store and scrambled into a booth, she sat at one end and eyed the newcomers warily. The two dark-haired boys looked so much alike they might have been twins, except one was shorter than the other. Lois was also dark, with glittering green eyes. Everything about her was smooth: her perfectly waved hair, her creamy white skin and her even features. Her voice had an ironic tone.

Norah tried to stay calm as Lois gave her a cool, appraising look. "That's a pretty purse you have, Norah," said Lois, as if Norah were a little girl pretending to be a grown-up. Sucking her milkshake hard, Norah glared at the other girl over the top of the container. She noticed how Lois continually drew Andrew's attention towards herself by touching his arm lightly or mocking him.

To her great relief the Mitchells left to meet their father. Now she had Andrew to herself again, but he still seemed to be with them in spirit. "What clowns," he laughed. "The whole family's like that—they're much less formal than *our* family. Everyone does what he wants and their grandmother is a scream. When Jack and I were little, she used to tell us wonderful stories about growing up in New York."

"Is Jack your best friend?" said Norah abruptly.

"I guess he is, although we've lived in different places for quite a while and we've—well, never mind. He's a marvellous fellow—the most intelligent person I know. One day he'll be a famous author. He already writes brilliant short stories and he's going to write about his war experiences—that will be something. He's the only friend I have who also wants to do something creative with his life. The difference is that *his* family is all for it," he added, his voice turning hard.

Norah was even jealous of Jack, and he was far away

fighting. All at once she felt tired and stale. The milkshake had made her more thirsty, not less, and her sandalled feet were clogged with dust. She had been with Andrew an entire afternoon but hadn't managed to say anything to bring them closer.

"Let's go and see if that pot is ready," said Andrew. A few minutes later they were lugging the heavy iron pot towards the car. Then Andrew drove fast out of town.

"Do you want to try?" he asked, slowing down.

"What do you mean?"

"Do you want to try driving? It's perfectly safe—this part of the road is always deserted and I'll take the wheel if you get into trouble. My father used to sometimes let me drive when I was your age—along this very road."

Norah was so overcome she could only nod with shining eyes. Andrew pulled over and changed places with her. Patiently he explained the functions of the pedals and gearshift. Her heart thudded as she turned the key and the engine responded. Slowly she let out the clutch as he told her, and pressed the gas pedal gingerly. The car jerked a bit and then, like an obedient animal, rumbled along the road. She managed to shift into second and third without stalling.

Norah clenched the steering wheel so hard her knuckles stuck out sharply. "You can go a *little* faster," Andrew chuckled. "At this rate we won't be home until dark!"

"But what if someone comes?" asked Norah, staring pop-eyed ahead of her.

"Just keep to your side of the road and you'll be fine."

Luckily no one did come. After a few minutes Norah relaxed a bit and began to enjoy driving. She liked the feeling of the car's power under her control and went a little faster, giggling when the car responded as if it had wanted to speed up.

"I'd better take over now," said Andrew. "We're coming

to a crossroad. You did very well," he added, as Norah geared down, turned into the side of the road and stopped.

"Thank you," she breathed. "That was super! When I grow up I'd like to be a chauffeur or something. But Clare says I can't."

"Why not?"

"She says only men can be chauffeurs."

"Don't listen to Clare," said Andrew, sliding into the driver's seat. "Women can do a lot more things than they used to. My mother drives a huge ambulance in Winnipeg. She loves it! Be a chauffeur, if that's what you want. Don't let anyone stop you—okay?"

"Okay," said Norah, too overcome to suggest that he should do what *he* wanted to as well. She sat beside him in a dream the rest of the way to Ford's Bay. She'd driven a car! Even her mother had never done that. The day had been redeemed; she put out of her head the disturbing sight of the prisoners of war and the unwelcome Mitchells.

"We'd better keep the driving a secret," said Andrew when they were back in the boat. "I don't think Aunt Florence would appreciate it." They exchanged a grin. As the boat slowed down to approach the island Norah kept sneaking looks at Andrew. His clear eyes were fixed on Gairloch and a peaceful expression was on his face.

Now she could say it. She could whisper, "I love you, Andrew," the way women did in movies. Then he would reveal that he loved her too, that he always had but thought she was too young to tell.

But the *Putt-Putt* arrived at the dock while Norah was still trying to pick exactly the right moment. The picnickers were back. Gavin and Sally jumped up from their fishing rods to greet them and the family engulfed her once more.

XII
THE PARTY

"The Elders want to see you, Flo," panted Janet. She had run all the way down from the cottage. "They're just finishing breakfast but they asked me to tell you to meet them in the living room in five minutes. What have you done?" she added curiously.

"Nothing!" Flo looked annoyed. "I wonder what they want. What a bother . . . I was just going to go to the mainland to get some more writing paper."

"Well, hurry up," said Janet. "Aunt Florence has that solemn look. I bet you *have* done something—something awful—and you won't tell us!"

She ducked to avoid Flo's pillow. Then they watched the tall girl meander up to the cottage, refusing to hurry.

"She sure has nerve," said Clare. "I wonder what's up."

Norah sat down heavily. "Maybe it's news—bad news! You know—about one of the boys she writes to."

They stared at her. "Oh, no," said Janet softly. "Oh, poor Flo . . ." Even Clare's face showed concern.

Norah twisted a corner of her sheet in her hands, the same choking fear filling her as in her nightmare about home. Last night, when Uncle Barclay had told her Churchill was in Canada for a conference, she had been irritated to be reminded once more about the war. Now its tentacles stretched toward them.

They sat on their unmade beds and waited. Then Janet leaned far out the window.

"She's coming! She's running and she doesn't look sad at all—she looks happy!"

Flo tore into the dorm and collapsed on her bed. "Listen everyone, I have *wonderful* news!" She glanced at their drained faces. "What's wrong?"

Janet bounced down beside her and gave her sister a squeeze. "Nothing!" she crowed. "Tell us!"

"Wait until you hear this. The Elders are abandoning us!"

"What?" Clare frowned. "Don't joke, Flo. This morning has been dramatic enough already."

"It's not a joke! You know that wedding they're all going to this Saturday."

They nodded. Aunt Anne's sister was getting married from the Royal Muskoka Hotel on one of the other lakes, and Sally was to be a flower girl.

"They were going to leave for the hotel on Saturday morning and come back the same day." Flo grinned. "Well, now they're staying overnight! They won't be back until Sunday evening because someone's having a lunch the next day."

"But that means—" began Janet.

"Exactly! We'll be alone. Andrew and I are in charge. We'll have the whole island to ourselves for almost two days!"

"But what about the Hancocks?" said Norah.

"They're going away too! Their nephew is home on leave and they're taking the train back to Toronto for the weekend."

"It's not that great," said Clare. "Won't we have to babysit George and Denny? That will take all our time—you know what brats they can be."

"They're going to the wedding! Aunt Anne thinks they should see Sally being a flower girl and her relatives have arranged a sitter for them afterwards. So it will just be us! Of course, there are the other little boys, but they're easy enough to look after. Now listen, I have a wonderful idea—let's have a party!"

"Now you're talking!" said Clare. "On Saturday night?"

Flo nodded. "Andrew and I can ask all our friends and you may too, of course."

Janet looked worried. "Are we *allowed* to have a party?"

"Of course not, silly! But no one will know, because almost everyone's parents will be at the wedding too!"

"I don't think we should do it," said Janet primly. "What if the Elders find out? Imagine how furious Aunt Florence would be..."

Flo grimaced but Clare said, "Don't be such a baby, Janet. We won't get caught, as long as we clean up afterwards. *I* think it's a swell idea. I've been waiting all summer for something exciting to happen and this is it!"

"It really will be all right, Janet," Flo reassured her sister. "Let's make a list!" She tore a page from her writing pad. "We'll ask the Mackenzies, the Laziers, Ceci Johnson and her friend from the States... We'll have to spend the next few days going around in the boat and passing the word—we can pretend we're going on a lot of picnics."

"Make sure there aren't too many girls," warned Clare. "And I'll ask Louise to bring all her records."

Janet and Norah listened quietly, scarcely believing that they were included as well. Then Janet added a few names to the list. Norah didn't have any friends up north to ask but that didn't matter—she was beginning to feel excited.

"Flo, do you think Andrew will want to do it?" she dared to ask, not looking at Clare.

"Oh, I'm sure he will," said Flo. "Andrew always likes to have a good time. It'll be nice to plan something with him again, the way we used to. We won't be able to tell him until he gets back from the Mitchells', though." She looked wistful. "He's always over there."

"Make sure you ask Jamie and Dick," said Clare.

"What about Peter and Ross and Gavin? What if they tell?" said Janet.

"Janet, will you stop worrying!" said Clare. "I'll manage Peter and Ross. I know enough things they've done to threaten them with. How about Gavin, Norah—can you trust him?"

"Of course I can!" said Norah indignantly. "He won't say anything if I ask him not to, and I don't have to threaten him."

"We'll give them something to do so they feel part of it," said Flo. "I know—they can meet the boats and help tie them up. Now *food* ... we need another list."

For Norah, the best part about preparing for the party was that Andrew was so enthusiastically involved. He stayed on the island and shared in their secret plans, even coming down to the boathouse at night to discuss them. He treated Norah to the same teasing banter that he did the other cousins; Norah was relieved that Clare didn't say anything.

While the cousins were keyed up with suppressed excitement about the party, the Elders were busy getting ready for the wedding.

"I'm sorry we have to leave you all behind, Norah," said Aunt Mary, as Norah helped her pin some new silk flowers on her hat. "It's going to be such a beautiful wedding—the wedding of the summer. But I suppose you'll like being on your own for a change."

"We will," Norah assured her. She wished she could tell Aunt Mary about the party; she was the only Elder who probably wouldn't mind.

"There!" Aunt Mary tweaked a bow on the hat. "That should match my new dress perfectly. I have to pick it up today."

Now that the dress was finished, Norah wondered what she'd use for an excuse to visit Tom. Would he be at the wedding? Would Aunt Mary have to pretend she didn't know him? Or perhaps they would decide that this was the occasion to announce their engagement. Quiet Aunt Mary was really the most romantic member of the family, Norah thought dreamily.

"Weddings! What a lot of fuss!" complained Aunt Catherine. Norah sat on the old woman's bed while she shook out an ancient beaded sweater and frowned at a moth hole in it. "They're bad enough in the winter but having to get all dressed up in the summer . . . I'm half-inclined to stay here with you young ones. I'm sure you'll have a better time than I will." She tugged on the sweater and grimaced at her reflection in the mirror.

"Oh," said Norah in a panic. But then Aunt Catherine added, "I have to go, though—the bride's parents are old friends. Weddings terrify me, you know."

"Why?"

"Because all my life I've had a recurring nightmare of standing in front of the altar and suddenly changing my mind—but not daring to say so because everyone would be disappointed. Whenever I see the bride and groom standing there I feel trapped. Much better to be independent, not saddled with someone for the rest of your life."

Norah was shocked. "But what about love?"

"Love!" Aunt Catherine chuckled. "Love's all very well, and none of us can do without it. We wouldn't want to, either. But it's like champagne—bubbly and sweet, but the effect doesn't last. Not the moonlight and roses kind of love, anyway. Look at our last king—Edward—where did love get him? It lost him the throne."

A dim memory stirred in Norah of sitting in the kitchen with her family, listening to the king's words from the wireless, words she had often heard grownups quote since then: that he could not be king "without the help and support of the woman I love."

"But why can't he marry her and still *be* king?" she had asked.

"Because she's divorced and they won't let him," Muriel had replied. "So he's sacrificing his throne for her. Isn't that romantic? It's true love..."

"Love! Puh!" Grandad had sputtered. He had sounded very much like Aunt Catherine just now. "What's so important about love? It's *duty* that's important. The fellow is neglecting his duty."

"You loved Granny," Tibby had said gently.

"That's different—that's *marriage*," Grandad had retorted.

"Don't you think *anyone* should get married?" Norah asked Aunt Catherine now, more bewildered each second.

"You poor child—what have I been telling you? Of course marriage can be splendid for some people. Look at Dorothy and Barclay—they've always seemed to me to have a good steady relationship. Marriage works when all the romance nonsense ends and you learn to give each other space and respect. But it's not for me. Everyone doesn't *have* to marry, you know. I could have, several times. But I'm just as happy—probably happier—alone. Not that anyone is going to propose to me now!" She struggled out of the sweater and shook herself like a small, fierce terrier. "But don't listen to the ramblings of an old woman, Norah. You'll fall in love one day and you might get married too. Just make sure you do what you want to do."

Norah walked slowly downstairs. She had always thought that Aunt Catherine wasn't married because no one had ever asked her. But to deliberately choose not to be... And she *was* happy, there was no denying that. Happier than some of the aunts, like Aunt Mar, who seemed only half-here with Uncle Peter away, or Aunt Anne, who fussed so much about being a perfect wife. But her own parents—now that she thought of it—had always seemed to be contented with each other. She wondered if Muriel and Barry would be.

Andrew waved to her as he walked by on the verandah. Norah's heart danced and she forgot her unsettling reflections. It seemed to her that love was much simpler than Aunt Catherine made out—and of course, *she* wanted to get married.

"Goodbye! Have a good time!" All the cousins stood on the dock and waved cheerfully. Uncle Gerald and his family had already left with a neighbour and the eight remaining Elders were crammed into the *Florence,* with Uncle Barclay at the wheel.

"They look like people in the movies," Gavin whispered to Norah. With their festive hats, bright floral-printed dresses, strings of pearls and crisp suits the aunts and uncles glittered with importance. A long time later, whenever Norah thought of the Elders she remembered them like this: "dressed to the nines," as Aunt Catherine said, looking as proud and excited as children going on an outing.

"Take good care of Bosley, Gavin," said Uncle Reg.

"You are only to leave the island for an emergency," said Aunt Florence.

"And remember, Flo—no visitors," added Aunt Dorothy. In the noisy farewells, Flo managed not to answer.

"Behave yourselves!" were the last words they heard. They waved dutifully until the launch was out of sight; then they grinned at each other.

"We're free!" laughed Flo. "Let's get going. Andrew, you have the list of food to get. The rest of you come up and start moving furniture."

By noon, when Andrew had returned from Ford's Bay with cartons of Orange Crush and Coke and packages of crackers and peanuts, the cottage was ready. All the living-room furniture had been pushed to the sides or put out onto the verandah. The rugs had been rolled up, leaving a bare expanse of painted floorboards. A stack of records lay ready by the new phonograph.

The little boys had listened solemnly while Flo told them about the party. "If you say anything, Peter and Ross, I'll tell Mother you were the ones who broke her sewing machine," said Clare.

"Don't worry—we'll never tell!" said Gavin earnestly. The three of them beamed with the honour of being included.

They all helped spread the crackers with cheese and a dab of jelly and arrange them on plates. Then Flo cooked them a huge batch of corn-on-the-cob for lunch. They devoured it in minutes, their faces gleaming with butter.

"Hanny will notice we've used all the butter ration," said Janet.

"We'll just do without it for the rest of the weekend," Flo told her.

"Come on, you three—I'll take you fishing in the rowboat while the women make themselves beautiful," said Andrew. Gavin, Peter and Ross ran after him.

As soon as the boys had left, the girls went skinny-dipping off the dock, playing catch with the floating bar of soap.

Then they washed their hair in the lake. Norah watched the other three put their hair up in pincurls.

"Shall I do yours too?" Flo asked her.

Norah wasn't sure how different she wanted to look, but she decided to risk it. Flo carefully twisted squiggly shapes all over her head. The four of them sat in a row to dry their hair and Flo began to shave her legs.

"Let me try," said Clare. "Mother says I'm too young, but if I start she won't be able to do anything about it."

Norah and Janet watched closely while Clare soaped one leg and drew the razor along it, leaving a gleaming bare patch.

"Ouch!" A line of red welled up. "Now look what I've done!" Clare splashed water on her leg to stop the bleeding but she had to press a wet towel on the cut.

"I'm glad I don't have to shave my legs yet," Janet whispered to Norah. "Mum says I'm so blonde I may never have to."

Norah looked down at her own smooth legs and gingerly touched the metal layer of bobby pins on her head. They were hot from the sun and they pinched. She let Janet paint the nails on her toes and fingers a shiny red and began to feel she was in disguise.

For the next hour they examined their clothes, trying on and trading until each person was satisfied. Flo passed around a jar of Odo-ro-no. "You don't want to have BO—the dancing will make you perspire," she warned. Then Flo and Clare covered their legs with some brown liquid called Velva Leg Film. Janet wanted some too, but there wasn't enough.

"I wish it wasn't so hard to get stockings," she grumbled. "You're lucky your legs are so brown, Norah. Mine are so white and freckled. And I look so *fat* . . ."

She did look fat—in her flowered print dress cinched at the waist, she resembled a sausage tied in the middle.

"You look . . . *curvy*," said Norah desperately. "Sort of like Dorothy Lamour."

"You look perfectly all right," said Flo. "And the point is not to worry about your appearance—just to have a good time. Now it's your turn, Norah."

After Norah had her dress on—an old one of Clare's that she had reluctantly lent her—Flo brushed out her hair and tied a blue bow on one side. Then she carefully applied some of her Tangee lipstick to Norah's open mouth.

"Wow! Have a look!" Norah went over and stood in front of the cracked mirror on the back of the door. The others gathered behind her as she drew in her breath with surprise.

Her hair was its usual dull brown, but now the ends burst into a froth that tickled her cheeks. The ribbon drew attention away from her nose. Her red mouth made her teeth look very white. Her dress was tight to the waist, then fell in soft folds, with Janet's silver pumps gleaming underneath.

"You're beautiful!" smiled Flo. "It's incredible—you could pass for sixteen at least."

"Oh, Norah, I wish I could look like that!" cried Janet. Clare didn't say anything but her pursed mouth looked grudgingly approving.

Norah crossed her arms over her chest. "Do you—do you think I need a bra? I'm getting one in the fall."

"That tight dress is fine without one," said Flo.

Norah let her arms hang free and continued to stare at the stranger in the mirror. Was that *her*? She smiled at her reflection and it grinned saucily back. What would Andrew think?

"Now there are fifteen!" panted Gavin. He collapsed beside Norah on the verandah swing, after racing full speed up the hill. He was almost hysterical with excitement; his eyes glittered and his cheeks were flushed a deep red. Aunt Florence would have called him overwrought and sent him to bed, but Norah didn't want to spoil his obvious enjoyment of the party. "Ten launches, three rowboats and two canoes," continued Gavin. "Peter and Ross are still helping tie them up."

All evening the little boys had greeted the boats and pointed the guests towards the party. That was unnecessary: the steps were dotted with candles and above them Gairloch's glowing windows beamed like a lighthouse into the darkness. Out of them drifted the strains of the Glenn Miller band, overladen with laughing chatter.

Teen-agers spilled out of the house onto the verandah, perching on the railing with cigarettes, bottles of pop or the beer that some of them had brought. Norah was studying a couple who were kissing close to her. The boy dived into the girl's neck; he seemed to be nibbling on it. Norah continued to stare as the couple's heads twisted and turned. "Necking" was a very accurate description, she decided. It didn't look very comfortable.

"Whoops—here comes another one!" Gavin tumbled down to the dock again as the lights of a launch streamed across the lake. Norah went over to the railing and gazed at the flotilla of boats, some tied to the dock and some to each other.

She wiped her sweaty palms on the skirt of her dress, took a deep breath, and plunged into the party again. She had only lasted a few minutes on her last attempt. Three times the noise and the grown-upness had overwhelmed her and she'd escaped to breathe more easily on the verandah.

Norah found Janet hugging Bosley on the windowseat, a dreamy look on her face. "Someone asked me to daance!" she whispered with awe.

Norah squished in beside her. "*Who?* Did you?"

Janet nodded solemnly and pointed. "With that boy over there—the one with glasses. He's Louise's cousin. But I stepped on his foot, so we stopped. I don't mind though—at least I was asked! I never have been before."

"What's his name?" The boy was sitting on the far side of the room, guzzling a Coke. He caught their eyes and scuttled out of the room.

"Now we've scared him away," sighed Janet. "Oh well. His name is Mark and he's only staying in Muskoka for another two days. I asked him lots of questions to draw him out, the way it says in *Ladies' Home Journal*, but he didn't seem to want to answer them."

"You were so brave to say yes," said Norah. "I hope no one asks *me* to dance. It would be so embarrassing."

"Have some peanuts." Janet had a bowl of them beside her. The two of them ate them all, throwing an occasional tidbit to Bosley, while they watched the party. Couples—some mixed and many consisting of two girls—jitterbugged before them, waggling their hands and almost leaping off the ground with energy. Some of the girls were dancing so hard that their leg make-up ran down in streaks; occasionally one would be lifted high above the crowd or swooped between her partner's legs. The cat collection shook precariously on the mantelpiece as the whole room seemed to jump and sway. The hot space was filled with a smell of cigarette smoke and sweat.

"Shall we?" suggested Janet.

"I'm not very good," said Norah.

"Well, you know I'm not. We should practise and maybe then I'll stop stepping on people's feet."

They slid off the seat and began to jitterbug. They had often practised dancing in the boathouse, but here it was different. Norah was sure everyone in the room was eyeing them scornfully. Her arms felt wooden and her feet kept stepping out of Janet's shoes. "That's enough," she said finally. "I'd rather watch." Janet seemed quite willing to stop and they went back to their post.

Norah had lost track of Andrew; the last time she'd seen him he'd been helping Flo uncap more bottles. Now she spotted him again and frowned. He was dancing with Lois; she hadn't even noticed the Mitchells arrive. Lois was teasing him about something, poking his chest while they danced. Andrew's deep answering laugh made Norah's insides lurch with jealousy. He had said hello to her in passing but he hadn't said anything about how she looked.

Someone put on "Stardust." The mixed couples came together like magnets and the single girls retreated to the sides of the room. Some of the couples kissed while they danced, barely moving to the hypnotic melody.

"Slow ones are such a bore," said Janet. "Look at Clare! Who's she with?"

Clare was snuggled into the shoulder of a tall blond boy.

"Aunt Mar wouldn't like that," said Janet. "He's too old for her." Then Flo steered a giggling Peter past them and they all laughed.

"Why are most of the girls older than the boys?" asked Norah suddenly. Some of the girls were as sophisticated-looking as movie stars, but many of the boys had skin pocked with acne and gangly arms and legs.

"Because the older boys are all in the war, silly."

Of course; now she remembered Flo saying how many of her friends were also writing letters to the front. Andrew and Clare's partner were the oldest. Norah let herself look at Andrew again; Lois was holding him so close Norah couldn't stand it.

"I need some air," she whispered, and slipped out into the night.

Gavin was on the glider, fast asleep. She half-carried him, half-led him to bed. Then she spent the next few hours swinging in her chair in time to the music, falling into a light sleep, then jerking awake again. She could go to bed herself, but she liked taking advantage of the fact that there was no one to tell her to. And she couldn't seem to leave the party; it was as if it were going to go on forever and she was stuck in it like a trance.

One after another the velvety melodies floated out to her: "Blue Moon," "Moonlight Serenade," and the whirling crescendo of "In the Mood." Again and again someone put on "You'll Never Know." That's *our* song, Norah decided. Most of the songs were about moons and dreams and partings and they all had a wistful edge to them. Being grown-up seemed to be one endless love scene where someone was in love and the other had left or didn't return the love.

Andrew's voice very close to her startled her awake. A strident female one answered it. "Come on, Andrew, just a short ride. *Why* can't you?"

Andrew and Lois were standing at the top of the verandah steps. Norah kept very still, rubbing her eyes. She must have slept for a long time. Now the party seemed to be ending; down by the water voices were calling out goodbyes.

"I told you," said Andrew, sounding as if he were controlling his impatience. "I'm supposed to be in charge and I don't want to leave my cousins alone."

"For Pete's sake, they're not babies! Can't we just nip over to Little Island? We'd have it all to ourselves. I'm beginning to think you're afraid of me."

They moved down the steps and into the shadows right below her. There was a long silence during which Norah, embarrassed and furious, hunched farther into the glider. She could see by their outline that they were locked in an embrace.

"There! Now will you take me?" wheedled Lois.

"*Lois* . . ." said Andrew, as if he were entreating her not to keep asking. Then a voice below called her name as well. "Lois! Are you coming or not?"

"There!" said Andrew eagerly. "Jamie and Dick are leaving—you'd better go with them."

"Oh, all right," grumbled Lois. "Sometimes you're a spoilsport, Andrew."

Norah leaned over the railing as the two of them went hand in hand down the steps. She listened to Andrew call goodbye, and sighed with relief as the boat carrying Lois chugged away.

XIII
A PROMISE

Norah expected Andrew to return to the party—there were still a few lingering dancers—but he strode around the side of the cottage. She slipped off the verandah and set out along the path by the lake to trail him.

After her sleep she was rested and alert. She had left behind her uncomfortable shoes and undone the pinching ribbon from her hair. The night air was warm and soft. A whippoorwill trilled its endless refrain, a startled raccoon lumbered out of her way and a few bats swooped in front of her. Crickets chirped in a reedy chorus. Norah slid through the lively darkness like a fish through water, her head up to admire the glittering sky. This was as magical and romantic a night as in the songs.

Finally she spotted Andrew, a dark, seated figure high up on her lookout. Norah stole through the trees and paused at the base of the rock. She could slip away again without him hearing her, but that would be cowardly.

"Andrew," Norah called.

He jerked around. "Who's there?"

"It's me—Norah."

"Norah! I thought you'd be in bed by now. Come and share the view—it's such a beautiful night."

Carefully Norah's toes found the footholds that were so familiar to her in daylight. She trembled with pleasure as Andrew reached out and took her hand.

"Thanks," she mumbled, flopping down beside him. Her cheeks were burning so much, she was glad it was dark. The rock still gave off a faint glow of heat from the day.

"This used to be my favourite place when I was younger," said Andrew.

"Did it? It's *my* favourite place!" Norah was so pleased, she forgot to feel awkward.

"I know—I've seen you up here."

Had he seen her spying on him? But Andrew was smiling. His eyes, dim by moonlight, were concentrating only on her.

"I meant to tell you how pretty you look tonight, Norah. Have you done something different with your hair?"

"Flo curled it," mumbled Norah.

"Hmmm . . . maybe you should do it like that all the time."

"It's too much trouble! I might later—when I'm sixteen or so."

"You'll probably be back in England when you're sixteen," said Andrew. "Surely the war will be over by then. Now that Sicily has been taken, it looks a lot more hopeful."

He didn't sound hopeful. He sounded, Norah realized, absolutely miserable. She remembered the night she'd seen him crying.

"Are you upset that the war might be over before you can be in it?" she asked carefully.

Andrew gave a dry, mocking laugh. "It's kind of the opposite. I'm afraid the war might *not* be over and I'll have to fight in it."

Norah swallowed hard. "Don't you want to, then?"

Andrew whirled around so fast that Norah gasped. "No, I do not! I've never wanted to do anything less in my entire life!" He leaned over and grabbed Norah's shoulders. "I don't *want* to kill anyone! I don't think it's right! But do you think my parents or anyone else in this damned family understands that?"

Andrew dropped his hands and Norah controlled the impulse to rub the painful places where he'd gripped her.

Andrew sighed. "I'm sorry, Norah. I didn't mean to scare you. Now you know. You're the only person I've ever told. I guess you're the only one I *can* tell, since you're not really part of the family. But I shouldn't bother you with my problems. I'm sorry," he said again. He sounded as if he were going to cry.

"It's okay," whispered Norah. "I don't mind." They were quiet for what seemed like an eternity, Andrew's fierce words echoing in the darkness.

"Aunt Catherine said that too," said Norah slowly. "She said that you weren't cut out to be a soldier and that you were born at the wrong time."

"Aunt Catherine is the only one who understands," said Andrew. "You know how kids play Cowboys and Indians and pretend to shoot each other? I never did—I used to pretend that my gun was a camera! It really upset my father—he was always buying me new, bigger guns to entice me. And I hated Cadets—all that stupid drilling. Do you know how many men were killed at Dieppe?"

"How many?" whispered Norah. She remembered the horror all the grown-ups had felt last August when so many Canadians had been lost. But she and the other cousins had been so busy playing games they hadn't paid much attention.

"Almost nine hundred! Think of that! Nine hundred men slaughtered like cattle—for what? Doesn't it seem intolerable and absurd to you that whenever human beings disagree they go out and *kill* each other?" His arms thrust wildly as his words rushed out.

Norah's head was whirling, but she tried to keep it above Andrew's rising passion.

"But what about *Hitler*? Don't we have to beat him?"

Beating Hitler had been ingrained in Norah's consciousness since she was nine. She remembered her own efforts to help. "I used to watch for his planes in England," she said softly. "All my friends did. We thought the war was fun then. I don't any more, but I still think we have to fight him. What would happen if he won?" Her voice rose in panic. "What would happen to *England*? And to my family?"

Andrew patted her knee. "You're perfectly right, Norah—don't worry. I know we have to beat him so people like your family can be safe. And we probably will. It's just too bad that war seems to be the only way." He sighed. "I feel like such a freak. Every one of my friends seems to take it for granted we'll all join up. Even fellows as bright as my friend Jack seem to be able to stomach it. We had a terrible argument the night before he left—*he* thinks I should fight. I don't know anyone who feels the way I do."

Norah was trying very hard not to think of Andrew as a freak herself. She'd never heard anyone express any doubts about the war—except for Aunt Catherine. But Andrew was a *man*, not an old woman. "Are you afraid?" Norah asked, almost angrily.

"I've thought about that a lot," said Andrew slowly. "I guess everyone must be afraid—you wouldn't be human if you weren't. But I think you could make yourself do it when the crunch comes— 'screw your courage to the sticking place' and all that. I *could* do that, I think—but it doesn't seem morally right to me. So I feel like such a phoney, with everyone thinking I'm going off to learn how to be an officer and then maybe join the war."

"But it's only maybe," Norah reminded him. "You might not even have to."

"Yes, I could avoid it—but don't you see how that makes me even more of a phoney? I'm not taking any sort of stand—everyone thinks I'm eager to get in on it, as Uncle Barclay keeps saying. If I'm lucky I won't have to fight, but then I'll spend the rest of my life pretending to be sorry I didn't. I just can't live that sort of lie!"

Norah listened to the pain in his voice. There was no way she could argue with his conviction.

She took a deep breath. All right, then. No matter how much she disagreed with him, she would accept his beliefs, if that was what loving him demanded.

"What do you *want* to do?" she asked.

"I want to be an actor, of course," said Andrew at once. "I want to do it *now,* not wait until after the war—to quit university and try to get on with some company."

"What would happen if you did that? Would someone make you fight anyway?"

"When I'm older I'd have to do service here in Canada, but they wouldn't make me go overseas. Do you know what they call guys like that? 'Zombies.' Can you imagine how the family would feel if I was a zombie? Their golden boy, their Hugh, being such a coward..."

All at once Norah saw everything very clearly. She felt older, not younger, than Andrew. "That wouldn't be being a coward!" she said firmly. "Standing up for what you believe in would be braver than fighting." She got up on her knees with excitement. "It doesn't *matter* what they think, Andrew! You should do what you want! It's not what I would do, or Flo or Uncle Barclay or most other people—but it's what *you* should do. Just tell them that you're never going to fight, so it's no use taking that course! Just tell them!" She didn't even realize she was shaking his arm.

Her face was so close that she could see his expression clearly—as if he were afraid of her. Then he threw back his head and laughed, laughter that was very close to crying.

"Oh, Norah, you are a wonder," he said, wiping his eyes. "*You'd* tell them, wouldn't you? You're much braver than I am. And of course, you're right. What you're suggesting is what I've been struggling with all summer. I *should* tell them and do what I want—but I don't know if I can! Isn't it ridiculous? I'm more frightened of this family than I am of the war!"

"Of course you can!" cried Norah. "Tell them tomorrow! Will you?"

Andrew shuddered. "Not tomorrow!" He was quiet again, and then he said slowly, "But maybe... yes, I will tell them, and very soon. I'll have to wait for exactly the right moment—when we're all together and I've worked up enough courage. Perhaps on our last night—then I can escape the repercussions. And believe me, there'll be plenty of them! I've been thinking that if I *did* decide to do this, I could live with some friends in Saskatchewan. There's a student company there I could try to join."

"But you'll do it? Do you promise?"

Andrew laughed again, but this time it was joyful. "Yes, I promise I'll do it. Thank you, Norah—you've helped me make up my mind. I was beginning to feel frozen—as if I'd *never* decide."

Norah thought she would burst with pleasure. "You're very welcome," she grinned.

"We'd better go—the others must be wondering why you're not in bed. I'll go down and make sure everyone's left." Andrew took her hand again as they stumbled down the rock.

"Good-night," whispered Norah. She flew down to the boathouse, her arms spread wide as if she were a bird. Minutes later, as she lay in bed and went over each burning word of their conversation, she realized she hadn't fulfilled her aim—she hadn't told him she loved him. But that could wait a while. Andrew had revealed his most intimate feelings to her. And he had entrusted her with an important secret. Surely that meant he felt something for her too.

XIV
UP THE RIVER

"Please pass the peanuts," said Gavin solemnly.

"And the pickles," giggled Ross. He sandwiched a pickle between two crackers and crammed it into his mouth. "Yummy! I wish we had this kind of breakfast every day!"

Flo yawned, had a sip of coffee and grimaced. "What did you put in this, Andrew? It doesn't taste like Hanny's."

Even though it was eleven, they were sprawled around the kitchen table in their pyjamas. Flo had begun by setting out bowls and a box of cereal, but the little boys had discovered the leftover food and now they were all enjoying it. The kitchen was a disaster: empty bottles, cigarette boxes and glasses took up every bit of space on the counters. The windows were wide open to get rid of the smoky smell.

"What a terrific party," sighed Clare. "Everyone said it was the best one of the summer."

"It was," agreed Flo. "I didn't realize so many people would come. Who *were* they all?"

"Friends of friends," grinned Andrew. "Word must have spread quickly. Some people even came from Huntsville!"

Flo turned to Clare. "Who was that boy *you* were with? He seemed a bit old for you."

Clare bristled. "He's not that old—twenty-two."

"Twenty-two!" gasped Janet, but Clare ignored her. "He's in the Norwegian Airforce. He's been training at the Muskoka Airport but he's leaving tomorrow so I won't be able to see him again. But he asked me to write to him," she added smugly. "Now I'll have someone in the war too."

"What about your boy friend in Montreal—what will *he* think?" Janet asked her.

"He can think what he wants. After all, Flo writes to more than one boy. Like she says, fellows who are overseas need to be cheered up."

Norah glanced at Andrew. He caught her eye and winked back; Clare's comments didn't seem to be bothering him.

"You just want someone to boast about," said Janet. "I don't think your mother is going to like you writing to someone so old. *I* enjoyed the dancing the most," she added, as if everyone had asked her. "Mark and I had a swell time trying the foxtrot."

Norah didn't think Mark had asked Janet to dance again, but she didn't say anything. She felt warm inside, as if a bright flame were burning steadily. In a blissful daze she listened to Andrew tease Janet about having a boy friend. Everything about this morning was special and new. She ran her hands over the smooth scrubbed pine of the table and took another delicious sip of Orange Crush out of its brown ribbed bottle.

They all lingered until Flo glanced at her watch. She leapt up. "It's almost noon! They'll be back in five hours! All right, everyone, we have to begin. Janet, you empty all the ashtrays. Norah and Clare, bring everything in from the living room and Andrew can put back the furniture. I'll start on the kitchen. You three boys scour every inch of the island for litter—especially cigarette butts!"

By four-thirty no one would have guessed there had been a huge party at Gairloch the night before. All of the living room furniture was back in its usual place. Every surface in the kitchen gleamed. They had burned most of the garbage and hidden the bottles for Andrew to sneak over to Ford's Bay the next day.

They sat in a row on the dock, drooping with sleepiness while they waited for the launch.

"No more freedom," complained Clare, when Peter sighted the boats. "Remember," she warned her brothers. "Not a word! I can hardly wait until I'm old enough to leave home and have parties whenever I want to."

"I wish we had just one more day," sighed Flo. "I love the feeling of having the island all to ourselves."

"It'll be fun to hear about the wedding, though," said Janet.

"Maybe they'll bring us presents!" added Ross. He jumped up and waved as the boat came closer.

The clan swarmed onto the dock and the usual kissing and exclamations began. Norah submitted to it all cheerfully.

"Look how neat and tidy everything is!" said Aunt Dorothy when they reached the cottage.

"We cleaned the whole cottage as a surprise," said Flo quickly. "It gave us something to do."

Everyone sat in the living room, the children exchanging guilty looks as the Elders praised them. Politely they listened to all the different versions of the wedding.

"Sally was the star," said her mother fondly. "She looked so adorable and she even sang a song at the reception, didn't you sweetheart?"

"I didn't want to," said Sally indignantly. "I only did it because you asked me to."

"But didn't you like being a flower girl?" Clare asked her.

"It was okay. But there was so much *waiting.*"

Each of the children was given a thin slice of wedding

cake. "I don't know how they managed such a big cake," said Aunt Dorothy. "Put it under your pillows tonight and whoever you dream of is the one you'll marry."

"I'm not *getting* married, so I may as well eat mine now," said Peter. All the Elders laughed as he gulped down his cake in one bite.

But Norah saved hers carefully. That night she went to bed early, but before she fell asleep she remembered to place the cake, wrapped in its paper doily, under her pillow. She always thought of Andrew last thing at night anyway, so she knew she'd dream about him.

The next morning she sat up in bed, nibbling thoughtfully at her flattened piece of cake. She had slept so soundly she couldn't remember her dreams. The other girls smiled secretly and said they wouldn't tell who they had dreamed about; Norah suspected they had forgotten as well.

She lay back in bed and nestled in her cosy blankets.

Andrew tells the family he isn't going to university and he's never going to join up. Then he goes to Saskatchewan and becomes the most promising actor in Canada. When the war is over he moves to England and begins acting there, so he can live close to Norah until she's old enough to marry . . .

Sally wandered in. "Hanny wants to know why you haven't come to breakfast yet."

"We're *tired*," giggled Janet. "But we can't tell you why."

"I know why. You had a party! Ross told me."

"I'll throttle him!" said Clare. "You'd better not tell, Sally!"

Sally looked at her slyly. "If you let me borrow your ukelele for the rest of the summer, then I won't tell."

"All right," sighed Clare. "But don't play it now," she protested, as the little girl began to strum the ukelele. "I want to put on a record."

They all lay back in their beds as the song began. "I'll be seeing you / In all the old familiar places..." Sally got into bed with Flo and the older girl whispered to her about keeping the party a secret.

"I'll be lookng at the moon / But I'll be seeing you." The melody lingered in the air after the song was over.

"Don't put that one on again, Clare," said Flo. "It makes me miss Ned too much."

"I wonder if I'll ever see Gunnar again," mused Clare.

"And Mark..." Janet said mournfully.

Norah tried to feel sad. Now that Andrew was going to Saskatchewan she wouldn't see him in Toronto this fall. When *would* she see him? But she couldn't seem to think beyond this blissful present, with his confiding words still ringing in her ears.

"I'm sure glad I'm not sleeping in here any more," declared Sally. "You're *still* talking about love."

"What should we do today? Everything seems so flat after the party," complained Clare. "And Louise has gone back to the city—I have no one to visit."

"Mum says I have to do some math," moaned Janet. "I have a whole workbook to get through. It's almost the end of the summer and I haven't even started it! Would you help me, Norah? You're so good at math."

Norah sat up again and looked out at the bright blue lake. It was much too inviting a morning to waste on schoolwork. And the summer *was* ending, she realized with alarm—only two more weeks! She wanted to do something special, something she'd never done before. Not with Andrew—now that she felt so sure of him she needed a rest from his intensity.

"No thanks, Janet," she said, as nicely as she could. "I have other plans."

"'I have other plans'—what plans?" Clare mimicked her

accent but Norah ignored her as she hurried into her clothes and ran up the steps.

"Good-morning, Aunt Florence," she said politely as, ten minutes later, she placed Aunt Florence's breakfast on her guardian's lap.

"Oh, it's you, Norah. Where's Gavin this morning?"

"He'll come up and take your tray. I wanted to ask you something."

"Well, ask away." Aunt Florence poured out her tea and leaned back against her plump pillows, looking as if she were already preparing to say no.

"Do you think Gavin and I could go somewhere today? On our own, I mean. The lake's very calm. I thought I could take him in the *Putt-Putt* to Mirror River and then go up it in the canoe—we could tow it behind on the way, like we did two years ago with Uncle Gerald."

"All the way to Mirror River? By yourselves? I don't think so, Norah. If you want to get Flo or Andrew to take you, that would be fine."

"But—" Norah tried to stay polite. "You see, this week is our anniversary."

Aunt Florence looked amused. "Your what?"

"Our anniversary. It's three years ago this week that we left England."

"Why so it is! I'd forgotten. It seems much longer than three years. I feel as if you've always been with us." She smiled fondly at Norah.

Encouraged, Norah smiled back. "I thought it would be nice if Gavin and I went somewhere by ourselves," she continued. "Sometimes I worry that he's forgotten about home. If we spent all day talking about it, he'd remember more."

That wasn't the real reason Norah wanted to go; she just felt like an adventure. And she'd been so obsessed with

Andrew lately; Gavin *did* deserve some of her time. She put on her best responsible-elder-sister role and waited.

Aunt Florence finished a piece of toast. "That's a very nice idea, Norah. And you'd probably like a holiday from all of us—I imagine that you sometimes find this family a bit overwhelming. But couldn't you just go to Little Island? Mirror River is quite a long journey. If it were just you and Janet I'd say yes, but I can't have you taking your little brother that far. What if you had engine trouble—or the weather changed? Remember how Mr Hancock and Gerald were caught in that fog last summer and had to spend all night on the lake."

Norah couldn't see how these dangers would be any worse with Gavin than with Flo or Janet. She knew the real reason—Gavin was too precious to Aunt Florence for her to risk it. She swallowed the jealousy she'd felt when she'd first arrived in Canada and Aunt Florence had favoured Gavin, then continued to try reasonable arguments.

Finally Aunt Florence compromised. If Norah could find an adult to take her and Gavin to the mouth of the river, they could be left alone there for the day with the canoe. Norah knew she wouldn't give in any more.

"Be sure to keep your life-jackets on," said Aunt Florence, standing on the dock to see them off. "Wear your sun hats and be very, *very* careful. Gavin, you are to do exactly as Norah says." She kissed him and handed him the lunch Hanny had packed.

"Don't worry—we'll be careful. Goodbye!" Norah called. Uncle Gerald backed out the *Putt-Putt* and they waved to Aunt Florence, Janet and Sally, all gazing plaintively after them.

Gavin hunched in the stern in his bulky life-jacket, his face radiant. Norah perched in the middle. Around them bobbed a few white sails, barely moving in the still air. Uncle Gerald drove slowly to avoid upsetting the canoe, which bounced behind them.

Gavin began a favourite game—counting islands. Big or small, they were all a smudge of grey rock topped by dark firs. Some had cottages on them but most were uninhabited. Norah studied the mainland cottages they passed. Many were grander than Gairloch, with low stone walls and two, or even three, boathouses hung with geraniums.

When they reached Eden House Resort, Norah and Gavin exchanged a conspiratorial look. They passed through the cut at Port Schofield and entered the other lake.

"Look!" cried Gavin. Close to the boat swam a deer. Its branched head ploughed beside them for a while as if it were having a race. Then it turned towards the shore.

"Poor *thing!*" said Gavin. "It's tired! Maybe it won't make it."

"Deer are good swimmers," Uncle Gerald assured him. "It's probably enjoying itself!" But Gavin kept his eyes on the deer until it was a tiny dot behind them.

Finally they reached the mouth of Mirror River. Uncle Gerald emptied the water out of the canoe, lowered it into the inlet and helped them load it. "I'll meet you right here at four," he said. "Have you got a watch?"

Norah nodded. After she and Gavin watched the launch zoom away, they grinned at each other and got into the canoe. "You can try steering," said Norah. She picked up her paddle and the canoe nosed up the river as if it were as eager to explore as they were.

Mirror River was aptly named. Its glassy surface reproduced exactly the surrounding foliage and sky. The water was so shallow in parts that the canoe barely skimmed the bottom. "We certainly don't need these!" laughed Norah, shucking off her life-jacket.

They rounded a few bends and the scenery and its reflections merged so seamlessly that Norah almost felt dizzy. Every leaf of the towering treetops was etched below; white and yellow lilies, soft brown cat-tails and delicate ferns were all part of the shifting picture on the surface.

I'm so *lucky,* thought Norah, to have come to a place in Canada where I can be in a boat on a river. Gavin was humming one of his odd little songs and they paddled dreamily in unison. A few other canoes passed them, their occupants calling out cheerful hellos.

"How long until lunch?" asked Gavin finally.

"There's no shore to sit on. Let's tie up and walk until we find a picnic spot." Hiding the canoe in some bulrushes, they took out the lunch basket and swished through a meadow.

"There!" pointed Norah. Ahead of them rose a grassy hill, crowned with a clump of aspens. The ground beneath the trees was cushioned with moss and they could see as far as the lake.

"This is like our own private lookout," said Gavin, digging out the sandwiches.

As usual, Hanny had packed a feast. Egg sandwiches and chicken sandwiches, carrot sticks and apples, and half a blueberry pie. They finished it all.

Gavin lay on his back and burped. "I don't ever want to go back to school," he said. "I want to stay up north forever and ever."

"Mmm . . ." agreed Norah, turning over on her back too. The trees formed a dappled canopy above them. "Let's not even *think* about school." She gazed up into the leaves and drifted into another daydream about Andrew.

"You look like a lady," remarked Gavin, glancing at her blouse.

Norah blushed. "I'm a teen-ager," she told her brother. "Everyone starts to look different then. You will too, some day. You'll have to shave, like Andrew!"

Gavin chuckled. "Andrew's not very good at shaving—he's always cutting himself."

Norah remembered why she had told Aunt Florence they wanted this day by themselves. "Gavin," she said, sitting up and looking at him. "Do you realize it's three years ago that we left England? You were only five! Do you remember?" A picture flashed in her mind of their peaceful, wooded village, surrounded by hop gardens and orchards. So different from this raw landscape, but just as beautiful. For the first time since the letter from home she felt a pang of homesickness.

Gavin thought carefully. "I sort of remember it . . . I remember going on the boat. Who was that lady who took care of me? She let me hold her baby."

Norah frowned. "Mrs Pym," she said quickly. Mrs Pym had taken care of Gavin because Norah had been neglecting him.

"I remember when Aunt Florence gave me a little airplane when I got here. And I remember when we ran away—but then we came back. *Why* did we run away?"

"Oh, I don't know," said Norah. Gavin was remembering the wrong things—all the confusion and misery of their first few months in Canada. "I meant, what do you remember about *home?* Do you remember Little Whitebull?"

"What's that?"

"Gavin! It's our *house!* It has a green door and chickens in the yard." The painful place inside her throbbed at the memory of the chickens; it had been her job to feed them.

"Mum talked about those chickens in her last letter."

Norah remembered something. "*Muv.* That used to be your special name for her. Why don't you call her that any more?"

Gavin looked confused. "I don't call her *anything.* I never see her!"

"How do you begin your letters?" asked Norah.

"'Dear Mum and Dad'", said Gavin timidly. "That's how I've always started them, ever since I learned to print."

"Well, I think you should start saying 'Muv' again. She'd like that." Norah stared at her little brother for a second, then added gently, "Do you *really* remember them? Mum and Dad and Grandad and Muriel and Tibby? Of course, neither of us knows Barry."

Gavin looked defensive. "Of course I do! They're our *family!* They live in England!"

Norah sighed and stopped nagging him. Sometimes the features of her family's faces grew fuzzy in her own mind. And since she'd been in love with Andrew she'd hardly thought of them. Gavin must think of them even less, if at all. To him, Mum and Dad were the "family in England" that he wrote to automatically when Aunt Florence reminded him.

"You know . . . ," she said slowly, hardly wanting to think about it herself, "some of the war guests are already starting to go back to England. Uncle Barclay read me a bit out of the paper. They think it's safe enough to go back now, even though the war isn't over."

"Go back to England!" Gavin sat up, looking scared. "Do *we* have to go back?"

"We won't go back until the war *is* over, because we were sponsored by the government and they won't pay for our passage until then. It's just the rich kids who are going back—the ones who can afford it."

"Aunt Florence could afford it . . ." began Gavin. Then he laughed. "*She'd* never send us back."

He looked so relieved that Norah hated what she had to say next. "But you know we *are* going back some day, don't you? Aunt Florence can't keep us forever. We have to live with our real family—with Mum and Dad and Grandad, in Little Whitebull. In Ringden." She felt as if her words were stabbing him, but they rushed out anyway.

Gavin's big eyes filled with tears that beaded on his lashes. He looked at Norah imploringly. "And never come to Gairloch again? And leave our house in Toronto? And Roger and Tim?" Those were his special friends at school.

"Oh, Gavin . . ." Norah patted him awkwardly. "I'm afraid so. But probably not for a few years."

"A few years is a long time," said Gavin desperately. "A *very* long time." He tried to smile at her.

They stared at each other helplessly. The future—that time "after the war" that the grown-ups kept talking about like a promised land—seemed unreal compared to this perfect day full of sunshine and gleaming water. At least Norah could daydream about Andrew meeting her in England—and she did want to see her family again. But now she realized how hard it was going to be for Gavin. He had always been more at home in Canada than she had.

"Let's not talk about going back to England any more, okay? I'm sorry I brought it up."

Gavin nodded. He scrunched up his face as if squeezing the unhappiness from it. Then he got up and tried to entice a chipmunk to eat some crumbs.

Norah lay down again. Why had she made him so miserable? She watched him crouch patiently until the chipmunk finally snatched a piece of bread from his fingers, and her love for him was so sharp it hurt her inside.

Then Gavin came back and sat beside her. "Norah, there's something very important I want to ask you."

"I thought we weren't going to talk about it any more!" What had she done? Was Gavin going to worry about this from now on?

"It's not *that.* It's about Creature." He pulled the elephant from his pocket.

Norah laughed. She sat up and took Creature from Gavin, sniffing him. "He doesn't smell bad any more—the sun must have baked it out of him. What's the problem? Does he need mending again? I don't think there are any places left to sew!"

"No, he doesn't need mending. It's just that—well, Peter says I'm too old for him," said Gavin. "He makes fun of me for carrying him around."

"But you only do here. In Toronto you leave him in your room when you're at school. And besides, it's none of Peter's business."

"No... but maybe he's right. It *is* sort of babyish to have a toy elephant when you're eight. Peter and Ross and Sally think I should *bury* him. They want to have a funeral with hymns and a cross, like we do for dead birds. But I *couldn't!*" He grabbed Creature back from Norah and stroked his trunk, close to tears again.

"Bury him! That's absurd. Don't you listen to them, Gavin. Do you still like Creature?"

"Of course," said Gavin in a small voice. "I've had him all my life. But I don't want to be babyish. Maybe I *should* give him up. The way Aunt Bea gave up cigarettes because of her cough."

"You don't have to give him up! Look, I have an idea. Why don't you make Creature your club mascot? Call it the *Elephant* Detective Agency and have an elephant flag and elephant badges. I bet they'd go for that."

"Yes...," said Gavin slowly. "We could tie him to a pole

and march around with him. He'd be a sort of—a sort of *joke.* Except to me, of course."

"And no one ever needs to know you feel differently," said Norah. She looked at her watch. "It's time to head back."

As they cleaned up their picnic and walked back to the canoe, she thought about Gavin's strange need for a toy. She'd never understood it. Even as a little girl, she hadn't liked stuffed animals or dolls—she only wanted to *do* things. She and Gavin were so different. But she was glad she'd thought of a way for him to hold on to his best friend.

On the way back they spotted some slate-coloured cranes and a swimming beaver, who slapped his tail as they glided by. Uncle Gerald was waiting at the mouth of the river with the *Florence.* He had George and Denny with him, who squealed with excitement when they saw them.

Before they reached Port Schofield they glimpsed a double-decker steamship with rounded ends and a striped smokestack: the *Sagamo,* returning from her daily Hundred Mile Cruise. As the boat came closer they heard piano music and voices singing "There'll Always Be an England."

"There you go, Norah and Gavin!" grinned Uncle Gerald, as they all waved at the passengers leaning over the railings. "A bit of home for you. Someone told me they sing that when they pass the German prison camp."

Norah sighed. She'd never liked that droning song and she was never going to be allowed to forget that she didn't really belong here. She didn't want to think about England any more. All she wanted to do was to keep "messing about in boats," like Ratty and Mole in *The Wind in the Willows.* To sit here with the lake breeze on her cheeks and the smell of fresh water in her nostrils; to hold on to these precious last weeks of summer—and to Andrew.

XV
LOIS

Once again Andrew was spending most of his time with the Mitchells. Norah decided he was probably avoiding the family until he told them his decision. When she pictured him facing the Elders on their last night she sometimes felt frightened for him. But she knew he would be splendid—he would address them regally the way he had when he'd played a prince.

She wondered if Aunt Mary was also going to reveal her secret soon. She hadn't been back to Port Schofield since the wedding and had begun taking long, solitary walks around the island. Perhaps she too was trying to work up her courage until the last evening—then she'd tell them she was going to get married.

For the first time it occurred to Norah that if Aunt Mary got married she wouldn't be living with them. She'd have to move to Regina—wasn't that where she said Tom was from? As much as she wanted Aunt Mary to be happy, it would be awful living with just Aunt Florence. But perhaps Tom would live with them in Toronto. Aunt Florence would probably insist on it, Norah told herself.

How shocked the family was going to be when these two bombshells exploded! Poor Aunt Florence—little did she know that her daughter and her great-nephew were about to make announcements that would shatter her assumptions that all was as it should be.

The cousins were spending every moment soaking up the last few drops of fine weather that the summer was squeezing out. They had several picnics and a late-night bonfire on the shore. Now it was dark by about eight and cool enough to put on sweaters and slacks.

"Brrrr!" shivered Janet one evening, as she and Norah and Clare walked down to the boathouse. "It feels like fall!"

They were escaping from the Elders. A boatload of neighbours had arrived after dinner and the girls had grown tired of sitting politely and responding to the usual inane questions. The worst was, "All ready for school?" One of the visitors was the mother of one of Flo's servicemen. She and Flo spent the whole of the evening deep in conversation about Frank. Flo seemed almost like an Elder herself as she took part in the maternal discussion.

"We're going to bed now," Clare announced finally, with a commanding look at Janet and Norah.

"So soon?" asked her mother, but they slipped away before anyone could say more.

"Thanks for getting us out of there," said Janet as they pounded up the boathouse stairs. "What should we do now? It's too cold to go swimming."

Clare looked mysterious and pulled out a thin, rectangular box from under her bed. "I know something we can do." She lit two candles and put them and the box on a low table. They sat cross-legged around it.

"Louise left me this," she explained. "It's called a Ouija board."

"It sounds rude," giggled Janet. "Is it one of those games where you have to tell things about yourself? I'm not playing if it is."

Clare frowned. "It isn't a game—it's real. Do you think you're brave enough to try?"

"Sure!" said Janet, her voice wavering a bit. "Aren't we, Norah?"

Norah shrugged. She wasn't going to let Clare's pose impress her. She eyed the strange board suspiciously as Clare unfolded it. The alphabet was printed in two curving rows in the middle of it, with a line of numbers underneath. YES was in one upper corner and NO in the other. Clare placed a small, heart-shaped wooden platform on top.

"This is the planchette. Two of us have to put our hands on it and ask Ouija a question. Then it moves to the letters or numbers and spells out the answer."

"All by itself?" said Janet, her eyes growing round.

"No, Clare moves it," said Norah. "I've heard of this—it's a trick."

"It is not!" cried Clare. "It really works! Louise and I found out all sorts of things—we know who we're going to marry! *You* don't have to do it, Norah," she added coldly. "Come on, Janet. Put your hands there. That's right, our fingers should just barely touch. Don't put any weight on it. Now—*Ouija, Ouija . . .*" Her voice sounded ridiculously ghoulish. "Tell us . . . tell us the name of Janet's future husband."

Janet giggled. "Quiet!" hissed Clare. "You have to concentrate."

They were all silent. The waves lapped softly outside. Then, very slowly, the planchette moved over the board on its three felt-covered feet.

Janet gasped. "Keep your hands on it!" Clare warned her. The tiny table went as far as the letter *H* and stopped.

"That's the first letter of his name," said Clare. "What's next, Ouija?"

Slowly the pointer moved to *A*.

"It's laughing at you," said Norah. "HA!"

The others ignored her. "Now *R*," whispered Janet. "But now it won't move—why not?"

"Is it another *R?*" asked Clare. The planchette swung over to the word yes.

"Har, har," whispered Norah.

"*Y!*" said Clare. "Harry! Is the name 'Harry', Ouija?"

Yes, answered the planchette.

Clare and Janet dropped their hands in their laps. "I told you it worked!" said Clare. "Do you know any Harrys, Janet?"

"No," whispered Janet. Her hands were trembling. "You mean, that's who I'm going to marry?" She began to smile. "That means I'll *get* married one day!"

Norah scowled. "Clare was moving it, Janet. I told you, it's just a trick."

Clare looked disgusted. "All right then—*you* try it, with Janet. Then you can't say I'm moving it. Janet wouldn't cheat."

Norah shrugged and placed her fingers on the planchette.

"Ask it who *you're* going to marry," ordered Clare.

"You ask it," retorted Norah. "I'm not speaking to some dumb board."

"No, it has to be one of you two."

"I'll do it, then," said Janet. "Ouija, Ouija," she crooned, her voice sounding even sillier than Clare's. "Tell us who Norah is going to marry."

Norah waited, confident that the pointer wouldn't move at all. Then it slid across the board so fast she could hardly keep her fingers on it. "Stop it, Janet!" she cried. "I thought you weren't going to cheat!"

"I'm not doing it!" whispered Janet frantically. "Don't let go, Norah!"

"*C!*" cried Clare triumphantly.

In an instant Norah's mind swept from disbelief to acute disappointment that it wasn't an *A*.

"*A . . . N . . . T . . . S . . . A . . . Y*," chanted Clare, as the planchette almost zoomed around, making a tiny scraping sound. "Is that all, Ouija? Yes."

"CANTSAY—what kind of name is that?" said Janet. "Maybe it's a last name."

"No," said Norah suddenly. "It's *can't say*. It doesn't know." That was almost a relief—it still left the possibility open for Andrew.

Then she shivered. It really did seem to work—she knew Janet hadn't been moving it. "Okay," she admitted to Clare. "I believe it now. But I don't believe it's magic. There must be some explanation."

"Louise's father says that we will it to go to certain letters. But *I* think it's supernatural. You can even talk to someone who's dead—do you want to try?"

"No!" shuddered Janet. "That's too spooky. Let's ask it how many children I'm going to have—me and Harry, that is," she snickered.

They crouched around the board again and Norah tried it once more with Janet. A strange thrill washed over her, as if they were doing something forbidden.

"Three!" said Janet. "Good, because that's exactly how many I've always wanted. Ask it how many Clare's going to have."

They couldn't stop now. Again and again they asked questions and the Ouija board obliged them every time. They found out that Clare would have no children and that Norah would have two (so I *will* marry Andrew, she concluded); that Clare would travel and Janet would pass math.

"Ask it when the war will be over," said Norah.

But the Ouija wouldn't budge. "I guess it doesn't know," said Clare. "It can't know everything."

Janet yawned. "I can hardly keep my eyes open."

They heard Flo brushing her teeth below them and hid the Ouija board under Clare's bed again, guessing that she wouldn't approve.

After the others were asleep, Norah tossed restlessly and finally got up again. She shrugged her clothes on over her pyjamas and wandered along the shoreline. Once she was back in the city she was going to miss this freedom of getting up at night if she wanted to.

Two loons called back and forth to each other in a yearning warble. Poring over the Ouija board had made her feel slightly sick, as if she had eaten too much rich food. It had been fascinating and strange, but she didn't want to do it again.

Up in the cottage the lower lights were off and the upper ones on; the Elders must be getting ready for bed. Norah fetched a flashlight from the boathouse and made her way to her rock. She studied the stars and found the Great Bear, which she had now learned to call the Big Dipper. The Northern Lights rippled across the sky in shifting bands of greenish-white. Their majestic, eerie beauty was almost frightening.

Norah glanced down at Andrew's dark cabin. Where was he tonight? If only he were up here, confiding in her again; she began to go over that whole magical encounter, as she had done a million times already.

Just as she began to feel too cold to stay out any longer, she heard the *Putt-Putt* arrive at the dock. Andrew's laugh rang out—someone was with him. A light female voice joined his in singing "Don't Sit Under the Apple Tree." Then two dark figures came into view behind the cottage. In the light from the back windows Norah could make out the other singer—Lois Mitchell.

The two of them hung onto each other and stumbled down the hill to Andrew's cabin. Its windows lit up after they went in. Norah couldn't help slipping down to eavesdrop, even though the longer she heard them together the worse it made her feel.

The window was open a crack. "I can't stay long," Lois was saying.

"Just a little while," said Andrew. "I managed to get two bottles of beer."

"Well... maybe half an hour," said Lois.

This was just the opposite of the party, when Andrew had been the one to want Lois to go. Now his voice was tender and Norah shook with jealousy. Why am I listening? she asked herself. She was filled with the same kind of self-disgust she'd felt over the Ouija board. But she couldn't seem to leave, and moved farther into the bushes by the window.

"It's so maddening that we're not going to the same university," said Lois. "Will you come and visit me at Queen's?"

Norah was glad to hear the hesitation in Andrew's voice before he mumbled, "I'll have to see." At least he'd only told *her* his secret.

She tried to calm herself. After all, it was normal for Andrew to have girl friends until Norah was old enough to be one. She knew he'd had them before—Janet had told her. And Lois was acting so silly, laughing and teasing—surely he didn't take her seriously.

Andrew and Lois began to dance to their own music, humming "You'll Never Know." That's *our* song! Norah whispered between clenched teeth. She was relieved to hear them sit down again but now it was worse—the whimpers and endearments of kissing began.

Norah couldn't stand this—she really had to leave. She began to unbend her cramped legs, but Lois's next words made her freeze.

"I'm so lucky that you picked *me,*" she said, in her ironic voice. "Do you realize how many girls are in love with you? Alma Field is crazy about you. So is Ceci Johnson. And that funny little English girl—I saw the way she looked at you that day in town. At the party too—she was watching your every move, and glaring at *me!*"

"Oh, *Norah,*" laughed Andrew. "Yes, she does seem to have a crush on me. I try not to encourage it, but she shadows me like a hawk! She's a good kid, though."

Somehow Norah managed to make her legs move. Forcing her body to be silent, she crept out of the bushes and stumbled up the hill and down the steps to the boathouse, forgetting to use her flashlight. She kicked off her shoes and crawled under the covers without taking her clothes off. Then she crammed her blanket into her mouth so the huge sobs bursting out of her wouldn't wake the others.

A kid. "Oh, *Norah,*" he had said in a dismissing tone. He had *laughed* at her. He had called her love a crush.

He didn't love her. He never had.

A wave of pain crashed over her. *"Ohhh,"* she wailed, hardly caring now if the others woke up. But they slept on. Norah cried until her whole body ached. Then she lay rigid and stared at the wall, not thinking or feeling anything at all.

XVI

"I'LL NEVER SMILE AGAIN"

The next day Andrew and Lois seemed to have become a couple. Andrew invited her for dinner and she came early to spend the afternoon swimming with the family.

"Such a pretty girl," said Aunt Dorothy.

"Very polite, too," added Aunt Bea.

"And she comes from a good family," pronounced Aunt Florence. "I must write to Constance and tell her how much we like her."

The aunts switched to the topic of possible husbands for Princess Elizabeth, as if she, too, were an acquaintance.

"So Lois gets the seal of approval," whispered Flo, lying beside Norah on the dock. "They'll have them married in no time! *I* don't think it's going to last long. She doesn't take him seriously, but he can't see that yet."

Norah glanced at her, surprised to hear Flo sounding jealous too. Maybe it *wouldn't* last. And maybe Lois wouldn't like him any more when she heard that he wasn't going to fight. But even if Andrew stopped seeing Lois, Norah could never forget what he thought of *her.* Andrew was as friendly as ever today but she could only hear "good kid" behind every word he said to her.

The trouble was . . . she still loved him. She watched him climb up the ladder, panting and dripping. He shook his wet hair at Lois and his musical laugh rang out when she shrieked.

I don't *want* to love him, thought Norah. But she couldn't help it. The rest of her life was ruined; she would always love him and he would never love her back. All day she kept having to escape from everyone to have a cry—she, who had always been proud of the fact that she *never* cried. She hid her face in her towel as tears threatened once more.

"I'll never smile again," crooned the phonograph they'd brought out onto the dock. Norah dived into the lake to cool her agony.

"Will you be our stage manager, Norah?" Gavin asked her that night. He and the rest of the Fearless Four were putting on a play for the last evening. "We need someone to pull the curtain and things."

"Sure," shrugged Norah. She listened dully while Gavin told her the plot. "Creature is the star!" he grinned.

"I'll help you make some costumes," Norah told him. At least it would give her something to do.

Picking blueberries was another distraction. "With jam about to be rationed I want as many as you can find," Hanny told the children the next morning. Aunt Anne, Aunt Dorothy and Aunt Mary joined Hanny for a jam-making marathon. For a couple of days the sweet heavy scent of cooked berries filled the cottage. Norah helped sterilize jars and melt paraffin. In Toronto she retreated to the kitchen with Hanny whenever Aunt Florence was too much to bear. Now she used this kitchen for a refuge from Andrew.

On the afternoon they finished all the berries, Norah sat dully on the dock wondering what to do with herself. *Wuthering Heights* lay abandoned beside her; it was too painful to read a story about love.

The *Putt-Putt* appeared around the point; Andrew's arm

waved. Norah jumped up to escape him, but he was calling her name and she had to wait.

"Would you like to go out in the canoe?" he asked as soon as he landed. "There's something I have to talk to you about." Norah flushed—whenever she encountered him she felt ashamed.

"No thanks," she said as coolly as she could manage. She ran up the steps before he could say more.

He tried again that evening, actually turning up at the boathouse when they were getting ready for bed. "Norah!" he called up.

She stuck her head out the window.

"Do you want to go for a walk?"

"No thanks," said Norah. "I'm already in my pyjamas." She withdrew her head quickly, but not before she had seen an apologetic look on Andrew's face. Part of her wondered what he wanted, but she was no longer strong enough to be alone with him, not when she knew what he thought of her.

He probably wants to talk about how he's going to tell the Elders, she decided. Well, he'll just have to work it out by himself. She tried to be angry with him, but she was filled with a rush of yearning. She put out her head again and watched his back as he walked slowly up the steps to the cottage.

"Imagine Norah turning down a walk with Andrew," taunted Clare.

Janet looked puzzled. "But Norah doesn't like Andrew."

"That's right—I don't," said Norah stiffly.

"Then you've changed," said Clare.

"Why did Andrew want to go for a walk with just you?" asked Flo.

Norah shrugged. "How should I know?" She hid under

the covers from their curious faces. Why couldn't they just leave her alone? For the first time all summer she looked forward to the privacy of her own room in Toronto.

The next morning Norah was relieved to hear that Andrew had gone to Huntsville for a few days. "Mr Hancock took him to the train station in Brockhurst," she heard Aunt Dorothy tell Flo. "He won't be back until our last evening. He said he was going to visit some friends of his parents."

Norah sat listlessly at the kitchen table while Aunt Bea and Aunt Mary discussed with Hanny the special menu for their last meal tomorrow.

"It would be lovely to have a roast," said Aunt Bea. "How I miss the supply boats! They came twice a week right to our dock, Norah. There were vegetables and flowers—even a butcher on board! I used to take Gerald down when he was a baby and weigh him on the scales. Now I suppose we'll have to go all the way into Port Clarkson—the best butcher is there."

"I'll go," said Aunt Mary. "If Norah will drive me. Will you?"

"All right," shrugged Norah.

She had never driven the *Putt-Putt* so far and her gloom lifted a bit when Aunt Mary let her manoeuvre the launch through the lock at Port Clarkson all by herself. But she quickly got bored with shopping and followed Aunt Mary around the stores in a dull daze.

"Would you like a cool drink before we go back?" asked her guardian.

"I don't care," said Norah.

They sat in a dim restaurant, sipping iced tea. Aunt Mary's kind face looked concerned. "You've been so pensive the last few days, Norah. Are you worried about going back to school?"

"No," muttered Norah, keeping her eyes down so Aunt Mary wouldn't notice her quick tears. If only she could unload her misery and be comforted! But she didn't want anyone to know how foolish she had been. She looked up, blinking rapidly. "There *is* something, but I can't tell you."

"I won't pry then," said Aunt Mary. "I hope it's not too serious." She sighed. "Perhaps going back to the city will be a good change for all of us. This summer has been so… *intense,* somehow. We need to get back to our regular routines. You'll be glad to see Paige and Bernard again, I imagine."

Norah nodded, puzzled by her words. Surely Aunt Mary wasn't going back to *her* regular routine—wouldn't she announce tomorrow that she would marry Tom?

Aunt Mary pulled out her handkerchief and blew her nose. It was already raw and her eyes were bloodshot. "What a nuisance this hayfever is," she sniffed. "Did you know that people used to come to Muskoka to avoid it? But now I'm sure there's as much ragweed here as there is in the city."

Then the colour slowly rose in Aunt Mary's face. She gave a small cough and looked down. Norah turned around to see who had startled her.

A man had entered the restaurant and was staring at their table, looking as bewildered as Aunt Mary. Then he came over and said softly, "Good-morning, Mary."

"Good-morning, Tom." Norah almost dropped her glass. "This is Norah Stoakes, who's living with us," continued Aunt Mary. "Norah, I'd like you to meet Mr Montgomery, an old friend of mine."

"How do you do, Mr Montgomery," said Norah automatically. She gawked at the man as he stood there.

Tom looked even older up close than he had at a distance.

His face was seamed with wrinkles and his sparse hair lay in thin white strands across his high forehead. He seemed as shy as Aunt Mary and pushed up his glasses nervously. "Um, shopping, were you?" he asked finally.

"Yes—we're having a big dinner tomorrow and I needed to pick up a roast."

"I borrowed one of the hotel boats to do some shopping myself. May I give you a lift anywhere?"

"No, thank you. We have our own boat. Come along, Norah, we'd better start back before the meat turns." Aunt Mary gathered up parcels and stood up.

"Goodbye then, Tom," she said, holding out her hand.

"Goodbye, Mary," he said gruffly. "Perhaps I'll see you again next summer." He held onto her hand a second, then Aunt Mary turned abruptly and walked out.

Norah hurried after her. What was *that* all about? Was the whole thing off? Aunt Mary sat in the boat facing backwards, so Norah couldn't see her face. But when they reached their own lake she tapped Norah's shoulder. "I don't want to go back to the island just yet. Could you stop in that cove?"

Norah turned the launch into a tiny cove and cut the engine. "Shall I tie it up?" she asked.

"Yes, but we don't need to get out. I just have to collect myself for a few minutes." Then calm, placid Aunt Mary burst into tears.

"Aunt Mary! What's wrong?!" Norah quickly tethered the *Putt-Putt* to an overhanging branch and sat beside her guardian, patting her shoulder awkwardly.

It only lasted a minute or two. Aunt Mary dabbed at her eyes with her handkerchief, blew her nose again, then turned to Norah with a weak smile.

"What a foolish woman I am, Norah! What must you think of me, carrying on like this? I hope I didn't scare you.

Perhaps I should explain. You see, I have been . . . keeping company with Mr Montgomery all month. I've known him for years—he grew up in Toronto—but he was living in the west."

Norah shifted impatiently. Aunt Mary seemed to have forgotten she'd already told her about Tom.

"Then I ran into him at the end of last summer—he'd been spending August at Eden House Resort. We wrote to each other all winter. He sent his letters care of one of my friends—it was the only way I could hide them from Mother. All those times I said I was getting my dress fitted I was also visiting Tom! It was so underhanded and deceitful. I half-expected Mother to catch on, but she didn't. I just couldn't let her know—not until I was absolutely certain of the relationship."

She looked so guilty that Norah cried, "Of course you couldn't!"

Aunt Mary's cheeks grew pink again. "We had such pleasant visits. He really is a remarkably decent man. And then . . . he asked me to marry him!"

"Oh, Aunt Mary!" Norah wriggled so much that the boat swayed. "That's wonderful! When did he ask you?"

"At Anne's sister's wedding. I knew he'd be there and we managed to slip away during the reception."

"When are you going to tell Aunt Florence?"

Aunt Mary smiled sadly. "I won't have to, Norah, because I said no."

"You said no! But you love him!"

"Probably I do love him. I must say, I came close to saying yes, but I thought about it very carefully. It's too late for me to get married. I'm happy the way I am. I *like* my life in Toronto, with my church and my Red Cross work. I have so many friends there. I don't think I could adjust to living somewhere else. And I'd miss you and Gavin dreadfully! I know you won't be with us forever, but I couldn't be the one to leave first."

"But why can't Tom—Mr Montgomery, I mean—live with us in Toronto?"

"He could never do that, Norah. He doesn't want to change his life, either. He has relatives in the west—he belongs there now. And there's Mother, of course. I couldn't ask anyone to put up with her and she'll need me more and more as she gets older."

"But that's just like *before!* You didn't get married *last* time because of Aunt Florence! You can't let her ruin your life again!"

"Perhaps, the first time, it was because of Mother," said Aunt Mary. "Not now. If I really wanted to marry him, I wouldn't let her stand in my way. No . . . even though she's obviously a factor in my decision, this time it's because of me. I've become used to my own company and my own ways. I don't think I'm prepared to change them, not even for someone I respect as much as I do Tom."

"But . . ." Norah's ready tears overflowed. "But you *love* him! And he must love you, if he asked you to marry him. He's your true love, just like all the songs. You have to be loyal to him!"

"Why, Norah! It's not like you to cry! Here, have what's left of my hankie. I shouldn't have told you all this—you're only thirteen, after all. Love seems different when you're young." She smiled. "Despite all those romantic songs, I don't believe that everyone has just one true love—why, look at me!"

"What do you mean?" gulped Norah. "You've only loved Tom! All those years!"

"All those years . . ." Aunt Mary looked puzzled, then she laughed. "Poor Norah, no wonder you're confused! That was a *different* Tom, that first man I told you about. That's Thomas Young. Now that would be loyalty, if I still loved *him.* I don't even know where he lives now."

"A different Tom?" repeated Norah weakly.

"Yes, it is rather a strange coincidence, isn't it? But after all, it's a common name."

"You mean, now you love someone else?"

"Yes, I do. You *can* love several different people in your life, you know. You will, I'm sure, until you find the right one."

"Never!" cried Norah. "I'll never love anyone but—" She clapped her hand over her mouth and her fingers became slippery with tears.

Aunt Mary picked up the sodden handkerchief and very gently wiped Norah's face. "So that's it," she said softly. "Who is it—Andrew?"

"Yes," whispered Norah. "He doesn't love *me,* though—he never did!"

Aunt Mary pulled her over for a hug. "Oh, Norah, you're so young—very young! This is just the beginning! I'm not going to say you only have a crush. I remember feeling the same way about one of my teachers—love is just as real at any age. But I promise you, you will get over it—and love someone else in time, someone who will love you back. Andrew is very fond of you, I'm sure, but he's so much older, you can't expect him to be interested in you. But wait and see—you're so full of spirit, so pretty. Lots of people are going to love you!"

"But I'm ugly!" burst out Norah. "My nose is too big!

"It's not big at all. Everyone thinks she's ugly at thirteen. *I* did—and when I look at snaps of myself then, I think I looked fine. Besides, it's what *inside* that makes people attractive."

Now she sounded too much like the Sunday School teacher she was. But her kind words warmed Norah. She remembered that pretty, confident girl in the mirror and hope flickered inside her.

"The meat!" said Aunt Mary. "We must be getting back."

"You won't tell anyone about Andrew, will you?" said Norah before she started the engine.

"Of course not! And I know you won't say anything about Tom. They'll both be our own special secrets."

As they drove back to Gairloch, Norah kept her eyes on the waves ahead, pondering the disappointing end of Aunt Mary's romance. She supposed Aunt Mary was doing what she wanted, though.

Her story wasn't going to be so boring. And she couldn't believe that she'd ever love anyone but Andrew.

XVII
THE LAST EVENING

They arrived back in time to say goodbye to Aunt Catherine. The whole family congregated on the dock to see her off, while the Nugents, who were going to take her to Ottawa, waited in their launch.

When it was Norah's turn to kiss her she wished she could tell Aunt Catherine what Andrew was going to announce when he came back tomorrow. She would be the only member of the family who would be pleased with him. But it was Andrew's secret.

"Goodbye," she said, suddenly shy.

Aunt Catherine kissed her firmly on each cheek. "There! You have a good year, Norah, and I'll see you next summer. In the meantime, don't grow up too fast! There's no hurry, you know—one day you'll be like me and wishing you were young again."

But her spirit seemed as young as ever as she waved vigorously from the departing boat. Norah watched it until it disappeared around the point. She usually forgot about the old woman until she was here again, but somehow, this year, she missed her already.

The family was in a flurry as they got ready to leave. Anything that could be nibbled by mice was put into the "tin room" above the stairs. Hanny packed boxes of jam for each family. Neighbours came by in their boats to say goodbye.

Everyone was leaving together on Sunday morning, and the precious moments rushed by. Too soon they were all sitting in the dining room for their last Big Dinner.

"Hanny, you've surpassed yourself." Uncle Reg leaned back in his chair and patted his stomach. "That was the best meal we've had all summer."

"Thank you, sir," said Hanny. She removed his dessert plate, stained purple from blueberry pie. The adults lingered at the table, smoking and chatting.

"The last time we'll all be together," sighed Aunt Bea.

"All except Andrew," sniffed Aunt Florence. "Why couldn't he have gone to Huntsville earlier in the month? And he really should have tried to be back in time for our last dinner. How is he getting here from Brockhurst?"

"He asked Mr Hancock to leave the *Putt-Putt* there for him," said Uncle Gerald. "He towed it over this afternoon."

"He did promise he'd be back as soon as he could, Aunt Florence," said Aunt Dorothy. She tried to change the subject. "I hope our tires will hold out long enough to come up next year. But I suppose we could take the train."

"It's the gas coupons I'm worried about," said Uncle Barclay. "We may have to run just one boat next summer."

"Why don't you do what we're going to?" said Aunt Florence. "Store the car all year and take streetcars. Then we can save our gas coupons for the trip north and use the rest for the boats."

"Do you want to have another contest, Florence?" asked Uncle Reg. "The first person to make *two* cushion covers by Christmas contributes fewer coupons." He smiled smugly; he'd beaten Aunt Florence by six rows.

"Oh, *you* . . . you're just like an old woman," chuckled Aunt Florence. "All right, you're on."

Uncle Barclay began explaining to them once more all the

details of the Allied invasion of Italy. Ever since they'd heard the news yesterday he'd talked of nothing else. Finally Gavin got up and whispered to Aunt Florence.

She stood. "All right, everyone, into the living room! I believe we're about to be entertained."

A few minutes later Norah stood behind a sheet pinned over a rope that was stretched across the alcove in the living room. Behind her the Fearless Four whispered last-minute instructions to each other. Norah remembered the unbearable excitement before the curtain rose. Janet, Bob, Alec and she also used to put on plays for the family. But last summer, suddenly feeling self conscious, they'd stopped.

"*Now,* Norah!" hissed Sally. Norah drew back the sheet in jerky movements, careful to keep herself concealed behind it. Then she slipped out at the side to watch the play.

Gavin stood in front of the audience dressed in Uncle Reg's tweed hat, Flo's trench coat pulled up over its belt and Uncle Barclay's pipe in his mouth. "The Fearless Four Detective Agency presents . . . The Case of the Stolen Elephant!"

The long play—Gavin had told Norah they couldn't agree on whose ideas to use, so they'd kept in everyone's—was complicated and far-reaching, with many costume changes and allusions to Johnny Canuck, Mussolini, Toad and Sherlock Holmes. They made up a lot of it as they went along, hauling up members of the audience to give evidence. Creature, of course, was the stolen elephant. He was finally given back in the end, returned by Roy Rogers—Peter, resplendent in a cowboy hat and holsters. Then the cast burst into song. "*Off* he goes, into the *WILD BLUE YONDER* ..." they shouted, hurling Creature up to the ceiling again and again. He lost his remaining ear on his final landing.

By the time they took their final bows the audience was

almost on the floor with laughter. They applauded wildly, wiping tears from their eyes.

"That was *superb!*" said Aunt Florence. "I haven't seen anything like it since Andrew and Flo performed *Dracula* for us. Come and give me a kiss, Gavin."

"Where *is* Andrew?" asked Clare. "Shouldn't he be back by now?"

"I can't think what's keeping him," said Aunt Bea, looking worried.

"Oh, he's probably having too good a time," said Uncle Reg. "You women coddle him too much. Now for some songs!" He pulled out the piano bench and they all gathered round.

For an hour they sang the family favourites: "You Are My Sunshine," "Waltzing Matilda" and "The Quartermaster's Store." All the Drummonds had strong voices. Norah let hers blend in with theirs, glad to forget herself and just sing. Squeezed in between Janet and Aunt Mary, she felt for a while as mindlessly content as she'd been in other summers.

"Here's one for you and Gavin, Norah," said Uncle Reg. He picked out a slow, sentimental melody as they all crooned "There'll be bluebirds over the white cliffs of Dover." Tears gleamed in Aunt Mary's eyes at the words "And Jimmy will go to sleep / In his own little room again." When Uncle Reg stopped playing everyone was looking at Norah and Gavin in the soppy way they sometimes did, when they remembered how far away from home the two of them were.

"I don't think there *are* bluebirds in England," said Norah, trying to change their mood.

"Maybe next summer the war will be over and you won't be here any more!" said Janet suddenly.

"Next summer?" whispered Gavin.

Aunt Florence frowned at Janet and pressed Gavin to her side. "Let's just take things one day at a time. Play something rousing, Reg. How about 'Roll Out the Barrel'?"

"... and the *GANG'S—ALL—HERE!*" they finished raucously. Everyone collapsed into chairs, while Aunt Mar and Aunt Dorothy handed around coffee.

Uncle Reg was staring intently at Gavin and Bosley. The dog's silky head rested on Gavin's knee; he stroked it sadly.

"I have a proposition for you, Gavin."

"What, Uncle Reg?"

"How would you like to take care of Bosley for me until the end of the war? I'll lend him to you! After all, he's much more attached to you than to me—aren't you, you fickle beast?" Bosley thumped his tail politely, then pressed his head harder against Gavin.

"Give Bosley to *me?*" the little boy breathed.

"*Lend* him. You'll have to give him back when you leave Canada."

"But won't you miss him?"

"Of course I will, but I think Bosley has shown whom he likes the best. I can see him in the holidays."

"Reg Drummond!" Aunt Florence glared at her brother. "Don't you see how cruel your suggestion is? *I've* sometimes thought of getting Gavin a pet, but then he'd have to go through the misery of giving it up. It's out of the question."

"Oh, *please,* Aunt Florence," begged Gavin. "I understand. I know it's just borrowing, really I do."

Aunt Florence looked at his pleading face and sighed. "Oh all right, sweetness. Reg hasn't left me any choice, announcing it this way. But you'll have to walk and feed him every day."

"I will!" promised Gavin. "Thank you, Aunt Florence and Uncle Reg! Did you hear that, Norah? Bosley's coming to live with us! *Aren't* you, Boz . . ." He buried his head in the dog's neck.

Norah agreed with Aunt Florence. Uncle Reg had set up a situation that was going to be wrenching sometime in the future. But Gavin's pleasure right now was too acute to deny. And it *would* be fun to have a dog in the house, especially a dog as agreeable as Bosley.

Janet and Clare had just started picking teams for Charades when a boat engine sounded faintly.

"Andrew, at last!" said Aunt Florence.

The family waited quietly while they listened to his footsteps on the verandah. Norah wondered why they thudded so heavily—almost like marching. The screen door clacked behind him and then Andrew made his entrance.

Aunt Bea shrieked. Then there was a stunned silence until everyone began to cry out at the same time. "Andrew! Oh, Andrew, my dear boy!"

Norah's arms and legs turned to mush. She shivered violently as she stared at him, her mouth twitching and tears escaping as she realized what he'd done.

Andrew was in uniform—encased from head to feet in thick wool khaki, his trousers billowing over heavy black boots. Worst of all, his beautiful wavy hair had been cropped close to his head, making him look tough and raw, as if all his former grace had been chopped away.

"I'm sorry to give you such a fright," he said quietly, sitting down beside Aunt Florence. "It was the only way I could think of to tell you. I've joined up. Tomorrow afternoon I report to training camp."

"But *why*?" cried Flo. "I thought you were going to wait until you could go over as an officer!"

"*I* know why—you're afraid of missing it, aren't you?" said Uncle Barclay. He clapped Andrew on the shoulder. "Good for you, boy. I don't blame you—I was hoping you'd do this."

Aunt Florence was finally able to speak. "You've given us all a dreadful shock, Andrew," she said sternly. "You could have at least consulted with us. Or your parents. Do they know?"

"Not yet," admitted Andrew. "I'll phone them tomorrow. Mother will be upset, but she'll come around."

Aunt Florence sniffed. "I should think she would be upset! Her only son, going off to war as a private!" Then she sighed. "I have to admit, I can't blame you either, Andrew. I was hoping—we all were—that you'd be an officer before you went. But Barclay is right—there might not be time for that. I think you've made a very courageous decision."

Then they all swarmed around him. The women were tearful and the men asked questions about training camp. Sally climbed on his lap and played with the tabs on his belt. Ross put on his cap and the other little boys gazed at him with awe.

Norah managed to slip out of the room before anyone noticed how hard she was crying. She ran up to her rock and threw herself down on it, her scalding tears running into the lichen.

How *could* he? He had broken his promise! He had betrayed her, but worse than that, he had betrayed himself—for she couldn't believe he had changed his beliefs so suddenly.

Lois must have talked him into it. She must have wanted him to be a hero—as Norah once had—and persuaded him to join the war like her brother Jack. That was the only explanation that made any sense.

She couldn't get out of her head the shock of seeing him standing there like a stranger. An anonymous soldier, who would crouch in a ditch and shoot people, like the scenes in newsreels.

Another picture flashed into Norah's mind, one she had also seen at the movies again and again. Soldiers lying inert on the ground. *Dead.*

"Doesn't it seem intolerable and absurd to you that whenever human beings disagree they go out and *kill* each other?" Andrew's words, spoken with so much conviction on this rock a short time ago, seemed to ring out again.

Norah thought of the picture of Hugh—Hugh in a uniform as well, gazing at the camera so cheerfully. He had never come back to Gairloch.

Andrew could be killed. His honest eyes, that had looked so enormous in his shorn head, could lose their sparkle forever. Norah had never seen a dead person, but she thought of the glazed eyes of lifeless birds.

War *was* wrong! She didn't care what the cause was. Aunt Catherine was right. It was wrong and wicked that the lives of boys like Andrew and Hugh could be extinguished as easily as snuffing out a candle. When she imagined Andrew lying dead in a muddy ditch somewhere, she knew that she had never really loved him until now.

Norah sat, shivering, drained and bitter, staring at the lake. All she wore was a cotton dress and her bare arms and legs were freezing; but she couldn't move.

"Norah?"

Andrew's voice was hesitant. "I knew I'd find you here." He climbed up beside her. She swivelled to keep her back to him.

"Look, let me explain! I tried to before, but you wouldn't let me."

"I don't want to hear," spat Norah. "Go away!"

"I'm sorry, but you *have* to hear. I know I broke my promise. But I think I have good reason to. And I thought you'd be pleased! After all, now I'm going to fight Hitler—and everything he represents. That's what you wanted me to do, isn't it?"

She whirled around. "Not any more! Now I think it's terrible that you're going to fight! I can't believe you've changed so much. How could you? Was it Lois? Did *she* make you?"

"It has nothing to do with Lois. She knows—I told her before I went to Huntsville—but she didn't affect my decision. It was Jack. I had an incredible letter from him. He *hates* the war—you're too young to hear some of the terrible things he described. Now he hates it as much as I do. But the point is, Norah—he's *still fighting.* He's still over there, doing all the dirty work—he and all the other poor guys—while I sit here smugly saying I won't go. It's not *fair* that they're all suffering—and believe me, they are—while I'm not. I don't want to do it one bit more than I did before but it has to be done. So I may as well do it *now.*"

"But you'll have to *kill* people!" cried Norah. "How are you going to do that, after all you said before?"

The muscle in Andrew's cheek jumped violently. "I can't answer that, Norah. All I can say is that—maybe—the end result will be worth it. Don't you see?"

"No, I *don't* see! What if everyone in the world just refused to fight? Then there wouldn't *be* any war! Then no one would get killed! Then y-you wouldn't..." she choked, starting to sob again.

Andrew pulled her close to him. "You're right. But we don't live in a world like that—not yet, anyway. But maybe if we win this war we'll never have to have another one."

"Aunt Catherine said people felt like that about the *first* world war!"

Andrew gave a weary sigh. "I guess they did . . . Norah, I've run out of arguments. All I know is, I've made up my mind. I don't *want* to do it. It's kind of like acting. I'll pretend to do it."

"But—" Then she looked up at his face and saw how determined it was. He wore a new firmness, as unyielding as his uniform. That was why he hadn't been able to tell them until he was wearing it, she realized; the uniform was part of the acting, like a costume. Surely the real Andrew was still underneath.

There was nothing more she could say. She continued to cry quietly, enclosed in the sheltering circle of Andrew's arm. At last she wiped her eyes with the rough wool of his sleeve.

"I'll never, *ever* agree with you," she muttered.

"I don't expect you to," said Andrew. "You're certainly unpredictable, though!" he added.

"So are you!" They exchanged wary smiles.

"Can I write to you?" whispered Norah.

"Of course you can! And you'll still be seeing me every now and then. I'll get leaves until we go over and I'll come and visit you all in Toronto."

Norah stood up and rubbed her goose-pimpled arms. Andrew stood too and they gazed out at the full moon streaming across the peaceful lake. "Whenever I see the moon I'll think of Gairloch," he said softly.

Whenever I see it, I'll think of *you,* thought Norah.

She took a deep breath. *Say* it. Quickly, while she still had him alone.

"Andrew, I—I . . ."

He bent over, put his hands on her shoulders and kissed the top of her head. "I know, Norah. I know. And I feel very flattered—I don't think I deserve it. But you're only—I hate to hurt your feelings but—"

Norah sighed. "I'm only thirteen."

"Well . . . yes! But the nicest thirteen-year-old I know." He looked apologetic. "I'm really beat, Norah. Are you okay now? Do you mind if I go to bed?"

"I'm okay."

He squeezed her hand, then slipped down the rock towards his cabin.

Norah watched him go, pressing the hand he had touched to her mouth. She stayed on the rock for a long time, the moon a watery blur through her tears.

XVIII
"YOU'LL NEVER KNOW"

Everything was packed. The piano had been pushed into its mouse-proof case and the water had been turned off. Already the launches had made several trips to Ford's Bay with suitcases and boxes. Now all the boats had been hoisted to the rafters of the boathouse. Most of the family was gathered on the dock and the verandah, waiting for Mr McGuigan from the store to appear with his boat and start taking them in batches over to the mainland.

Uncle Gerald and Andrew were fastening the heavy shutters back on the windows. Norah always hated this part about leaving. It was as if the cottage were having its eyes covered.

"School the day after tomorrow!" gloated Clare. "I can hardly wait to see John."

"Oh, Norah, I'll miss you!" wailed Janet. "Christmas seems so far away."

"I think you should all have Christmas with *us* this year," smiled Aunt Dorothy. "Would you like that, Norah? You could come on the train. After all, you should see Montreal before you leave Canada."

"That would be fun," said Norah. She grinned at Janet. "You can play me all your new Frankie records."

"Next summer I'll take you all on a canoe trip to Algonquin Park," said Flo. "If I'm not in the RCAF by then," she added, avoiding her mother's look.

"*Nor*-ah... Aunt Florence says it's our turn first," called Gavin from the dock.

After an almost sleepless night, Norah had risen at dawn, circled the island and said her customary goodbye to every rock and tree. She had kissed all the Elders and now she hugged Janet and Flo.

"What about *me?*" demanded Clare. They stared at each other, then each managed a tight smile.

Then Norah looked around to say goodbye to Andrew. She found him at the far end of the verandah, putting up the last shutter. His ugly uniform still made her quake. In the daylight she noticed the white strip of skin around his haircut where his tan stopped.

Andrew turned around. Norah's heart thumped so loudly she was sure he could hear it. She had rehearsed her last words all night but all she could manage was, "Goodbye, Andrew."

He took her hand, smiling ruefully. "Goodbye, Norah. I'll see you in Toronto." She sped down to the dock.

Gairloch receded into the distance. Aunt Mary sat in the stern of the boat and looked sadly back at the island. Gavin clutched Bosley. Norah's eyes were fixed on the tall boy who stood on the verandah of the cottage and waved after them, looking smaller and more fragile every second.

"Do you think we *will* be back next summer?" Gavin whispered to her after they had landed at Ford's Bay.

"I'm sure we will," said Norah, as much to reassure herself as him. "Don't worry about it any more, Gavin. Let's just enjoy being in Canada. Think of school—you'll be glad to see your friends, won't you?"

"Sure! And wait until they meet Boz! Will you like seeing *your* friends?"

Norah nodded. She crouched by the shore and dabbled

her hands in the lake one last time, while the others walked towards the car. She wondered how Paige's summer in Cape Cod had been, and if Bernard and his mother had been able to get away from the hot city. Then she pictured describing *her* summer to them. There was so much of it she'd never be able to explain.

What would the next years bring? Andrew would go off to the war . . . and *surely,* she prayed, return. She and Gavin would go back to England. Now that she had someone new to worry about, the future seemed more scary and uncertain than ever.

But one thing wasn't uncertain. She would always love him, she told herself fiercely. It was just like her favourite song; he would never know how much. Whatever the future brought, all she could do was hold on to the hope that, one day, he would know—and love her back.

I'm only thirteen, thought Norah. I can wait.

"Norah Stoakes!" called Aunt Florence's exasperated voice. "Are you going to stand there daydreaming all day?"

Norah ran to the car and climbed in. "Sorry," she said cheerfully. "Aunt Florence . . . when we get back to Toronto, could you buy me a pair of saddle shoes?"

ACKNOWLEDGEMENTS

For their encouragement, advice, memories and cottages, many thanks to: Sue Alderson; Miza Jean-marie; Mary and George Johnson; Carol, Paul, Mollie and Connie Johnson; Vicki, Stuart, Sanders—and Bosley!—Lazier; Claire Mackay; Hugh, Anne and Matthew Mackenzie; Lee, Mike and Megan Mackenzie; Kay and Sandy Pearson; Linda Shineton and Gordon Mitchell; Hope Thomson, and Calla and Josie Haynes; and Maggie Wedd.

PERMISSIONS

THE LIGHTS GO ON AGAIN

For Ian

He who would valiant be
'Gainst all disaster

John Bunyan and others

CONTENTS

I

WHAT AM I GOING TO DO?

The large boy hulked in front of Gavin on the sidewalk, blocking his way.

"Hold it right there, Stoakes."

Gavin looked behind him, to where he'd just left Tim and Roger at the corner. They were already too far away to call back. And it was no use running. Mick could easily catch him.

"What do you want?" Gavin breathed.

Mick's mean face came closer. His eyes glittered like hard blue marbles. "I want you to do me a favour."

"Wh-what?"

"I need some cash. Bring me two bucks tomorrow morning. You can meet me at the school flagpole before the bell. Understand?"

"But I haven't got *two* dollars!"

"Then get it. I know your ma's rich."

"She isn't really my mother," said Gavin. "She's not even related to me. She's just looking after me and my sister until the war is over. My real mother lives in England."

Mick grabbed Gavin's arm and gave it a savage twist. "So what? You live with her in that fancy house, doncha? Bring me the money by tomorrow morning—or you'll be jelly!"

Gavin tried to curb his tears. Pain blazed up his arm. "Okay, Mick. Could you please let go? You're hurting me!"

Mick gave one more tortuous twist, then freed Gavin's

arm. Gavin picked up his speller out of the snow and fled, the bigger boy's words shouting behind him, "Don't forget—tomorrow morning before the bell!"

The icy December air made his lungs ache, but Gavin didn't stop running until he reached the towering house at the end of one of the winding streets. He pounded up its wide steps and slammed the door behind him. Safe!

"Is that you, Gavin?" Hanny, the cook, came out of the kitchen, wiping floury hands on her apron. "Why are you so out of breath?" She pulled off his tuque. "And look at your hair—you're sweating!"

"I—just—felt—like—running," panted Gavin. "Where's Bosley?" Usually his springer spaniel waited for him at the end of the block.

"Norah took him for a walk. She got out of school early today. And your aunts are having tea at Mrs Bond's. Would you like something to eat?"

"Yes, please. Can I have it in my room?"

Hanny gave him a glass of milk and an apple. Gavin carried them carefully up the stairs. He changed out of his school breeks, rubbing the itchy places behind his knees where the wool chafed. He sat down on the rug beside his bed and tried to eat.

But his tears escaped. They burned against his cold cheeks, as his chest still heaved.

"Stop it!" he whispered fiercely. "*Crybaby . . .*" Gavin sniffed deeply, wiped his eyes on the bedspread and began to nibble the apple. *Think . . .*

Two dollars! He'd never be able to find that much money by tomorrow. He glanced at the iron bank shaped like a bear on his desk, but he knew it only contained the fifteen cents he was saving to go to the movies on Saturday.

Tomorrow was the day Aunt Florence gave him a quarter

to take to school for his weekly war savings stamp. If he kept that and the fifteen cents and next week's stamp money and allowance quarter...

He counted on his fingers. That made only ninety cents. Besides, it was stealing. And he knew Mick wouldn't wait.

He couldn't ask Aunt Florence for two whole dollars without telling her why he needed it. And he knew enough not to tattle on Mick. Ken Cunningham had last month. Mick got the strap and Ken appeared in school the next week with a black eye. He told everyone he'd fallen playing hockey.

Gavin winced as he lifted his glass to drain it. His arm still smarted. Why was the meanest boy in the school suddenly picking on *him?*

Ever since Mick Turner had arrived in September he had been the terror of Prince Edward School. He was large for grade seven—even the grade eights were afraid of him. He bullied alone, stalking the corridors, the washrooms and the playground for his victims. So far Gavin and his friends had managed to avoid him—until today.

Gavin found *The Boy's King Arthur* on his shelf, climbed onto the bed and opened the book to the picture of Sir Launcelot facing Sir Turquine.

"I am Sir Launcelot, the bravest knight in the world," he whispered. Then he read what Sir Launcelot had done to Sir Turquine, how he "leaped upon him fiercely as a lion, and got him by the banner of his helmet, and so he plucked him down on his knees, and anon he rased his helm, and then he smote his neck asunder." For a second or two Gavin felt as satisfied as if he had cut off Mick's head. Then he clapped the book shut.

In real life he wouldn't even attack Mick with his fists. It wasn't just that Mick was so much bigger. It was because Gavin hated fighting. Lots of the other grade five boys got into fights. But it made Gavin feel sick to think of hitting someone, or being hit back. He was such a coward! Sir Launcelot wasn't afraid of fighting. Or of bullies like Mick.

But fighting was dangerous. Once a long time ago, when Gavin had been five, *everything* had been dangerous. Then there was talk of Hitler invading England, and bombs, and enemy planes crashing. But after he and his older sister Norah had come to Canada as "war guests" he'd been safe.

Lately, though, even his security in Toronto had begun to crumble. The war, which had been going on as long as Gavin could remember, was ending. The grown-ups talked about how the Germans were being driven farther and farther back. Troops had landed in France on D-Day and now Paris was liberated. In school they sang songs about the end of the war: "It's a Lovely Day Tomorrow," "The White Cliffs of Dover" and "When the Lights Go On Again."

Of course Gavin wanted the Allies to beat Germany and Italy and Japan. But once the war was over, there would be no reason for him and Norah to stay in Canada. They'd have to go back to England, to that place where he had felt so *unsafe.* To a scary new country and a scary new school. To a family he barely remembered, though Norah talked about them all the time.

Gavin shivered and, as usual, tried not to think about it. But it was so hard not to, when his parents' letters talked about their return, when Aunt Florence and Aunt Mary kept giving him sad looks and when Norah, especially, was so excited about going back.

"Just wait, Gavin," she said. "You'll really like our village. There's a pond where you can fish and woods to play in."

I like it *here,* Gavin wanted to answer—but that would show what a scaredy-cat he was.

He tried to think of how brave all the men were who were fighting in the war. Like Andrew, Aunt Florence's great-nephew—he was a soldier stationed in Italy. Gavin and Tim and Roger often pretended they were fighting in the war, but Gavin knew he'd never have the guts to really do it. Just as he didn't have the guts to fight Mick.

Gavin flipped up his eiderdown on each side, forming a snug cocoon around him. He tried not to cry again. If only Bosley were here to comfort him. Or *Creature* ...

Creature was the name of his small stuffed elephant. When Gavin was little he took him everywhere and talked to him as if he were real. He'd never do that now, of course—not now that he was ten. But he wished he still had him.

A year ago he'd lost Creature. The family had helped him search the whole house. "He must have fallen out of your pocket outside," said Aunt Florence. "Would you like me to buy you a new elephant?"

"No, thank you." Gavin had smiled and pretended he didn't care...

He sat up and wiped his eyes. *Think!* Think about *Mick,* not about a stupid toy elephant! He had only this evening to find the money.

"Norah... can I talk to you?" Gavin stood in Norah's doorway after dinner.

"Sure! I need a break anyway." Norah turned around from her desk and stretched as Gavin came into her room. It was in the tower, the highest part of the house. Whenever he was up here he felt safe; like being in a fortress.

Should he tell her about Mick? He studied his sister. Now that Norah had started high school she had turned into a "bobby-soxer." She and her best friend, Paige Worsley, looked like twins, in their Sloppy Joe sweaters, saddle shoes and pleated skirts. Norah wore lipstick whenever she was out of the house. Photographs of Frank Sinatra plastered her walls. Last month, when Aunt Florence had been away in Montreal, Aunt Mary had let her have a slumber party. The house had resounded with the shrieks of six teen-age girls, as they played records, curled each other's long hair and talked on the telephone all evening. Aunt Mary, Hanny and Gavin had retreated to the kitchen to escape the racket.

But underneath her teen-age disguise Norah was still Norah: his kind older sister and his best friend. She was also the bravest person he knew.

That was why he couldn't tell her about Mick. She'd be so furious that someone was picking on her brother that she'd tell on Mick. Then he would be even meaner to Gavin.

"Well?" smiled Norah. "Why are you staring at me like that? What did you want to talk about?"

"Do you have any money?" Gavin asked quickly. "I need two dollars really fast."

"Two dollars!" Norah looked apologetic. "I'm sorry, Gavin, I'm broke. Why do you need so much?"

"I can't tell you."

"Oh. Well, why don't you ask Aunt Florence?"

"I can't tell her either," said Gavin, "and you know she wouldn't give it to me unless she knew why." He shrugged, as if it wasn't important. "It doesn't matter."

Aunt Mary's voice called up the stairs. "Ga-vin . . . it's almost time for your programme."

"Coming down to listen to 'The Lone Ranger'?" Gavin asked her.

"Not tonight—I have to study! Maths is the first exam and I'm not nearly ready."

"I thought maths was your best subject." It was Gavin's worst.

Norah looked sheepish. "It usually is. But I missed some important parts of algebra when I was—um—out of school."

In October Norah had been suspended from high school for two days. She'd written an essay about how she didn't believe in war and how killing people was always wrong. When her teacher had given her a low mark she'd protested to the principal.

Gavin remembered how steadfast she'd been all through the huge fuss both at school and at home. The adults had called her "disrespectful," both to them and to her country, but not once had Norah faltered in her firm beliefs. No one, not even Aunt Florence, had been able to squash her. Finally her mark had been reluctantly raised and she'd returned to school in triumph.

Gavin sighed; if only *he* were unsquashable. "You'll do okay, Norah," he told her. "You always do."

"Thanks, Gavin." Her clear grey-green eyes searched his face. "Are you *sure* you don't want to tell me why you need so much money? Are you in some kind of trouble?"

Gavin almost told her. But he thought of Norah confronting *his* principal the way she had hers, and of Mick's reaction.

"I'm sure," he mumbled, turning to go.

Norah swivelled her chair back to her desk. "All right, then. I'd better get on with maths. I'm not looking forward to tomorrow morning!"

Neither am I! thought Gavin as he trudged down the two flights of stairs to the den.

Gavin tried to forget about Mick as the galloping music and the Lone Ranger's call of "Hi-yo, Silver... away!" began his favourite Monday evening radio programme. He held open his speller as he listened but he couldn't concentrate on the list of words he was supposed to learn for tomorrow. Instead he let his mind fill with images of cowboys who always beat their enemies.

Aunt Florence and Aunt Mary knitted as they listened—long grey scarves for soldiers. Gavin put down his book and ran his fingers through Bosley's silky fur. The dog's loose skin was dark under his black patches and pale under his white ones. His long ears were the softest part of him; Gavin massaged one between his palms and Bosley thumped his tail in ecstasy.

When the programme was over, Gavin lay down on the floor and rested his head on the soothing warmth of Bosley's side. I wish I was a dog, he thought, as the problem of Mick came rushing back. Dogs never had to worry about anything.

"Turn to the news, Mary," Aunt Florence told her daughter. As usual, Gavin didn't listen. For most of his life he had sat with grown-ups around a radio while an announcer droned on about the war.

He watched his two guardians. Quiet, plump Aunt Mary, her greying hair in a neat bun, had a peaceful expression on her plain face. When her mother wasn't around she let him and Norah do whatever they liked, as if all three of them were Aunt Florence's children. She was always ready to listen or to laugh at a joke. *Safe* ...

Aunt Florence was even safer. Gavin remembered the only other time in his life he had felt this scared: travelling on a big ship to Canada, then living in a hostel with lots of other children while they waited to be assigned to a home. During those endless, confusing days he had clung to one person after another for protection, but they had all been temporary. He'd had to leave the nice women on the boat and at the hostel who'd taken care of him. And Norah had been so wrapped up in her own misery, she hadn't noticed how much he needed her.

Then he had stepped into this solid house where majestic Aunt Florence had welcomed him warmly and claimed him as her own.

"Why do you like her so much?" Norah sometimes asked Gavin. She preferred Aunt Mary. Although she and Aunt Florence secretly respected each other, they had always had a stormy relationship.

Gavin couldn't explain. The older he got the more he realized how conceited and snobby his guardian was. She was often unfair to both her daughter and Norah, and she drove Hanny wild with her bossiness. But whenever Norah and Hanny sat in the kitchen making fun of Aunt Florence, Gavin defended her. Her utter, rock-like confidence—and knowing that he was the most important person in the world to her—protected him.

"You let her baby you too much," was another thing Norah told him. "You should stand up to her more."

But he didn't mind all the hugs and kisses and mushy nicknames. Aunt Florence often told Gavin how much he was like Hugh, her son who had been killed long ago in another world war. Sometimes she went on too much about his clothes, or how blue his eyes were. But when he politely objected she would laugh, hug him, and stop.

Aunt Florence thought he was perfect—coward or not.

"You're growing so fast, sweetness," she smiled when the news was over. "That shirt is much too short in the sleeves. We'll have to get you some new clothes, so your parents don't think I haven't been taking good care of you."

She almost grimaced when she mentioned his parents. But quite often lately Aunt Florence had brought up the subject of Gavin and Norah's return to England, even though it was obviously painful to her. Gavin had overheard the social worker from the Children's Aid Society who had visited last month warn the aunts that they had to prepare them.

He turned over and buried his face in Bosley's neck, sniffing in his warm, musty smell. He couldn't imagine his life without these two women. It was even harder to think of leaving Bosley. He'd known, ever since Aunt Florence's brother Reg had "lent" him the dog the summer before last, that he'd have to give him back one day. He knew in his head that Bosley wasn't really his. But in his heart he was.

Moping over leaving Canada wasn't any help. The end of the war might be soon—but facing Mick was tomorrow!

"I've been thinking, Gavin," said Aunt Florence. "Now that you're ten, I don't see why you can't stay up until nine. Would you like that?"

"Oh, yes, *please!*" Gavin sat up with surprise, and both the aunts laughed. The more Aunt Florence made herself talk about the coming separation, the more she filled Gavin's life with treats to cushion the pain.

Gavin knew he was spoilt; his friends often told him so enviously. He probably *could* ask for two dollars and get it; but only for a good reason. If he could think up a convincing lie, Aunt Florence would believe it. She trusted him. She thought that he was worth trusting; that he was good. And he liked being good—like Sir Launcelot, and the Lone Ranger, and the Shadow, and the pilgrim they talked about in Sunday School.

If only he could be brave, as well.

It was swell to be able to stay up later. But Gavin's stomach lurched as he thought of the bully's words: "... or you'll be jelly." Which part of him would Mick hit first?

"Oh, Bosley," Gavin whispered, "What am I going to do?" He almost started crying again.

Aunt Mary got up and peeked out the window. "It's

snowing again! You'll have good tobogganing tomorrow, Gavin."

Gavin didn't answer. All at once he had thought of a solution—for the time being, anyway.

He would pretend to be sick. Aunt Florence would let him stay home from school if he said he didn't feel well. That wasn't really a lie... he *didn't* feel well, not when he thought about being pounded by Mick.

Gavin opened his speller again, limp with relief. It was a coward's way out, but it was all he could think of.

II

THE BIG SNOW

That night Gavin dreamt he was Superman. He picked up Mick by the scruff of his neck, flew to the top of a high building, whirled the bully around his head three times, and dropped him. Mick screamed all the way down until he landed with a *SPLAT*—just like in the comics.

Gavin woke up tangled in his sheet. His clock said six-thirty but he hadn't heard the milkman's horse clomping in his dreams the way he usually did. His windowpane rattled and a branch scraped against it.

He hopped out of bed and opened the curtains. Snow raged against the glass, as if trying to get in. A blizzard!

Gavin grinned—then frowned, as he remembered his plan. If he pretended to be sick, he couldn't enjoy the fresh snow. But he could go out *now,* then get back into bed before anyone was up.

"Come on, Boz!" Bosley looked up from his basket with sleepy surprise. He stretched his long front legs out of it, leaving his hindquarters in place as he decided whether or not to wake up. He lumbered to his feet, then stretched again with a complaining groan.

"Lazybones," chuckled Gavin, flinging on his clothes. "Get up. We're going *out.* For a *walk!*"

At the word "walk" Bosley jolted awake. He danced and whined around Gavin, his stubby black tail wagging furiously.

"Shh!" Gavin held the dog by the collar as they crept downstairs. In the hall he put on his jacket, ski pants, tuque, mitts and galoshes. Then he unlocked the front door and pushed at it. It wouldn't budge.

"That's funny." He went into the kitchen and unlocked that door. But it, too, was stuck. He peeked out of the window.

"Wow..." The snow came halfway up the panes and the back yard was a whirling landscape. Gavin pushed at the door again but the snow blocked it. Bosley scratched at it and whined.

"You need to go out, don't you boy? But we're trapped!"

Gavin thought a minute. Then he hauled the kitchen table over to the window, stood on it, pulled down the upper sash and pushed out the storm window. Snow and cold air rushed into the warm kitchen. He poked out his head and looked down. The drifts were so high it probably wouldn't hurt to simply fall into them.

"Come on, Boz, you go first." Gavin lifted Bosley onto the slippery tabletop, climbed up himself and put the dog's front paws on top of the open window. His hind legs scrabbled for a foothold and he whined again, his liquid brown eyes looking back imploringly at Gavin.

"Be *brave,*" Gavin told him. "Jump!" But Bosley kept whining and trying to get off the table. Gavin sighed. His dog was a coward too. "Come on... pretend you're Lassie." With great difficulty—Bosley was almost as big as he was—Gavin hoisted the protesting dog and spilled him out of the window. Then he tumbled out after him.

Down they both dropped, like stones into water, until the snow stopped their fall. They emerged caked in white, Bosley sneezing violently and Gavin laughing.

He brushed off his face, but the wind blew more snow

into it. He struggled to the front of the house; it was like wading through waist-high mud. Then he stopped in awe.

Gavin had seen lots of snow since he'd lived in Canada, but never as much as this. He blinked through the swaying curtain of flakes. The street, sidewalks and front yards merged into one white expanse. Each house had several feet of snow heaped on its roof, with tall drifts blown against its doors and lower windows. Every car was buried. Snowflakes scraped against his jacket, melted on his eyelashes and tickled his nose.

Gavin stood spellbound in the dim morning light. He put out his tongue to catch the flakes, feeling like an Arctic explorer —Nansen, he decided—setting foot in an untouched land.

Bosley had followed gingerly in Gavin's path. Now he began to play, springing out of the snow like a jack-in-the-box. Gavin leapt and stumbled after him, throwing sprays of snow into the air. His laughter and Bosley's barking rang out in the silent street.

The snow was seeping into Gavin's cloth jacket and he began to shiver. He started towards the house, then stopped.

How was he going to get back in? The open window was too high to reach and both doors were blocked. And if he were trapped outside, that meant Norah and Aunt Florence and Aunt Mary were trapped inside!

What would Sir Launcelot do? Or Nansen? He floundered to the back yard and looked around. Then he spied the snow shovel under the porch, where Hanny's husband had left it the last time he'd shovelled the snow. He picked it up and began working on the four-foot drift blocking the back door.

His sore arm made it difficult to lift the shovel and he had to keep stopping to pound snow off the blade. Sweat ran down his forehead and his breath steamed around him. He pretended he was Nansen again and hummed to himself as he imagined freeing his fellow explorers from their igloo. The snow blew back almost as fast as he cleared it, but finally he had shovelled away enough to jerk open the door. He and Bosley ran through the kitchen into the hall.

"Wake up, everyone!" Gavin shouted. "I've rescued you!"

By breakfast the glow from the family's praise, which made Gavin feel like a hero, had worn off. While he was outside he had completely forgotten about Mick. He couldn't pretend to be sick now that he'd demonstrated so much healthy vigour.

"I've never *seen* so much snow!" marvelled Aunt Mary. "It must be a record!"

Aunt Florence brought in their breakfast. "I'm sure Hanny won't make it in at all today. And the milkman probably won't either, or the bread wagon. We're almost out of both. Only one piece of toast each, please."

Gavin looked out the window at the shifting white world. He glanced across the table at Norah, who smiled back. She was obviously hoping for the same thing he was. Then the radio confirmed it: all Toronto schools were closed.

"Hurray!" shouted Norah. "No exams!"

Gavin couldn't stop grinning as his fear rolled away. It would return tomorrow, but right now he had a whole day of freedom from Mick.

The holiday stretched to two days; two days when the city was paralysed by what everyone later called "the big snow." The grown-ups looked grave as calamities kept being reported on the radio. Several people died of over-exertion as they struggled through the drifts. A streetcar was overturned on Queen Street, trapping everyone inside. By Wednesday thirteen people had died and all deliveries were still delayed.

But for Gavin and his friends the blizzard was a profitable

adventure. He and Norah strapped on their skis and struggled to the local store, where the owner allowed one quart of milk a customer. After the snow finally stopped falling, every young person in the neighbourhood began to shovel. They shovelled paths to doors. They shovelled sidewalks. They shovelled out cars. Gavin thought his arms would fall off, they ached so much. But it was worth it to feel like a hero again, as the people he shovelled out thanked him warmly. Best of all, many of them insisted on paying.

"You shouldn't take money," said Norah sternly, when he told her how old Mr Chapman had given him a quarter. "This is an emergency!"

"I tried to refuse but he said I had to!" said Gavin.

"Oh, all right. I guess it's okay as long as you don't ask."

By Wednesday afternoon Gavin had $3.15—more money than he'd ever had in his life. Now he could face Mick when school opened again, and even have some left over.

"You'll always remember this, Norah and Gavin," said Aunt Mary that evening. "You can tell your grandchildren you experienced the worst storm Toronto has ever had."

They were relaxing in the den after dinner, as usual. The house had a huge living room but the family spent most of their time in the smaller, more comfortable den. Gavin sprawled on the floor, reading the funnies. Aunt Florence and Norah were huddled over a game of cribbage. Aunt Mary was unpacking Christmas tree ornaments, inspecting each one to see if it was broken.

"I think we should all be very proud of ourselves," said Aunt Florence. "Mary and I are pretty good cooks, aren't we? I believe my biscuits are even better than Hanny's. And you children were splendid, the way you got us milk and shovelled all that snow. I'm going to write to your parents and tell them."

They all beamed at each other, even Norah and Aunt Florence.

"I hear there's a shortage of Christmas trees and turkeys this year," said Aunt Mary.

"Then we'll do without a tree and have a goose instead of a turkey," said her mother calmly. "After all, we already do without using the car to have enough gas coupons for the summer." She put away the cards. "Beat you again, eh, Norah?" Norah grinned ruefully.

Aunt Florence took out *Oliver Twist* and began where she'd left off last time. This fall she had started reading aloud every evening, the way she did in the summers at Muskoka.

Gavin settled back against Bosley, who was snoozing peacefully. The snow pressing against the house made the den even cosier than usual. Sitting here listening to Aunt Florence's rich, reassuring voice was like being on an island. An island of safety in a world of dangers—Mick, and having to leave Canada. He closed his eyes and tried to will the evening to last forever.

But Mick finally had to be faced when school reopened on Thursday. The streets were still glutted with snow. Gavin kicked a hole in a snowbank as he waited at the usual corner for Tim and Roger. The money was safe in his mitt but he shivered inside. What if Mick wasn't satisfied?

"Hi, Gav." Tim threw a soft snowball at Gavin's stomach. "I was thinking about Mick." While they were shovelling together yesterday Gavin had told his friends all about the bully's threat.

"What about him?"

"Why don't we ambush him with snowballs? From behind the school fence so he won't see us. Then you could keep your money."

Tim was always suggesting things like this. *He* was brave

—but too impulsive. "That wouldn't do any good," Gavin told him. "It might put Mick off for a while but he'd still look for me later to get the money. And if he found out it was us he'd be even madder."

Tim looked disappointed. "I guess so. Jeepers, why are people *like* Mick? Mean like him..."

Gavin shuddered. "He's even meaner than Charlie was." Charlie had been last year's bully, but now he went to Norah's high school.

"Remember when Charlie and his gang beat up your sister's friend just because he had a German last name?" said Tim.

"They cracked his rib!" said Gavin indignantly.

"I wonder if Charlie still picks on Bernard. Does your sister ever talk about him?"

"Bernard doesn't live in Toronto any more," said Gavin. "He and his mother moved back to Kitchener." Gavin remembered how Bernard had always been nice to him. He could have told *him* about Mick.

Roger joined them, out of breath from running. "Sorry I'm late. Mum couldn't get out of bed and I had to make breakfast." As usual Roger looked worried. His mother had a bad back and his father, an officer in the navy, was fighting overseas. Roger was the only child—sometimes he even had to do the grocery shopping.

"What were you talking about?" he asked, as they started walking the remaining two blocks to school.

"Mick," sighed Gavin.

"Oh, him." Roger looked even more worried. "I just saw him."

The other two stared at him. "Where?"

"Hanging around by the store. He was making a kid in grade three eat some snow that had dog pee on it."

"He's such a creep!" cried Tim. "He's like a Nazi."

"A nasty Nazi," said Roger quietly.

Tim grinned. "Mick's a *nasty Nazi* . . . Mick's a *nasty Nazi* . . ." He and Gavin and Roger goosestepped along the snowy sidewalk as they continued the chant. But not too loud, in case Mick was lurking nearby.

Gavin felt braver now that both of his friends were with him. Norah called them "The Three Musketeers" and they often pretended they were. They'd been friends since grade one.

Tim Flanagan was the middle one of six. He was round and emotional, but despite his frequent outbursts, he never let anything bother him for long—except for being hungry, which he always was.

Skinny Roger, on the other hand, appeared calm and quiet, but he constantly picked at the skin on his fingers and usually had an anxious frown on his face. "That Hewitt boy looks like a little old man," Aunt Florence said. Roger got high marks in all his subjects but after each report card he always said they could have been higher.

Three was a perfect number for games. Besides the Three Musketeers, they often played they were Sir Launcelot, Sir Galahad and Sir Gawaine, or the army, the navy and the air force. Gavin was the best at making things up, Roger knew the most facts, and Tim was the most daring.

"Should we stay with you while you give Mick the money?" asked Tim as they approached Prince Edward School.

If only they could; but Gavin shook his head. "Mick wouldn't like it if he knew I'd told you."

"Then we'll hide behind the fence. Come on, Rog!"

"No snowballs!" Gavin called after them. He watched them push through the excited crowd of kids playing in the snow. Then he went up to the flagpole—no Mick. He stood there alone for a long time, wishing he could be invisible like the Shadow.

"Hi, Gavin." Eleanor Austen came up to him.

"Hi, Eleanor." Gavin forgot his fear for a moment as he smiled at her. Eleanor was even smarter than Roger, and she was the prettiest girl in his class. Her eyelashes were so long she could balance eraser crumbs on them; last year she'd demonstrated. This morning her cheeks were the same colour as her red tam; her long brown braids hung in neat polished ropes from under it.

Some girls were unbearable. Like Lucy Smith. She was a grade ahead of Gavin and also a war guest, from the same English village as him and Norah. She and her sister and brother, Dulcie and Derek, had come over on the same ship. Now Derek had gone back to England to join the army, but Lucy and Dulcie still lived a few blocks away from the Ogilvies', at Reverend and Mrs Milne's.

Lucy acted as if she owned Gavin, bossing him in front of his friends. And Daphne Worsley, Paige's youngest sister, was even worse; Aunt Florence called her "a holy terror." At least Daphne went to a different school.

Eleanor, however, was *interesting.* She wrote dramatic stories, which she sometimes read aloud in class. And instead of a dog or a cat she had a pet monkey called Kilroy, which she had once brought to school.

Eleanor looked at Gavin urgently. "Quick!" she whispered. "They dared me to kiss you! So I'm just going to pretend, okay?" She smacked the air in front of his cheek, then rushed back to her friends watching from the girls' playground.

Gavin did what was expected of him. "Yech!" he cried, pretending to wipe off the kiss. The girls giggled.

Gavin's cheeks burned as much as Eleanor's had. Girls often dared each other to kiss him—him, Jamie and George, whom they had decided were the best-looking boys in grade five. Gavin had never liked it—but it had never been Eleanor before. He almost wished she hadn't just pretended.

A teacher came out and rang the first bell. The snowball fights stopped and everyone began to line up at the boys' and girls' entrances.

Where was Mick? Gavin was just about to dash into school when a rough voice behind him snarled, "Hand it over, Stoakes."

Gavin tore off his mitt and held up the red two-dollar bill. He was ashamed at how much his hand trembled. Mick grabbed the bill.

"Okay. You're safe. For now . . ." Both of them ran to their classrooms.

"Did you do it?" Tim whispered to Gavin, as they stood beside each other during "God Save the King."

Gavin nodded, trying to catch his breath. "But now I wish I hadn't. It's so unfair that he gets away with it!"

"At least you won't get beaten up," said Tim.

Mrs Moss directed one of her piercing glances at them. They clamped their mouths closed, then opened them again to chant "The Lord's Prayer."

"Any more talking, Tim and Gavin, and you'll be visiting with me after school today. Do you understand?" the teacher said after roll-call.

"Yes, Mrs Moss," they murmured. Mrs Moss was a new teacher this year and they still weren't sure whether to rate her as "nice" or "mean." She smiled more than "Sourpuss Liers," whom she'd replaced, but she was also strict; she always meant what she said.

"Now, because we had no school for the last two days, I wonder how many of you remembered to bring your quarters..."

Gavin had been so busy worrying about the money for Mick, he'd forgotten his war savings stamp money. He watched as some of the pupils exchanged their quarters for a stamp. They were allowed to paste it on one of the squares drawn over the large cartoon drawing of Hitler's face. Since September they had covered up almost half of it.

"There!" said Mrs Moss. "The rest of you please bring your money tomorrow. Now... I wonder if by any chance anyone has any news for this morning?" She looked mischievous; of course, *everyone* had stories about the blizzard.

Mrs Moss let six pupils recount their adventures of being stuck, looking for milk and bread, and shovelling people out. Gavin didn't contribute; he was still seething over the injustice of Mick. It was much easier to feel revengeful now that he was safe.

"I'm sure that many people were very grateful to you for helping," said Mrs Moss. "And now *I* have some news. You've probably noticed that Colin Porter hasn't been here this week. He and his sister Rose have returned to England. I just found out that they sailed last weekend."

The room buzzed as everyone turned around to stare at Colin's empty desk. But because Colin had been a prig and a tattle-tale, no one looked upset.

During arithmetic Gavin bent over his workbook, but he wasn't thinking about addition. He and Colin had been the last war guests in grade five. In grade one there had been three others in his class, but in the past two years they had all returned.

"Are you daydreaming again, Gavin?" asked Mrs Moss.

Gavin tried to concentrate. They were supposed to add a

long column of three-figured numbers. He had always found it hard to think of numbers as just numbers. In grade one he had decided that some numbers were male and some female, and that each had a definite personality. He still couldn't help thinking of Six as a prissy woman who didn't like being next to pompous Nine. So how could he add them up?

They had to hand in their workbooks while Gavin was settling an argument between Three, a howling little girl, and Ten, a wise old man. That meant he'd have to stay in at recess tomorrow to finish it.

Next was a spelling test. Gavin waited for the monitors to fill his inkwell, rattling the little silver lid confidently. He'd had two extra evenings to study his speller and got every word right.

"When do you think *you'll* have to go back to England, Gav?" Roger asked him at recess. His dark eyes looked worried again.

"Not for a long time!" said Gavin hastily. "Not until the war's over. That's what the social worker told us last month. Our parents don't think it will be safe until then. There's a new kind of bomb and lots of them fall over Kent."

"*Flying* bombs!" said Tim eagerly. "I know about those. I saw them on a newsreel."

"Maybe Colin will see a flying bomb," said Roger. "I bet he'll be scared."

Tim gave Gavin a friendly shove. "I hope the war is *never* over, Gav! Then you'll never have to leave Canada."

"But then my father wouldn't come back!" protested Roger.

"Oh yeah. Sorry, Rog."

"Let's stop talking about the war," said Gavin desperately. "Want to build a snow fort after school?"

III

NEITHER CALM NOR BRIGHT

Gavin and Tim and Roger were careful to stay out of Mick's way for the rest of the term. Then the Christmas holidays started and they were free from worrying about him for a while.

Now there was lots of time to play in the huge amount of snow that still covered the ground. The three friends tobogganed, made snow forts and jointed the highly organized snowball fights in the school playground. But as Christmas Day approached, Gavin became more and more uneasy.

"What's wrong with you, Gav?" Tim asked him. "You haven't been listeneing! I said, I *think* I'm getting a chemistry set. How about you? You always get such keen stuff."

Gavin couldn't explain how everything was different this year. Although no one could bear to talk about it, everyone in the Ogilvie household was aware that this was Gavin and Norah's last Christmas in Canada. It was hard to ignore the sad looks he kept getting, not only from Aunt Florence, Aunt Mary and Hanny, but from the five Montreal relatives who'd come to stay—"cousins" and "aunts and uncles" that he knew from Gairloch, the island they went to in Muskoka every summer.

On Christmas Eve afternoon Gavin sat in the living room having a game of checkers with Uncle Reg. Aunt Florence had managed to find a tree. It was much spindlier than usual but it still glittered with the same glass balls and bubble lights that covered it every year. The same angel perched on top and the usual hill of presents buried its lower branches. Gavin kept glancing at the tree, taking whiffs of its piney smell for reassurance.

Uncle Reg reached down and fondled one of Bosley's ears. "Well, Boz, do you miss me?" Bosley raised one paw and shook hands politely, but then he pushed under the table and put his head in Gavin's lap.

"He certainly prefers *you* now," chuckled Uncle Reg. He jumped his checker over one of Gavin's, then looked up, unusually serious. "Gavin, I want you to know that when you have to return to England I would give Bosley to you for good—if he was allowed to go."

A flash of hope filled Gavin. "*Is* he?"

"I'm afraid not, son." The old man looked sorrowful. "I even made inquiries. Dogs aren't allowed into Britain without going into quarantine for months. We couldn't do that to Boz."

"No," agreed Gavin sadly. "He'd be too lonely." He swallowed hard. "I know I have to give him up, Uncle Reg. You said that when you lent him to me. It's okay."

Uncle Reg smiled at him. "You're a brave boy." Then he sighed. "I think Florence was probably right. I shouldn't have given Bosley to you in the first place. I should have realized how hard it was going to be when the time came for you to go back."

"But I'm *glad* you gave him—lent him—to me! He's one of my best friends!" Then Gavin couldn't help sniffling.

Uncle Reg handed him a large, soft handkerchief, looking as if he were going to cry too. "I promise you I'll take very good care of him and I'll always think of him as *your* dog—as if you've lent him to *me!* I'll send you reports and pictures of him."

Gavin blew his nose, handed back the handkerchief and tried to smile. Then Uncle Reg might stop talking about Bosley.

"I have a perfect word for charades this year," chuckled Uncle Reg. "Let's try to get on the same team." Gavin cheered up as Uncle Reg told him how he planned to use the word to trick Aunt Florence.

That evening a crowd of visitors filled the living room. At one end the teen-agers gathered: Aunt Florence's great-nieces, Flo and Janet, Paige, Paige's sister Barbara, Dulcie and Norah. They shrieked with laughter as Paige, the tallest and wildest, imitated the headmistress at her girls' school. The adults sat with their drinks and cigarettes at the other end of the room, praising Uncle Reg for managing to get a bottle of rye.

Gavin was stuck with Daphne and Lucy. He slouched between them while they chattered about tomorrow morning.

"I always get up at five o'clock and open my stocking," declared Daphne, spitting out crumbs of shortbread as she spoke. "They make me go back to bed until seven, but then we *run* downstairs and rip open all the presents."

Lucy looked prim. "*We* have to wait until Uncle Cedric gets back from early service, then we have to get dressed and have breakfast before we have the tree. Then we go to church. That's exactly how we did it in England."

Daphne pinched Gavin's leg. "Ouch!" he protested. "I wish you wouldn't always do that, Daphne."

"I bet you'll miss my pinches when you go back to England," she smirked.

"That'll be the only good part about going back," he retorted.

"But don't you *want* to go back, Gavin?" Lucy asked him. "I can hardly wait to see my parents again! I'll miss Canada and the Milnes, of course, but England is our *real* home."

Everything Lucy said always sounded like something she was copying from the grown-ups. Gavin shrugged. Daphne pinched him again and he got up indignantly.

If only the Montreal cousins who were his age—Peter and Ross and Sally—had come this year. He found a chair in a corner and curled up in it, thinking of all the good times he had with those three at Gairloch every summer. But if the war was over by next summer—and everyone seemed to think it would be—he wouldn't be in Canada.

In August Norah and Gavin had walked around the island by themselves on the morning they'd left. Norah had been in tears. "This is going to be the hardest part of Canada to give up," she said, gazing greedily at every rock and tree. "It's probably the last time we'll ever be here." Gavin hadn't believed her. Now he did.

And if he would probably be back in England this summer, that meant he'd be there for sure by next Christmas... Gavin glanced at the brown paper parcel from his parents under the tree. It always looked so plain compared to the other presents in their bright paper and ribbon. Next Christmas, when he and Norah were with their parents, would *all* their presents be wrapped in plain brown paper?

Uncle Reg went over to the piano and everyone gathered around to sing carols. Gavin tried to make himself feel Christmassy, especially when they sang "Good King Wenceslas." It had become a family tradition for Uncle Reg and Gavin to sing the parts of the king and the page. Usually this was Gavin's favourite part of Christmas Eve, imagining himself following a king "through the rude wind's wild lament/And the bitter weather."

Sire, the night is darker now,
And the wind grows stronger:
Fails my heart, I know not how,
I can go no longer

sang Gavin when it was his turn. But this year the song seemed unbearably sad, even after the king's reassuring answer.

"That was wonderful, pet!" Aunt Florence whispered. "You really made the words come alive!"

They had just begun "Silent Night" when all the lights in the house went out.

"Oh, *no!* Not on Christmas Eve!" someone cried.

The girls giggled in the darkness and Daphne pinched Gavin again. But soon one of the adults had found candles and the living room became a soft, flickering cave.

"Let's carry on," said Uncle Reg. "I can see well enough."

"All is calm, all is bright," they sang.

"It certainly isn't calm and bright tonight!" laughed one of the aunts at the end.

The family sat down and sipped eggnog. Gavin snuggled up against Aunt Florence. In the last few years Toronto had often had power failures. He liked the way the house seemed to shrink around him, enclosing him in a safe cocoon.

"This is what it must be like all the time in England," said Aunt Mary.

"*I* remember," said Dulcie. "We had to cover every inch of the window with black curtains. People came around and inspected to make sure not one chink of light showed."

"Well, soon they won't have to do that any more," said Mr Worsley. "Just like that song—what is it?"

"When the Lights Go On Again," said Lucy importantly. "We sing it in school."

"But then you'll all have to go back," said Janet. She clutched Norah's arm as if she'd never let her go.

That made everyone look sadly again at Norah, Gavin, Dulcie and Lucy. Gavin shivered. He *never* wanted the lights to go on.

Christmas morning was different too. Usually Peter and Ross shared Gavin's room and they inspected the stockings on the ends of their beds together. This year he opened his stocking all by himself. After he had spread everything out on his bed—a cap gun, pencils, comics, a package of Chiclets, two rolls of Lifesavers, notepaper, and an orange in the toe—he put it all back carefully in the stocking and went up to the tower. There he spilled it out again with Norah, Janet and Flo.

As in Lucy's house they had to get dressed and eat breakfast before they had the tree. Gavin always relished the delicious suspense while they waited for the adults to finish. This year, at least that part was the same. As he waited on the stairs in front of the closed living-room door he felt Christmassy for the first time.

But when they were finally allowed to dash in, he tried to hide his disappointment. Usually there was something large under the tree for him: one year it had been skis, another year a new bike. But this Christmas all his presents were wrapped—and small.

The presents themselves were okay: a baseball glove, several airplane models and some books he had wanted. But he'd hoped for a new hockey stick. And his present from Aunt Florence was baffling: two tiny, engraved gold circles lying on cotton batting in a small blue box.

"They're much too old for you, pet," said Aunt Florence. "But they're very valuable and I want you to keep them safe until you're grown up. They belonged to my husband."

Aunt Florence looked so proud he couldn't hurt her feelings by asking what the strange objects were. "Thank you very much," he said. "I'll take good care of them."

"I'm sorry that all your presents are so small, sweetness," she said. "But we didn't want to give you anything this year that you couldn't take home with you." Then her strong face crumpled.

So that was why. Gavin tried to be grateful. After all, he already had plenty of stuff—more than most boys his age. It wasn't that he didn't like what he'd received; it was just the *change*.

Norah, too, got something that was old, but at least you could tell what it was: a short string of pearls.

"They were given to me when I was your age," smiled Aunt Mary.

"They're real, so take good care of them," warned Aunt Florence.

"I will. *Thank* you!" Norah tried on the pearls while Janet admired them.

At ten o'clock they all gathered around the radio for the King's Christmas message. The young people squirmed but the adults listened intently.

"We do not know what awaits us when we open the door of 1945 . . ." said the hesitant, English voice. "The darkness daily grows less and less. The lamps which the Germans put out all over Europe, first in 1914 and then in 1939, are being slowly rekindled. Already we can see some of them beginning to shine through the fog of war that still shrouds so many lands."

"That was his best speech yet," said Aunt Dorothy at the end, wiping her eyes.

"And hasn't his voice improved! He never stutters any

more," said Aunt Florence approvingly—as if King George VI were her personal responsibility.

While the family was walking along the snowy sidewalks to church, Gavin lingered behind the adults with Norah.

"You know those little gold things I got," he muttered. "What *are* they?"

"They're cuff-links, silly! You use them to keep your cuffs together."

"But I have buttons on my cuffs!"

"Later you'll just have holes, and then you'll use cuff-links. Look at Uncle Reg's shirtsleeves."

Gavin sneaked a look at them during church. Sure enough, Uncle Reg's sleeves were held shut with two gold circles, just like his. He sighed. What a boring present.

Beside him Norah ran her fingers along her pearls. "Isn't it strange to think that next Christmas morning we'll be in church in Ringden?" she whispered, as Reverend Milne talked about the growing possibility of world peace.

Gavin nodded miserably. Norah, however, looked eager, not miserable. That made him feel even more alone.

After church they had Christmas dinner. Hanny roasted a goose and everyone commented on how it was just as good as a turkey. Gavin ate as much as he could to fill up the empty space inside him.

When the meal was over Uncle Reg and Uncle Barclay fell asleep in front of the living-room fire, still wearing the paper hats from their crackers. Hanny went home to her husband, and the aunts and cousins did the dishes. On other Christmases this was the time of day when Gavin and the younger cousins played with their new toys. This year he wandered into the living room, wondering what to do. He sat down and opened up one of his new books. It was called *Rabbit Hill* and it looked good, but he couldn't concentrate. The uncles snored gently. He could hear the women singing "We all want figgy pudding" in the kitchen. He had offered to help, but they'd shooed him out.

Finally the dishes were done and the others came into the living room, teasing the uncles as always for falling asleep. Flo, the oldest cousin, stretched out her legs and sighed. "What a nice break. I wish I didn't have to go back tomorrow." She was in the RCAF and only had two days' leave.

"I wonder what Andrew's doing right now?" said her younger sister, Janet.

"His mother said his last letter was dated October," said Aunt Dorothy. "All we know is that he's somewhere in Italy."

"I hope he got my parcel," said Janet. "I knit him some socks."

"We sent him some food and books but so many parcels don't seem to ever reach him," sighed Aunt Mary.

"I hope you girls are all writing to Andrew regularly," said Aunt Florence.

"I do—every month," said Flo.

"I write *twice* a month," boasted Janet.

"Do you hear that, Norah? Norah says she doesn't need to write to Andrew because she's not related to him," sniffed Aunt Florence. "But the dear boy needs all the letters he can get to keep up his spirits."

Norah ignored Aunt Florence's disapproving frown. Gavin was careful not to look at his sister. He knew that, ever since Andrew had spent the summer before last with them at Gairloch, Norah had been writing secretly to him. He occasionally wrote back, to Paige's address.

Gavin also knew that Norah was in love with Andrew.

She'd told him that one night after Andrew had gone to fight overseas and he'd found her in tears.

"Don't tell anyone," she'd said. "They'll tease me and say I'm too young. But I won't be too young when he comes back."

If he came back. That was why everyone looked so grave at the mention of his name, and why Norah always snatched the paper and scanned the casualty lists before the aunts saw it. Whenever Gavin watched a newsreel showing dead soldiers he closed his eyes in case one of them was Andrew.

Gavin squirmed. Norah wasn't quite fifteen. She wasn't even allowed to date. If the war was over soon, surely she would still be too young for Andrew. Surely she couldn't get *married*—would she?

When the family switched from Andrew to news of other relatives Gavin let himself glance at Norah. She was staring into the fire dreamily. She looked as grown-up as Flo, he realized with alarm. Aunt Florence had let her wear lipstick and stockings and her long hair was carefully curled at the ends. Did Norah have to change along with everything else?

Norah didn't look very grown-up after supper, as she helped her team act out the first syllable in their word for charades. She and Aunt Mary huffed and puffed, their hair in their eyes, as they jumped around the room with their feet together, clutching the sides of their dresses.

"Can-can!"

"Hop!"

"Rabbit!"

"Give up . . ." gasped Norah. "We can't do this forever. And it's only one syllable!"

"I know!" said Janet. "It's a sack race! *Sack!*"

"Right!" laughed Aunt Mary, collapsing on a chair.

But no one could guess the next two syllables. First Aunt Dorothy and Flo dressed as tramps, then everyone on the team drank something and held their imaginary glasses up to their ears. For the whole word they carried in Norah, her hands and feet tied up, and pretended to burn her on a fire.

"Aha!" said Aunt Florence. "Sacrifice!"

"You *always* guess," grumbled Flo.

"But what was the second syllable?" asked Janet. "The third was 'ice,' but what were all those rags you were wearing? 'Riff'?"

"The first part of riff-raff!" said Flo, as the others groaned.

"Our turn," said Uncle Reg. "For our first word I want to change things a bit. We'll do the whole word at once, with no syllables. And only Gavin and I will know what the word is."

"But why can't the rest of your team know?" demanded Aunt Florence.

"You'll see," said Uncle Reg. He took the dressing-gown belts that had been used to tie up Norah and formed them into a figure eight on the rug. Now, Florence, you sit down in one circle facing outwards, and, Barclay, you sit in the other."

"This sounds like one of your tricks, Reg," said Aunt Florence.

"It's just charades, Florence. Will you please sit down?"

Finally she lowered her large rear into one of the circles. Uncle Barclay stoically sat down in the other.

"That's the word," grinned Gavin. "It has four syllables."

Everyone tried half-hearted guesses but no one came near.

"Really, Reg, I feel very foolish sitting here," complained Aunt Florence.

"Not as foolish as you're about to feel!" smiled her brother. "Give up?" Everyone nodded. "Tell them, Gavin."

"Assassinate!" crowed Gavin. The uproar that followed—even Aunt Florence laughed—made Gavin forget for the only time that this was his last Christmas in Canada.

The visiting relatives caught the train back to Montreal on Boxing Day. Gavin spent the morning at Roger's, but after lunch he had to stay in to write his thank-you notes. He sat at the desk in the study, staring at the list Aunt Florence had given him and swinging his legs. Bosley snoozed at his feet. Writing thank-yous was so tedious, but Aunt Florence always insisted it be done right away.

Finally he dipped his pen into the inkwell and began the first letter on the list. "Dear Mum and Dad. Thank you for the wooden truck and the hat. I like them very much." He put down his pen. Didn't his parents realize that he was much too old for wooden toys and that he already had plenty of hats? Then he wiggled with guilt. He knew that Dad had carved the truck and Mum had knit the hat. Their letters often said how impossible it was to find new toys in England. Norah's eyes had filled with tears when she'd unwrapped the homemade blouse Mum had sewn her. Gavin wished they wouldn't send anything at all—then he wouldn't have to feel so ungrateful.

He closed his eyes and tried to remember his real family, but their faces were blank. They were simply names: Mum, Dad and Grandad; his sister Muriel, her husband, Barry, and their new baby; and his other sister, Tibby. They were like distant relatives he never saw, as distant as a cousin of Aunt Florence's in Manitoba, who always sent him a small Christmas present, but whom he'd never met.

He picked up his pen and finished the letter, describing

Christmas Day and his other presents. Then he scribbled his other notes as quickly as he could to get them over with.

Finally he blotted the last envelope. He piled them on the hall table and went up to his room to read. But Bosley wouldn't stay with him. He kept going out of the bedroom, then coming back to Gavin and whining.

"What's the matter, boy? You've just *been* out."

He got up and followed the dog into the upstairs hall. Bosley was standing at the half-open door of Aunt Florence's room. He looked back anxiously at Gavin.

Gavin listened for a moment. Surely it couldn't be… crying. Not Aunt Florence. She *never* cried.

But the sound was unmistakable. He peeked through the crack of the door and saw Aunt Florence sitting at her dressing table. Her back was towards him and her shoulders were shaking. One hand clutched the woven paper mat he'd made for her in school. He'd written "Merry Christmas to Aunt Florence from Gavin" on it in his best handwriting.

Gavin scurried back to his room. Aunt Florence wasn't *ever* supposed to cry! He read his book intently, letting the story carry him away from her weeping.

IV

AN ORDINARY WINTER

Nineteen forty-five began with the coldest January Toronto had had in twenty-five years. Whenever Gavin went outside he had to wear extra clothes: long underwear, another pair of mitts, a fleece-lined leather cap with flaps, and a scarf tied over his mouth and nose. The scarf kept falling down, freezing into a hard woolly clump where his mouth had wetted it.

At least the cold weather slowed down Mick. No one stood still long enough for him to threaten, and many recesses were spent indoors, where teachers supervised them more than usual.

Every morning Mrs Moss talked about how the Germans were being cornered by the Allies—but still the war didn't end. Aunt Florence stopped mentioning Gavin and Norah's return to England. Gavin decided to pretend it wasn't going to happen.

The winter days and months slipped by like beads on a string—orderly and normal. Gavin threw himself into his activities in a sort of dream.

The city streets were still so blocked with snow that the scrap-paper pick-ups were halted. Instead the schools had a competition to see which one could collect the most paper. Gavin and Tim and Roger hauled paper to the schoolyard on their toboggans, then bundled and stacked it until their arms ached. The piles in the schoolyard grew and grew. Mr Evans, the principal, told them proudly that even though they hadn't won, Prince Edward School had collected several tons of paper.

Gavin and Tim and Roger went downtown to see the helicopter that was being exhibited in Simpson's department store. If you brought some war savings stamps with you, you were allowed to climb inside and sit at the controls.

Gavin got three more badges in Cubs and two goals in hockey. Roger turned eleven, and Tim ate so much at his party that he threw up all over the rug and was sent home in disgrace. Gavin and Tim were caught chewing gum by Mr Evans. He made them stay after school and scrape off enough gum from under the desks to fill up a piece of paper each.

On February 2 the groundhog saw his shadow. Tim's parents took him and Gavin to the Ice Follies. The Ogilvie household celebrated Norah's fifteenth birthday by all going to see *Blithe Spirit* at the Royal Alexandra Theatre.

Mick got the strap again, for beating up Russell Jones in the washroom. A teacher had been walking by and heard the commotion.

Norah had an argument with Aunt Florence about staying out late at the new canteen that had opened for teenagers. "*Everyone stays* until midnight!" she protested, but Aunt Florence just said, "Fiddlesticks! You're not everyone and I want you home by ten-thirty."

Norah won first prize in her school speech contest. The topic was "My Hero." Norah spoke clearly and fervently about Amelia Earhart, the first woman to fly an airplane across the Atlantic Ocean.

"You were very good, my dear," said Aunt Florence.

"You were wonderful!" cried Aunt Mary. "I never could have stood up in front of all those people when I was your age. And what a fascinating woman! Why did you choose her?"

"Miss Gleeson at the library gave me a book about her." Norah grinned, stroking her trophy. "Maybe I'll be a pilot too, one day."

"A pilot!" spluttered Aunt Florence. "Don't be absurd, Norah." But Norah looked thoughtful.

Three more girls in grade five kissed Gavin. Jamie and George kept getting kissed too. Then Jamie tattled and Mrs Moss told the girls they had to stop "all this kissing nonsense."

Gavin got fourteen valentines—the same as the number of girls in his class. Roger and Tim teased him and he pretended to despise the valentines. But he went through them all at home, trying to guess which one was Eleanor's.

One Saturday evening a boy turned up at the Ogilvies' front door, asked for Norah, and was ushered into the hall.

"This is—um—Michael Carey," Norah told Aunt Florence.

Michael shook hands nervously as Aunt Florence inspected him. Gavin sneaked a look at him and Norah as they sat together in the living room. Both had flushed faces and neither spoke much. Norah seemed relieved when Michael left half an hour later.

"Is he your boy friend?" Gavin asked her.

"No! He's just a boy in my class," muttered Norah.

Aunt Florence came into the hall. "He seems like a presentable young man, Norah. I know his grandmother." She smiled. "Now that you're fifteen, my dear, I will allow you to go out with boys, as long as I meet them first."

"Thanks, but I don't *want* to date," retorted Norah.

"Very well . . . it's up to you, of course." Aunt Florence walked away huffily; she didn't like having her favours refused.

"Why don't you want to date?" asked Gavin. "You do other things with boys."

Norah lifted her chin proudly. "I like dancing with boys at the canteen and I like talking to them when we go to Murray's for a milkshake. But I refuse to be attached to anyone! There's only one person I'm interested in. Michael and the other boys in my school can never come up to *him.* But don't forget, Gavin, that's a secret."

"I know. Norah..."

"Mmm?" Norah looked dreamy.

"Do you—uhh—do you think ten is too young to like girls? I mean for a boy." The minute he said that he regretted it. What if she teased him?

But Norah regarded him seriously. "Nope. If you like someone, you like them. It doesn't matter how old you are." She took his hand. "Come on—I'll teach you how to play crib."

In March the snow finally melted. Gavin and Tim and Roger spent most of their after-school time fixing up their fort in the ravine behind the Ogilvies' house. Bosley tried to help by chasing away squirrels.

Mick cornered Roger one afternoon in the ravine. He forced him to take off all his clothes and ran away with them, leaving Roger shivering and crying in the fort.

When the others found him there, Gavin raced up the hill to the house to get some of his clothes while Tim wrapped Roger in his jacket.

"We *should* tell on Mick!" said Gavin when he'd come back. He turned pale at the thought of his friend's ordeal. "He shouldn't get away with this!"

"No!" cried Roger. "The more he's punished the worse he gets!"

"He should be *expelled,*" said Tim.

"That's the only solution," said Roger. "But how can we

be sure Mr Evans *would* expel him? He's never expelled any-one before." He looked down at the sleeves of Gavin's sweater dangling below his wrists. "What am I going to say to my mother? That jacket was brand new! I'll have to make something up so *she* won't tell."

"From now on we have to stick together all the time," said Gavin.

"All for one and one for all!" cried Tim. But Roger just sat on a log looking wretched.

The weather became warmer and warmer. The grown-ups smiled and said it was a good omen. Tulip bulbs sent green swords up through the damp earth, and Aunt Mary ordered seeds for this year's Victory Garden. In school they kept singing "When the lights go on again/All over the world." But all over the world the war carried on.

V
THE TELEGRAM

"See ya later, alligator," called Tim as the three of them parted at the corner.

"After a while, crocodile," Gavin answered.

"Don't forget your glove," came Roger's distant cry. They were meeting again in twenty minutes to play baseball.

Gavin peeled off his jacket as he walked home. The soft spring air was almost hot. His shoes felt wonderfully light on the bare sidewalk, after trudging along it in galoshes all winter.

He turned into Sir Launcelot, rescuing a princess from a dragon. The princess looked just like Eleanor. He whacked a bush with a stick as the dragon's head fell off.

"Oh, Sir Launcelot, you are the bravest knight in the kingdom!" the princess cried. A passing woman smiled at him and Gavin realized he'd been muttering to himself.

"Wave, Boz!" he cried as he neared the end of his block. The dog lifted his paw in a comical salute, then hurtled towards Gavin, jumped all over him and licked his face. He led Gavin the rest of the way to the Ogilvies', his tail beating. The two of them raced up the stairs and into the hall. Gavin stopped to check the mail.

A letter for him! He tore it open. Good—his Mysto-Snapper Membership Badge for Orphan Annie's Secret Guard had arrived. Tim had got his two days ago. Gavin crammed it back into the envelope. Then he noticed something else lying on the hall table.

A yellow envelope. The kind of envelope a telegram came in.

Everyone knew what a telegram meant. Gloria Pendleton's family had received one last year when her father had been killed in France.

Bosley whined and looked anxious, the same way he had when they heard Aunt Florence crying. Now Gavin realized that, again, someone was crying. The sound came from the den. Aunt Mary, he guessed, listening hard.

"No-o-o..." she wailed. Then Norah said, "It's not true! I just can't believe it's *true!*" Aunt Florence's voice, broken and bitter, croaked, "What a waste. What a *wicked wicked* waste."

Hanny came out of the kitchen. At the sight of Gavin she sobbed and held up her apron to her red, swollen eyes.

"What's wrong?" said Gavin. "What happened?"

"I can't bear to tell you. Go into the den. They're all in there." She ran back to the kitchen, crying even louder.

Andrew... It must be Andrew.

Gavin thought of Andrew's laughing face two summers ago when he'd taken them all sailing. Then he thought of Norah. Tears formed in his eyes.

He should go straight into the den and join them, but his feet seemed stuck to the floor. He stood there and stared at the yellow envelope. The silver bowl of roses on the hall table gave off a heavy, dizzying smell.

Sir Launcelot would be brave. *He* wouldn't cry; he would go and comfort his sister. Gavin took a deep breath and walked into the den.

Norah was sitting stiffly on the edge of the chesterfield. When she saw him she winced as if she'd been stabbed. Her eyes were filled with such acute pain he had to look away. This was how much she had loved Andrew.

"I can't tell him," she whispered.

"*I'll* tell him," said Aunt Florence. "Come here, sweetness." She sat down and held out her arms. Gavin walked slowly towards her. It was just like the day he'd entered this room for the first time and Aunt Florence had summoned him into the protection of her strong embrace.

He stood in front of her. Her firm hands gripped both his shoulders while she spoke. On the small table beside her chair lay the telegram, but he couldn't see the print clearly.

"Gavin, I have something terrible to tell you. You're going to have to be very brave."

"Yes, Aunt Florence," said Gavin. "Is it Andrew?"

"Andrew!" She looked bewildered for a second, then let go of his shoulders and sighed heavily. "No, pet. It's not Andrew. It's—it's your mother and father. They've been killed by a flying bomb in England."

He couldn't have heard her properly. He stared, then finally whispered, "Killed?" Aunt Mary began sobbing again.

"Yes, pet," said Aunt Florence gently. "Your grandfather sent us a telegram. Do you want to read it?"

Gavin took the telegram from her. For a few seconds the black letters danced against the yellow background, then were still.

REGRET MY DAUGHTER AND SON-IN-LAW KILLED BY V-I STOP PLEASE TELL CHILDREN AND CONVEY OUR LOVE AND SORROW STOP LETTER FOLLOWING JAMES LOGGIN

Gavin handed it back. "Do you understand, pet?" Aunt Florence asked him.

"Yes," he whispered. Aunt Florence pulled him onto her

knee as if he were five again. He felt babyish, perching there, but he couldn't protest.

"*Damn* this war!" sobbed Aunt Mary. "Damn, damn, *damn!* Why should such a monstrous thing happen to two innocent children?" Gavin gaped at her. Aunt Mary *never* used words like that!

He slid off Aunt Florence's lap, but she kept her arm around him. Norah still sat in her frozen position; he couldn't look at her face again. Aunt Mary was beside her, but she seemed afraid to touch her.

Hanny brought in a tray of tea. "You and Norah have some too," she urged them. "I made it good and sweet—who cares about rationing at a time like this?" She sat down with them while the adults talked in low, shocked voices.

My mother and father are *dead*, Gavin said to himself, sipping the hot sugary liquid. He tried to make himself cry.

"I think you two should go up to Norah's room," said Aunt Florence, when they'd finished their tea. "I'm sure you want to be alone together. We'll call you for dinner."

Gavin trudged up the stairs after Norah, thinking regretfully of Tim and Roger waiting for him in the park.

Norah sat on the window-seat in the tower, staring at nothing. Gavin tried to think of something to say.

"Is it really true, Gavin?" She kept her eyes away from him.

Gavin shivered at how strange her voice sounded. "It must be," he said carefully. "The telegram said so."

"But maybe... maybe it's the wrong family! Maybe they sent it to the wrong address!"

"It had our grandfather's name on it."

"Yes. So it must be true," she said dully.

She was quiet for a long time. So was Gavin. Bosley had followed them to the tower. He jumped up beside Norah and rested his head on her knee.

Finally Norah broke the silence. "I *knew* it."

"What do you mean?"

"I knew they'd be killed," she said slowly. Her voice was singsongy and faraway. "I've had a nightmare about it for years—I never told you. A nightmare that their house was bombed and they were all killed. Except *Grandad* isn't dead. That's right, isn't it?" she asked, as if she were asking herself, not him. "He sent the telegram, so he can't be dead. That's the only thing that's different from my dream. And listen to this, Gavin." She twisted a corner of the curtain in her hands and her voice became shrill. "I dreamt it again *two nights ago.* I hadn't had the dream for almost a year, but then I did. Maybe that's the day it happened! Maybe—"

"Stop it, Norah!" Gavin put his hands on her shoulders and shook her hard. "I don't think you should *talk* about your dream!"

She looked right at him for the first time—as if he'd woken her up. "Sorry, Gavin," she said softly. "I didn't mean to scare you." She sighed. "You're right. What's the use of talking about it *now?*" She picked up his hand. "Oh, Gavin... I just can't *believe* it! Can you?"

Gavin shook his head.

Norah went over to her bedside table and took out a letter from the drawer. She brought it back to the window-seat and gazed intently at it. "This is Dad's writing. The last letter from them before they died. Do you want me to read it to you?"

"If you want," whispered Gavin.

Norah began to read the letter. Gavin had already heard its contents, of course, when it arrived in February. His parents were full of excitement about the black-out finally beginning to be lifted in England: churches could let their stained-glass windows show and car headlights no longer had to be masked. The Home Guard was disbanded, so Dad could stay home in the evenings. "The world is getting brighter and soon you will be with us again," read Norah's quavering voice. "Best love to you both, D-Dad and Mum."

Norah began to shake. Then she erupted in tears. She threw herself on the window-seat's pillows as her body heaved and shuddered. "Oh Dad . . . Mum . . ."

Gavin clenched his fists, trying to stop the wave of fear that broke over him. "Don't cry, Norah," he said, patting her back as if she were Bosley. "Don't cry." Bosley tried to lick her.

But she kept on crying for a long time while Gavin sat awkwardly beside her. Then she raised her wet face. She stumbled into the bathroom and blew her nose loudly. "I'll tell you one thing, Gavin," she sniffed, coming to sit down again. "Wh-whatever—whatever happens to us, we'll always stick together. No one is going to s-separate us, all r-right?" Her body shook with dry sobs.

"Of course not!" said Gavin with surprise. "What do you think will happen to us?" he added. A wonderful thought came to him. "Will we—will we stay in Canada now?"

"No, we won't!" Norah's anger froze her sobs. She looked so fierce that Gavin felt ashamed. "Don't *ever* think that! We're *English!* England is our home! We'll go back and live with Grandad, of course."

"Oh." So everything was the same. When the war was over he still had to go back to England.

Norah thumped the pillows. "I wish we knew more about how it happened! Then it would be easier to believe. Why didn't Grandad say more?" She sighed. "I guess we'll just have to wait for his letter."

"Why don't we phone him?"

"They—M-mum and Dad—didn't have a phone. And we don't even know if Grandad is in the house any more. We don't even know if the house is still *there* ..." She picked up Dad's letter again. "I still can't believe it! I need to be alone, Gavin. Tell them I don't want any dinner, okay? We'll talk again in the morning. Will you be all right?"

Gavin nodded. He wasn't all right, but he could never tell her why. Not because he felt sad about his parents. Because he didn't feel anything at all.

Gavin and Norah stayed home from school for the rest of that week. Aunt Florence arranged a memorial service for Saturday. "They'll be having a funeral in England, of course, but *we* have to do something too. It's important for the children to go through a ritual," Gavin heard her say to Aunt Mary. Both of them seemed grateful to throw themselves into getting ready for the service.

Norah stalked around the house with puffy eyes, breaking into torrents of tears with no warning. The adults kept handing her fresh handkerchiefs and tried to comfort her. Gavin wished he could escape from her pain, but he forced himself to listen every time she wanted to talk.

"If only I'd *told* them!" she agonized.

"Told them what?"

"Told them about my dream! Then it might not have happened!"

Other times she talked about how she shouldn't have argued so much with her mother. "I was awful to Mum our last night at home," she moaned. "I hardly spoke to her, I was so mad they were sending us to Canada—and that was almost the last time I saw her!"

Gavin tried to comfort his sister, but his words bounced off her grief—as if Norah were enclosed in a box that shut him out.

Almost worse was how everyone in the family kept asking how *he* was. He muttered, "I'm okay," but they didn't seem to believe him. He knew they wanted him to cry. But however hard he tried, he couldn't.

If only he could go out and play with his friends as if this hadn't happened! Aunt Florence even suggested it, but Gavin didn't know what he'd say to them.

Instead he spent long hours in his room, making a difficult model or reading until his eyes stung. At least next week he'd be allowed to go back to school. But that would be different as well, he thought drearily. Now *everything* was different.

St Peter's Church was packed. Gavin sat in the front pew with Norah, the Ogilvies, Hanny and her husband, and Uncle Reg, who'd come to represent the Montreal relatives. He sneaked some looks behind him while they were singing "The Lord Is My Shepherd." Tim was there beside his parents, and Roger with his mother. He avoided their eyes. He also spotted Mrs Moss, Mr Evans, Paige and her family, and Dulcie and Lucy. Even Miss Gleeson, the public librarian whom Norah and Gavin had got to know over the years, was there.

Gavin tried to pay attention to when he was supposed to stand and sit and kneel. He tried not to think about musketeers or baseball or the new trick he was teaching Bosley.

"Let not your hearts be troubled," said Reverend Milne. He looked down at the front pew with such a concerned expression that Gavin flushed and hung his head.

The last hymn was "Abide With Me." Aunt Florence and Aunt Mary kept dabbing their eyes with their handkerchiefs. Norah didn't sing but held her head high. "She's being *so* brave," Gavin heard Hanny whisper to her husband.

"Where is death's sting / Where, grave, thy vic-tor-y . . ." Gavin shifted with impatience; what a *slow* hymn. Half the people in the church were weeping while the ponderous melody droned on. Gavin could feel the whole congregation's pity pressing against his back. Why did his parents have to go and die and put him through this?

A grave, dark-clothed crowd filled the Ogilvies' house after the service. Norah was safe in a corner; Paige and Dulcie and their sisters surrounded her protectively, warding off sympathetic adults. Gavin wasn't as lucky. He had to shake hands and say "thank you" again and again, as one person after another came up and said "I'm so sorry." Women kept glancing at him and wiping their eyes.

Tim and Roger approached with their parents. Gavin turned as crimson as if he'd been found out about something he'd done wrong. His friends looked just as embarrassed.

Tim's father put his hand on Gavin's head and Tim's mother hugged him wordlessly. Roger's mother clasped his hand and murmured something about "this terrible war." Then the three adults waited for Tim and Roger to say something.

"I'm sorry about your parents," mumbled Roger, his head down and his fingers scratching rapidly at the skin on his thumbs.

"Me too," said Tim. "Was it a V-1 or a V-2 bomb?"

"Tim!" cried his parents, pulling him away.

"He hasn't cried yet," Aunt Mary was telling Paige's mother. "We're not sure it's sunk in."

"He doesn't *have* to cry, Mary," said Aunt Florence. "He hardly remembers his parents. *I'm* much more of a mother to him now."

Gavin chewed on a sandwich, the crumbs sticking in his throat. Aunt Florence was the only one who understood.

VI

TRY TO REMEMBER

On Monday Norah said she couldn't face school yet and no one made her go. Gavin, however, was out of the house as soon as he finished breakfast. He took his bike and didn't pause to wait at the corner for Tim and Roger.

After the bell he sat at his desk, lowering his flushed face, while Mrs Moss told him in front of the whole class how sorry they were. At recess all of grade five avoided him, as if he had some disease. At lunchtime Tim and Roger gave him clumsy smiles, then quickly bicycled away.

Finally Gavin couldn't stand it. After school he went up to Tim and Roger at the bike stands.

"Hi." He tried to smile nonchalantly, but his cheeks burned.

"Oh, hi, Gav," mumbled Roger.

"How are you?" added Tim.

"I'm all right. Look . . ." Gavin paused. Then he rushed out his words before he lost his nerve. "Look, let's just *forget* about my parents. I mean, not forget about them . . . but let's just act like before. Okay?"

"Okay!" said Tim. "Do you want to go to the fort? One wall needs fixing."

"Sure!" said Gavin.

"Uh-oh . . . Mick's standing over there by the corner of the school," whispered Roger.

Tim swung his leg across his bike. "Who cares? All for one and one for all!"

Gavin glanced at Mick. The bully was staring intensely, at *him.* He cycled fast to catch up with Tim and Roger.

All week teachers and some of the older girls came up to Gavin to say they were sorry. But now that he had his friends back he didn't mind as much. He was practised at smiling sadly and saying "thank you" every time someone mentioned his parents' death. Otherwise he acted so normal that soon everyone at school seemed to forget about it.

When the letter from Grandad finally arrived, Norah asked Aunt Florence to read it to them. She sat beside Gavin on the chesterfield, gripping his hand and crushing his fingers together.

Aunt Florence's voice was quiet and steady as she read:

> Dear Norah and Gavin,
>
> I find it very difficult to tell you about Jane and Arthur's death, but it has to be done. There isn't much to say about it. On Monday, March 12 your parents were having their noon meal at home. I was out at the pub when I heard the infernal ticking of a doodle-bug. We thought they were all over. There's a few seconds of quiet before the damned thing drops. When the explosion came so close we all rushed out of the pub and I ran home.
>
> The house was smashed—just like my house in Camber was. So this is the second time I've escaped a Jerry bomb by being out. I want you to know I would gladly have gone in their place. It's so bloody unfair that an old man like me survived and they went.
>
> They were killed instantly and would have felt no pain. Thank God you young ones weren't there as

well. I never wanted you to go to Canada but since it probably saved your lives, I'm glad you went.

But now it's time for you to come back. The war's nearly over and you belong here. I know there still could be some danger, but everyone says that bomb was a fluke. We haven't seen any since and anyway, lightning never strikes twice in the same place. I am living with Muriel but I'm planning to rebuild the house. There's a lot that can be salvaged. I would like you both to live there with me. It's where you belong. Muriel and Barry and Tibby agree that would be best. We will all look after each other.

Regards to the Ogilvies. Please let me know immediately when you are coming back. We can all stay with Muriel until the house is rebuilt.

Your affectionate grandfather,
James Loggin

A heavy silence filled the room. Gavin pretended to inspect Bosley's toenails. What did his guardians think of this rough-sounding man who said "damned" and "bloody"?

Aunt Florence spoke first. "Norah, dear, do you want to read the letter again alone?"

Norah took the piece of paper from her. Her face was almost as white as it was. "I'll read it again but we can talk now. How soon can we leave?"

"Norah!" gasped Aunt Mary.

Norah turned to her. "I'm sorry, Aunt Mary. I didn't mean to sound ungrateful. But we have to go home! Grandad needs us. And we can help him build the house again," she added, her voice breaking.

"Building the house isn't going to bring back your parents, Norah," said Aunt Mary gently.

"I know . . . but we have to go *home,*" Norah pleaded. "Don't you understand?"

Aunt Florence had been unusually quiet. Now she patted Norah's knee and said in a strained voice, "Of course we understand. We've always known you would have to leave us. Now it's just more urgent. But *you* have to understand, Norah, how hard it's going to be for Mary and me. You're part of the family. We—we *love* you," she added stiffly.

Norah began to cry again. "I know that, Aunt Florence. And we can't thank you enough for all you've done for us. But now it's time to go! *Isn't* it, Gavin . . ."

Gavin gulped and because Norah looked so desperate he nodded. "Uh-huh."

Aunt Florence glanced at him and then back at Norah. "Listen to me, Norah. I understand why you want to go back right away and why your grandfather wants you as soon as possible. Your family has had a terrible loss—you need to be with each other. But we can't just decide when you'll go. You heard what the social worker said. The ships are very erratic. If we tell them you want to go now it could be next week, or three weeks, or three months. None of us can live with that uncertainty."

"But—" protested Norah.

"Hear me out, please. I couldn't sleep nights if I thought we'd sent you back before the war's over. I don't agree with your grandfather about it being safe. What if there *are* more bombs in Kent? And it's important for you to finish your school year. You have final exams in June, which will help you get placed in an English school."

Aunt Florence sat up straighter, her voice growing more and more decided. "Here's my suggestion. Stay until the end of school. I'll tell the social service people we'd like to apply for a ship that sails *after* that—if the war's over by then, of course. You and Gavin have had a dreadful shock. I think you need time to recover before the additional change of returning to England. What do you think? I'm sure your grandfather and sisters can wait a few more months," she finished grandly.

It took half an hour to convince Norah; half an hour in which Gavin sat in silent agony, praying she would agree. Finally she turned to him wearily. "What do *you* think, Gavin? Do you want to go back now or later?"

"Later, please," whispered Gavin. *Never,* he added to himself.

"All right. We'll wait until school's over." Norah sounded exhausted. She looked down at the letter in her hand and her face twitched.

"Come along, dear," said Aunt Mary. "I'm going to put you to bed with a hot drink and then I'll read to you."

Gavin twiddled the radio knobs after they'd left the room. He looked up to find Aunt Florence staring at him. Not with sorrow, which he would have expected, but with a kind of triumph. "What's wrong?" he asked.

"Nothing's wrong, pet," she smiled. She kissed the top of his head. "Nothing's wrong at all."

After that Norah acted more and more strangely. She alternated between profound sleepiness and bursts of anger. Hanny kept tempting her with her favourite food, but she scarcely ate. She yawned through meals and dozed on the chesterfield when they were all in the den.

"How is she ever going to get through her studies?" whispered Aunt Mary, as they looked at Norah curled up like a little girl in the cushions.

"I've written a note to her teacher to excuse her from homework for a week or so," said Aunt Florence. "He agrees with me that this is just a reaction to help her get over the shock."

Gavin tried to think up ways to make Norah feel better. He suggested they go to see *House of Frankenstein* but she refused. She never left the house except to go to school, and whenever Paige called on her she made up some excuse not to see her.

One afternoon Gavin was sent up to the tower to wake Norah for dinner. He sat on her bed while she got ready, chatting to her about school and normal things.

"How can you act as if nothing has happened?" she snapped.

She hadn't spoken to him like this since that long ago time when they'd first arrived.

"I'm sorry, Norah," whispered Gavin. "But I keep forgetting about it."

"Forgetting about it!" Norah glared at him. "How *could* you?"

"I guess . . . because . . . I don't feel as sad as you do. Because I don't remember Mum and Dad very well."

"*Try* to remember. It was only four and a half years ago that you saw them. *I* remember them perfectly! If only you remembered, we could talk about them. You're the only other person in this whole country who knew them!"

"I'm sorry, Norah. I'll try harder."

That night in bed he tried to envision his parents' faces and voices: nothing. What was the matter with him? Roger hadn't seen his father since he was seven, and he often talked about things they had done together.

When Gavin tried to remember, a wall seemed to rise up between England and Canada. On one side was danger; on the other side, safety. The danger was worse than before: a bomb could smash a house and kill your relatives. That made the safety even more precious.

On Saturday Gavin borrowed his parents' letters and

photographs from Norah. Surely if he studied these as intently as he studied for a social studies test it would *force* him to remember.

He began with the six photographs. The whole family before the war—Gavin smiled at Norah as a skinny little girl and himself as a solemn baby. Mum and Dad standing in front of "Little Whitebull," the house that was now demolished. Dad in his Home Guard uniform. Tibby in her A.T.S. uniform. Muriel and Barry holding their baby—Richard, the first grandchild. My nephew! thought Gavin. He'd forgotten about Richard. Mum and Dad and Grandad last summer.

His parents looked older than other people's parents. That was because there was such a gap between Norah and Gavin and their older sisters. Mum wore a kind of turban in all the pictures, so he couldn't tell what her hair was like. Her face was pretty but tired-looking. Dad's dark hair was streaked with grey. His beaky face was a lot like Norah's. Norah often told Gavin that *he* looked like Mum, but he couldn't see the resemblance.

He would have recognized them if he saw them, because he'd had their faces pointed out in each new photograph as "Mum and Dad." But he recognized them the same way he did a picture of a famous actor or hockey star: someone familiar but not intimate.

Norah had kept all the letters in order, packed neatly into a wooden box Aunt Mary had given her. It took Gavin all day to read them. "What are you up to, all by yourself?" asked Aunt Florence when he went downstairs for a snack.

"Oh... just a special project." She smiled and didn't press further. That was one thing he'd always appreciated about Aunt Florence. Despite her constant shower of affection, she always respected his privacy.

The letters portrayed two people bravely struggling from

day to day in war-torn England. Both his parents were extremely busy. Mum spent mornings at the Women's Voluntary Services and afternoons waiting in lines for food as rationing got worse. Dad worked all day as a bookkeeper in Gilden, the town near their village, and every evening at his Home Guard duties. But in between the hardships—and as he read Gavin sensed that there was a lot left out besides the sentences that had been blackened by the censor—his parents seemed to have had a lot of fun. There were dances that the American GIS put on in the village hall. Fetes to raise money, a community pig to feed. Marriages—including Muriel's—and other celebrations. Everyone in Ringden seemed to know each other and help each other get through the war.

Mum and Dad had taken turns to write. Every letter said how much they missed Norah and Gavin and looked forward to having them back.

They seemed like nice people to have as parents. He would have liked to know them. Now he never would. Now he was an *orphan*—like Oliver Twist. That felt important.

Reading the letters was like seeing a movie of the years he'd been in Canada. Each one commented on something Norah and Gavin had told their parents. "Congratulations on learning to swim, Gavin! . . . By the time you get this you will be back from your trip across Canada and enjoying Gairloch again . . . How exciting that you've begun skiing . . ."

Every time Gavin read words like this he remembered the thrill of learning to swim and ski, the exciting train journey west and every blissful summer at Gairloch. After he finished reading the letters he did have a clearer idea of what his parents had been like. But he was also left with a far stronger sense of what good years he'd enjoyed in Canada.

That evening he returned everything to Norah. "Did it

help you remember them?" she asked, gazing sadly at the photographs.

"Not really," Gavin admitted. "But now I know them better." It was the best he could offer her.

The social worker came to see Norah and Gavin. She suggested that they both talk to a psychiatrist—"to sort out your feelings about this tragedy." One afternoon they got to miss school while Aunt Florence took them to the university on the streetcar.

Gavin felt strange when they walked past the green space in front of an old stone building called Hart House. He vaguely remembered playing games on this grass the week they had stayed at the university until they'd gone to live with the Ogilvies. It seemed like centuries ago.

They entered another old building. Gavin sat with Aunt Florence in a waiting room while Norah was led into an office and a door closed. Gavin swung his legs and tried to read a babyish children's book that was on a table. Aunt Florence stared into space, unusually vague.

After a long time Norah came out, looking angry and proud. Then it was Gavin's turn. A woman with a chirpy, brisk voice invited him to sit down on a slippery chair in front of her desk.

Aunt Florence had told him that a psychiatrist was like a doctor who took care of your feelings instead of your body. "In my day we didn't need to talk to strangers about our personal affairs," she sniffed. "But they seem to think it will be helpful."

The woman—she told Gavin to call her Dr Wilson—started by asking him to tell her about the things he did every day. He wondered why she was so interested, but he chatted to her about his friends and Bosley and Cubs. Every time he sounded enthusiastic about something, like getting a home run or enjoying a book, she smiled and said "Good for you." So he was careful not to tell her anything that would make her stop smiling—nothing unpleasant or confusing about Mick, or Eleanor.

At last she came to the subject of his parents. "Do you feel sad about what happened?" she asked kindly.

Gavin squirmed. He couldn't tell her he didn't—then she wouldn't think he was a good person. He nodded, trying to look doleful.

"How much do you remember about them?"

Gavin swallowed hard. "Well, of *course* I remember them—but not as much as Norah does."

"It would be very natural if you didn't remember much," she said. "Or if you don't feel *very* sad. After all, you were only five the last time you saw them."

She smiled and Gavin gave her a timid smile in return. So he didn't have to remember—that was a relief. He would have liked to tell her how much he *wanted* to remember, for Norah's sake. But he thought of Aunt Florence's words. This woman was a stranger; he didn't know her at all.

"And how do you feel about going back to England?"

Gavin thought fast, so she wouldn't find out what a coward he was. "I'm sad about leaving the Ogilvies of course, but I'm *English,*" he explained, remembering Norah's words. "That's where I belong."

She seemed to believe him. "Good for you!" she repeated. She sighed. "It's going to be much harder for your sister. Being home will bring back so many sad memories for her."

She stood up. "*You* seem to be coping very well, Gavin. You're a brave little boy, and I've enjoyed talking to you." She shook his hand and walked him to the door. Then Aunt Florence went in.

"She was so nosy!" said Gavin. "What did she say to you, Norah?"

"Oh . . . nothing worth mentioning." Norah buried her nose in a *National Geographic* magazine. Gavin left her alone. Finally Aunt Florence came out and they all went home.

"Dr Wilson says that Norah's reactions are completely normal," Aunt Florence told Aunt Mary that evening when Norah was upstairs. "We just have to wait. She assures me she'll get over it with time."

"The poor dear," sighed Aunt Mary.

Aunt Florence smiled at Gavin. "And she says you're doing fine, pet."

Gavin felt as if he'd passed some sort of test—a test he'd cheated on.

VII
THE DOG SHOW

Easter passed very quietly in the Ogilvie household. Usually they went to the Royal York Hotel for Sunday dinner after church, followed by a walk on the boardwalk at Sunnyside. But this year they just came home and had a small ham. Gavin munched on it gloomily. He didn't like ham, but he couldn't complain when it was so hard to get.

Today was April Fools' Day as well as Easter. But this year he couldn't subsitute salt for sugar at breakfast, or tell people things like "There's a spider in your hair" or "Your shoe lace is undone." The family was still too sad for jokes. Since April the first was on a Sunday he couldn't even enjoy the tricks they always played in school. And now it was past noon and April Fools' was over anyway.

Norah had refused to go to church. "I don't believe in God any more," she told the aunts bluntly.

"But Norah!" cried Aunt Mary. "It's understandable that you would feel that way, but when something terrible happens you *need* to go to church!"

"Well, I'm not," said Norah. "I'm never going again and you can't make me."

Aunt Florence opened her mouth to scold Norah, then closed it and gave her a disapproving look instead.

Gavin was awed by Norah's nerve. But she was right, he thought. They couldn't make her go to church. Aunt Mary offered to make an appointment for her to talk to Reverend Milne, but Norah firmly refused.

A few days later Paige persuaded Norah to go over to her house. But Norah was back in twenty minutes. "She says I sat down on her favourite record on purpose," she told Gavin. "How was *I* supposed to know it was on the chair? What a stupid place to leave a record! I'm not speaking to Paige any more." She ran upstairs.

Then Norah's teacher asked Aunt Florence for a conference. "He says you're being rude in class," Aunt Florence told her. "He's trying to be as understanding as he can, but you are really testing his patience, Norah. We all know you're grieving for your parents, but you must try to co-operate."

"Why should I?" snapped Norah. "Who cares? I'll soon be finished with this crummy school anyway." Again, she fled to her tower.

"I don't see why she should get away with this rudeness," snorted Aunt Florence.

"But Mother," objected Aunt Mary, "didn't Dr Wilson say it's healthy for her to be angry?"

Aunt Florence sighed. "I suppose so. If Norah were really my child I'd insist on her being polite to her elders. But I guess we'll just have to put up with it."

Gavin wished he hadn't overheard this. Aunt Florence had always treated Gavin and Norah as if they *were* her children. Now she seemed to be letting Norah go.

Was she letting him go too? Was that why she wasn't making more of a fuss about him leaving in a few months? But maybe she just wanted to ignore that as much as he was.

Gavin tried to enjoy the unusually early spring as if it were like any other April. After he saw the movie *Thunderhead,*

Son of Flicka he named his bicycle Thunderhead and rode it along the road like a real stallion. The gardens in Rosedale blazed with yellow forsythia and by the third week in April the new green leaves had already popped open.

At school, Mick had suddenly stopped bullying. He began combing his hair and tucking in his shirt. Everyone was relieved, but puzzled. Then Roger found out why.

"You know Terry Fraser, who's in the chess club with me?" Tim and Gavin nodded. "Well, he told me Mick's in love with his sister Doris!"

"Mick? In *love*?" giggled Tim.

Roger grinned. "Yes! He keeps asking her for dates but she won't go. He follows her home every day and writes her notes. Doris just laughs at them. She showed them to Terry—he says they're really corny."

"Poor Doris!" said Tim.

"At least it keeps him busy," said Gavin. Now they didn't have to keep out of Mick's way. But every once in a while Mick would give Gavin that strange look—as if he wanted something from him.

Aunt Mary took Gavin with her on the train to visit an old friend in St Catharines. She was in rhapsody over the cherry blossoms but Gavin was more interested in Niagara Falls, where the friend, Mrs Butler, drove them. He had been there several times before, but he always found the falls a thrill.

He stared in wonder at the powerful roar of water, his face soaked with spray. The biggest waterfall in the world. It just kept going—thundering endlessly over the rocks, oblivious of tourists or wars or ten-year-old boys. Somehow its indifference was comforting.

Gavin turned around to the two women. "The Canadian falls are *much* bigger than the American falls."

"Listen to him!" chuckled Mrs Butler. "He sounds like a real Canadian!"

Gavin was offended. Of course he was a Canadian! Then he remembered that he wasn't.

The grown-ups' lives revolved around the news. President Roosevelt had died. War brides began to arrive in Canada. The world held its breath with excitement as it waited for the final defeat. Everyone began guessing the exact date when the war would end.

Tim showed Gavin and Roger a clipping from the paper. A Junior Dog Show was to be held at Poplar Park that Saturday. "Why don't we enter Bosley?" said Tim. "The first prize is a book of movie tickets!"

Gavin studied the announcement. There were six categories Bosley could enter: Most Obedient, Waggiest Tail, Best Costume, Best Groomed, Funniest Expression and Best in Show.

Every day that week he brushed Bosley until his coat gleamed like black-and-white satin. He found one of his outgrown Hallowe'en costumes for Bosley to wear: a clown suit trimmed with orange and green ruffles. He cut holes in the orange wig for Bosley's ears.

Bosley had always been obedient. Gavin practised his "wave," "trust and paid for" and "play dead" tricks. He worked out a routine where the dog jumped over a box to fetch a ball, then came back with it to perch on the box. "You're such a *good* dog," Gavin whispered to him the night before the show. "You're just as clever as Lassie. I know you'll win everything."

Bosley bounded beside the three boys on the way to Poplar Park. Gavin carried the box and the others the ball and costume.

As they approached they could hear barking and yelling. Kids and dogs were everywhere. A small girl tried to keep up with an excited Newfoundland dragging her on its leash. Three golden retrievers panted at their owners' feet, grinning at everyone. A tiny papillon huddled inside its owner's jacket.

"Please control your dogs!" shouted one of the adults in charge, as a pug and a curly-haired mutt tumbled in a fight around her feet.

Bosley took one look at the noisy crowd and pressed against Gavin's knee. A cairn terrier snapped at his feet. Bosley whimpered and put his tail between his legs. Daphne Worsley ran up and picked up the terrier's leash.

"It's all right, Boz," said Gavin, as Bosley tried to hide behind him. "It's only Thistle. You *know* Thistle!"

"Bosley's such a coward," said Daphne smugly. "He's always been afraid of my dog."

"He is not a coward!" said Gavin.

"He's going to win everything—just wait," said Roger.

Daphne picked up Thistle. "Huh! Just *you* wait. Thistle'll win way more ribbons than Bosley."

Gavin turned his back on her and tried to calm Bosley, as a man with a megaphone announced the first category: The Dog with the Waggiest Tail. Bosley kept his tail firmly planted between his legs.

"Come on, Boz—want a biscuit?" Gavin cried desperately. He always wagged his tail for a biscuit—but not today. Tim tried to hold up the spaniel's tail but when he let it go the tail snapped back out of sight.

"Do something!" said Roger. "They're all in the ring!"

"I can't," sighed Gavin. "He'll just have to skip this category." They watched with disgust as Thistle, his tail straight up and whipping back and forth like a metronome, won first prize.

Next was Obedience. "He'll win this," said Gavin confidently. He pulled Bosley into the ring. The dog reluctantly rolled over and played dead, trembling the whole time. When Gavin ordered "Trust" he obediently sat and ignored the biscuit in front of him; but at "Paid For" he wouldn't touch it, despite Gavin's pleading. He half-heartedly jumped over the box to retrieve the ball, but it landed beside Thistle. The terrier growled and Bosley raced back to Gavin without the ball, yelping with fright while the audience laughed.

"What's *wrong* with him?" asked Tim.

"He's just not used to being here yet," said Gavin. "He'll improve." They watched Daphne and her dog prance into the ring. "Thistle will be worse than Bosley," whispered Gavin. "He *never* obeys."

But Daphne had worked out a routine involving the one thing Thistle was excellent at: jumping. She arranged three boxes in a row and Thistle bounced back and forth over them like a dog on springs, yipping proudly. The audience loved it and the terrier won another First.

They watched Toby the papillon and Amos the Newfoundland win for smallest and largest dog. Then they decked Bosley out in his clown outfit and paraded him around the ring for Best Costume. Bosley dragged his feet and Gavin had to pull him. Then he sat down and pawed off his wig. Ahead of them strutted Thistle, wearing a tiny kilt tied around his middle and a Scottish beret with holes cut out for his ears. Daphne wore a matching kilt and hat.

"First prize for Thistle again!" groaned Tim when the event was over.

"It's not fair," said Gavin. "The rules didn't say anything about the *owners* dressing up."

"We'll never get Best in Show now," said Roger sadly. "There go the movie tickets."

But then Bosley improved. He was third for Best Groomed and first for Funniest Expression. "To Bosley, the springer spaniel, because he looks so dejected about being here," said the judge.

"Just ignore them, Boz," whispered Gavin as everyone laughed again. "At least you won."

He and Tim and Roger watched as Daphne took Thistle up to receive the ribbon for Best in Show—and the book of tickets.

"Don't worry, Boz," said Gavin. "*I* know you're the best dog in the world!"

Bosley whined at him pleadingly, as if he were saying "Can't we go home now?"

"We'll go soon," promised Gavin. "First we're getting popcorn and you can have some."

Eleanor was standing beside the popcorn stand. Her monkey sat on her shoulder, playing with one of her braids. "Hi," she called.

"Can I hold Kilroy?" asked Tim.

"Better not," she said calmly. "He bites strangers. I tried to enter him in the show but they said only dogs were eligible. It's so unfair! Kilroy is as good as any dog."

The monkey was dressed in a green suit, like a little man. He even wore a tie. He bared his teeth and chittered at Bosley and Bosley got as far away from him as he could.

"He's a swell monkey," said Gavin. He smiled at Eleanor while Tim and Roger were buying their popcorn. She smiled back. "Your dog's nice too," she said.

Eleanor's sister led her away and the boys sat on the grass, wolfing down popcorn. Bosley wouldn't eat and still gave Gavin beseeching looks, but Gavin didn't want to go home yet. The Ogilvies' house was so dismal and boring these days, with Norah wretched and Aunt Florence and Aunt Mary wrapped up in the news.

Today was the first day since Gavin's parents' death when no one had come up to him to mention it. The sun was out, the duck pond sparkled in the bright air, and dogs panted and played around him. Bosley hadn't done very well, but it didn't matter. Nobody in the crowd around him would ever guess that Gavin wasn't a Canadian boy and that Bosley didn't really belong to him.

VIII
THE LIGHTS GO ON

"Have you heard?" shouted Tim before he reached Gavin. "Hitler's dead!"

"I know!" said Gavin. Hanny had burnt the toast at breakfast while Aunt Florence read aloud the newspaper. Mussolini was dead too. There was a photograph of his body in the same paper.

Adolph Hitler . . . the evil man they had been fighting against as long as Gavin could remember. When he'd first come to Canada he'd had nightmares about Hitler, but after he started school he had made fun of him like everyone else: a silly little man with a stubby moustache. But one of Hitler's bombs had killed his parents . . .

"Aren't you glad?" said Tim, while they waited for Roger.

"Of course!" said Gavin. But the paper had also said that a German surrender was "imminent."

That meant the war could be over this week—so he and Norah would have to go back to England as soon as the school year finished.

"My Mum bought me a flag for VE Day," said Roger after he'd joined them.

"We should get some bunting and decorate our bikes so we'll be ready," said Tim.

Mrs Moss spent half of arithmetic talking about the news. "You are a privileged generation," she told them. "You'll inherit a world of peace that your elders won for you."

The class grew more and more restless as they thought of victory—and a holiday from school. "What if it happens on the *weekend?*" worried Roger.

The next day Berlin fell. Norah stopped Gavin on the stairs. "We can go home soon," she said quietly.

"Uh-huh," gulped Gavin.

"I finally had a letter from Andrew," said Norah. "Now he's in Holland. He says he'll visit us in England if we're there before he comes back to Canada."

"How is he?"

"He always *says* he's fine. It's hard to tell how he really is. I bet he isn't fine. I bet he's hated it, having to kill people. But at least *he* wasn't killed," she added bitterly. "He said to tell you how sorry he is about Mum and Dad."

"Mmm," said Gavin. He tried to imagine Andrew visiting them in England but he couldn't even picture himself there.

And what would happen with Andrew and Norah? He couldn't tell from his sister's voice whether she still loved Andrew.

Everything was happening much too fast, like the last of the water rushing out of a tub. Gavin wanted to put in the plug. At the same time, he couldn't help being infected by the joy of victory that was sweeping the city.

Next Monday morning Gavin stood outside Mr Evans's office with the other messengers for that week. When you were a messenger you waited there every day to take news back to the classroom.

The principal was usually a vague, subdued man. But this morning he actually ran out of his office, a smile creasing his tired-looking face.

A few seconds later Gavin skidded along the wooden

floor back to his classroom. He pushed open the door and cried, "The war's over! Mr Evans just told us! He wants to see you right away, Mrs Moss."

Class 5A leapt to their feet, pounded on their desks and cheered. Mrs Moss didn't even try to stop them. She ran out of the room and returned quickly.

Then she asked them to sit down. Everyone became quiet when they noticed her wet eyes. Cheers and thumps were still coming from other classrooms down the corridor.

"The war in Europe is indeed over," said Mrs Moss. "The Germans surrendered last night. I think it's especially appropriate that you were the one to tell us, Gavin, when your family and country have suffered so much." She beamed at them. "Now . . . Mr Evans has informed me that today *and* tomorrow will be a holiday . . ."

"Hooray!" Pandemonium broke out again, but Mrs Moss waved it down. "*Quiet,* please . . . that's better. I know you're eager to go out and celebrate, but before we go we'll have a short service of thanksgiving."

She read aloud a prayer about peace, then they sang "The Maple Leaf Forever."

"All right," she smiled. "Off you go."

Gavin, Roger and Tim galloped home, leaping into the air and shouting. The sidewalks teemed with released children.

"Okay," panted Tim at the corner. "Get your bikes and meet here in fifteen minutes. Then we'll go downtown!"

Gavin kept running. His heart pounded so much he had to stop and catch his breath before he dashed up the steps and pushed open the door.

"Aunt Florence! Aunt Mary! Hanny! The war's over!" He forgot that he had wished it would never end.

They all came out of the den. "We know, pet," said Aunt

Florence, hugging him. "We've just been listening to Mr Churchill."

"School's closed!" said Gavin. "Can I go downtown on my bike with Tim and Roger?"

Aunt Florence smiled. "I suppose so, if you're careful. Hanny, why don't you go home and celebrate with your husband? Mary and I will stay here and listen to the news."

"Thank you, Mrs Ogilvie," said Hanny. "I'll just pack Gavin a sandwich before I go."

"I'm going to put up that old Union Jack that's in the attic!" said Aunt Mary. Her face looked as excited as a girl's.

Norah walked slowly into the hall, dropping her books. "The war's over. I guess you already know," she added in a dull voice.

Aunt Mary kissed her. "Yes, dear Norah. This long, terrible war is finally over. Are you going to go downtown and celebrate, like Gavin?"

"Celebrate? Why would I want to celebrate?"

Gavin left the aunts trying to comfort her.

The three boys rode to the corner of Bay and Queen, then hid their bicycles under the stairs of a building and joined the noisy crowd around City Hall. A tall red thermometer decorated its clock tower, keeping track of the Victory Bond Drive.

Above them people threw ticker tape from high office windows and Mosquito aircraft dropped bags of paper scraps, until the air looked like December's snowstorm. Music blared from loudspeakers and the Mayor stepped onto a platform and led the crowd in singing "God Save the King."

Gavin and Tim and Roger pushed their way through the

swaying, cheering crowd. Adults ruffled their hair or pulled them into impromptu dances. They caught sight of other kids from their school and waved. Then they spotted some boys hitching a ride on the front of a streetcar.

"Come *on,*" shouted Tim. When the next streetcar arrived they perched in a row on its front fender for a few minutes, then hopped off—right in front of a policeman. But he just grinned at them.

They stayed downtown until their throats were sore from shouting and singing, their legs ached from standing and their stomachs rumbled. As they pushed their way back to their bikes, Gavin noticed a soldier standing on the sidewalk. He was watching everyone quietly, his sombre expression a contrast to the giddy crowd. One khaki sleeve was pinned up neatly where the soldier's arm was missing.

When he got home Gavin told the aunts and Norah all about the downtown celebrations. "May I go out again after dinner?" he asked. "They're having fireworks in Poplar Park!"

"Norah's going to watch them," smiled Aunt Mary. "Paige phoned and asked her. Aren't you, Norah dear . . ."

Norah looked indifferent. "I guess so. Gavin can come with us if he wants."

Aunt Florence shook her head. "I think you've had enough excitement, pet. And I've hardly seen you all day! You can watch the fireworks from here."

"But how?"

She smiled mysteriously. "You'll see. You'll have a better view than anyone in Toronto!"

When Paige called for Norah she looked as if she wanted to change her mind about going out. But Paige dragged her away before she could refuse.

Then Aunt Florence led Aunt Mary and Gavin up the

back stairs to the former maid's room. Gavin stared at it curiously. When he'd first come here there had been a sulky live-in maid called Edith. But Edith had left to work in an airplane factory and Aunt Florence had never found a replacement.

Now Aunt Florence stood on a chair and pushed open a trap door in the roof. A ladder swung down. She laughed at Gavin's surprised face. "Come on, pet—you'll have to go first and help us up."

Gavin scurried up the ladder and stepped onto—the top of the house! There was a flat roof area covered with a thin layer of gravel. He leaned back into the cavity and pulled up the chairs they handed him. Then he gave a hand to Aunt Mary and together they heaved up the bulk of Aunt Florence.

"I didn't know you could come up here!" said Gavin. "Why didn't you tell me?"

Aunt Florence chuckled. "Because I didn't want you—or your unruly sister—to come up on your own. You're never to do that, do you understand? It's a very long way down."

Gavin nodded reluctantly. He explored the whole of the roof while his guardians set up the chairs. Then the three of them sat in a row and looked down at the lit-up city.

The Ogilvies' house was one of the tallest in the neighbourhood. A sea of black roofs and green treetops was spread out below them in the dusk. Gavin could see the Worsleys' yard, where Thistle raced around yapping. Daphne came out and called him and Gavin smiled to himself. She didn't know she was being watched.

"Hugh and I sometimes came up here," said Aunt Mary. "On the maid's day off."

"What?" Aunt Florence stared at her daughter. "I didn't know you even knew about it!"

"Hugh found the door when he was twelve and I was nine. We came up for years. Once even at night!"

"Mary! I simply cannot believe you would do such a thing!" spluttered Aunt Florence—as if Aunt Mary were *still* nine.

"Well, we did."

Aunt Mary smiled calmly at her mother and, very slowly, Aunt Florence smiled back. "I guess I can't do anything about it now. That Hugh . . ." she added sadly, gazing at Gavin in the hungry way she always did when she mentioned her son.

"The fireworks are starting!" said Gavin. A silvery fountain burst in the distance, then a blue streak and a pink star. The screeches and crackles reached them a little later than the flashes, like a movie where the sound didn't match the picture. After the fireworks they could hear sirens, ringing church bells and faint, distant singing.

"The lights will be blazing in England tonight," said Aunt Florence. "Your grandfather and sisters will be glad of that, Gavin."

"The European war over at last," sighed Aunt Mary. "Now if they can just finish the war with Japan as well, maybe that will be an end to this madness. It's hard to feel happy when it's brought so much tragedy. Especially to you and Norah, Gavin." She pounded the arm of her chair. "Oh, *when* will people ever learn that war doesn't solve anything?"

The other two stared at this unusual outburst. "Now, Mary . . . let's count our blessings," said Aunt Florence. "We got rid of that brutish Hitler. Gavin and Norah were free from danger in Canada. Andrew is safe. And Gavin was too young to be in it. Let's hope you'll *never* have to be in a war, sweetness." She patted his knee. Gavin was once again surprised that she was not saying anything about him going back to England.

He looked up at both of them: ridiculous, loving Aunt

Florence, and good Aunt Mary. These two women were his parents now. He got up and pretended to look at some revellers coming home from the fireworks, but he was blinking back tears. How could he leave them?

The next day—the *official* VE Day—Gavin and Tim and Roger went downtown again but it was quieter than the day before. They bicycled to Queen Street and watched a parade, then went to Tim's house for lunch.

"I want to show you something," Tim told them, after his mother had gone out with his younger brothers. He led Gavin and Roger to his parents' room and pulled out a magazine from under the mattress.

"I heard Mum tell Dad she was going to hide this from us," said Tim. "So I sneaked in and found it."

Gavin recognized the cover. "Why would your parents hide *Life?*"

"This issue is so creepy, I guess they thought it would scare us. It is scary. Are you brave enough to look?"

Of course the other two had to say they were. They knelt on the floor and leaned on the bed while Tim opened the magazine. Then they stared in silence, while he slowly turned the pages.

The full-page photographs were of bodies. Terrible, emaciated, naked bodies. *Hundreds* of bodies. In one picture they were being shovelled into a mass grave.

Gavin swallowed. "But—but who are they?" he croaked.

"It says they're in some camps in Germany called Belsen and Buchenwald," said Tim, sounding out the names with difficulty. "But it doesn't say who they are or why they're dead. Or why there's so many of them."

Gavin turned back the pages and read some of the text. "It says they're 'slave labourers.' What does that mean?"

"I didn't know the Germans had slaves," said Tim. "Do you think they were Allies?"

"We could ask a grown-up," said Roger.

"But then they'd find out we were looking at this when we weren't supposed to," said Tim.

They continued to stare at the hideous pages. Gavin shivered. "Let's put it away. Maybe one day we'll find out who they are."

Tim shoved the magazine under the mattress and they went out to play in the sunshine.

IX
A PROPOSAL

"Gavin, I'd like to talk to you in my room," said Aunt Florence the next evening.

Gavin finished putting on his pyjamas and went in to sit on the soft loveseat in her bedroom. Aunt Florence sank down beside him. "You may have noticed," she began, "that I've been out a lot lately."

Now that he thought of it, she had gone downtown for many "appointments" in the past few weeks. But Aunt Florence was often out, visiting friends or meeting with one of her charity groups.

"I've been working out a plan, Gavin, and now I need your advice. It's an idea that came to me as soon as we heard about your parents. It wouldn't have been appropriate to bring it up then. But now it's time, especially since the war's over."

"What is it?"

"I know that Norah has to return to England," said Aunt Florence slowly. "She's never felt totally at home in Canada, although she's adjusted as well as she could. It's understandable that she wants to go back. She was old enough when she left to remember her own country."

She paused. "But you're different, Gavin. You feel like a Canadian now—am I right?"

Gavin nodded. What was she getting at?

"And I think you're happy living with Mary and me." Her eyes gleamed, knowing the answer.

"Of course!"

"I know you are," she said warmly. "From the moment you came here you belonged—much more than Norah did. Now, Gavin, I'm going to ask you something that will startle you. You don't have to answer right away." She put both her hands on his shoulders and looked into his eyes. "Would you like to stay in Canada and live with me always?"

Gavin started to shiver, the joy that filled him was so intense. "Stay in Canada? But how?"

"You've been like a son to me these past years. Now I'd like you to be my *real* son. I want to adopt you, Gavin. I would never have suggested this, of course, when your parents were alive. I knew it was going to be difficult for you to return, but they were your parents—you belonged with them. But now that they've gone, you can stay here! If you'd like to, of course."

Gavin took a deep breath. "Could you adopt Bosley too?"

Aunt Florence threw back her head and laughed. "Of course I'll adopt Bosley, you funny boy! I know Reg would give him to you for good. Everything would be the same. You and Bosley would keep on living here with Mary and me and you'd become a real Canadian."

"But what about *Norah?*"

"That's the hard part, pet," said Aunt Florence gently. "You and Norah would be separated. I know how much you love your sister. But she's growing up. She'll be leaving you one day anyway. We would certainly have her back to Canada whenever she wanted to come. And we could visit her often in England."

"But why can't you adopt Norah too?"

Aunt Florence sighed. "I would. I really would, Gavin, despite our differences, but you know she wouldn't want it. She wants to return to England and I don't blame her."

Gavin thought of something else. "Will my grandfather *let* you adopt me?"

"You've hit upon the one problem we might have. No, he might not let me, and if he objects I won't be able to—he's your legal guardian now." A familiar stubborn expression appeared on her face. "But I think I can persuade him—him and your older sisters and maybe even Norah. I'll see that you get a good education. In grade seven you can start St Martin's, which is the best boys' school in Ontario. And then university. And you could take piano lessons and French lessons—you'll have every advantage. And, most important—you would become my heir."

"Your air?" said Gavin. "What does that mean?"

"It means that one day—along with Mary, of course—you'll inherit this," smiled Aunt Florence, waving her hand around her. "Surely your family wouldn't want to deny you *that.*"

She leaned over and kissed him. "I know this is a lot for you to take in, pet. I don't want you to give me an answer yet. Think about it until the weekend, all right?"

"But can't I tell Norah?"

"If you want. But I don't think you should tell her until you're sure of your decision. You know she'll be against it. Why wouldn't she? And this is a secret, all right? I've told Mary, but I don't think you should discuss it with anyone else but Norah."

Gavin could hardly make it into bed, he was so stunned. He put down one arm and fondled Bosley, grinning into the darkness.

He didn't need any time to think about it. He had never wanted anything as much in his life. If Aunt Florence adopted him everything would stay the same! He could keep Bosley! He would be safe and secure in Canada instead of living in a scary country where people had been killed by bombs. There would be no Norah, but as wave after wave of relief swept over Gavin he tried not to think about that.

For the rest of the week Gavin thought he would burst with the excitement of Aunt Florence's proposal. "We'll be able to keep going to Gairloch every summer, Boz," he whispered to the dog. "We'll always know Tim and Roger. Next year you can go in the Dog Show again, and this time you'll win!"

He didn't think he wanted to go to a posh boys' school and wear a uniform, but that was two years away. Maybe by then he could talk Aunt Florence out of it.

The future, which had been a black tunnel, now seemed like a long vista of sunny days. Gavin walked around holding a bubble of happiness inside him. Every time he looked at Aunt Florence or Aunt Mary they exchanged secretive smiles. He knew that Aunt Florence guessed what he'd decided, but he'd promised to wait until the weekend to tell her.

And he *should* talk to Norah before then. But every time he began to climb the stairs to her room he thought of a reason to wait until later. In the daytime it was easy to revel in the joy of staying in Canada. But at night he twisted in his sheets, thinking about Norah.

If only she could stay too! But he knew she wouldn't, not even for him. He tried to reassure himself with what Aunt Florence had said—that Norah would be leaving him anyway. She was getting as grown-up as his other sisters. One day she might get married, like Muriel, or get a job, like Tibby.

But Norah was the only sister he knew. She was his best friend. How could he face those clear eyes and tell her he was staying behind?

He could picture exactly how she'd react. They were so different from each other. Norah always knew what she wanted. She was so sure about everything, so brave. He was so wishy-washy... such a coward.

He couldn't tell her.

"I've decided," he announced to Aunt Florence on Saturday morning. "I'll stay. I'll stay and be your son."

"Oh, Gavin." Aunt Florence clasped him so hard that Gavin couldn't breathe. "Let go!" he laughed.

She loosened her hold. There were tears in her eyes. "You have made me very, very happy. And I'll make *you* happy, you'll see. You'll be the happiest boy in Canada!" she crowed, kissing him firmly on each cheek.

"There's still Norah and Grandad," Gavin reminded her.

"Did you talk to Norah?"

Gavin hung his head. "I couldn't," he whispered. "Could *you* tell her?"

For a second a flicker of fear passed over Aunt Florence's face. Then she straightened her blouse and said briskly. "All right, pet. Why don't you send her down to me right now? We might as well get this over with."

"What does *she* want?" demanded Norah, when Gavin appeared at her door. "I'm trying to finish my essay."

"Just go and see her," said Gavin. He put his hand on Norah's arm as she brushed past him. "And Norah... listen to her, okay?"

Norah gave him a quizzical look and flounced downstairs. Gavin followed slowly. His mouth was dry and his stomach churned. He sat on the floor outside his room and watched Aunt Florence's closed door. Bosley's warm side pressed against him.

At first he heard the low, reasoned murmur of Aunt Florence's words. Norah's response was swift and sure:

"*No!*" Gavin clutched Bosley as her voice grew louder. "He's not staying! You can't *do* this!"

"What's going on?" Aunt Mary had come out of her room.

Gavin gave her a desperate look. "Aunt Florence is telling Norah."

"The poor child," murmured Aunt Mary. "I wonder if this idea of Mother's is right..."

Gavin couldn't bear to be left out any longer. He stood up and opened the door. Norah and Aunt Florence were facing each other like two opponents in a boxing ring. Both pairs of grey eyes flashed with determination. Norah looked much angrier, however, while Aunt Florence was struggling to stay calm.

"I knew you'd react this way, Norah," she said. "But I think that once you've thought about it, you'll see it's the best thing for Gavin. Isn't he the one we should be thinking about?"

"Gavin is not staying in Canada!" shouted Norah.

Desperation filled Gavin. Norah was standing in his way—destroying his only chance of safety and happiness.

"Listen to me, Norah!" They all stared at him with surprise. "I *want* to stay! I *want* to live in Canada!" Her hurt expression melted his anger into tears. "Oh, Norah... why can't you stay too?"

"I have already suggested to Norah that I adopt her as well," said Aunt Florence stiffly. "She says she would rather go back to England."

"But *I* want to stay here!" begged Gavin. "*Please,* Norah..."

Norah looked around at all of them. Her face was bleached of colour and her voice icy. "All right, Gavin—stay. You can have him, Aunt Florence. And you can all just—go—to—hell!" She spun around and ran out of the room.

By the evening they were limp from spent emotion. Aunt Florence had gone up to Norah's room and stayed there a long time.

"She wants to speak to you now," she told Gavin. She shut herself up with Aunt Mary and Gavin trudged up the stairs to the tower.

"Come in," said Norah weakly. She was lying on her bed. "Listen, Gavin," she muttered. "I'm sorry I said that awful thing. I didn't mean it. Do you believe me?"

"Yes," whispered Gavin, although he didn't think he'd ever forget the sting of those words. Words *hurt.* He sat down on the end of the bed, keeping as far away from Norah as he could. Her voice still sounded bitter and she looked as terrible as when they'd heard about their parents. Her hair was in uncombed strings over her tear-marked cheeks and her nose was raw from crying. *He* had made her feel this way.

"Do you really want to stay here?" Norah asked him.

Gavin nodded miserably. He was wounding her even more but he had no choice.

"Are you sure Aunt Florence hasn't just brainwashed you into saying yes? She's always had some sort of weird power over you."

"I made up my own mind. I'm sorry, Norah. I *have* to stay, don't you see? Canada's my *home.* I don't *remember* England. I don't even remember—" He stopped, afraid to hurt her again.

"You don't remember Mum and Dad," she sighed. "I know that now."

"I don't want to lose *you,*" said Gavin. "But Aunt Florence said we can visit you, and you can visit us too."

"She told me that too." Norah sat up. "Aunt Florence is offering you a lot," she said tightly. "You'll get a good education and one day you'll be rich."

And I'll get to keep Bosley, Gavin added to himself.

"She seems to think it's the best thing for you," continued Norah. "I don't! But Aunt Florence always gets what she wants. I just hope Grandad refuses—I bet he will."

She finally managed a small, clenched smile. "But I also want you to be happy, Gavin. Aunt Florence says I shouldn't upset you about it. So I'll keep quiet until we hear Grandad's decision. That's the best I can offer."

"Thank you," whispered Gavin. He had to leave before he cried. He ran down to his room and crawled under his eiderdown.

What a horrible, horrible day. It was even worse than when his parents died, because this time all the anguish revolved around *him.* He gazed around his neat room, at his models and soldiers and books arranged exactly as he liked them. In Muriel's house in England he probably wouldn't even have his own room.

Surely Grandad would say yes and Norah would accept it. Then maybe he could stop feeling so guilty.

Aunt Florence sent Grandad a cable, asking him to telephone at her expense. To Norah's fury, the call came through when they were in school. "I wanted to talk to him!" she cried.

"He's going to phone back again," said Aunt Florence. "Maybe you can talk to him then. His voice was amazingly clear."

"But what did he *say?*" demanded Norah.

She looked embarrassed. "He was... well... surprised, of course. He said he'd think about my proposal and phone back. I did most of the talking."

"I bet you did," Norah muttered, so low that only Gavin heard her.

Then a cable arrived:

MUST CONSULT REST FAMILY STOP WILL NOT TELEPHONE UNTIL JUNE

JAMES LOGGIN

"June!" spluttered Aunt Florence. "That's too long! Doesn't he realize how hard it is on Gavin to wait? And we can't make any arrangements for a ship until we know if one or both of you are going."

"But Mother," said Aunt Mary timidly, "you can understand how Mr Loggin needs time to think about it. After all, you're asking him to give up his only grandson." Aunt Florence frowned at her.

Gavin stole a glance at Norah. She looked as frustrated as the rest of them not to *know.*

"Well, he's left us no choice," sighed Aunt Florence. Later she told Gavin in private not to worry. "He didn't sound negative, pet—just rather shocked, which is understandable. Let's assume you *are* staying. I'm going to write a long letter to your grandfather. I'm sure I can convince him. But until we know, remember it's still a secret."

But Gavin couldn't keep the secret bottled up any longer. One afternoon, when he and Tim and Roger were in the fort, he told his friends that he might stay in Canada.

"Hooray!" shouted Tim. Roger just grinned.

"Don't tell anyone," warned Gavin. "It's a secret! And my grandfather might *make* me go back."

"He must be really mean to do that," said Roger.

This was exactly how Gavin had been imagining Grandad lately—a mean old man who wanted to spoil his happiness.

"He *is* mean," said Gavin. "It would be awful to have to

live with him. We don't even have a house! We'd have to squeeze into my sister's house. And she and her husband are probably mean too," he added wildly. He looked at their sympathetic faces. "But wouldn't it be keen if I stayed in Canada? Then we'd always be friends!"

"I have an idea," said Tim. "Let's make a pact, just in case you do have to go back. A pact in blood."

"Blood!" the other two cried.

"Just a little bit of blood," said Tim. "We'll prick our fingers and be blood brothers, the way they did in *Secret Water.*" They were all avid readers of the Arthur Ransome books.

Roger looked nervous when Tim took out his jackknife and placed it on a log.

"Will it hurt?" he asked.

"I don't think I want to," said Gavin.

"Don't be such cowards," said Tim scornfully. "Look, I'll go first."

He opened up the knife and scratched the blade tentatively on the ball of his forefinger. Then he jabbed. Gavin closed his eyes.

But nothing happened. Tim jabbed again: two, three, five times. But the blade was too dull to penetrate his skin.

"Oh, well," said Roger. "We can just *say* a pact."

"No, there has to be blood," insisted Tim. He rooted in his pockets and pulled out a safety pin. "This should work." Placing the point of the pin on the same place, he pushed slowly and withdrew the tip. "There!" They all peered at the tiny gleam of blood on his finger.

"Hurry!" said Tim. "Do yours before mine dries!"

Roger took the pin and pushed it in quickly. "Ouch!" He stuck his finger in his mouth.

"Don't waste it!" said Tim. "Now you, Gavin."

Gavin held the pin over his fingertip. “Do it!” ordered Tim.

He pressed the pin into his finger. It really hurt and he withdrew it quickly. Some blood welled up and pooled along the lines in his skin.

How strange to think that his body was full of gallons of this bright red liquid. Blood *flowed;* that’s what they learned in school. It meant you were alive—life blood. A gruesome thought came into his head. His parents’ blood would have stopped flowing when they were killed. That was what death was.

“You can get way more if you squeeze,” said Roger. They pinched their sore fingers until half a red globule hung from each one.

“Okay, rub them together,” said Tim. He smeared his bloody finger over Roger’s finger, then Gavin’s. The others did the same.

“Now I have blood from both of you mingled with mine,” said Tim, examining his finger with satisfaction.

“We should say something,” said Gavin.

Roger looked solemn. “We three swear, by the mingling of our blood, that we will be blood brothers and friends forever.”

“I swear,” said Tim, choking with laughter.

“I swear,” said Gavin fervently. “Now we really *are* like the Three Musketeers. All for one and one for all!” They were musketeers until dinner time.

X

A SURPRISE VISITOR

The family tried to carry on as if they weren't waiting for a decision that would change their lives forever. By unspoken agreement no one talked about it, but the whole household itched with prickly suspense. Aunt Mary was overcome by spring allergies and took to her bed. Hanny served dull, badly cooked meals and sat around the kitchen morosely nursing her tea and cigarette. Norah had to study for her final exams. Sometimes Paige persuaded her to go to a movie or the canteen, but most of the time she escaped into her books. Aunt Florence took Gavin to the Riverdale Zoo on Firecracker Day. They were both relieved when the outing was over, after the strain of pretending that everything was normal.

But when June came and there was still no word from Grandad, Aunt Florence broke the silence. "When is he going to phone?" she asked Norah angrily. "It's unbearable, keeping us in suspense like this! If he hasn't phoned by Monday I'm going to send another telegram."

"How should I know why?" said Norah sullenly. "It isn't *my* fault he hasn't phoned yet! I want to know what he's decided just as much as you do." The two of them were as antagonistic as when Norah and Gavin had first arrived, as if their four years' truce had never happened.

Gavin began to daydream so much in class that Mrs Moss had to keep him after school several times to finish his work.

"Are you worried about going back to England?" she asked during one of these detentions. She looked up from her desk as he tried to concentrate on a page of long division.

He couldn't tell her his secret. He just whispered "Yes, Mrs Moss" so sadly that she let him leave.

Gavin walked home slowly, kicking at the sidewalk and scuffing his new oxfords. He didn't care. *Waiting*. It seemed that all he had done in 1945 was wait. He felt as dry and wrung-out as the twisted dishcloths that Hanny hung on the line.

Today was Monday—the day Aunt Florence said she'd send Grandad another telegram. That cheered him up a little. At least they were *doing* something.

The house was silent when Gavin got there. Hanny told him the aunts had gone out to vote in the Ontario election. "Norah's at the library. I'd like to nip out and vote myself before I start dinner. Will you be all right by yourself for half an hour?"

"Sure." After Hanny had gone, he wandered upstairs, Bosley padding behind and whining for a bite of his cookie. Gavin was rarely alone in the house. He decided to explore every inch of it, as if he had never been here before.

First he climbed on a chair and tried to open the trap door to the roof, but he couldn't quite reach it. Then he made his way slowly downwards, from Norah's tower to the musty basement.

He even ventured into the aunts' rooms, careful not to touch anything. He examined the childhood photograph of Aunt Mary and her brother Hugh, which she always kept on her chest of drawers. On her bedside table lay a Bible and a library book called *The Building of Jalna.* A watercolour picture of Gairloch hung on one wall. Surely he'd be back in that magical place this summer...

Aunt Florence's room smelled like the flowery perfume she always wore. It was stuffed with cushions, soft furniture, family photographs and hat boxes. Beside *her* bed was a book about the Royal Family. Almost everything in the room was pink. Being in here always made Gavin feel as if he were enveloped in a soft pink cloud of security.

As he continued his expedition through the house, its solid presence held him like a hug. If Aunt Florence adopted him he would own this house one day! He'd own part of Gairloch too. Not until he was grown up, of course.

Bosley would be dead by then. It was so unfair that dogs didn't live as long as humans. But he'd always have a springer spaniel, Gavin thought dreamily. They would all be black-and-white and they'd all be called Bosley.

After his tour he lay on the den floor, listening to "Terry and the Pirates" on the radio. Bosley's freckled muzzle rested on his stomach. Then the door knocker banged and Bosley jumped up with a warning bark.

"Shhh! It's probably Norah, silly. Hanny must have locked the door." Gavin got up to open it.

An old man stood there. He was short and tubby, with a white fringe of hair under his crumpled hat. Heavy brows fell over his eyes and his stiff moustache was stained with tobacco. He wore a grimy suit and a bedraggled blue tie. His shoes needed polishing. In one hand he held a battered suitcase, in the other a pipe.

Gavin backed off with alarm. He must be a tramp! Tramps usually came to the kitchen door and begged for some food from Hanny. Would this man expect him to give him something? Bosley growled and Gavin put one hand on his collar.

The man stared at Gavin with a curious, searching expression. Then he said softly, "Is it Gavin?"

"Who are you?" whispered Gavin. "How do you know

my name?" Suddenly the man's face looked familiar—where had he seen it?

"Don't you recognize me? I'm your grandad! I've come to take you home."

Half an hour later everyone sat in the living room, staring dumbfounded at Grandad.

Except for Norah. She pressed against her grandfather, hanging onto his arm like an anchor. Gavin would never forget the look of utter relief on her face when she'd come through the door, minutes after Gavin had awkwardly invited Grandad into the hall. She had screamed, then collapsed sobbing in his arms, as if she were sobbing away four and a half years' homesickness as well as the grief over her parents. "*Grandad!* Oh, Grandad..."

"There, there, my brave Norah. I'm here now. Everything is going to be all right. Just look how you've grown! Both of you!"

Norah kept hold of Grandad while they stumbled into the living room and collapsed on the chesterfield. Then Hanny and the aunts arrived. Grandad introduced himself gruffly. Aunt Mary cried out with delighted surprise. Aunt Florence stiffened, then shook Grandad's hand without a word. She stared coldly at the old man while Hanny brought them tea and stayed to listen to his story.

"A fellow I know in the navy got me onto a ship for Canada. It was a cheap passage and I've made a bit of money this year doing carpentry. It was some voyage, I can tell you! Full of war brides and babies. The whole ship reeked of nappies!" He wiped his bald forehead with his handkerchief.

"We are *so* glad to meet you after all these years," Aunt Mary said again. "Norah has told us all about you and you can tell what a comfort it is for her to see you again." She smiled warmly at Norah.

Finally Aunt Florence spoke. "You're very welcome to stay here, of course, Mr Loggin. But I'm curious. Why did you journey all this way when Norah is about to return to England anyway?"

Gavin froze; even Bosley seemed to hold his breath.

"Your request put me into such a dither, Ma'am, that I couldn't think straight. I've never been one for letters or telephones, so I decided to come over and talk to you in person about . . . this matter. But let's wait until tomorrow for that. Right now I want to catch up with these young ones."

"Of course you do!" said Aunt Mary giddily. "We'll leave the three of you alone until dinner's ready." She and Aunt Florence and Hanny left the room.

Gavin shoved piece after piece of Hanny's gingerbread into his mouth while Norah found her voice. She and Grandad talked and talked, interrupting each other with excited comments about the rest of the family.

Grandad had an English accent, of course, but he wasn't easy to understand like some of the English teachers in school. His speech was garbled and rough and Mrs Moss would have been shocked at some of the words he used. Every once in a while he stopped and stared at Norah and Gavin. "I can't believe how much you've both changed! But of course, it's been almost five years. Do you remember me, Gavin?"

"Yes, sir," lied Gavin.

Grandad laughed. "You don't have to say 'sir' to your own grandad! And listen to your accent! Norah's not as bad, but you sound like the Yanks we had in our village."

"I'm Canadian, not American," mumbled Gavin.

"Gavin!" Norah frowned at him. "You're *not* Canadian, you know that. You just sound like one."

Grandad grew solemn and talked about their parents'

death and the funeral that the whole village had attended. Norah cried again. Curled up against Grandad she looked even younger than Gavin.

"It's such a damned tragedy," exclaimed Grandad. "My only daughter... how I miss the arguments Janie and I used to have! And Arthur, always so cheerful and calm. He never agreed with me on much, but he always accepted me." Tears formed in his sea-blue eyes.

"It's all right, Grandad," said Norah softly. "You've got us now. I'm going to quit school and take care of you."

"You'll do no such thing, young woman!" bristled Grandad. "You'll finish your education. I've heard about your good marks—it would be a bloody waste. And I'm pretty good at housekeeping, myself. Wait until you taste my meat pies, young Gavin!" He looked up at Gavin slyly. "If you search in my pockets you might find a sweetie."

When Gavin didn't respond Grandad looked embarrassed. Gavin lowered his head. A "sweetie" must be a candy. Did his grandfather think he was still five?

Was Grandad really going to take him back to England like he'd said? Was that what he was going to tell Aunt Florence tomorrow?

He glared at the grubby old man sitting on Aunt Florence's sleek chesterfield. He smelled! He used bad words! Gavin edged away from him as he and Norah talked and laughed. This *stranger* wanted to remove Gavin from the only home he had ever known.

Grandad didn't look nearly as grubby after a bath and a shave. But he still wore the shiny suit and the frayed tie at their late dinner. Gavin could tell that Aunt Florence was embarrassed to have him in the house. He thought of Uncle Reg's meticulous dark suits and snowy shirts. To Gavin's horror Grandad tucked his napkin under his chin and slurped his soup.

"A super meal," he told Hanny, as she took away his dessert plate. Hanny smiled—she seemed to like him as much as Aunt Mary did. "You wouldn't believe the food in England," said Grandad. "Rationing's getting worse instead of better. Of course the parcels you've sent us have really helped."

He glanced at the mahogany table and the silver gleaming in the candlelight. "Norah and Gavin were certainly lucky, to come to such a fine house. I'm sure they wouldn't look so fit if they'd stayed in England." He cleared his throat. "I know Jane and Arthur would want me to thank you. We can never repay you for the kindness you've shown our young ones."

Aunt Mary dabbed at her eyes. "It was *our* privilege, Mr Loggin. They're wonderful children and it's changed our lives to have them with us for so long." She and Grandad beamed at each other. Grandad lit his pipe and puffed foul-smelling smoke into the room. Norah sniffed it in and sighed happily.

But Aunt Florence and Gavin sat stiffly in their chairs, one disapproving and the other afraid.

XI
A DECISION

Grandad was put into the spare room next to Gavin's. Gavin tossed all night, his dreams interrupted by the snuffle and wheeze of loud snores.

Their grandfather was still asleep when Gavin and Norah left for school. "The poor man must be exhausted after such a long journey," said Aunt Mary.

When Grandad got up, thought Gavin, he would tell Aunt Florence he was taking Gavin back to England. By the time he got home for lunch it would all be decided.

At least they had lantern slides in school that morning. Gavin sat woodenly in the darkened classroom, while Mrs Moss's voice droned on about daily life in Lapland. Tim sneaked Gavin a package of Lifesavers. Gavin just held it in his lap, until Martin snatched it, hissing, "What's the matter with you, Stoakes? Pass it on!"

"No talking! Remember there will be questions afterwards," warned Mrs Moss. Luckily she didn't call on Gavin; nothing from the slides had sunk in.

He thought of asking himself to Tim's house for lunch. But that would just stretch out the agony of not knowing.

When Gavin got home, however, no one was there but Hanny. She gave him a peanut butter sandwich alone in the dining room.

"Where *is* everyone?" he asked.

"Norah took her lunch as usual. Mrs O and Mary had

their Red Cross meeting. And your grandfather has gone out to buy some tobacco. My, he's a card. He says I cook eggs better than his wife did!"

"Did—did he and Aunt Florence talk to each other?"

Hanny sat down beside him. "Yes, Gavin, they did. They were in the den for an hour. You're worried about your grandfather wanting you back, aren't you..."

"What did Aunt Florence look like when she went out? Mad?" He could picture exactly her affronted expression when she didn't get her way.

"I'm sorry, Gavin, I was doing the dishes when she left. Your grandfather seemed fairly cheerful, though, when he came in to ask me directions."

"But that's bad!" cried Gavin. "If he was cheerful, maybe he got what he wanted!"

"Now, now..." Hanny patted his arm. "We don't know that yet." She sighed. "It's such an impossible decision. You can understand why both he and Mrs O want you. *I'd* like you to stay, of course, but I wonder what's best..."

"It's best that I stay!" Gavin pushed away his sandwich and ran up to his room. If even Hanny wasn't sure he should live in Canada, maybe he wouldn't be allowed to.

"Gavin?" Hanny had followed him up. "Are you all right?"

"I feel sick." His head was whirling and his stomach felt queer. "Can I stay home from school this afternoon?"

"Of course you can. I don't know how you'd sit through it, waiting to hear the decision. Shall I bring the kitchen radio up?"

"All right."

He lay on his bed and listened dully to "The Happy Gang." Then he turned off the radio and tried to read, but soon he slept. His dreams were a jangled repetition of big hands reaching out again and again to snatch him and pull him apart. He woke up sweating. Red lines were etched in his cheek from pressing against the pattern in his bedspread.

The house was silent. Gavin crept to the door of his room and listened. Footsteps sounded in the downstairs hall and Aunt Florence's voice said, "Very well. I'll see if he's awake."

She started up the stairs, then saw him standing at the top. "There you are, sweetness! Are you feeling better? Hanny said you weren't well."

"I'm okay."

"Come into the den, please, Gavin. Your grandfather and I want to talk to you."

This was it. He followed Aunt Florence's erect back down the stairs. He couldn't tell from her voice what the decision was.

Gavin sat down in the den, his legs trembling. He was curiously relieved; at least he was finally going to *know.* Bosley lifted his head from the rug and gave his tail a sympathetic thump.

"Gavin..." Grandad looked as fierce as Norah did when she knew what she wanted. "As you know, Mrs Ogilvie has offered to take you permanently into her family—to adopt you." A strained politeness came into his voice. "It's a very generous offer, especially after all she's already done for you. She also says that you *want* her to adopt you. Is that right?"

Gavin lifted his head. "Yes, sir," he said clearly.

Grandad winced. "I can understand that. You've obviously been happy here and you don't remember your real home. And if you stayed in Canada you'd have a lot of advantages our family could never give you."

Hope stirred in Gavin. Was it possible that Grandad was going to agree?

But then Grandad sat up straighter. With a stubborn look at Aunt Florence he said, "Perhaps it's unfair of me to deprive you of those advantages, Gavin, but I can't give you up. Neither can Norah or your other sisters. Even though you've lost your parents, you still have us. We're your family. I know you don't remember us—but we remember *you.* We love you. You *belong* with us. So I'm afraid..." He wiped his forehead and carried on firmly. "I'm afraid that I can't allow Mrs Ogilvie to adopt you."

For a few seconds the room spun. "But I want to stay here," Gavin said weakly. "Please, sir—Grandad—can't you let me?"

"Gavin, old man, I know you want to stay. But you're only ten. You don't know what's best for you. You'll get used to me—*and* to England. Believe me, in a year or two you'll be glad I made this decision for you. And I *am* your legal guardian," he added, with another defiant glance at Aunt Florence. "I'm supposed to make decisions for you."

"Aunt Florence!" cried Gavin. "Don't let him take me!"

Aunt Florence's voice was low and furious. "There's nothing I can do about it, pet. We've gone over and over it all day, but he won't budge."

The two adults stared at Gavin greedily, as if they were pulling him apart—just like his dream.

Gavin jumped to his feet. "*No!*" he shouted, facing Grandad. "I won't go back with you! It's *not* fair! I'm happy *here!* I belong *here!* Why can't you let me stay where I'm happy?" Tears streamed over his cheeks, but he didn't even notice, his anger was so overpowering.

"Gavin!" Aunt Florence pulled him over to her. "Calm down! You're getting hysterical!"

"Oh, Aunt Florence . . ." Gavin buried his face in the haven of her soft front and sobbed frantically. "Aunt Florence, I don't want to leave you! I don't want to live with him! Don't let him take me away from you! *Please!*"

He kept on crying for a long time, while Aunt Florence tried to soothe him. Finally Grandad spoke, his voice broken. "Am I so awful, then, Gavin? I'm not an ogre, you know."

"I'm s-sorry," gulped Gavin. "But I don't want to leave!"

Grandad wiped his forehead again. "I can't think," he mumbled. "This room is so bloody—" he glanced at Aunt Florence—"this room is so warm."

Aunt Florence stood up and took Gavin's hand. "Your grandfather and I need to talk alone again, pet. Go and ask Hanny to bring us some lemonade. I'll call you when we're ready for you again."

Gavin stumbled out and gave Hanny the message. Hanny gave him some lemonade too, and he sipped it at the kitchen table. Hanny chattered to him about her husband's model trains; her voice seemed to come from far away.

It was a long time before Aunt Florence finally called him. Gavin made his frozen legs walk back into the den.

"Your grandfather has come to a decision," said Aunt Florence. Her face was bent and her voice so low that Gavin gave up hope.

Grandad's eyes were bleary and red. "Gavin, my boy . . . you looked at me back then just like Janie used to, when she wanted something desperately. I knew you were close to Mrs Ogilvie. But I suppose . . . I suppose I didn't realize *how* close. I don't mean to be cruel . . ."

Gavin took a quick breath while Grandad continued.

". . . and I can't bear to make you this unhappy. Are you absolutely certain that you want to stay?"

"Yes!" whispered Gavin.

"After all, your happiness is the most important thing," said Grandad slowly, as if convincing himself. He sighed. "All right." He threw Aunt Florence a bitter look. "You can stay. But I've given Mrs Ogilvie one condition."

"What?" breathed Gavin.

"That she doesn't start legal adoption proceedings until after Norah and I have left. I want you to have that time to change your mind if you want to."

"I'll *never* change my mind!" said Gavin. Then he flinched at Grandad's hurt expression. For the first time, he felt sorry for the old man.

"You certainly seem to know what you want," said Grandad gruffly. "But remember, Gavin, even if it's the day we leave—even if it's after we're back—you can still decide to live with Norah and me, all right?"

"All right," whispered Gavin to the floor.

"Now, if you'll both excuse me, I'd like to go to my room." He walked out stiffly, holding his white head high.

Aunt Florence stared at the chair where he'd been sitting. "This is very hard for your grandfather," she murmured. "It's extremely generous of him to give you up."

A warm glow slowly filled the numb space inside Gavin. "I'm going to stay," he whispered.

Aunt Florence smiled at Gavin as if she couldn't believe her luck. "Yes, pet... you're going to stay!"

Gavin let out a long sigh. "*Jeepers...*"

"Jeepers is right!" she laughed. "That's exactly how *I* feel!"

"Can I tell Tim and Roger?"

"I don't see why not. You can tell whomever you like. But Gavin—try not to act too excited while Norah and Mr Loggin are still here. It will hurt their feelings if you're too happy about staying. Remember that you aren't going to see them for a while."

Gavin couldn't think of that. He was going to stay!

"This is going to be a difficult time," mused Aunt Florence. "Especially saying goodbye to Norah. But after that... oh, come over here and give me a kiss."

Her arms were shaking when she hugged him. It was as if they had been through a battle—like another kind of war. But they'd *won,* thought Gavin gleefully. He and Aunt Florence had won!

"I'm staying!" Gavin told Bosley, after Aunt Florence had also gone up to her room. He got down on the rug and tickled Bosley's stomach. "You're going to be my dog forever and ever!" Bosley licked Gavin's face, as if he wondered what all the fuss was about.

Gavin lay against the dog—*his* dog. Relief bubbled through him like warm water. He was staying. He was *safe.*

Once again he was afraid to tell Norah. But he knew Grandad had told her already from the anguished looks she gave him all through dinner. Afterwards she invited him to go for a walk around the block.

"Grandad said you're staying," she muttered, staring straight ahead. She stopped walking and faced him. "Gavin, are you *sure* this is what you want?"

"Yes!" Why did everyone have to keep asking him that?

"I thought seeing Grandad again would make you change your mind. But you don't even remember *him,* do you?"

"No. I'm sorry."

Norah's eyes filled with tears. "I can't bear to leave you behind! You're my brother!"

"I'm sorry," said Gavin again.

"Gavin, when we left England D-dad and Mum . . ." Norah swallowed a sob. "They told me to take care of you! At first I forgot." She blushed. "I was too wrapped up in my own misery to think of you. But then when I realized how much—how much I loved you, I promised myself that I'd *always* take care of you. If I leave you here I'm breaking that promise! It's like breaking a promise to Dad and Mum! Can you imagine what *they'd* think of us separating?" Her sobs overtook her and she flung herself down on someone's lawn.

Gavin crouched beside her. "*Please,* Norah! You *have* taken care of me—good care!" He thought desperately. "But if you let me stay, then *that's* taking care of me too—because that's what I want! And you'll still be my sister, no matter where we live." He took her hand.

She clutched it with both of hers. "I just don't know! I suppose you're right, in a way. I suppose your happiness is the most important thing. It's so mixed up. I'm so *tired.* I'm so sick of trying to decide what's right." She let go of his hand. "I give up, Gavin." Her voice was broken. "I can't fight you any more. If you really want to stay, I guess Grandad and I will just have to accept it. All I can do is hope that you'll change your mind."

Gavin shuddered. How could he hurt her like this? Especially when she'd already suffered so much. But he had no choice "I'm sorry," said Gavin for the third time, "but I won't change my mind."

"I guess there's nothing I can do about it, then," she said wearily. They walked back to the house in miserable silence. Norah wasn't angry with him. But there was a new distance between them, as if they already lived in different countries.

XII
GRANDAD

"You're staying?" cried Tim.

"Forever?" said Roger.

Gavin grinned at his friends. "Yes! Aunt Florence is going to adopt me! And I get to keep Bosley!"

"Hooray!" Tim threw his baseball glove into the air, then pounded Gavin on the back.

"Now we really *are* blood brothers," laughed Roger. The three of them linked arms and continued to walk to school.

"Will you change your last name to Ogilvie?" asked Tim.

Gavin hadn't thought of that. He had been Gavin Stoakes all his life.

Before he sat down at his desk he went up to Mrs Moss and said shyly. "I'll be here again this fall, Mrs Moss. The Ogilvies are adopting me!"

"Why, Gavin! What a nice surprise! May I tell the whole class?"

"All right." He blushed when everyone clapped, but their grins warmed him. Someone passed him a folded note.

"I'm glad you're staying. I hope we'll be in the same class again next year. Eleanor." He sneaked a look at her, but she was bent over her desk.

Gavin told everyone he knew: the policeman at the crosswalk, the woman in the store where he bought gum and comics, and Miss Gleeson at the library.

"If that's what you want, I'm very happy for you," said

the librarian, as she stamped out *Homer Price* for him. "But what about Norah? Is she staying too?" Miss Gleeson had been one of Norah's first friends in Canada.

Gavin flushed. "She's going back to live with my grandfather," he mumbled.

"Oh." Miss Gleeson looked surprised, but she didn't say anything else.

The more Gavin talked to people about staying, the less he had to think about Norah leaving. But he kept his promise and tried not to talk about it at home.

Aunt Florence, Aunt Mary and Hanny gave him special smiles; but more often they watched Norah desperately, as if she were disappearing before their eyes. At least Norah still had to spend most of her time cramming for exams. Then Gavin could avoid her.

Grandad, too, holed himself up. He had taken over the late Mr Ogilvie's study. Aunt Florence had requested that he not smoke his pipe anywhere else in the house. "It's very hard on my daughter's allergies," she said stiffly. Even though she had won, Grandad's continued presence seemed to irritate her.

"But Mother, I like the smell of pipe tobacco," protested Aunt Mary. "My father used to smoke a pipe," she explained to Grandad.

"It's not good for you," repeated her mother.

Grandad seemed relieved to have a place to escape from her. When he wasn't visiting a downtown beer parlour he'd discovered, he sat in the study for hours, reading every line of the newspapers. All the way up in his room Gavin could hear the ringing tap of his pipe as he emptied it into the ashtray.

When Norah wasn't working she retreated to the study with Grandad. Talking about their parents or making plans for England, Gavin supposed. He knew he'd be welcome to join them, but he preferred to listen to the radio in the den.

"Mary, I've decided to cancel our Sunday bridge evenings for the time being," Aunt Florence told her daughter as they sat in there one evening.

"But Mother—why?" Aunt Mary was an avid bridge player.

Aunt Florence glanced at Gavin. He pretended to be absorbed in his book. "I don't think Mr Loggin would feel comfortable with our friends," she murmured.

"But he's a delightful man!" said Aunt Mary. "And don't you think they'd be interested in hearing about England?"

"That may be, but I've made up my mind."

Aunt Mary looked as if she'd like to protest, but as usual she didn't dare. From then on none of the Ogilvies' usual friends visited the house—as if Grandad were something to be ashamed of. Gavin knew Aunt Florence was being snobby. But he told himself that Grandad probably didn't want to meet her friends anyway.

"What are you up to today, Gavin?" said Grandad one Saturday morning. "I thought we could take in the pictures, and have a bang-up tea somewhere afterwards."

"The pictures?" said Gavin.

Grandad smiled. "The movies, to you. How about it?" He almost looked afraid as he waited for Gavin's answer.

Gavin thought fast. "Uhh—I was going to do something with Tim and Roger today."

"They could come too! Ring them up. I'll treat you all."

There was no choice. Tim and Roger were both delighted that they didn't have to pay for a movie. They pressed beside Grandad on the streetcar, listening avidly while he told them how his house had been bombed by the Germans in the summer of 1940.

"That's why I ended up living with my daughter's family. I'll never forget the look on your mother's face when I turned up at the house!" he said to Gavin. "They took me in with no hesitation."

Gavin sat quietly while the other two plied Grandad with questions. Norah had often talked about the time Grandad had arrived so unexpectedly on their doorstep; that was the day before their parents told them they were going to Canada.

Gavin had been there too, of course—but he couldn't remember it at all. He wondered if his mother had felt as surprised and shocked then as he had when Grandad appeared at the Ogilvies' door.

And had the old man really been wanted? His parents' letters had sometimes complained about Grandad: spending all day in the pub, never wiping his feet, arguing with his son-in-law about the American soldiers. Gavin glared at his grandfather. Why did he have to keep turning up uninvited, disrupting other people's lives? If he hadn't come, maybe Norah would have decided to stay after all.

They went to see *A Tree Grows in Brooklyn* at Shea's. Gavin liked the first part the best, when Francie and her brother Neeley—who looked just like Tim—ran wild around the slums of New York. But after the father died, the movie got uncomfortably serious. Francie's sharp grief was just like Norah's. When she finally cried, Gavin felt guilty all over again that he never had. He looked around the audience. All the adults were sniffling, including Grandad.

"What a fine picture!" said Grandad when it was over. He wiped his eyes. "Did you boys like it?"

"It was okay," said Roger. "Except for the soppy parts."

"I liked it when Neeley said 'cut the mush,'" grinned Tim.

"The family reminded me a bit of *our* family," said Grandad. "The way they made do in a hard time."

Was their family that poor? wondered Gavin. If so, he was even gladder he wasn't going back.

They walked along the crowded sidewalk. Tim and Roger were squeezed ahead and Gavin was stuck beside Grandad.

"I didn't realize the film was about a death," he said. "I hope it didn't bother you too much. I'd better warn Norah not to see it."

"There's Murray's," pointed out Gavin. He ran ahead to catch up with the others.

"Is anyone hungry?" Grandad asked when he reached them.

"I am!" cried Tim.

They went inside and each had a milkshake and as many doughnuts as he wished. Tim managed four.

Gavin was surprised at how easily shy Roger talked to Grandad. He began telling him about his father. "He might be home next week! Mum has all his favourite food ready for him."

"And you haven't seen him since you were seven?" said Grandad. "Do you remember him?"

"Of course I do!" said Roger. "The week before he left he taught me how to play chess. Every time he writes he says I'll probably beat him in our first game." Roger stopped eating and sat in a happy daze. Gavin had never seen him look so carefree.

He sipped his milkshake jealously. Lucky Roger. He had a father and he sounded nice. Tim's father was nice, too. He always had time to throw a ball with Tim and his brothers.

Would he have remembered *his* father when he finally saw him in person? But it was too late to wonder about that now. His father was dead. All he had was this grandfather who had tried to yank him away from a family and a place he loved.

"Your grandfather's swell!" whispered Tim on the way home. "He said he'd send me a piece of shrapnel when he gets back! You must feel real sad that he's leaving soon."

Gavin shrugged. "Hey, wasn't it great when Francie and Neeley got the Christmas tree?"

Grandad kept on trying to make friends with Gavin. He invited him into the study, but Gavin stayed there for as short a time as possible, then made up an excuse to leave. Still, he took Gavin to the museum and to Casa Loma.

"No wonder you like this city," he said. "It's so clean and modern. You should see London—it's a mess of bombed-out buildings. I wish I had time to see some of the rest of Canada. You and Norah are lucky children. You've been west and to Montreal and a cottage in the north every summer."

The worst part of spending time with Grandad was that he went on and on about Ringden and the family there. He seemed to expect Gavin to know about things like cricket and pig clubs. "Muriel and Barry's house is only a few minutes away from Little Whitebull," he told Gavin. He chuckled. "Your nephew Richard is a real bruiser. He looks like his Dad but he has the Loggin stubbornness. Like Janie and Norah—like me! When Richard doesn't want to eat something he clamps his lips closed."

Gavin grunted a reply. Why would he be interested in a baby?

"Do you remember your friend Joey?" continued Grandad.

Gavin shook his head impatiently.

"You and he were inseparable. He's a bit of limb, Joey is. Just before I left he got into a lot of trouble for breaking a window in Mrs Chandler's house."

"I don't remember him," Gavin repeated.

Often Grandad gave him a sad, pleading look. Then he'd say *sneaky* things. "Ringden's a great place for young ones. You can run wild there—hardly any cars and lots of woods to play in. And there's always Gilden to go to for the pictures. When our house is rebuilt I was thinking we could get ourselves a dog. Joey's mother has a pointer cross who's expecting pups."

Grandad was trying to bribe him! And he'd *never* have a dog that wasn't a springer spaniel.

He can't make me change my mind, Gavin thought. Grandad wasn't the only one who could be stubborn.

Gavin developed a hacking cough that wouldn't go away. He felt well enough, but he sounded terrible. Aunt Florence made him stay in bed for two days. As always when he was sick, she brought him special food and new toys and read to him for hours.

"How are you feeling?" Grandad stood at his door on the morning of the second day.

Gavin made himself cough weakly. "All right, I guess."

"This is quite a room you have," said Grandad. He came in and glanced at all of Gavin's stuff. "English kids haven't been able to get toys for quite a while."

Was that *his* fault? He wished Grandad would leave; this was the first time he'd ventured into the one place Gavin could escape from him.

"You don't seem very sick to me," said Grandad quietly. "These women coddle you too much."

Gavin glared at him. "I *am* sick! The doctor said so."

Grandad just raised his bushy eyebrows. He dropped a new comic on the foot of Gavin's bed and left without a word.

XIII
MICK'S PLAN

The social worker phoned and said Norah could sail on a ship that left on July 13. Grandad would have to pay his own way, but there was space for him also.

"But that's only four weeks away!" cried Aunt Mary. "Oh, Norah, I can't bear it..." She stifled a sob.

"Now, Mary, we knew it would be short notice," said Aunt Florence. "I certainly don't want you to leave so soon, Norah, but who knows when another sailing will be available? And Dulcie and Lucy are going on the same ship—that will be pleasant for you."

"I'm sorry it's so soon too—but it's what we planned," said Norah. Her eyes shone with excitement but she avoided looking at Gavin.

"I'm going to have a large farewell party for you," said Aunt Florence grandly. "You can ask whomever you like—your whole class, if you want!"

"Really?" Aunt Florence didn't approve of many of the teen-agers in Norah's class. "*Thank* you!" Norah looked daringly at her guardian. "Can we roll up the rug for dancing?"

"I suppose so," smiled Aunt Florence. "But leave sitting space for the adults."

She and Aunt Mary began to pack a trunk for Norah. Every day Aunt Florence brought something home for her. "I want you to be the best-dressed girl in Ringden." Norah didn't even object that she hadn't picked out the new clothes herself. Gavin was amazed that she and Aunt Florence, now that they were parting, were suddenly so easy with each other.

Aunt Florence hardly paid any attention to Gavin—as if she were putting him off until later. Gavin knew he should be spending as much time as he could with his sister; he wouldn't see her for a long time. But he still couldn't talk to her. And all Norah seemed able to do was to give him the same yearning looks that Grandad did. Gavin kept on avoiding both of them.

His relief at staying in Canada had turned sour. Guilt gnawed at him constantly, as if he had a small wild animal living inside him. He tried to reason the guilt away. If he left he'd make five people miserable—Aunt Florence, Aunt Mary, Hanny, Tim and Roger. Not to mention Bosley. By staying he was only hurting Norah and Grandad. And surely after they left this guilt would disappear. Aunt Florence would focus on him again and he'd be safe.

The reasoning didn't work. He skulked around home and school like a criminal.

"What's eating *you?*" complained Tim, when Gavin snapped at him for accidentally ramming into his bike.

"Quit worrying, Gav," smiled Roger. "He didn't even scratch it."

Roger was blissful these days. His father was back and every afternoon Roger ran home to play chess with him. And Tim had just got a dollar in birthday money. He had endless, gloating discussions about what he'd buy with it.

Gavin scowled at his friends. Why did they have to be so cheerful?

"I get to go on a shi-ip, and you do-on't!" taunted Lucy one morning in the schoolyard.

"I don't *want* to go," retorted Gavin. "I'd rather stay in Canada."

"But you're English, not Canadian!" said Lucy. "The Milnes don't think it's right that Mrs Ogilvie is keeping you here."

"She's not keeping me! I *chose* to stay!"

"Well, I think you should come back with us. We all came over together—we should leave together, too. I can hardly wait to see my family." She looked at Gavin curiously. "Of course, it's different for you when your parents aren't there any more. But don't you want to see Ringden again?"

"Just leave me alone!" Gavin turned his back on her, only to face Eleanor.

"I'm having a birthday party this Sunday, Gavin," she said. "Would you like to come?"

"I don't go to parties with girls," he answered stiffly.

"Then don't come!" She flounced away.

Why had he said that? It was as if someone else had said it.

Then he found out that Eleanor had asked Tim and Roger too. They pretended to be scornful but Gavin could tell they were pleased. Only six boys, including Gavin, had been invited. It was the first mixed party in grade five.

"*I* wouldn't go to a sissy girls' party," Gavin told his friends at recess. Maybe he could change their minds.

"I'm only going because Tim's going," Roger protested.

"And I'm only going because Eleanor's mother is such a great cook!" said Tim. "Remember that cake she brought last year?"

"You're going because you're *sissies,*" pronounced Gavin. "A musketeer wouldn't go."

Roger turned pale. "If you feel like that, maybe we shouldn't be blood brothers any more. Right, Tim?"

"Right!" muttered Tim. There were hurt tears in his eyes. The two of them left Gavin standing alone.

He kicked at the dirt. *Now* what had he done? In only a few minutes he had alienated his best friends.

I don't care, he told himself.

"Hey, Stoakes." Mick was slouched by the bike stand, watching him. "Come over here."

Mick was back to his cruel self these days; Doris had laughed at him in front of her friends. Once again, everyone stayed out of his way.

But Gavin made his feet walk over. He met Mick's eyes and tried to sound cool. "Yeah?"

Mick's ugly mouth sneered. "Wanna make a few fast bucks?"

"How?"

"I have a plan, but I need someone to help me with it. If you do I'll give you a share of the profits."

"What is it?" whispered Gavin.

"Meet me here after school and I'll tell you."

For the rest of the day Gavin wondered if he would. Mrs Moss scolded him for forgetting his blackboard monitor duties. When he said sullenly, "It wasn't just *my* fault. Marit forgot too," she frowned at him. "That's not like you, Gavin. You know Marit was sick for half the week." Gavin almost wished she'd keep him after school so he wouldn't have to meet Mick, but she just looked disappointed and told him to fill the inkwells.

When he came to Eleanor's desk she deliberately shoved his arm. Blue ink splattered over the desk, Gavin and Eleanor, and the floor. The class snickered.

Then Mrs Moss was really cross. "Gavin! What's wrong with you this week?"

"It was Eleanor's fault," Gavin tried to tell her, but she made him get a wet rag from the janitor and clean up every spot.

By tattling on both Marit and Eleanor, Gavin had broken the most sacred class rule. For the rest of the day no one spoke to him. He remembered when the class had acted like this towards snooty Colin. Now he knew how Colin must have felt. Hurt. *Angry.*

If no one in 5A liked him any more, then he might as well do what Mick wanted.

After school he waited by his bike, watching Tim and Roger get on theirs and ride away without a word. All the other bicycles were gone by the time Mick appeared.

His leering face actually looked pleased. "So you came. I had to write stupid lines, or I would have been here sooner. Follow me. I'll explain on the way."

Gavin didn't dare ask where they were going. He walked his bike and tried to keep pace with Mick's long legs. He hoped no one noticed him. And he hoped that this wouldn't take too long. He was supposed to report home first before he went anywhere after school, and it was already late.

"Okay, here's the deal." Gavin had to strain to hear Mick's low voice. "You know Sullivan's Hardware on Yonge Street?"

"Uh-huh."

"There's an old dame who works in there. I want you to go and chat her up while I look over the goods."

"What do you mean?" asked Gavin.

Mick looked impatient. "Women *like* kids like you, Stoakes. They think you're cute. So go in there and talk to her. Ask her for something and get her into a long conversation. In the meantime I'll stash one of those expensive fishing reels in my pocket. Don't stop talking until after I've left the store. Then just go home. I'll sell the reel—I know a guy who'll buy it—and I'll give you, say, a third of the price, okay?"

Gavin stopped walking. "But that's stealing!"

Mick glared at him. "*Yes,* Mister Goody-Goody, it's stealing. But I'm the one who's doing it, so you don't have to worry your pretty head about it. All you have to do is sweet-talk the lady for a few minutes and you'll get some cash." He sniggered. "After all, I sort of owe you, don't I?"

Was he right? Was it only Mick who would be stealing? Gavin *pretended* he was right. A sick kind of excitement filled him, replacing the guilt.

Why not do something wrong for a change? Everyone—Aunt Florence, Aunt Mary, Mrs Moss—thought Gavin was good. But he wasn't. He was letting his sister go away without him.

He reminded himself of what Mick had done to Roger. But a reckless voice inside him said, "I don't care."

"So, do you have enough guts to do it?" asked Mick. "Or are you as yellow as you look . . . ?"

"I'll do it," said Gavin quickly.

Mick slapped him on the back and looked friendly again. "Good for you, Stoakes!"

"But what if you get caught?"

"I've *never* been caught," boasted Mick, making Gavin wonder how many other times he had stolen something. "But if I am, just pretend you weren't with me. I'm the one who's taking the risk. *You* have nothing to lose."

They turned up Yonge Street. "So, kid . . ." said Mick, in an interested voice.

Gavin looked at him with surprise. "Yeah?"

"So how do you like being an orphan?"

Gavin shrugged.

"I'm an orphan, too, you know. My folks were killed in a car accident in Nova Scotia."

"When?"

"Five years ago. I lived with my grandfather but he died too. So I had to move to this rotten city and live with my aunt. All she does is holler at me and she never gives me any money."

"Oh." Why was Mick telling him all this? Mick looked as if he wondered too. He spat on the sidewalk. Gavin worked up some saliva in his mouth and spat too. Mick gave him a sudden, warm grin.

They reached Sullivan's Hardware. Gavin had often noticed it when he'd gone to the library, but he'd never been inside. Mick ordered him to park his bike by the door. Gavin needed more time to think, but Mick shoved him inside.

Just as Mick had said, an older, white-haired woman was sitting on a stool behind the counter. She looked up from her knitting and smiled at Gavin. "Hello, dear."

"Hello," Gavin squeaked, trembling so much he could hardly answer. But his fear made her warm to him.

"Don't be shy. May I help you?"

"I want—" Why hadn't Mick given him enough time to think of something? Gavin looked around desperately at the tool displays and lawn mowers. Behind the counter were dozens of open bins full of nails and screws.

"I need some... nails," he said.

"What kind of nails, dear? As you can see, there are lots of sizes."

"Umm... about this long." Gavin held his hands a little way apart. The woman laboriously got down from her stool and picked some nails out of a bin. Gavin could hear Mick entering quietly behind him. "This size?"

"Those are a bit too long." Gavin made her go back three times to pick another size. But the old woman was wheezing so much he couldn't ask her again.

"These are okay," he said. He paused. Out of the corner of his eye he could see Mick prowling the fishing section.

"I need them for my costume," he said wildly.

"And what costume is that?"

"There's a costume parade on the last day of school."

"That sounds like fun. Do you go to Poplar Park?"

"No, Prince Edward. I'm going to the parade as—as Sir Launcelot, so I need to make a sword." Suddenly inspired, Gavin added, "My dog, Bosley, is going as my horse."

The woman laughed. "Bosley! That's a funny name."

Now Gavin had no trouble talking to her, for he no longer needed to lie. He chatted easily about how Bosley had been already named when he got him, and how he had been a borrowed dog but now belonged to Gavin permanently. When the woman found out he'd come over as a war guest she asked him the usual questions about how he liked Canada. "I suppose you'll be going home soon," she said.

"Actually, I'm staying in Canada. That's why I get to keep Bosley. My parents were killed in the war so the family I've been living with is adopting me."

Her kind eyes filled with pity. "You poor dear! What a lot you've been through!"

Gavin suddenly realized that Mick had left the store. "Um, I have to go now," he said, turning to leave.

"But what about your nails?"

"Oh, yes." Gavin dug in his pockets, then flushed. "I'm sorry—I forgot my money. I'll come back for the nails later."

"It's such a small amount." The woman smiled. "Take them now, dear, then you can get started on your sword. You can come back tomorrow and pay me—you look like an honest little boy."

"No, that's okay." Gavin tried not to run out. Once he was outside he took a deep breath to steady his lurching stomach. He hopped on his bike and rode home as fast as he could.

"Gavin! Where have you been?" asked Aunt Mary as soon as he came into the hall.

"I—I had to stay after school again," mumbled Gavin.

"But you should have phoned and told us, the way you usually do!"

"I'm sorry. Please don't tell Aunt Florence."

Aunt Mary looked grave. "All right. But it's not like you to be naughty. And I'm worried about how many times you've been kept after school this term. Is something wrong?"

Gavin shook his head and escaped to his room. "Naughty" sounded so tame. Stealing and lying weren't naughty; they were *wrong*.

All the same, he was filled with a strange, defiant exhilaration. He and Mick hadn't been caught, and he'd done the most daring deed in his life. He'd been as brave as a knight, he thought proudly, the way he'd talked to that woman without faltering. Wait until he told Tim and Roger! Then he sighed. Tim and Roger weren't speaking to him.

He wondered if Mick really would give him some of the money. If he did, Gavin would buy a whole lot of comics and gum and invite Tim and Roger over to share them. Maybe then they could be blood brothers again.

XIV
HOT WATER

Gavin sat in class the next afternoon colouring a map of the British Isles. "Make England red, Wales purple, Scotland yellow, the Irish Free State green and Northern Ireland orange," Mrs Moss instructed.

Why those particular colours? wondered Gavin. Ordinarily he would have asked the teacher, but now he just filled in England with his red pencil crayon. Colouring was soothing, like being back in grade one.

He was especially careful when he got to the area where Kent was. A year this summer he'd be visiting Norah there. He'd be eleven and a half then and going into grade seven, maybe to a fancy boys' school. Norah would be sixteen! Would she look the same?

Someone knocked on the door and Mrs Moss took a piece of paper from a messenger. She read it and looked up. "Gavin... Mr Evans would like to see you in his office."

Gavin froze. The whole class stared at him, the way it always did when someone was in trouble.

"Run along, Gavin," said Mrs Moss gently. "He probably wants to talk about your staying next year. Carry on with your work, everyone."

Gavin forced his legs to stand up and take him out the door. Maybe Mrs Moss was right, he thought frantically.

His steps resounded on the wooden floor. The office

seemed miles away, unlike the time he had sped along the same corridor to announce the end of the war.

When he reached the outer office his slender thread of hope snapped. Mick was sprawled on the bench where you waited to see the principal.

Gavin sat down beside him, his pulse pounding in his throat. "Hi, Mick," he whispered.

"Shut up, Stoakes," Mick growled. "Just remember—we were each on our own."

Gavin didn't have time to think or reply. The secretary came out of the inner office and said, "Mr Evans will see you both now."

She closed the door behind them. They had to stand side by side in front of the principal's desk. He sat behind it, leaning back in his chair, his usually absent-minded face intent with anger.

"I've called the two of you in to discuss an incident that occurred in Sullivan's Hardware after school yesterday. Mrs Sullivan noticed a fishing reel missing after two boys had been in the store. She said the younger boy talked to her while an older boy came in. The younger boy said he went to Prince Edward School."

How could I be so *stupid?* thought Gavin.

Mr Evans cleared his throat and leaned forward. "She also said that the younger boy was a war guest. Therefore I have no doubt at all that the boys were you two. Gavin, you are the only war guest of that age left in this school and Mick, you're rather accomplished at this sort of escapade, are you not? What I *don't* know is whether this was a set-up. It certainly looks like it. But I find it very hard to believe, Gavin, that a boy like you would do such a thing. Did you? Or did you just happen to be in the store the same time as Mick... ?"

Gavin could say that. He knew Mr Evans would believe him—he *wanted* Gavin to be innocent. Although the principal was remote, he had always been kind.

Gavin remembered the friendly way Mick had talked to him on the way to the store, and how Mick was an orphan like he was. He remembered a phrase he had heard once: "honour among thieves." He knew Mick wouldn't tell on him.

But why should Mick get all the blame?

"Well, Gavin, I'm waiting."

Gavin hung his head. "Yes, sir. I—I helped Mick steal the fishing reel."

"I'm deeply shocked, Gavin." He turned to Mick. "Do you admit to this crime?"

"I have to, don't I?" muttered Mick. "Now that he's squealed on me."

Gavin gasped. That wasn't what he'd meant to do!

"This is the last straw for you, Mick," said the principal. "You are out of this school. I've given you enough chances. I don't want your kind here to influence younger boys. Go and wait outside. Your aunt will be here shortly. *And* a policeman. We'll talk again when they both arrive."

Mick slouched out. Gavin tried to catch his eye. I'm sorry! he wanted to plead. Then he looked at Mr Evans and began to tremble.

"You're in very hot water, young man. Sit down over there." Gavin sat in the chair Mr Evans waved to. Was he going to have to see the policeman too? Would he be put in jail?

Mr Evans seemed to read his mind. "You're lucky, Gavin, that you're not going to be involved with the police as well," he said sternly. "But you have such an unblemished record that they said I could deal with you myself."

Gavin waited to be dealt with. But instead of being stern,

Mr Evans's voice became kind—so kind that Gavin's tears spilled over.

"I know you've had a difficult time this term," said the principal. "Your parents' death and your guardian's decision to adopt you must have disrupted you considerably. But do you understand what a terrible thing it is that you've done?"

On and on went his tired, disappointed voice. "Yes, sir," whispered Gavin at intervals. He wanted to sink into the floor with shame. Sir Launcelot or a musketeer or the Shadow would never have stolen—*or* betrayed someone. On the radio the Shadow always said that crime didn't pay—he was right. Gavin promised never to steal again. He apologized tearfully over and over until Mr Evans seemed satisfied.

"All right. I believe you, and I know that you would never have done it if Mick hadn't put you up to it. However..." Mr Evans's voice was stern again. The principal was pulling open a drawer in his desk, the drawer that every boy in the school dreaded...

"You know that I can't let you get away with this without punishment, Gavin. Stand up, please, and hold out your hand."

Gavin didn't think he *could* stand up, his legs were so wobbly. His hand shook just as much. Mr Evans came around the desk holding the strap. Gavin had never seen it but it was familiar from other boys' descriptions: thick, black and rubbery, about the length of a ruler.

He was hit six times on each palm. His hand sunk under the force of each blow, but Gavin knew you were supposed to bring it up again on your own, or else the principal would hold your wrist. Finally it was over. Gavin couldn't stop blubbering as he frantically rubbed his stinging palms against the sides of his pants.

"All right," said Mr Evans gruffly. "Go to the boys' washroom until you've calmed down. Then go back to your classroom. I'm going to have to phone Mrs Ogilvie and tell her about this. But I don't want to hear that you've talked to anyone else about it, do you understand? The matter is closed."

Outside the office Mick was sitting beside a sour-looking woman and a grave policeman. Gavin scuttered past them, hanging his head to hide his tears.

He rushed into the boys' washroom, sat in a cubicle and sobbed. Then he held his flaming, puffy hands under cold water until they felt a bit better. He splashed water on his face too and slowly walked back to the classroom.

After you got the strap you were supposed to grin while you swaggered back to your seat. Gavin couldn't manage it. Everyone murmured with surprise when they noticed his hands. "Back to work, class," said Mrs Moss, but she looked as shocked as the rest of them. Gavin bent over his map but his throbbing fingers couldn't grasp the pencil crayon.

At recess he was surrounded. "What did you *do*?" they all asked.

Gavin reddened. "I'm not allowed to say."

"How many times?"

"Six on each hand."

"Wow… the most I've ever had is three," said Tim. "Meet Roger and me after school, okay?" he added in a whisper.

"Okay," said Gavin gratefully.

When they lined up to go in Eleanor came over and demanded to look at his hands. "Strapping's so mean!" she shuddered. "And it's not fair that only the boys in this school get the strap when the girls don't. Are you *sure* you don't want to come to my party, Gavin?"

"I'll come," said Gavin, trying to return her smile.

Mrs Moss kept him after school for a few minutes. "I've heard all about it, Gavin," she said quietly. "I'm sorry you had to be punished. I think you know that Mick has been permanently suspended."

"What will happen to him?" asked Gavin.

"He'll go to a special school." Mrs Moss sighed. "Maybe they can help him."

It's my fault he had to go, Gavin thought. But it wasn't really. Mick would likely have been caught even if Gavin hadn't squealed; if not for this incident, for something else.

He would probably never see Mick again. He thought once more of the strange bond between them on the way to the store.

On the way home Gavin told Tim and Roger a condensed version of the robbery. He knew he could trust them not to tell anyone else.

"I can't believe you did it!" said Tim, half-horrified and half-admiring.

"Why did you?" said Roger. He seemed more certain than Tim of the enormity of Gavin's crime.

"I don't know," said Gavin. "I guess I just wanted to see what it was like. But I never will again!" he added sheepishly.

"Want to come over to my house?" Tim asked.

Gavin shook his head. It was a comfort to have his friends back, but now he had to face the music at home. What if Aunt Florence was angry too?

XV
LEAVE ME ALONE

Norah was modelling a new coat for Aunt Florence and Aunt Mary in the den. The three of them greeted Gavin so normally he knew Mr Evans hadn't phoned yet. He decided he might as well tell them first.

Slowly he stuttered out the whole story. Aunt Florence's stout figure shook with fury as she listened. Then she pressed Gavin's wounded palms between her large, plump hands. "How *dare* someone hit you!"

"I didn't think old Evans would ever strap *you!*" said Norah. "Did it hurt a lot?"

Gavin nodded and Bosley put one paw on his knee.

"First thing in the morning I'm going to go to the school and give that man a piece of my mind!" snorted Aunt Florence. "He has no right to hit you! Especially when it was Mick's fault, not yours!"

"Why didn't you *tell* me about Mick?" fumed Norah. "I could have done something about him! Is that who you had to get the money for in December?" Gavin nodded again.

"What money?" demanded Aunt Florence. "What else has this Mick done?"

In a halting voice Gavin told them about the money, then about Roger being left naked in the ravine.

"But you should have told us!" cried Aunt Florence. "You poor little boy, putting up with him all this time!"

"Imagine letting a bully like that stay in the school!

Someone who forces younger boys to help him steal!" shuddered Aunt Mary.

"It's completely unjustified!" said her mother. "Gavin should never have been punished. I'm going to demand that Mr Evans *apologize* to you, pet—to you *and* to me."

"Hold it!" said Grandad. Gavin didn't realize he'd come into the room. "I think we're getting things a little out of proportion here."

"What do you mean?" said Aunt Florence coldly. "Gavin has been *struck!*"

"I heard," said Grandad quietly. "And I'm sorry he has. But listen to me for a minute, Gavin. This is the usual punishment at your school when someone does something wrong, am I right?"

"Yes," whispered Gavin.

"So it seems to me the question is whether or not you deserved to be punished. Do you think you did?"

Gavin gulped at how stern Grandad's eyes looked under their bushy brows. "Yes, sir."

"He *didn't* deserve it!" cried Aunt Florence. "That boy *made* you go along with him, didn't he?"

Gavin started to agree. Then he looked back at Grandad. "No, Aunt Florence. I didn't have to do it."

"But you'd never do such a thing of your own free will!"

"I did, though," said Gavin, wincing at the shocked expression that came into her eyes.

Everyone was quiet while they digested this. "But *why*, Gavin?" Aunt Mary finally asked.

"I don't know. I just... did! I promise I never will again," he said to Aunt Florence.

She bridled. "Well, you may *think* you chose to—to steal —but I don't believe it! That boy brainwashed you! And no child of mine is going to be strapped! I'm still going to ask Mr Evans to apologize to you."

"But—" Gavin could well imagine her marching into the school and giving Mr Evans a "piece of her mind." He'd never be able to face his classmates again.

"I can't let you do that, Ma'am," said Grandad.

Aunt Florence looked as if she hadn't heard properly. "What did you say?"

Grandad's voice was low but angry. "I won't let you embarrass my grandson by saying anything to his principal. In the first place he *isn't* your child—not yet. And you heard what Gavin said. He was wrong. He knew very well what he was doing—he could have refused. I don't believe in hitting children myself, but we have to accept the school's methods. Gavin deserved his punishment. And after school tomorrow he and I are going to that hardware store so he can apologize to the owner."

"He is *not!*" cried Aunt Florence. "Why should he have to suffer any more than he has? He's coming to Mr Evans's office with me first thing in the morning!"

"No!" Gavin wondered who had shouted so loud, then realized it was himself. He glared at Aunt Florence and shook with anger. "I don't *want* you to go to his office, Aunt Florence! Everyone will laugh at me if you go! And Grandad's right—I *did* steal! I'm not always good! I'm *tired* of being good! Stop treating me like a baby! Just—just *leave me alone!*"

He was still shouting, standing in front of her and clenching his fists.

Aunt Florence wilted against the cushions of her chair, as deflated as if he had poked her with a pin.

"Thatta boy, Gavin!" whispered Norah. They all waited for him to continue. But his fury had fallen as quickly as it had risen. "Please, Aunt Florence," he continued wearily. "Please don't say anything to Mr Evans."

"Very well, Gavin," said Aunt Florence stiffly. "If that's what you want, we won't discuss the matter any further." She marched out of the room.

Never, in the whole time since Gavin had known her, had she spoken to him so coldly.

Grandad met Gavin after school the next day. It was raining and the gloomy weather added to Gavin's dread as they approached the hardware store.

"What shall I say to her?" he asked outside the door.

"Just say you're sorry."

"But she might be really mad!"

"I wouldn't be suprised if she was," said Grandad. "Would you like me to come in with you?"

"Yes, please," said Gavin.

He kept as close to Grandad as possible as they went over to the counter. The woman looked up, then frowned.

"So it's you."

"I'm very sorry I helped Mick steal the fishing reel," said Gavin as fast as he could. But his tongue was like a piece of wood and his words came out fuzzily. "It was wrong. I promise I'll never do it again."

"How can you expect me to believe you? And to think I thought you were such an honest-looking boy! I won't be fooled like that again, I'll tell you!" She scowled at both of them. "And who's this?"

"My grandfather," said Gavin, taking Grandad's hand. The skin on it was rough but warm.

"Huh! I bet he's pretty ashamed of you."

"If my grandson says he'll never steal again he won't," said Grandad quietly.

"Don't be so sure." She glared even harder at Gavin. "You'd better be careful you don't end up in reform school like that other boy! Get out of my store! I never want to see you in here again!"

Gavin pulled Grandad out of the store. "She wasn't very nice!" he said when they got outside.

"Well, you weren't very nice to *her*, were you? She's angry because she trusted you and now you've betrayed that trust."

Gavin sniffled and Grandad handed him his handkerchief. "Never mind, old man. You've apologized—that's the most important. You were brave. I'm proud of you." Gavin kept hold of his hand all the way home.

"I'm sorry I shouted at you, Aunt Florence," said Gavin that evening. She hadn't spoken to him all day.

Aunt Florence's voice was remote and sad. "I accept your apology, Gavin. Perhaps I was slightly precipitate."

Gavin didn't know what "precipitate" meant. She didn't call him "pet" the way she usually did. "Pet" *was* an awfully babyish nickname, though . . .

"Give me a kiss and run along, then." She held out her cheek but she didn't add a hug the way she usually did.

After that Aunt Florence did what he'd asked her to—she left him alone. She was as polite and distant to him as if he were a visitor.

Gavin wondered if he really wanted this. It was like standing in a bright open field instead of in a protective forest. He could tell she was still hurt by his words. But surely, after Norah and Grandad left, her old easy affection would return.

All weekend Gavin sat in the study with his grandfather and sister. They were leaving him alone as well; they no longer made him feel pressured to change his mind. Like Aunt Florence, they seemed afraid to upset him.

As usual Grandad and Norah talked about home. Little Whitebull the way it used to be . . . Ringden with its shops, cricket green and surrounding hop-fields . . . various people in the village . . . and, of course, their family. As Gavin listened, faint outlines of these places and people formed in his mind. He didn't know whether he was remembering or imagining.

"I feel sorriest for Tibby," said Grandad, "because most of her things were still in the house. Do you remember the watercolours she used to do, Norah? They were all lost."

"She painted a picture of a cow," said Gavin suddenly. "With brown spots."

"Gavin!" cried Norah with delight. "*I* remember that picture! She painted it for *you!* For your fifth birthday!"

Gavin scrunched up his face to hold onto the memory, but it sank back into his mind as quickly as it had bobbed up.

The next day, though, a few more things came back to him—like a blurry film coming into focus. He remembered the tinkle of the bell in the village shop and the sour smell of the scullery in their house. When he told this to Norah and Grandad they hugged him.

"Oh, Gavin . . ." said Norah, but Grandad gave her a warning glance.

The three of them chatted together quietly, enjoying their fragile new harmony. No one dared mention they only had three weeks left together.

XVI
THE BIRTHDAY PARTY

That Sunday Gavin, Tim and Roger walked slowly along the sidewalk to Eleanor's house.

"*How* many boys are going?" Roger asked again.

Gavin counted on his fingers. "Us three, Jamie, George and Billy."

"And *all* the girls," groaned Tim.

"I don't think I'll come after all," said Roger when they reached Eleanor's house.

Gavin tugged him up the steps by his sleeve. "Come on, Rog. All for one and one for all!" He banged the knocker before Roger could flee.

Mrs Austen stood in the doorway, an apron over her dress. "My, don't you all look spiffy! Let's see... I know Tim from church. Are you Roger?" Roger nodded shyly. She put her hand on Gavin's shoulder. "Then you must be the poor little English boy who lost his parents—Gavin, isn't it? Come and join the others in the living room."

Now Gavin wanted to leave too, but they had to follow Eleanor's mother along the hall.

Fourteen girls were crowded together on one side of the living room, whispering to each other. Jamie, George and Billy sat silently on the other side.

Gavin sneaked a look at Eleanor after they had joined the other boys. Like all the girls she wore a fluffy dress and had a large bow tied on one side of her head. Her dress had tiny pink flowers dotted over it. He had never seen her hair loose before. It waved around her face.

The only sounds were stifled giggles from some of the girls. Eleanor looked as if she wished she hadn't decided to have a mixed party. Gavin tried to catch her eye and reassure her.

Mrs Austen bustled back into the room. "What's all this shyness about?" she cried, with a silly, tinkling laugh. "Let's have a game and break the ice!" She clapped her hands. "Everyone into a big circle!"

They all had to stand in a circle as if they were three years old. Gavin manoeuvred himself so he was next to Eleanor.

"Hokie Pokie!" cried Mrs Austen. "You put your right hand in, you put your right hand out..." She flung her hand in and out in time to the tune. No one sang, and only two girls copied her.

"You put your left hand in..." She faltered, then stopped singing. "I guess you don't know that one. Sit down where you are and we'll play Button, Button."

Mrs Austen reached into her pocket and showed them a small white button. "Now, who wants to be It?"

When no one volunteered, she looked at her daughter. "How about the birthday girl!"

Eleanor blushed. She took the button from her mother and knelt in front of each person in turn. "Button, button, who's got the button?" she muttered, placing her palms together and passing them through each person's praying hands.

Gavin smiled at her when she reached him and she gave him a tiny smile back. Then she opened her hands slightly and let go of the button. He pressed his palms against it tightly.

"Can anyone guess who has it?" asked Mrs Austen.

"Gavin," said Tim accusingly. He must have seen their exchanged smiles.

Gavin opened his hands to reveal the button.

"Good for you, Tim! Now you're It."

Gavin grinned as poor Tim had to touch each of the girls' hands. He knew he would give the button to Roger; but he didn't want to guess and have to be It next. Everyone else refused to guess too.

Mrs Austen sighed. "Well, if you're tired of Button, Button, I have another game. Don't go away!" She hurried out of the room and returned with a tray filled with small objects. "Kim's Game! I'll give you five minutes to memorize the contents."

This was better; they could separate into boys and girls again while they examined the tray. Gavin had always been good at Kim's Game. He concentrated hard: an apple, a pair of scissors, a china cat, a handkerchief...

Mrs Austen took the tray away and they each tried to remember its contents. Roger got them all and won a small bag of candy.

"Now that was really fun!" said Mrs Austen, flushed with success. "How about London Bridge?"

"Please, Mum," begged Eleanor. "Can't we stop playing games and open the presents?"

Mrs Austen looked disappointed. "No more games? All right, then, sweetheart."

They sat on the floor around Eleanor while each person handed a present to her in turn. The girls all began talking as if they were by themselves, oohing and ahhing at the hair ribbons, necklaces, small dolls and ornaments that Eleanor unwrapped. The boys sat forgotten at the edge.

"Why do girls like such boring stuff?" whispered George. "My mother bought her a pincushion!"

"Mine got her a comb and brush set," said Tim scornfully.

Gavin smiled to himself. He had chosen Eleanor's present himself: a copy of his favourite book, *Lassie Come Home*.

"Thanks, Gavin!" Eleanor looked over at him when she had unwrapped it. "I've seen the movie but I've never read the book."

"The book's just as good," he assured her.

Mrs Austen stood at the door. "Everyone into the dining room!"

"At last!" whispered Tim.

Eleanor blew out the eleven candles dotted over the large chocolate cake. Mrs Austen helped her cut it and passed cake and ice cream to everyone.

"Have you all had enough?" she asked after second and third helpings. They looked up from their scraped plates and grinned at her.

"Now you can go back into the living room and amuse yourselves until it's time to go home," said Mrs Austen. She looked relieved as they filed out.

Once again the girls and boys sat on separate sides of the room. But their full stomachs made them relax. Jamie let out a noisy belch and everyone laughed. Suddenly they acted ordinary, as if they were in the classroom.

"Do your blushing trick, Tim," said Sylvia.

Everyone watched Tim while a slow pink wave ascended from his neck to his forehead.

"How do you *do* that?" asked Wendy.

Tim shrugged. "I don't know. I've always been able to do it."

"Hey, can anyone do this?" Billy bent his fingers backwards. "I'm double-jointed," he boasted.

Then George showed them how he could make his arms rise on their own by standing in the doorway, pressing his wrists against each side of it, then letting go. Everyone had to try.

"Can we see your monkey, Eleanor?" asked Corinne.

They followed Eleanor to her room where Kilroy crouched in a cage, glaring at them with beady black eyes.

"He's mad because he's locked up," said Eleanor.

Gavin looked curiously around her room. There were the usual girls' things—dolls and frilly curtains—but he noted with approval that she had a microscope and many of the same books that he had.

"Let's play Murder In the Dark!" suggested Charlotte.

"It's not dark enough," said Eleanor.

"How about Sardines?" said Lizzie. "I'll be It. Is it all right if I go anywhere in the house?"

"Anywhere but the kitchen," said Eleanor. "Then we won't bother Mum."

Lizzie ran out to hide. The rest of them sat on the bed and the floor in Eleanor's room, counting to one hundred in unison. Then they fanned all over the house to search for her.

Gavin tried the basement, the den and the living room before he heard faint giggling coming from Eleanor's parents' bedroom. He ventured in and discovered Lizzie, Charlotte, Jamie and Frances under the bed. He squished in with them and stifled his laughter while they watched Tim's feet come into the room and go out again.

By the time ten of them were crammed under the bed they were giggling so much that the rest had no trouble finding them—except for Tim. When he was the only one left they screamed his name until he came back into the bedroom. "But I *looked* in here!" he grumbled.

"Charlotte's It," said Lizzie. "She was the first one to find me."

"What's all this?" Mrs Austen came into the bedroom. "Now, Eleanor, I really don't think you need to be in here. If you all go back into the living room I'll bring you some ginger ale."

Everyone sprawled in friendly comfort in the living room, gulping down the welcome drink.

"Do you know who I saw the other day?" asked Marit. "Miss Wright! She was in Woolworth's and guess what she was buying—an eraser!"

They all shrieked with laughter. Old Miss Wright had been their grade three teacher. Every day she had confiscated someone's eraser and a rumour had started that she ate them after school.

"Do you think we'll get Miss Mackay or Miss Hood next year?" asked Shirley.

"Miss Hood's *really* mean," shuddered Frances.

"Maybe we won't get either of them," said Eleanor. "Mrs Moss told me there'll be a bunch of new teachers next year, especially for the older grades—men who've come back from the war."

"A man teacher! That'ud be swell!" said Tim.

"Did you know that soon we'll have *television* in Canada?" asked Meredith.

"I know about television," said Roger timidly. It was the first time he'd spoken. "Everyone will have a screen in their living room with sound and pictures."

"My mother says it won't last," said Jean. "You have to look at it all the time. You can't do other things, like when you're listening to the radio."

"And you have to make the room really dark," said Wendy.

"And the screen's really tiny," said Gloria. "Why would anyone want to watch a tiny little screen when you can go to the movies? Did anyone see *The Three Caballeros?*"

Gavin leaned against a chair, listening to the chatter. They were all friends with him again. Most of them had been in his class since grade one. Now that he was staying in Canada, they'd be in his class next year as well.

"I have an idea," said Sylvia. "Let's dance!"

"Dance?" cried some of the girls with excitement.

"Dance?" said Tim in horror.

"Okay," said Eleanor. "My sister has lots of records, and we just got one of those automatic record players." She went over to it and in a few seconds Doris Day was crooning "Sentimental Journey."

Sylvia drew the curtains and turned off the lights. Some of the girls retreated to a corner, but others looked determined. "Come on, Jamie. Come on, Billy." They dragged the boys into the middle of the room and pulled them around in the dim light.

Gavin backed away from Meredith and quickly turned to Eleanor. "Would you like to dance?"

In a few minutes even Roger was dancing. The other girls danced with each other, giggling as someone stepped on a clumsy foot.

Gavin steered Eleanor carefully. He had practised dancing every summer with the older cousins at Gairloch. "You're good!" whispered Eleanor as someone put on "There, I've Said It Again."

"Isn't there something faster?" complained Joyce, but Gavin was glad he could still hold onto Eleanor. Her hand was soft and she smelled like Ivory soap.

Mrs Austen hurried in. "Dancing! Don't you think you're too young for that? It's time to go, anyway. Mrs Anthony is here to pick up Jean and here comes Mr Everett up the walk."

Gavin and Roger and Tim walked home, past lawns sparkling with greenness in the hot June air.

"That wasn't *too* bad," admitted Roger.

"The grub was super!" said Tim. He'd stuffed his pockets with peanuts and they nibbled them as they walked.

Gavin just smiled, thinking of how Eleanor's hair had brushed against his cheek.

XVII
THE FAREWELL PARTY

Mrs Moss gave up on regular lessons for the last few days of school. Instead 5A listened to her read *Tom Sawyer.* They also helped clean the classroom, by taking down the maps, perfect spelling papers and drawings pinned up on the walls and sweeping out and scrubbing the ledges, floors and desks.

On the last afternoon Mrs Moss stood in front of them holding a sheaf of white cardboard. "I'm happy to tell you that everyone has been promoted to grade six," she smiled. She passed out the report cards in order. Eleanor, as usual, was first, then Roger.

The class examined the report cards as Mrs Moss poured out glasses of lemonade. Gavin had good marks in English and socials but he only got 61 in arithmetic. He was afraid to look at conduct, but to his relief he got a B. Underneath Mrs Moss had scribbled, "Gavin has bravely overcome the difficulties he's had to endure this term. We are delighted he will be back with us for the next school year." She didn't say anything about him getting the strap.

Gavin looked up at his teacher, as she merrily chatted with the girls who were helping her pass out cookies. If he were marking *her,* she'd get all A's.

After the treats were finished and the empty glasses collected, each pupil waited to be released.

"You'll always remember this school term," said Mrs

Moss. "The term the war ended. Now it's up to your generation to grow up and make a world where there *aren't* any wars."

There was a solemn silence while the class digested this. Mrs Moss looked apologetic. "What long faces! You don't have to do it *yet.* Enjoy being young first! I've liked teaching you very much," she continued. "I hope you all have a wonderful summer and come back ready to work hard in the fall."

Tim writhed with impatience. "Three cheers for Mrs Moss!" he shouted. He jumped to his feet and everyone else followed. "Hip Hip *Hooray!* Hip Hip *Hooray!* Hip Hip *Hooray!*"

"Thank you!" Then at last came the phrase they'd been longing for. "All right... you may go."

Everyone rushed out the door, lugging book bags and calling back goodbyes to Mrs Moss.

Mr Evans smiled at Gavin, Tim and Roger as they passed him in the hall. "All ready for your holiday, boys?"

"Yes, sir," they mumbled, slowing their run to a walk. Gavin avoided the principal's eyes. He would never be able to forget what nice Mr Evans had done to him.

A chant echoed all over the playground:

No more pencils
No more books!
No more teacher's
Dirty looks!

"What are you doing this summer, Gavin?" Eleanor stood by the bike stands as Gavin tried to fit his bulging schoolbag into his basket.

"We're going to the cottage like we always do," said

Gavin. "But this year we have to wait until after..." He swallowed. "Until after my sister and my grandfather go back to England."

"When's that?"

"July the thirteenth."

Eleanor glanced at Tim and Roger approaching and said quickly, "I'll be in Toronto all of July. Maybe you could come over before you go to the cottage."

"Maybe," said Gavin. "See you, then."

"See you." She rushed away to join her friends.

"What did *she* want?" said Tim.

"Oh . . . she just wondered what I got in English," said Gavin.

"She always beats me in that," muttered Roger. "If it wasn't for English, *I'd* have the highest marks."

Their bags were so heavy they had to walk their bikes, balancing the loads on their handlebars.

"This is the fourth best day of the year," pronounced Tim. "First is Christmas, then your birthday, then Hallowe'en—then today! Let's ride our bikes to Hogg's Hollow tomorrow."

"We're leaving tomorrow," Roger reminded him. He and his parents were going to stay with relatives in Collingwood for July. Roger's father had been told to take a complete rest. "He wakes up at night shouting," Roger had told them. "He dreams he's still fighting. And sometimes he just sits in a chair for hours, not saying anything." He looked as anxious as he had before his father returned.

"I guess we won't see you until September, then," Gavin told Roger as they neared the corner.

"I guess not. Have a good summer. 'Bye!"

"I'll come over tomorrow after breakfast," Tim told Gavin.

After they separated they each turned around and shouted, "All for one and one for all!"

On Dominion Day Gavin and Tim went to see *Son of Lassie* at Loew's. Gavin had been longing to see it but he couldn't pay attention. All he could think of was Norah leaving.

Ten more days, ten more days . . . The refrain pounded relentlessly in his head. A week from Friday Norah and Grandad would go to Union Station to catch the train to Montreal. They'd stay overnight with the Montreal relatives, then continue to Quebec City, where they would board a ship called the *Strathern* for Liverpool.

"Are you all right, Gavin?" asked Aunt Mary a few days later. She sat down on the stairs beside him. He had moped there since breakfast, staring at Norah's trunk packed and ready in the hall. Today it was going to be picked up and shipped ahead of her.

Gavin shrugged, and Aunt Mary put her arm around his shoulder. "Even though we've been prepared for this for so long, I still can't believe the time has almost come."

They were quiet for a few minutes. "You can still change your mind if you want to," said Aunt Mary softly.

Gavin looked at the trunk. It stood near the closet he used to play in when he was younger, pretending that the late Mr Ogilvie's canes were horses. The silver bowl on the side table and the red Persian carpet glowed in a beam of sunlight. Very soon the trunk would be taken away from this peaceful hall that smelled of roses. It would start its long journey to an unknown country. "No!" he shuddered.

Aunt Mary pulled him closer. "As long as you're sure. *I* certainly don't want to lose you—not you as well as Norah." She sighed. "Soon you and I and Mother and Hanny will be at Gairloch. That will cheer us up."

"And Bosley," whispered Gavin, as the dog nudged his knee. "You'll be glad to get to Gairloch, too, won't you boy?" Bosley had been lying sadly by the trunk all week.

"Where *is* Norah?" asked Gavin. "I haven't seen her all morning."

"She went downtown with Mother to buy a new dress for the party."

At least getting ready for the party gave them all something to do. Hanny and Aunt Mary spent hours in the kitchen. Gavin helped Norah move back the furniture and roll up the rugs.

"I hope Paige remembers all her records," she said. How could she think about records at a time like this?

Aunt Florence continued to be distant with Gavin, but she put on such a good act of being affectionate that no one but Gavin knew how much she'd changed. Norah and Grandad, on the other hand, could scarcely let Gavin out of their sight. Grandad took him to Centre Island for the day and Norah even dragged him over to Paige's with her. Now they talked about what they'd do when Gavin visited England next summer.

"We'll go to Camber, of course," said Grandad. "Wait until you see the beach—miles and miles of sand! When you were a little tyke you used to bury me in it."

A dim memory of holding a tin pail and shovel tugged at Gavin's mind—then let go.

"Andrew is coming to visit me for sure!" Norah told them. "I sent him Muriel's address. He says he has a surprise—for all of us! You'll probably see him at Christmas, Gavin."

Grandad went upstairs for more tobacco. "Norah, what will happen with you and Andrew?" blurted out Gavin.

"What do you mean?"

"Will you—will you *marry* him?" He shivered. If Norah had to live so far away, he wanted her to stay exactly the same.

Norah grinned in the carefree way she used to before their parents' death. "Marry him! I'm only fifteen!"

"But I thought..."

She blushed. "I know I told you I loved Andrew. But I was different... then. Now I don't expect anything from him. I still like him a lot. But he's probably changed—just like I have. I'm just going to wait and see how I feel when I see him."

Grandad came back and began telling them how he planned to add a new room to the house. "For you, old man," he smiled. "It will always be there for your visits."

"When you come next summer I'll show you where I saw a crashed German plane," said Norah.

How could they chatter on so cheerfully, when they were going to leave so soon? Then Gavin heard the pain in their voices. They were only pretending to be cheerful; pretending for him.

The family sat in the living room, waiting for the guests to arrive. The house was spotless and the dining-room table was heaped with food and drink. It was a hot night and Gavin's short wool trousers itched. Norah looked much older than fifteen in her new yellow-and-white polka dot dress and bright lipstick. Even Grandad was dressed up, in a clean shirt and a blue tie. He fanned his sweating face with the evening paper. With an exasperated look at Aunt Florence, he fingered his empty pipe.

"I can't believe you'll only be with us for five more days, Norah!" said Aunt Mary, fumbling for her handkerchief.

Aunt Florence frowned at her. "Now, Mary, none of that. Here's someone arriving," she added with relief.

Paige and her sisters and parents filled the hall. "Do you want me to show you how to do a Chinese burn?" Daphne whispered to Gavin. "I take your arm and..."

"No!" he said, backing away from her. If only she were Eleanor. Aunt Mary had asked him if he wanted to invite his friends, but he'd shaken his head. After all, the party wasn't for him.

More and more people filled the house. It was just like after the memorial service—but now everyone was laughing instead of acting solemn. Gavin scowled. Why were they all so cheerful? Norah and Grandad were *leaving*—that wasn't a reason to celebrate!

The adults—friends of the Ogilvies and a few of Norah's teachers—sat on the furniture around the edge of the living room. Teen-agers danced on the cleared space in the middle. When there was a slow dance some of the adults got up and joined it.

Gavin tried the jitterbug with Norah and the foxtrot with Aunt Mary. Daphne and Lucy kept asking him to dance. He refused, but he couldn't shake off Daphne. She followed him everywhere and never stopped talking. Finally he sat nursing a Coke while Daphne stood in front of him, describing in gloating detail how she'd almost been expelled from her school after she filled her teacher's desk drawer with worms.

"I don't know how Paige is going to *exist* without Norah," Mrs Worsley was telling Aunt Mary behind them. "She's wept buckets of tears all week."

"We're hoping Norah can visit Toronto in two years," said Aunt Mary. "We'll go over there first next year, and then she can come here. If we carry on taking turns, at least we'll see her once a year. And that will keep her in touch with Gavin." She lowered her voice. "Sometimes I feel it's wrong, separating them. I know it's what Gavin wants, but I still wonder... I don't know how he's going to bear saying goodbye to his sister."

Gavin ducked his head as the women looked at him. He watched Norah teach Grandad how to jitterbug. The two of them were laughing so hard they could hardly stand up.

How could they laugh?

Gavin glanced back at Daphne; now she was talking to her mother. Very carefully he slipped out of the living room. He tiptoed across the hall, then ran up the carpeted stairs to his bedroom.

Bosley stuck his head out from under the bed. "Poor Boz," said Gavin. "You don't like the party either, do you? I don't blame you. It's a *stupid, boring* party..." He sat on the floor in the dark, leaning against the bed. Bosley emerged all the way and rested his heavy head on Gavin's leg. The party noises floated up from below: talking and laughter and the jaunty melody of "Mairzy Doats."

Tears slipped down Gavin's cheeks. Bosley struggled to his feet and licked them away.

Gavin clutched him. He was all alone . . . except for Bosley. Norah and Grandad were leaving him. But that was his fault. He had chosen to stay in Canada to be safe.

But he didn't *feel* safe any more. The big old house, which had always been such a secure fortress, seemed empty and cold, as if Norah had already left. And Aunt Florence, who had been an even safer haven, had changed. That was his fault, too. He had driven her away with his anger.

Now he heard "Three cheers for Norah, Dulcie and Lucy!" Then the voices began singing "We'll Meet Again."

"Oh, Boz . . ." Gavin squeezed the dog again, but so tightly that Bosley whined in protest and went back under the bed. Gavin crawled in after him. Maybe he'd feel better where it was dark and confined.

He hadn't been under his bed for years. It reminded him of hiding under Eleanor's parents' bed. That time he'd been happy, squashed in with his friends.

Now he just felt silly. His bed wasn't as high as Mr and Mrs Austen's; he could barely raise his head. Bosley watched curiously while Gavin slithered around on the bare floor, trying to get comfortable. Finally he managed to turn over on his back. He stared at the mattress bulging between the springs. His tears dribbled into his ears.

Then he stopped crying. On the far side of the bed, against the wall, a lumpy shape was squished between the spring and the mattress. Gavin slid himself over, reached out his arm, and forced his hand between the wires. He closed it around a small wool form, something he knew very well. As gently as he could he tugged it out—Creature!

He scraped his head in his haste to get out. Then he sat on the edge of the bed, brushing off the dustballs from his worn, stuffed toy elephant.

"Creature . . ." whispered Gavin. The elephant must have been stuck between the mattress and the wall, and worked itself under the mattress when the bed was changed. He stroked Creature's grimy trunk. He looked just the same: both his ears were missing and his tail had worn to a frayed string.

Gavin curled up on the bed, rubbing Creature against his cheek the way he used to when he was little. Creature smelled the same too—a mixture of musty wool flannel and sawdust.

A sharp image came to him, like a movie in his mind. He was sitting in a little room holding his elephant up to his face and sniffing him, the way he was now. Sitting in a high, hard chair, swinging legs that didn't reach the ground, while two grown-ups told him solemnly that he was going with Norah on a ship to Canada.

Mum and Dad. He could *see* them. Mum's tired face struggling with tears and Dad's trying to be cheerful.

" . . . and remember old man," Dad's voice was saying, "whatever happens, I want you and Norah to stick together like glue! Promise?"

"I promise," whispered five-year-old Gavin.

Gavin bounced into a sitting position and tried to remember more. But that was all. The rest was a confused blur of going on a train and a ship and another train, the way it had always been.

But he remembered them! He focused on the scene again—his parents breaking the news to him as they all sat in the front room. There was a faint odour of ammonia in the air, mixing with Creature's smell. Mum wore a faded blue blouse. *Muv . . .* that's what he called her then. Her hands were red and chapped from always washing dishes. Her hair fell into her eyes. Dad had a long nose like Norah's and a warm, reassuring voice. He called him "old man" like Grandad did. Muv called him "pet" like Aunt Florence.

Gavin pressed Creature to his cheek as he held on to the memory-picture. Then his parents' images dissolved. He remembered them—but they were gone. They were dead. He would never see them again.

"*Muv . . .*" Gavin turned over and sobbed into his pillow, still clutching Creature. "Dad . . ."

He cried for a long time, until his insides were light and empty. Then he dried his face on his pillowcase and stumbled to the window. Some of the guests were leaving.

"Goodbye, Norah! Have a safe journey!"

Gavin leaned out the window and the night air cooled his hot cheeks.

"I want you and Norah to stick together . . ."

Finally he knew what to do.

XVIII
WE'LL MEET AGAIN

Gavin had stumbled out of his clothes and fallen into bed and a deep, thick sleep. He woke up all at once, full of energy. It was only six o'clock.

He stuck his head into the hall. Everyone's door was closed and the usual snoring came from Grandad's room. They went to bed last night and forgot about me! he thought indignantly. But maybe he'd already been asleep when they'd come upstairs.

Gavin put on his dressing-gown, put Creature in his pocket, told Bosley to stay, and padded up to Norah's tower. Her new dress was flung over a chair and she was buried under her blankets. It was a shame to wake her, but he couldn't wait.

"Norah!" He touched her shoulder.

She groaned and shook his hand away, burrowing farther in.

"Norah, wake up!"

Norah opened her eyes halfway and gazed blearily at him. "What do you want? What time is it?"

"Six o'clock."

"Six! Go *away* ..."

"*Norah* ..." Gavin giggled as she put her hands over her ears. "Listen, I have to tell you something! It's really important!"

Finally she struggled awake, leaning against the head-board and yawning. "What could be so important at six in the morning?"

Gavin grinned and climbed onto her bed. "Oh, nothing. Just that I'm coming back to England with you..."

"*What?*" She leaned forward and clutched his arm. "Really?"

"Really and truly," he laughed. "I've decided to go back with you and Grandad."

Norah looked stunned. "But you were so sure you wanted to stay here! What made you change your mind?"

Gavin shrugged. "I just did. I can't—I just can't let you go without me. We have to stick together! Like glue! Dad told me that before we left. I promised I would, but I forgot for a while."

"But are you sure you can give up Aunt Florence and Aunt Mary? And your friends, and this house..." Norah looked afraid to believe him.

"I'm sure," he said. "I'm very, very sure. I want to stay with *you.* It's where I belong. And we have to take care of each other, like Muv and Dad asked us to."

"Muv... that's what you used to call her," said Norah softly. "Oh, Gavin..." She hugged him. "Look at me, I'm crying! I was wishing so much you'd change your mind but I'd given up hope! I'm so *happy!*" she said in wonder. "I never thought I'd feel really happy again." She wiped her eyes. "Wait until Grandad hears!"

"Let's tell him!"

The two of them crept hand in hand down the stairs to Grandad's room. "Listen to him snore!" chuckled Gavin.

Grandad woke up quickly. He leaned against his pillows while Gavin told him. Then his old face broke into a wide grin.

"You're coming with us?" he cried. "My dear boy... what wonderful news!" There were tears in his eyes. "You've made a very brave decision, old man."

Old man ... Gavin heard Dad's voice again and smiled at his grandfather.

"I think it's the right decision," said Grandad slowly. His face became serious. "But since I've been here I've seen how much you love the Ogilvies—especially Mrs Ogilvie. It's going to be hard for you to leave them."

Not as hard as leaving *you*, thought Gavin, looking at Grandad and then at Norah.

"England's in a sorry state right now," continued Grandad. "The food is scarce and terrible. You can't buy new clothes or toys. We'll be squashed at Muriel's, then we'll be living in a half-finished house that would fit into the living room of this house. And we don't have much money. You'll have to try for a scholarship to grammar school."

"I don't care!" said Gavin.

"Can you give up all this?" Grandad waved his hand around the room—at the spool bed, ornate wallpaper and mahogany wardrobe. "This fancy house? And the summer one?"

"And you'll have to leave Bosley behind," said Norah gently. "Did you remember that?"

Gavin gulped. Why were they trying to discourage him?

"I know that! Bosley will have to go back and live with Uncle Reg. But he likes Uncle Reg. I know it will be hard—but it won't matter as long as I'm with you. Don't you *want* me to come?" he added tearfully.

"Of course we do!" they cried.

"We just wanted to make sure you'd thought about it carefully," said Grandad. "But I can see that you have. Thank you," he said gruffly. "Thank you for choosing us."

Gavin and Norah climbed onto the bed and sat cross-legged on the foot of it. The three of them beamed at each other.

"Will Gavin be able to get on the same ship?" asked Norah.

"We'll enquire about that first thing on Monday morning," said Grandad. "If he can't we'll cancel our ship and all go together on a later one."

"How am I going to tell Aunt Florence?" shuddered Gavin. "I think she's already mad at me."

"It won't be easy," said Grandad. "But we'll be with you all the way."

Gavin pulled out his elephant.

"Creature!" cried Norah. "Where did you find him?"

"Trapped under the mattress," grinned Gavin.

"I'd forgotten all about your elephant," murmured Grandad. "Your Grannie made him for you when you were born, just before she died. She would be glad you still have him. He's as old as you are! He certainly looks the worst for wear. What happened to his ears?"

"He looks fine!" said Gavin indignantly. Then he laughed with them. "I'm going to keep him forever and ever and give him to *my* children!"

Gavin knew he had to tell Aunt Florence as soon as possible. He decided to wait until after church. All through the service he daydreamed, trying to find the best words. He only paid attention when Reverend Milne asked the congregation to say a prayer for Dulcie, Lucy and Norah. "We have been privileged to have the care of these fine children for the past five years," he said, gazing sadly at Dulcie and Lucy in the front pew. "We wish them a happy future and a safe crossing to England."

"Yeck! How embarrassing!" muttered Norah.

"That prayer is for you as well, Gavin," whispered Grandad.

Then Gavin's favourite hymn was announced: "To Be a Pilgrim." "He who would valiant be / 'Gainst all disaster," he sang out. A pilgrim was sort of like a knight or a musketeer, he decided.

Gavin couldn't eat his lunch. "Are you sick?" asked Aunt Mary.

"I'm not sick." He looked at Aunt Florence. She had touched hardly any of her meal either. "Aunt Florence . . . I need to talk to you in private."

"Very well." Aunt Florence's voice was icy as she and Gavin went into the den and shut the door.

Gavin looked around at the comfortable, cluttered space. So many important things had happened in this room. Their arrival, the news of their parents' death, his decision to stay... He thought of all the evenings he'd spent in here listening to the radio or to Aunt Florence read. Then he remembered the valiant pilgrim and took a deep, steadying breath.

"Well?" Aunt Florence sat down heavily in her favourite deep armchair. Her voice was shaking. Then she looked at Gavin and he realized that she knew what he was going to tell her.

"Aunt Florence... I'm so sorry... but—"

"It's all right, Gavin." He'd never heard her sound so defeated. "You want to go with them, don't you?"

Gavin nodded. How could he hurt someone so much? "How did you know?" he whispered.

"I've seen how you've been clinging to Norah and your grandfather in the past few weeks. I've seen how you've changed. I think I've known ever since the day you got into trouble at school. You've been growing apart from me. I should have encouraged you to talk about it but I just—I just couldn't! Come over here..."

Gavin came closer and she took his hand. "I love you

dearly, Gavin. I hope you know that. You've been like a son to me. But you *aren't* my son. Perhaps I've tried to hold on to you too much."

"You haven't," sniffed Gavin. "You've made me happy."

"I'm glad of that. But you don't need me any more. The war is over. And even though you've lost your parents, it's still right that you go back. It was selfish of me to try to keep you here."

She looked like a tired old woman. "Aunt Florence," whispered Gavin. He pushed into the chair beside her and the two of them sat together in silence.

The next day, after a morning of frantic telephone calls, a space was found for Gavin on Norah and Grandad's ship. Now there were only three days left. Aunt Florence seemed relieved to spend all that time doing Gavin's packing.

Gavin told Bosley he was leaving him. He wasn't sure if Bosley understood his words, but he certainly understood the open suitcases and piles of clothes in Gavin's room. He followed Gavin everywhere, gazing accusingly at him.

"You'll be all right, Boz," Gavin told him. "Uncle Reg loves you just as much as I do." He had read once that dogs didn't have long memories. Bosley would probably forget all about him.

But he'd never forget Bosley.

There was so little time for goodbyes. Some of the family friends who had been at the party dropped by with small gifts for Gavin when they heard. But others didn't even know he was going—Mrs Moss, all the people in his class, and Roger. Gavin thought sadly of how casually he'd said goodbye to Roger when he thought he'd see him again in September. At least there were two people he could say goodbye to in person—Tim and Eleanor.

Tim's face turned red without him willing it to as he stared furiously at Gavin. "But you said you were *staying!*"

"I changed my mind."

"But *why?* You're Canadian, not English! You don't even talk like someone who's English! You said you didn't even remember England!" They were lying on the floor in Tim's room; Tim kicked one of his bedposts.

Gavin sighed. "I know I don't remember it. I don't *want* to leave you and Roger. I don't want to go back, but I have to stay with my family—my real family. Don't you see?"

"I thought the *Ogilvies* were going to be your real family now!"

"I thought so too, but I was wrong."

They lay in silence, Tim's face buried in the rug. Gavin knew he was hiding his tears. "I'll write to you, Tim," he said desperately. "And the summer after next, Norah and I will probably come back for a visit."

"You'll spend it in Muskoka like you always do," Tim muttered into the rug.

"Well, you can come! You and Roger! You can both come up north for the whole summer, okay?"

"I guess so... I like Gairloch." Tim had come for a week last year. "But that's two years away—that's forever!" He looked up at Gavin, tears gleaming on his round face. "All for one and one for all, eh?"

"All for one and one for all *forever,*" said Gavin.

Eleanor was more difficult; he had to lose her just as she was becoming a friend. It would be easier to just leave without telling her. Gavin kept putting off phoning her but he finally made himself do it the day before they left.

"May I please speak to Eleanor?"

"Just a minute—*Eleanor!*" a voice shouted in his ear. Her older sister.

Then Eleanor answered. "Hello?"

"Uh? this is Gavin."

"Hi, Gavin! Are you having a good summer?"

He had meant to tell her on the phone but as soon as he heard her voice he wanted to see her one more time. "Can I come over? Right now?"

"Sure. Why does your voice sound so funny?"

"I'll tell you later."

Gavin ran all the way to her house. His shirt was sticking to his heaving chest by the time he got there.

"Let's go into the back yard," said Eleanor after she answered the door. "Mum made some lemonade."

Gavin drained two glasses of lemonade while Eleanor sat quietly in a chair and watched him.

"So what did you want to tell me?" she asked finally.

He stared at her. Her braids were pinned around her face in a circle. It made her look like a flower.

"I came to say goodbye," he mumbled.

"Oh, you're going up north. But I'll see you in September."

"You *won't!*" said Gavin, close to tears. "I'm going back to England. I decided not to stay in Canada. My sister and grandfather and I are leaving tomorrow."

"Oh." Eleanor's expression didn't change.

"I may come back and visit Canada in a while, though," said Gavin.

"We'll be older then," she said matter-of-factly.

"Uh-huh." Maybe when they were older he'd know how to talk to her more easily. "I'll write you a letter," he said.

"Okay." Eleanor still looked as calm as if Gavin were only going away for the summer.

"So . . . goodbye, then."

She just sat there. Didn't she care at all? "Goodbye," she mumbled, staring at the grass.

Gavin walked away quickly. His legs quivered as he stomped to the front of the house and along the sidewalk.

"Wait!" He was almost at the corner when Eleanor reached him. He turned around and she stood in front of him, trying to catch her breath. One of her braids had come loose. "Good luck, Gavin," she said gravely. "I'll never forget you." She leaned forward and kissed him lightly on the lips. Then she walked away.

Gavin watched her go. Her lips were soft, like tiny cushions, and they tasted of lemonade.

That evening everyone spoke in tender, careful voices, as if afraid the other person would break. Hanny made Norah and Gavin's favourite foods for dinner. Then they sat in the den quietly, listening to a concert on the radio. Every once in a while Aunt Florence or Aunt Mary or Grandad would ask each other if some item or another had been packed.

When the concert was over Gavin fiddled with the radio dial, wondering what the programmes were like in England. Then the door knocker sounded and everyone was relieved when the Worsleys marched in noisily.

"I have a present for you, Gavin," whispered Daphne. Gingerly, Gavin took the small box she handed him. It probably contained something disgusting.

But to his surprise Daphne had given him the jackknife she always carried with her. "It's to protect you in England," she grinned. "You never know what wild animals you'll meet there. You can use it to skin them."

"Thanks, Daphne!" said Gavin. "I'll take good care of it."

When the Worsleys got up to go everyone was crying, especially Paige. "Oh, Norah, I can't bear it! You're the best friend I ever had!"

Norah wiped her own eyes. She took Paige's arm. "I'll walk home with you—then we'll have a little more time."

The rest of them went back into the den. Aunt Florence opened up *Sunshine Sketches of a Little Town* and began to read. She had begun it earlier in the month to try to cheer everyone up. But although the words she was reading were amusing, her voice was not. Gavin stared at her strong face and at Aunt Mary's gentle one.

"Excuse me," he murmured, and slipped from the room. He went into the dim living room and curled up on the window-seat.

Bosley hopped up beside him and collapsed in a silken pile at his feet. Gavin stroked him all over, from his smooth head to the ends of each of his fluffy feet, memorizing every freckle and patch. Bosley rolled over on his back with pleasure and Gavin tickled his stomach in the place he liked best. Then he pulled Creature out of his pocket. He was much too old to carry him around the way he used to, but tonight he needed him.

Glancing out the window, he saw all the streetlights come on together. He had never seen that happen before. It was like that song, "When the Lights Go On Again."

The war was over and the world's lights could shine again. That was good, of course; but the light was cruel as well as hopeful. It exposed all the bad things that had happened in the war—all the suffering. His parents crushed under their house, soldiers dying in the mud . . . and those mysterious, terrible bodies in *Life* magazine.

Gavin shivered. Tomorrow he had to venture into that glaring new world. He had to leave behind the people and places he was so used to—that he loved. Bosley whined, and Gavin kissed the white streak between his eyes. Then he huddled against the warm dog.

He couldn't do it. He would go back into the den and tell them he was staying. In two days he and Bosley could be out in the canoe at Gairloch. He was only ten. How could he be expected to give up so much? He *would* stay.

"Gavin? Are you all right?" Grandad came into the dark room and sat down beside him.

"I'm scared," whispered Gavin.

"That's understandable," said Grandad. "You're leaving everything that's familiar to you. But *what* are you afraid of?"

"Of England—and the war—and people getting killed like Muv and Dad—of everything!"

"The war's all over now, Gavin," said Grandad gently. "You know that."

But England had always meant the horror of war. It was so hard to believe that the horror wouldn't still be there.

"What else are you afraid of?"

"Starting a new school."

"That's scary," agreed Grandad, "but you've always done well and made friends in school here. I don't see why it should be any different in England. It'll *seem* different for a while, but you'll soon get used to it. Anything else?"

Gavin stroked Bosley's head. "Everything ahead is so—so *blank.* I don't know what's going to happen! It's so hard! Having to leave everybody, not knowing what it'll be like."

"Life *is* hard, old man. I'm sorry the war has made you have to find that out so soon. And nobody *ever* knows what's going to happen." He chewed on the end of his pipe. "That's what makes life interesting! I can't tell you there won't be bad times, but I promise you there will be lots of good times too. Think of this as an adventure!"

An adventure... like the pilgrim fighting his giants, or Sir Launcelot setting out on a quest. They were beginning the adventure by going on a ship. And then he'd see his other sisters again, and his new nephew... A small flame of excitement flickered in Gavin.

Maybe Sir Launcelot had to leave people he loved too. Maybe he'd even had a dog. He had to hurt them. But that didn't keep him from his quest.

"Feel better?" said Grandad.

Gavin nodded. "A little. I'm still afraid, though." He sighed. "I'm such a coward, aren't I, Grandad..."

"A coward!" Grandad's moustache quivered. "You listen to me, young man—you're the bravest boy I've ever known! Everyone's afraid. Being brave is going ahead *despite* your fear. It seems to me you've done that all along. Just look at all the difficulties you've faced in this war! You're *not* a coward!"

"Really?" grinned Gavin.

"Really!" Grandad took Gavin's hand. "Let's go back into the den. You can't leave those two alone on your last night."

The train was waiting. Aunt Florence, Aunt Mary, Hanny and Norah were all crying.

Gavin had hugged Bosley for the last time as they were leaving the house. The spaniel would travel up north with the Ogilvies tomorrow, and at the end of the summer he'd go back to Montreal with Uncle Reg. Gavin could still feel the warm, wet touch of his dog's tongue on his face.

A short distance away from them Dulcie and Lucy and the Milnes were also saying tearful goodbyes. "All aboard!" a man's voice called.

Norah kissed Aunt Florence last. "I will miss you *so*

much!" cried Aunt Florence, releasing Norah from a bear hug.

"Thank you for *everything!*" cried Norah, laughing and crying at the same time.

Grandad kissed Aunt Mary's cheek.

"Thank you for lending us your children," she sobbed.

The old man turned to Aunt Florence, hesitated, then firmly kissed her cheek as well. Aunt Florence looked startled, then she gave him a rueful smile. "Thank you from me as well, Mr Loggin," she said quietly.

Gavin was passed from Hanny to Aunt Mary. Then he stood in front of Aunt Florence. "Goodbye," he whispered.

"Oh, my dear, *dear* little boy . . ." She pulled him into a deep, soft embrace and he inhaled the smell of her perfume. She clung to his arms as she held him out and said gruffly, "Be brave and happy, Gavin. We'll see you next summer." Then she let him go.

"Come on, Gavin." Norah took his hand and led him onto the train, just as she had done five years earlier. They found their seats. Grandad lifted their luggage onto the rack as Norah and Gavin leaned out the window, calling and waving to their Canadian family.

"Goodbye! Goodbye!"

"Goodbye! See you next summer!"

Then the train moved out of the station and they began the long journey back to England.

EPILOGUE

September 28, 1945

Dear Aunt Florence, Aunt Mary and Hanny,

Thank you for your last letters. I'm glad Bosley is still okay. Uncle Reg sent me a picture of him. He looks fat! I hope Uncle Reg isn't feeding him too much.

Our house's walls are almost fixed. Grandad and his friends work on it every day. We're going to give the house a new name—Gairloch! When you come next summer it will be finished. And as soon as we move in I'm getting a dog! I've already picked it out—he's part pointer and part retriever. I've named him Kilroy.

Everyone in England rides bikes, even the grown-ups. I am using Norah's old one. It's heavy and black and not nearly as nice as my Canadian bike.

School isn't too bad. There's only six other kids who are ten and only thirty-three in the whole school. We are the oldest age. My teacher's name is Mr Maybourne. He's also the headmaster—that's what they call "principal." He's quite strict and he complains because I'm behind the others. Some of the kids tease me about my accent and call me "Yank." I told them they should call me "Canuck" instead. Joey said I was a coward because

I left England during the war. But another boy called James stuck up for me. Yesterday James came for tea. He likes all my models. You can't buy models in England any more.

Norah goes to school in Ashford. She takes the train. Next year I'll go there too, to a much bigger school where there are only boys. I'll have to wear a uniform like Norah does.

My sisters and Barry are fine. They talk about our parents all the time. Muriel says to tell you she will write soon.

The baby is funny. His hair sticks straight up. I'm trying to teach him to say "Gavin" but he won't.

Andrew came to see us! He looks just the same. He is safe and didn't get any wounds. He gave me a German badge. I'm the only person in the school who has one.

Norah has a boy friend! His name is John. He's sixteen and he goes to school in Ashford too. She met him on the train. Norah and John say they are pacifists and that the Allies shouldn't have dropped the atomic bomb on Japan. I haven't decided about that yet.

Andrew told us he's going to marry a Dutch girl called Alida. She has gone ahead to Canada to stay with his parents. They're going to live in Saskatchewan while he takes acting. I guess you know that.

Andrew and Norah and John and I went to London on the train. We saw Westminster Abbey and Big Ben. We looked for the King at Buckingham Palace but he didn't come out. Lots and lots of the buildings in London were smashed in the war, just like our house. Andrew took us to a fancy restaurant.

He let me have three desserts. Then we said goodbye to him and came back all by ourselves on the train.

Gavin put down his pen and read over what he'd written. There was so much he'd left out. How the puppy he'd picked seemed afraid of him. How small and drab England was. How crowded they all were in Muriel and Barry's tiny house. The meagre food. The bitter coldness inside, now that fall—*autumn*, he corrected himself—was here. Most of all, his constant, burning homesickness.

He looked around the kitchen. Muriel was stirring a vile-smelling stew. Drying diapers were draped in front of the fire. Grandad sat in a corner behind his newspaper, puffing on his pipe. Norah was trying to concentrate on her homework at the other end of the table from Gavin.

The baby toddled over to Gavin and grabbed his leg. "Ga—win," he said clearly.

"Did you hear that?" cried Gavin. "Richard said my name!" Everyone looked up and smiled at Richard and Gavin.

Gavin picked up his pen again.

I miss you very much and I miss Canada.
I am being brave.

Thank you to Jean Little, Kay and Sandy Pearson, Patricia Runcie, Linda Shineton, Elizabeth Symon, Joan Weir—and especially to Claire Mackay for her generous advice.